The Arctic Cruise

Caroline James is the celebrated author of later-life fiction and her vibrant storytelling stems from her colourful career. Before becoming a full-time writer, she carved out a fascinating path in the hospitality industry, owning a lively pub then a charming country house hotel. As a media agent, she worked closely with celebrity chefs, giving her an insider's perspective on the glitz, glamour, and grit of the culinary world. When she finally turned her focus to writing, she discovered her true calling, penning best-selling novels that have garnered her legions of fans.

Also by Caroline James

The Cruise Club
The Cruise
The French Cookery School
The Spa Break

The Arctic Cruise

CAROLINE JAMES

avon.

Published by AVON
A division of HarperCollins*Publishers* Ltd
1 London Bridge Street
London SE1 9GF

www.harpercollins.co.uk

HarperCollins*Publishers*
Macken House, 39/40 Mayor Street Upper
Dublin 1, D01 C9W8, Ireland

A Paperback Original 2026
2
First published in Great Britain by HarperCollins*Publishers* 2026

For those who dream of far horizons, may your journeys bring friendships and memories to last a lifetime.

Acknowledgements

I have always been enchanted by cold weather. There is a special kind of magic in winter, and I love curling up warm indoors while a cold wind howls outside, or walking with Fred, my Westie, as snow crunches beneath our feet and frost tingles my cheeks. Those wintery moments made it an easy choice for my next cruise story, and I decided that my characters would sail somewhere cold and head into a world of snow, ice, and the magical northern lights, bound for the Arctic.

But to capture their journey, I first had to experience it myself.

On a crisp winter's morning, Eric and I set off for Newcastle, staying at the welcoming Little Haven Hotel in South Shields. I was enchanted by the *Beach Ladies* sculptures that greet travellers there and found them so delightful that they found their way into my story. Early the next day, I woke to see the silhouette of the cruise ship *Borealis* etched against the horizon. As she slipped gracefully into the narrow channel of the Tyne, I gazed in awe. Soon, I would be standing on her decks, sailing into an Arctic realm of polar nights, where the aurora borealis would dance like ribbons of fire across the sky.

That moment was the beginning of our Arctic adventure. Over the following two weeks, as the days and nights unfolded and vast seascapes revealed their stark, frozen beauty, my characters, Joy, Henry, and their fellow passengers came alive on the page, each inspired by the wonder, stillness, and grandeur of the Arctic.

The Arctic Cruise was born.

My grateful thanks for their generous support go to:

Lorella Belli, my wonderful agent. I am truly indebted to you and your talented team. With you in my corner, my stories could not be in safer or more capable hands.

Helen Huthwaite, my editor at Avon. Your wisdom, generosity, and keen insight are beyond measure. I am deeply grateful to you and your brilliant team for your kindness, guidance, enthusiasm, and unwavering support.

Dear readers, I hope you enjoy this story as much as I enjoyed writing it, and once again, thank you for joining me on this journey.

I am deeply grateful to the remarkable team at Fred Olsen Cruises who made this voyage unforgettable. From the warmth of the crew and their superb service who create memorable journeys that stay in the heart, to the companionship of lovely fellow travellers Pamela and Barry, who began the voyage as strangers, but I know will be friends for life. Every encounter enriched our experience and helped transform my research into a new story.

And last but never least, Eric, you are my rock. My

companion throughout our travels, trials and tribulations, the love of my life and best friend.

An Arctic cruise is not just a magical journey, but a reminder that adventure has no age.

Happy cruising!

With love,
Caroline

www.carolinejamesauthor.co.uk

Caroline James would also like to express her gratitude to:
Wil Cheung of www.wilphotography.co.uk for his invaluable advice, expertise, and inspiring talks during her research aboard the Fred Olsen's ship, *Borealis*, while travelling to the Arctic.
Fred Olsen Cruise Lines (www.fredolsencruises.com) for their generous assistance in enhancing her cruise experience on board *Borealis*, which in turn enriched the storyline of *The Arctic Cruise*.

Disclaimer

The *Emerald Dream*, its crew, passengers, and all other characters depicted in this story are fictional creations of the author's imagination. Any likeness to actual individuals, or ships, is purely coincidental. While the story draws inspiration from locations the author has personally visited while cruising, the ship's itinerary reflects artistic licence and does not represent actual cruise routes, destinations, or events.

Descriptions of the polar night and the aurora borealis are based on careful research and aim to be authentic. However, artistic interpretation has also been applied.

Chapter One

*To travel through Arctic waters is to witness
nature's majesty – where the mountains whisper
stories, every sunrise brings wonder, and
dusk drapes the world in mystery.*

Joy Bradley stood at the window of her hotel room at the Inn on the Beach in Little Haven and stared out at the horizon. Despite the stillness of the sea, unease tightened her stomach, and her fingers dug into her palms as the weight of inevitability crept closer.

Beneath the early morning sky, a ship appeared, sailing smoothly towards the harbour. In the soft light, the rising sun caught the gleam of its hull cutting through the misty morning, and as it moved nearer, Joy imagined a predator closing in on its prey.

Was it too late to gather her cases and hurry from the hotel? Back to the home where memories still haunted her.

Taking steadying breaths, Joy closed her eyes and counted slowly. She *could* do this. She *would* embark on a holiday. It was a cruise that Tom had planned and something her daughter demanded when she thrust the glossy brochure into her mother's hand.

The dream cruise for their fortieth wedding anniversary. The memorable holiday that Joy had carefully planned with Tom. Christmas aboard a floating paradise to share the wonder of the Northern Lights doing what they loved best.

'We'll book an Arctic cruise,' Tom had said as he'd scanned the brochure. 'Let's celebrate the milestone of our marriage and go somewhere snowy at Christmas – after all, we got married on Christmas Eve.'

But the much-anticipated anniversary was not to be.

As she watched the *Emerald Dream* enter the channel of the River Tyne, Joy remembered the warm September night beneath a Mediterranean sky strewn with stars when, to the gentle sway of the ship, Tom fell asleep in their balcony cabin.

He never saw a sunrise again.

Joy felt tears trickle down her cheeks. The pain of Tom's death was still raw. Despite the months that had turned into more than a year, she'd never forgotten the agony of touching his cold skin and lifeless body. His death so sudden, leaving Joy in a widowed world she hadn't been ready to enter.

Now, that world was a place she found difficult to leave.

Would Tom have wanted her to join this cruise? To remember their years together and all their holidays at sea? The idea felt almost unbearable. There was an ache in her chest that wouldn't go away, and pain hung like a heavy coat. It was only through the incessant nagging of Susan, their daughter, that Joy found herself about to board the cruise. Tom had paid upfront for the Arctic cruise, and Susan insisted that Joy should still go.

'Mum, I can't come with you,' she said. 'You know how Hugh insists that his family spends Christmas with us. Perhaps you can find a pal to join you?'

Joy knew only too well that Christmas in Susan and her husband Hugh's home was a highlight of the year. Wild horses wouldn't drag Susan away from the ritual her husband adored. Joy thought of the bustling kitchen, with endless mouths to feed, and the hours Joy spent chained to the sink, only to return home utterly drained. As for finding a travelling companion, she had no 'pal' in mind and, in truth, preferred it that way. The thought of a double-berth cabin all to herself was oddly comforting.

Had Susan and Hugh had children, Joy would have leaped at the chance to join the Christmas festivities in London, despite all the hard work. But Susan's focus had always been her high-flying career, and Joy felt the ache of a missed opportunity. She'd never have the chance to cradle a grandchild; that small, private pleasure had never come her way.

Now, the *Emerald Dream* was close by. So close, she could see passengers on upper decks who waved to those watching on the banks of the Tyne. Outside, a woman bundled in a quilted coat, returned the greeting excitedly as the magnificent ship cruised slowly towards the port.

At least someone is happy to see the Emerald Dream, Joy thought.

She walked to the bed and fastened her suitcase, then, reaching for her coat, thrust her arms into the sleeves and wrapped a scarf around her neck. Checking that her gloves were tucked safely in her pockets, Joy heaved the case to the floor and took a last look around. The room was so cosy and welcoming, with its seaside-pastel shades and mock porthole windows, that she felt reluctant to leave.

But Susan's words echoed. 'It will be good for you,' she'd said. 'Dad wouldn't want you to be miserable. I miss him too, but I've managed to move on.'

Well, bully for you! Joy loved her daughter and knew she meant well, but Susan could sometimes be less than sympathetic. Susan didn't wake every day to an empty space where her husband used to be and feel the panic that followed.

Joy felt weighted down, a feeling as heavy as the suitcase beside her. Yet amid her grief something had shifted and the panic attacks that stalked her had faded. She hadn't had one in months and was at least able to leave the house to make this trip – something that had felt almost impossible in the aftermath of Tom's death.

She made her way to the hotel reception, where jolly Christmas decorations hung, and a pretty tree laced with lanterns stood in one corner, while a miniature Santa sat beside the tree. Its pointed hat was crooked, and its fur-trimmed coat a faded shade of red. Santa's smile was worn, his cheeks chipped, and Joy knew that Tom would have joked that Santa had seen better days.

Acknowledging the young man behind the desk, Joy settled her account. She struggled to summon up any Christmas spirit as he ordered a taxi for her as she waited in the warmth of the hotel lobby. Very soon, she would arrive at the port and, unable to face breakfast here in the hotel, Joy planned to settle in the ship's departure lounge and read a book before the embarkation process began. But as she traced the edge of her wedding ring on her finger, she wondered if this holiday would be the beginning of anniversary memories or another painful reminder of Tom's death.

A few minutes later, the taxi's horn beeped outside, and with effort, Joy forced herself to move. Holidays were for leaving cares and woes behind, and the *Emerald Dream* awaited, but as she climbed into the cab and the vehicle pulled away from the hotel, she knew that no matter how far she travelled, some things refused to be left behind.

* * *

Leticia Scott was excited. After hurrying out of her hotel room at the Inn on the Beach in Little Haven, she was in awe of the magnificent sight of the *Emerald Dream* as it entered the mouth of the Tyne, passing the iconic red and white of the South Shields lighthouse, sailing slowly down the river to the port. Passengers who would soon disembark stood on deck, and Leticia waved her hands. 'Hello!' she called out excitedly.

After a few minutes, the ship became distant as it continued to its destination, and Leticia gathered her quilted coat tightly and turned to the narrow path leading back to the hotel, bracing herself against the freezing Tyne wind. Ahead, nestling by the sand dunes, she was intrigued to see a collection of sculptures. The life-like human figures appeared to be conversing. Captivated, she hastened her pace until she stood in the middle of the bronze munchkin-like characters.

'What fun!' Leticia laughed and saw that someone with a sense of humour had placed cosy knitted Santa hats and seasonal fur-trimmed scarves on the figures, as though protecting them from the harsh weather whipping in from the North Sea.

A notice board alongside explained that this was the *Beach Ladies* – a public artwork created by the artist Juan Muñoz, and the ladies were to welcome visitors from both land and sea. They reminded Leticia of Weeble toys with egg-shaped, weighted bottoms. 'Just like me.' She smiled. She stared at their faces and ran her gloved fingers over their old-fashioned clothes, the surface smooth and cold.

'Weebles wobble, but they don't fall down . . .' she sang.

Reminding herself that she must tell Jim about the sculptures, Leticia hurried back to the hotel just as a taxi pulled away from the front door. Inside, the lobby was warm and welcoming, and as Leticia removed her gloves, she noticed a pretty Christmas tree, hung with colourful lanterns. Beside the tree stood a miniature Santa with a pointed hat and fur-trimmed coat. Leticia reached out to stroke Santa's rosy cheek. 'Happy Christmas!' she whispered.

Turning to a young man in reception, Leticia called out, 'Good morning, we're checking out shortly.'

The young man returned her greeting then produced a bill. 'Any plans for Christmas?' he asked.

'We certainly have,' Leticia grinned. 'We're off to Norway on a cruise.'

Moments later, she tucked her receipt in her bag, reached for her keycard, and let herself into her room. 'Jim, you'll never guess what I've just seen . . .'

As the door closed behind her, Leticia looked towards the port hole window, where the morning sun suffused the room in a warm glow. Seated in his wheelchair, her husband looked peaceful, his eyes closed. The light caught the shine of his sleek black hair, and the lines on his face appeared soft.

How handsome he is! Leticia stood, drinking him in.

She watched Jim's hands, resting on the arms of the chair. Hands that were no longer strong or active. Leticia silently cursed the illness that had caused Jim's disability and swallowed the lump rising in her throat. Life had dealt her handsome husband a cruel blow.

Jim turned, his eyes now open and a knowing smile on his lips. 'You've seen the ship,' he said, 'I've been watching you.' He picked up his glasses and perched them on his nose to gaze at his wife.

'Yes,' Letitia replied, 'I'm glad we were up early, I never expected such a wonderful surprise.'

'It was quite a sight,' Jim agreed, 'and now the *Emerald Dream* will prepare for a speedy turnaround, with a brand-new passenger list.'

'Including us.' Leticia reached out to cradle Jim's face and lovingly kissed him.

'I hope I'm not too much of a burden.' Jim frowned. 'This damn wheelchair is so restrictive and hard for you to manage.'

'Don't be silly.' Leticia brushed off the comment. 'Now, we need to sort ourselves out, and I'm sure you're ready for breakfast.'

As she tidied their room, Leticia told Jim about the *Beach Ladies* and how they reminded her of herself. 'If there's time before we check out, we'll whizz over to them, and you can see for yourself,' she said.

'My whizzing days are over, my love, but I'd enjoy seeing the sculptures.' Jim placed his hands on the wheels of his chair and attempted to turn around. 'But first, I need the bathroom.' Frustration etched itself on his face as the chair barely moved.

Some days were better than others. Some days Jim could stand and walk independently. But today was not one of those and, swift to react, Leticia took control.

Giving Jim space, she waited by the window and stared at the long sandy beach of Little Haven. Despite the sunshine the temperature outside was just below freezing. Several hardy swimmers were in the sea, and Leticia shuddered at the thought of the icy water. In days long gone she knew that Jim would have joined the swimmers, enthusiastically grabbing opportunities, his energy unlimited.

But despite Jim's condition being life-changing for them both, Leticia refused to be downhearted. She embraced every day with hope and was determined that Jim did the same. Their cruise was a much-anticipated Christmas gift to each other, a holiday to tick off their bucket list, and would be a wonderful break.

In the hotel restaurant, Leticia watched as guests ate their breakfast. She wondered how many, like herself and Jim, had chosen to spend the night before the cruise in a hotel. The drive from Bath the previous day had been pleasant but long, and it made sense to have a leisurely overnight stop before boarding the *Emerald Dream*.

Jim was chatting to a couple seated at an adjacent table. The couple nodded as they listened to his words.

Thank goodness he makes the effort, Leticia thought, watching the exchange with a mixture of affection and relief.

She smiled as a server poured coffee and, sitting back, Leticia felt herself relax. The cruise was truly beginning, and Christmas felt full of possibility. Should they be lucky enough to witness it, perhaps the beauty of the aurora borealis would cast a spell that eased Jim's pain. Whatever the outcome, Leticia made a promise to enjoy every moment and make the most of this Arctic cruise, while ensuring that despite his fading strength, Jim did too.

Time was no longer a companion but more like a silent thief, stealing precious days that they once took for granted. But when Jim turned to face her, she beamed, and taking his hand, her dark brown skin a striking contrast to Jim's pale complexion, Leticia leaned closer. 'Here's to our dream cruise, my darling,' she whispered, 'and I simply cannot wait.'

Chapter Two

*A cruise is where you lose yourselves in the waves,
only to find yourself in the journey.*

In the crew section of the *Emerald Dream*, Simon Blake sat in his office on a lower deck and studied his programme for the day. As cruise director, Simon had already attended the morning briefing to coordinate the ship's officers and department heads, and any matters that team members raised had now been dealt with.

Simon was buzzing and as he worked, he hummed a popular Christmas song. Christmas was his favourite time of year and he couldn't wait to set sail to Norway, where the snow-capped mountains and winter scenery would be the perfect backdrop for this festive voyage.

Simon enjoyed this time of year in Norway and found a fascination in the dark polar days, as though he were sailing into an unknown world. They would cross the Arctic Circle, where the sun slipped permanently below the horizon and only at midday would the land become briefly bathed in a dim blue twilight, before darkness returned and took hold.

Running a hand over his smooth head, Simon studied the passenger list, noting frequent cruisers, higher-tier loyalty members, and VIPs. He saw that Kenneth and Barbara Montgomery Jones had booked a Dream Suite, and housekeeping had been instructed to ensure fresh flowers, fruit and champagne were in place for their arrival. The couple often sailed with the Diamond Star Line, the company that owned the *Emerald Dream* and her sister ship the *Diamond Star*. Like many who chose to travel on these ships, the Montgomery Joneses were of a certain age.

Simon loved his job, and seeing the world and getting paid for it was part of the charm. But he thrived on the thrill of creating special memories for their guests and especially enjoyed cruises with mature passengers because they appreciated the old-school glamour that the Diamond Star Line retained. Many were seasoned travellers and often returned year after year. The *Emerald Dream* was quite unlike the party boats Simon had worked on in previous jobs, where the younger passengers of the vast floating cities treated their cruise like a reality TV show. It wasn't that the guests of the *Emerald Dream* didn't get into mischief, but the chaos was calmer, and Simon easily coped.

He reached across his desk and picked up a draft copy of the *Emerald Dream Daily Times*. Compiled by Penny, the assistant cruise director, she'd left it for his approval. Each evening, a copy was placed in every cabin, detailing events over the next twenty-four hours. Beginning with the weather forecast, the evening entertainment, restaurant times, and dress code, Simon then studied the bar specials, live music venues, and onboard activities.

Tomorrow would be a sea day, when passengers had the day entirely onboard, and Simon noted that the ship's fitness instructor, Kyle, had an early morning session for seniors entitled Frost & Flex. They were due to sail into much colder weather, and Simon hoped Kyle wasn't planning to frog-march the participants out on deck. On a previous Arctic cruise, Kyle had kept the medical team busy with over-eager seniors risking life and limb during his Silver Fox Stretch. Kyle's Brrrr-lesque Bootcamp resulted in two elderly ladies spending three days in the medical facility suffering from hypothermia.

But despite adding to health and safety concerns, Simon knew that Kyle was popular and always scored high on passenger feedback forms. Some guests even commented that they'd like to take Kyle home to exercise together in the comfort of their cosy sitting rooms.

Simon leaned back and thought of Kyle's perfectly toned abs, his muscles a work of art. A fitness magazine model brought to life. With his soft blonde hair, baby blue eyes, and mischievous smile, Kyle's endless energy was a magnetic force. If they weren't both crew members, Simon might have tapped Grindr's heart icon on Kyle's profile on the dating app. Not that he'd expect Kyle to respond. After all, who wanted to date an overweight Teletubby lookalike? Simon might hold a position of authority on the ship, but he wasn't on anyone's eye candy list. Besides, work and pleasure didn't mix, and Simon was married to his job.

Penny popped her head around the door, bringing Simon back to reality. 'Excuse me,' she called out. 'Embarkation is going smoothly, and we're almost full. It looks like sail away will be on time.'

'Thanks, Penny, I'll let the captain know.'

Gathering paperwork, Simon pushed back his chair. Checking that his desk was neat and tidy, he stood and straightened his tie. Buttoning his uniform jacket, Simon tapped his portly tummy. 'Showtime,' he said and fixing a wry smile, stepped out to welcome the newly arrived guests to their Arctic cruise.

* * *

Henry Halliday's worn leather suitcase was neatly placed beside his hand luggage when he stepped into cabin 3344, situated on the promenade deck of the *Emerald Dream*. Opening the wardrobe doors, he checked several drawers before studying the contents of the minibar and hospitality tray. Peering into the bathroom, Henry stroked the thick towels and noted the toiletries, then moved into the sitting area of his terrace room and pulled open the wide glass doors that led to the deck, where two steamer chairs lay side by side.

'This will do very nicely,' Henry muttered.

He politely nodded to passengers strolling by, who, like Henry, were familiarising themselves with the layout of the ship. A woman, bundled into a quilted coat, pushed a wheelchair and paused to ensure a blanket was securely tucked around the occupant.

'Hello,' she said, 'isn't it a beautiful afternoon.'

'Indeed,' Henry replied.

Returning to his room, he unpacked and carefully tidied his personal items and cold-weather clothing. As he placed a dinner suit on a hanger, he felt slightly guilty that he'd invested in a new formal outfit that might not see much wear. But his previous suit had last been worn at his retirement party, almost a decade ago, and to his discomfort was somewhat tight. These days, he'd no occasion for such a get-up and preferred more casual clothes, and his old cords, woolly jumpers, and tweed jackets served him well. Still, the cruise itinerary stated that there was a dress code for formal nights, and Henry, known to adhere to rules and regulations, would comply.

Glancing at his watch, Henry realised that he hadn't eaten since breakfast, and his tummy was making it known. A mid-afternoon cup of tea and a biscuit would pacify the rumbles until dinner, and he decided it was time to explore. With his cabin ship-shape and his precious camera and valuables secured in the safe, Henry straightened the collar of his plaid shirt. Patting the pockets of a tailored tweed waistcoat, he felt for his glasses and cabin card, then reached for his well-worn Barbour and set off.

In the corridor, he almost crashed headlong into a housekeeping trolley. He apologised profusely to the uniformed lady who peered out from a tower of sheets.

'Terribly sorry I didn't see you there,' Henry said.

'Is no problem. My name is Jennifer. I look after you,' she replied. 'Anything you want, you tell me, I take care of cabin, keep it good for you.'

Jennifer's smile was welcoming, and her voice carried a soft lilt. Henry noted her name badge, which had a Philippines flag printed alongside it.

'Well, I'm much obliged. Thank you, Jennifer, and it's a pleasure to meet you.' Henry stumbled backwards. Women often made him clumsy, and he hastened to move away.

Emerging from the corridor, Henry paused. He'd entered the lower level of the central atrium, where a grand staircase circled the space around a vast clock. It reminded Henry of Big Ben, and as he walked around to study the ship's landmark, he saw several ornate clock faces displaying time zones in different countries. The magnificent structure, decorated with Christmas swags of red and gold, was topped with an enamelled globe wrapped in a tartan bow.

Henry checked his floor plan then began to ascend the thickly carpeted, sweeping staircase that connected different levels of the ship. By the guest services desk, a Christmas tree sparkled with silver lights, which were as bright as the smiles of the staff who greeted him. A spacious bar and lounge area was busy, and guests gathered around low tables, already enjoying cocktails of the day. Acoustic music played, and picture windows framed the view of the port outside.

In the Botanical Room, the decoration reflected nature, and Henry thought the serene setting would be an ideal place to relax. Other rooms had interesting names, and the Planet Room and Oriental Tea Room both looked inviting, but Henry was led by a delicious aroma of coffee coming from a serving counter in the Bookmark Café, surrounded by bookshelves.

'Perfect,' Henry said, and found an armchair beside large windows, where he placed his Barbour jacket as a steward came to take his order.

'I'd like a cappuccino and a shortbread biscuit if you have one,' Henry said.

'Freshly baked today.' The steward smiled and made a note of Henry's cabin number.

As he sat back, Henry began to unwind. The stress of the journey was behind him now, and the closure of the Tyne Tunnel that had delayed his progress and caused an anxious hour's diversion was soon forgotten. His trusty Morris Traveller was safely parked until his return, and all Henry needed to do was look forward to the holiday.

Henry Halliday had never been on a cruise. It hadn't appealed to the history teacher who'd devoted decades to shaping young minds. Henry's hobbies lay in photography, wildlife, and stargazing, and the Scottish Highlands were his favourite destination. Wonderful species of red deer, golden eagles, otters, and wildcats could be found there and, in the Cairngorms National Park, he'd witnessed incredible views of the night sky, including on one occasion, the dense region of stars located in the Milky Way. But Henry had never seen the Northern Lights.

In the summer, at his camera club meeting, a member had talked about this marvel, showing photographs and inform-ing colleagues that the spectacle was best seen in Norway, especially in Tromsø, which was described as the gateway to the Arctic. Here, the sun didn't rise in December and the polar night offered perfect conditions. When Henry learned that Bill Zhang, an astrophotography expert much talked about by club members, would be on board the *Emerald Dream* as a guest speaker for the Arctic cruise, he took advantage of an offer in his club magazine and booked his place.

The coffee arrived and Henry sipped. It was delicious, and the shortbread was perfect too. Fussy about his coffee and a dab hand in the kitchen, Henry enjoyed taking a freshly baked batch of biscuits or cakes to his club meetings, where the members devoured the treats. Miss Audrey Aston, Henry's elderly neighbour, also enjoyed his culinary efforts during their weekly afternoon tea together at home in the North Yorkshire town of Skipton. Over the years, Audrey had become both a close friend and trusted neighbour and Henry enjoyed the old lady's feisty nature and her love of life almost as much as she loved his shortbread and spicy carrot cake.

As he eased into the deep leather armchair, Henry smoothed a silver-streaked strand that had fallen onto his forehead. Despite his years, he was proud of his full head of hair, unlike the many comb-overs of his contemporaries. With lots of walking and a careful diet, Henry kept himself fit, and his eyes, a deep shade of blue, still held a twinkle. He didn't look his age and felt at least a decade younger than his seventy years. Audrey, also a retired schoolteacher who'd taught art, told him he was still young enough to find a good woman and settle down, but Henry flinched at the thought.

It wasn't that he didn't like women, quite the opposite in fact. Over the years, Henry had been in several relationships, and two had been serious, but he had been devoted to his intellectual life and reluctant to commit. He'd never felt a conviction strong enough to marry, and with no signs of wedding bells ringing, his partners became impatient and eventually drifted away, and Henry decided he was better off alone.

As Henry finished his coffee, he thought of Audrey. She lived in a detached house alongside his own and took care of his plants in his absence. The weathered red brick Edwardian properties with curving bay windows had been built to last and were surprisingly spacious, with a deep cellar, two living levels, and several attic rooms. Henry loved his home almost as much as he'd enjoyed his job teaching at the grammar school in Skipton and had been bereft when his retirement came around. It was Audrey who encouraged Henry to take up new hobbies, and she took an interest in his photography and star gazing.

'You must make the best of the cruise,' Audrey had been adamant. 'You never know what might happen or who you might meet,' she insisted, flicking crumbs from her lace-trimmed blouse with fingers as gnarled as driftwood. 'Go and have an adventure, Henry Halliday, before it's too late!'

Now, Henry reached for his Barbour and rose from his chair to head out on deck to watch the ship sail away from the port. But his neighbour's words lingered.

An adventure? He wasn't so sure.

With a sharp tug, he opened a door and stepped outside. As the ship's horn bellowed, Henry shrugged into his coat, bracing against the crisp air. He'd planned a holiday with sightings of the Northern Lights, perhaps some wildlife photography, and excellent meals. After all, he thought, as he joined other passengers and the *Emerald Dream* moved slowly away from Tyneside, these simple pleasures were predictable and safe.

And for a retired schoolteacher like Henry, that was adventure enough.

Chapter Three

Taste the world where the sea is your companion,
and every course tells a story.

Dinner in the Emerald Dining Room was a formal experience, and as Joy entered, she noticed that everywhere sparkled with glamour, Christmas cheer, and abundant colourful decorations. A Christmas tree stood beside the reception desk which was framed in an archway of festive swags and tartan bows.

Joy wondered what Tom would have thought of the atmosphere, as she noted candlelight flickering on polished silver and crystal chandeliers, casting a warm glow over the guests as they arrived to take their place at tables set for the evening. Stewards in smart uniforms moved efficiently, their steps whisper-like across the carpet as they glided from table to table. Joy was wide-eyed as she stared at the dome-shaped dining area which hummed with gentle conversation against the backdrop of music from a string quartet playing soothing tunes from a balcony above the main room.

Fearing that it was a mistake to enter the room as a solo traveller, Joy was nervous as the maître d' greeted her, and instinctively she wanted to double-back to the safety of her cabin. But it was too late to change her mind. Not wishing to sit alone, she'd chosen a communal table and allowed herself to be guided to table number twenty-eight, situated in a balcony position overlooking the extended restaurant below. Her steps were hesitant, and she gripped her clutch bag tightly to her chest. When the maître d' pulled out a chair, Joy sat down with a shy nod to a couple already seated.

So far, so good.

Joy knew that Tom would expect her to join in, but he wasn't the one plunging alone into a cruise with strangers. She'd almost cancelled her dinner reservation, preferring to go to the buffet restaurant where food was served at all hours. Choosing a table for one in a corner, Joy would have dined then headed back to her cabin to settle down with a book and bed. But as she'd dressed, her phone had rung. It was Susan checking on her mother to ensure all was well.

'Now make sure you have a decent dinner, Mum,' Joy's daughter had instructed. 'You've paid a lot of money for the cruise, so don't go sloping off to the buffet where you can sit anonymously in a corner picking away at a salad.'

Joy had rolled her eyes but knew that her daughter was right. She promised Susan that she'd take her place in the main restaurant at a table with other guests. And yes, she *would* go to the show after dinner, too. Smoothing her simple A-line dress over her slim hips, Joy had slipped her feet into ballet pumps and smiled dryly. At least they would soon be far away, and the signal on her phone would no longer be available. Wi-Fi on the ship was expensive, and Joy had no intention of upgrading her package to take ticking-off calls from Susan.

Now, as the dining room filled, Joy placed her clutch bag on her lap and turned to her dining companions.

'Hello,' a woman said, offering her hand, 'I'm Leticia Scott, and this is my husband, Jim.'

Joy felt her hand pumped and noted that the woman filled her space at the table. 'Pleased to meet you both,' Joy said as she leaned in to acknowledge the couple. 'I'm Joy Bradley.'

'What a lovely name, and what a coincidence!' Leticia beamed. 'My name comes from the Latin word meaning joy or happiness, and everyone says that I'm full of joy.'

'Too much joy, at times,' Jim laughed.

'So, you're a Joy too,' Leticia said. 'I hope we'll be cruise buddies.'

'Oh, that's interesting,' Joy replied, feeling flummoxed by this woman's instant engagement. *Cruise buddies?* Joy wasn't sure about that.

She gave a half-glance at Leticia, noting her striking dress, a shade of red that perfectly flattered her dark skin. Her lips, glossy and plump, were red too, and her large oval eyes seemed to light up the room. Leticia's hair was intricately plaited into cornrow braids threaded with pretty beads and piled elegantly high on her head. On her wrists, an assortment of silver bangles gleamed.

Wearing a beige dress, Joy felt dowdy next to this vibrant woman and thought that she should have chosen

21

something more glamorous or added a bright scarf. But Joy lacked the confidence to stand out like Leticia. It had abandoned her many years ago. She half-wished that she'd done more with her own hair, which, though still a vibrant shade of chestnut, was fashioned into an easy to manage cut that lay primly on her shoulders. With her beautiful braids and colourful clothes, Leticia was larger than life, and Joy felt herself sink low in her chair.

While Leticia greeted another couple who'd joined the table, Joy stole a glance at Jim. In a smart suit and open-necked shirt, Leticia's husband was as handsome as she was vibrant. But noting that Jim was sitting in a wheelchair, she wondered what ailed him. When Jim turned and caught her eye, he removed his glasses and grinned, and Joy hoped his condition wasn't serious.

A man sat down beside Joy, and she turned to introduce herself.

'Kenneth Montgomery Jones,' he announced.

His spicy aftershave was so overpowering that Joy wondered if he'd bathed in it. Dressed in a dark blazer with gold buttons, Kenneth wore a bow tie with a white shirt and as he moved his head, Joy saw the thick crown wobbled independently.

Was he wearing a wig? When Kenneth turned, his hair, the colour of a conker, was a split-second behind.

Kenneth summoned the sommelier with a snap of his fingers and Joy winced. She disliked seeing anyone treat staff disrespectfully.

When Kenneth's wife, Barbara, leaned forward to say hello, Joy set her face in a smile. Barbara's bosom was bursting from a silver sequinned top, and her ash-blonde hair, neat in a chignon, was topped off with a black velvet band. Joy couldn't imagine the worth of Barbara's dazzling diamonds and covered her own modest wedding ring with her fingers.

'We were almost late for dinner,' Barbara began. 'Kenny and I were enjoying complimentary champagne and canopies in our Dream Suite and didn't notice the time.' She gave a snort that passed as a laugh and fluttered unnaturally long lashes.

Contemplating Barbara's age, Joy studied her smooth, taut skin which looked as though it had been lifted, and her eyebrows seemed permanently raised. Instead of reducing her years, Barbara seemed to have fast-forwarded them, and Joy guessed she was in her early sixties.

Meanwhile, Kenneth was asking the sommelier what was drinking well, and Joy wondered if he meant the wine or the waiter.

Confirming his order, Kenneth turned to Joy.

'Château de Pizay Morgon,' he began. 'A good red wine from Beaujolais. Babs and I often take holidays there,' he added. 'It's made with the Gamay grape, don't you know.'

Joy didn't know at all and had no clue what Kenneth was talking about. She was about to tell him that she knew little about wine, but another guest was being shown to their table, and everyone turned as a man sat down.

'Good evening, everyone,' Henry Halliday said as a steward skilfully flicked a napkin and placed it on Henry's knee.

Oh Lord, Joy thought, *is the maître d' matchmaking?*

23

She'd been placed on a table with two couples and a man who might be single like herself. Thank goodness Henry Halliday was on the opposite side of the table, and she wouldn't have to make small talk. Between Leticia, Barbara and their spouses, Joy hoped that the dinner table chatter would be all the conversation they needed.

Tomorrow, Joy decided, she would ask to move tables. Surely, she wasn't obligated to share with the same guests every night.

Their steward Jhamille introduced his assistant, Ryan, and they handed out menus. Moments later, with choices ordered, the sommelier poured Kenneth's wine, inviting him to sample it. Kenneth held his glass to the light, making a grand performance of swirling, and Joy wondered if he was summoning up spirits. Perhaps Tom would appear at any moment to haunt her, like a genie from a lamp!

Diplomatically silent, the sommelier stood alongside, waiting for Kenneth's approval.

'Mmm, a classic Cru Beaujolais. I detect blackcurrants and a hint of raspberry,' Kenneth murmured, 'there's a slight edge and a fine tannin . . .'

Joy thought that Kenneth could be describing a glass of Ribena and holding up her own glass, nodded to Jhamille, who held a pitcher of iced water.

'The acidity is almost playful,' Kenneth continued, his eyes closed.

As the sommelier waited, his expression remained neutral, although Joy thought she detected an amused twitch at the side of his mouth.

'But what about the body?' Barbara interrupted.

Kenneth opened his eyes, 'Generous and extremely ostentatious,' he replied.

Joy caught Leticia's eye, and it was all she could do not to smile as Leticia whispered that Kenneth might be describing his wife.

Leticia passed Joy a silver dish and as Joy spread butter on a warm, seeded roll, she considered her dinner companions. Leticia and Jim might be fun, but Kenneth and Barbara would be more of a challenge. As the first course arrived, the couple discussed their wine and made it clear that the bottle was for their sole enjoyment. When Leticia ordered a bottle of prosecco and offered it to Joy and Henry, Joy accepted. However, Henry said he'd prefer a pint of beer.

Kenneth raised his eyebrows. 'Beer and fine dining?' he commented, clearly not approving. As he shook his head, his toupee lifted slightly at the corners.

Turning to her starter, Joy tucked into crab pâté, served with slithers of melba toast.

Leticia struck up a conversation with Henry and they learned that he was a retired schoolteacher – a department head, who'd taught history at a grammar school in Skipton. Henry admitted that he'd loved his job and missed it. He spoke fondly of his classroom years, recalling lively debates about historical events and his satisfaction in helping students learn.

'I miss the routine,' Henry admitted, 'and also the camaraderie of colleagues and the sometime chaos of school life. Teaching gave me a purpose in a way that few other things have in the years that have followed.'

Jim was fascinated and told Henry that he envied him. 'My career was in computers,' Jim said, 'I didn't really enjoy it, though it gave me a decent living, and it is refreshing to hear from someone who loved his job and made such a difference to young lives.'

When they learned that Joy had been a teacher too, at a secondary school in Lancaster, Jim proposed a toast.

'To teachers,' he stuttered, 'the guiding lights who inspire our futures.'

Kenneth looked bored but soon perked up when Barbara announced that after leaving the diplomatic service, her husband was in international finance, and they'd lived all over the world.

'Yes, Hong Kong, Dubai, Jo'burg and a long stint in Zurich,' Kenneth sighed, 'all gruelling stuff.' He shook his head. 'Let's face it, you've not lived until you've negotiated a bond deal in Mandarin. A bit different to staid old Skipton, eh Henry?' Kenneth stared at Henry.

Joy wondered what international finance meant and presumed it involved laundering money and hedge funds. She turned to Kenneth and asked, 'What exactly did you do?'

'Started as a junior officer in the British Diplomatic Service and was posted to various embassies,' Kenneth replied. 'Worked my way up with a bit of this and that, trade negotiations here, political reporting there . . .'

Barbara butted in. 'When Kenny left government, he moved into the lucrative private sector, joining a merchant bank in the City.' She smiled smugly, no doubt concealing the fact that her husband had greased many palms to nudge regimes into taking on loans, keeping his kickbacks safely offshore.

'Ah yes,' Kenneth sighed, 'my international contacts and knowledge of local politics were invaluable in negotiating finance and managing debt deals.'

It sounded improbable, and everyone stared, clearly wondering if Kenneth had spent decades drinking other people's whisky, shuffling papers, and collecting frequent flyer airmiles.

When the main course arrived, Kenneth picked up his knife and poked at his steak before taking a bite and half-heartedly chewing. 'Not like the steak we had at Don Julio in Palermo, is it Babs?' he said. 'Argentinians worship their beef and know how to serve it.'

Leticia smiled at Jim. 'We enjoyed the Wagyu in Japan,' she commented, raising her glass to her husband.

'Yes, the Kobe melted like silk,' Jim replied.

Joy remembered an episode of *MasterChef* where Kobe beef had been revered by Michelin-starred chefs, and she turned to Leticia and Jim. 'Japan holds the crown for the most expensive steak in the world. How amazing that you got to try Wagyu.'

Kenneth had been upstaged and swiftly steered the conversation away from meat and back to wine one-upmanship instead.

As Kenneth droned on, Joy looked at Henry, who was quietly eating his meal. She hoped he hadn't taken offence to Kenneth's comment, and when Henry looked up, she gave him a hesitant smile.

To her surprise, he returned her smile with a wink.

Feeling her cheeks flush, Joy took a sip of iced water. Wanting to know more about the couple on her right, she turned to Jim and asked what job he did with computers.

'I was a programmer,' Jim explained.

'Ah, a geek!' Kenneth rudely chirped up.

'And I was a nurse,' Leticia added.

'You still are,' Jim said, reaching for Leticia's hand. Raising her fingers to his lips, he kissed them tenderly.

Joy watched Barbara as she stared at the couple, noting the kiss.

'My goodness, all this talk of work makes me weary,' Barbara said. She'd finished her meal and now drained her wine. 'Let's talk about the cruise and the trips we're going on when we get to Molde, our first stop.' She pushed her plate to one side. 'We've chartered a boat for our own private cruise of the fjords. What's everyone else doing?'

Joy wondered why Barbara and Kenneth didn't take advantage of the wonderful tours offered through the *Emerald Dream* guest services but assumed that they didn't want to mix with the passengers going ashore in Molde.

'I'm looking forward to the coach trip along the Atlantic Ocean Road,' Henry said, 'I understand it to be one of the world's most beautiful drives, and I'm hoping to photograph wildlife.'

'You'll see plenty of wildlife on the coach.' Kenneth chuckled. 'Babs and I prefer to be more independent.'

'Jim and I are going to travel on the Rauma Railway,' Leticia said. 'There's a lunch included too.'

Kenneth turned to Joy. 'And what about you, old girl?' he asked. 'You'll be staying put on the ship, I suppose?'

Joy bristled. She didn't enjoy being called 'old girl' and being patronised. Despite her years, she didn't consider sixty-three to be old, nor did she take kindly to Kenneth's assumption that she wasn't adventurous enough to step off the ship.

Taking a deep breath, Joy said, 'Actually, *Kenny*, this old girl is looking forward to the trip that Henry is taking, and I can't wait to see the eight-kilometre stretch of road that links the islands with so many breathtaking bridges.' Joy paused. 'But then again, your trip with Babs to the fjords will be stunning. Let's hope it doesn't snow, and the icy Molde Mist, which is almost certain at this time of year, obliterates the view during your private excursion.'

Joy saw Barbara's eyes narrow, and her plumped-up lips press into a tight smile. Had Barbara realised that Kenneth might have misread the private tour information when he booked it?

Barbara declined a dessert and told Kenneth he shouldn't overindulge either. Taking his arm, they rose. 'Mustn't be late for the show,' Barbara said. Short in stature, she barely reached Kenneth's shoulder. 'Simon, the cruise director, has reserved seats for us at the front,' she added smugly. 'Enjoy the rest of your evening, everyone.'

With a curt nod that raised the fringe of his toupee, Kenneth guided the couple out of the dining room.

'It's a good job the ship is steady tonight,' Leticia mused, 'I'd hate to be around Kenneth's hairpiece during a storm. More prosecco, Joy?'

Joy stifled a laugh and saw that Henry was smiling, too.

'What's the Molde Mist?' Henry asked, 'I've never heard of it.'

'Neither have I.' Joy shrugged and tipped back her glass to drain it. 'I made it up.'

Henry stared open-mouthed at Joy, but Leticia and Jim had begun to laugh. Seconds later, Joy heard Henry laugh, too.

As Joy watched her dinner companions, she experienced a strange sensation, as though her long forgotten sense of humour had woken within. Like a flicker of light from a room darkened for too long, Joy felt a tiny glimmer of hope.

And tonight, for Joy, that was enough.

Chapter Four

Beyond the fjords lies a world untouched, where every step is an Arctic adventure.

On the first full day of his cruise, Henry woke early. To his surprise, he'd slept well. As he pulled himself into a sitting position, Henry patted the comfortable covers around him and reached for his glasses, then, taking his copy of the *Daily Times*, he began to read.

Today would be spent at sea as the *Emerald Dream* travelled north to Norway. Henry studied the day's itinerary, beginning with the weather forecast, which stated that the sea was moderate, the skies partly cloudy, and the wind a northerly gale force six to seven.

'It might get choppy, but nothing to worry about,' Henry said and stared out at the view, where the murky water of the North Sea was a white-capped, steel-grey expanse.

Henry was glad that he'd had an early night, opting not to go to the show. Instead, after a tiring day, he'd retired to his room and settled down to spend his first night onboard.

As Henry studied the rhythmic swells, a man, speed-walking, appeared beyond the one-way mirrored sliding glass doors that opened onto the promenade deck. Wearing a T-shirt, walking boots, and shorts, the man paused to catch his breath, and Henry saw that he carried weights in each hand.

'Ah, someone who enjoys the cold, a Jack Frost,' Henry named the vision, 'and he's a fitness fanatic . . .' He wondered at the man's ability to brave the weather wearing only a flimsy shirt. It was bitingly cold on deck and Henry snuggled further into his warm duvet, enjoying the luxury of watching the world outside without being seen himself.

Audrey had been insistent that Henry upgrade his cabin. In her day, she'd been a frequent cruiser. With long school holidays, Audrey spent many years travelling the world on various ships, visiting far-flung destinations such as Patagonia and Kyoto and the delights of Europe closer to home.

'Don't be cooped up in a cubby hole,' she'd implored as she studied Henry's cruise brochure. 'You don't need a grand suite or a private balcony, but the terrace cabins are generally more spacious with the luxury of stepping out onto the deck whenever the fancy takes you.'

Henry agreed that Audrey's advice had been sound, and he was enjoying his terrace cabin. Returning to the *Daily Times*, Henry planned his day.

An interdenominational church service would soon take place, followed by a chef's demonstration in the auditorium. Henry didn't feel the need for a blessing, but as chocolate was Henry's guilty pleasure, a chef's take on chocolate ganache cake might be interesting. He saw that a presentation of forthcoming excursions would be held mid-morning in the Triton Lounge, followed by a *Beginner's Guide to the Night Sky*.

Further reading detailed various classes, including exercise with the ship's fitness instructor, bowling, bridge, and a book club. There was also indoor curling and something called Killer Darts. Henry considered the age of the passengers he'd so far encountered and decided that a pensioner with a dart in their hand was something to avoid at all costs.

But first, he would enjoy a good breakfast.

Henry swung his legs out of bed and went to the bathroom, where he stood before the mirror to shave. Remembering the previous evening and the guests he'd met at dinner, Henry considered the Scotts a nice enough couple, but he had misgivings about the Montgomery Joneses.

Audrey's pre-cruise warning rang clear. 'Never judge a book by its cover!' she'd told him and said that a cruise ship held a sea-going sample of humanity and there would be people he would like and those he might not. Henry decided not to judge the Montgomery Joneses but to chat more with them at dinner. In the same conversation, Audrey had also reminded him that he was still young enough to find a good woman and settle down.

Rinsing his razor under the tap, Henry wondered why Audrey was so intent on Henry finding a partner. Surely, he was too old. After all, when Audrey was in her mid-sixties, she'd 'found a good woman', but the lady in question, a headmistress from a neighbouring school, had run off with a large share of Audrey's savings to settle down with a children's nanny in Nuneaton.

As Henry dressed, he thought of his friend.

The eighty-three-year-old, with depleted savings, could no longer afford her love of travel, but she expressed no regrets about her failed relationship, explaining that the 'good woman' she'd known had been extremely good in bed. 'Don't knock it until you've tried it, Henry Halliday,' Audrey said. 'Same-sex relationships are sensational!'

Henry chuckled. He didn't doubt his friend but considered himself too long in the tooth to have any experimental dalliances.

Opening his wardrobe, Henry chose a navy sweater that Audrey had gifted for his Christmas cruise. The thick cable-stitch had an ambitious pattern of frolicking red reindeers knitted into it, amongst snowflakes and fir trees.

'Perfect for Christmas in Norway, and toasty and warm. I ordered it on Etsy, it's hand-made,' Audrey commented, nodding with pleasure after insisting that Henry model his gift.

Henry was grateful that Audrey hadn't knitted the gift herself and thought of the erratically stitched, voluminous cardigan that she regularly wore. Knitting and Audrey were like oil and water and not a good match. He smoothed the sweater over his tummy and glanced in a mirror, hoping that it didn't cling to his midsection.

As Henry opened a drawer to find a scarf, he thought about Joy, the other guest at dinner who was also a solo traveller. She'd seemed nervous, and he wondered if, like himself, Joy had thought twice about joining a shared table. As it turned out, the dinner conversation had gone well, and Joy seemed to relax by the time desserts were served, perhaps due to the prosecco that Leticia generously shared.

But Henry thought Joy had an air of sadness, and he

wondered if she'd lost someone close. She might be a widow, and he'd noted a ring on her wedding finger, but whatever Joy's circumstances, he hoped she enjoyed the cruise. It took courage to travel alone at a certain age. Confidence can diminish as one gets older. He remembered her smile across the table when he'd winked, and a flush crept over his face. What on earth had made him do that? He wasn't in the habit of winking at women and Joy probably thought that Henry had a nervous tic.

Ready for the day, Henry closed his cabin door and stepped into the corridor, where Jennifer, neat in her uniform with a starched white apron, was making her way towards him.

'Good morning,' he greeted the housekeeper cheerily.

'Good sleep?' Jennifer asked.

Jennifer's jet-black hair was pulled sharply into a ponytail, and her smile was kind. Henry studied Jennifer's heart-shaped face and golden complexion and thought how attractive she was.

'Excellent, thank you,' he replied, returning her smile.

'I make up room good.'

'You did, and I'm very grateful. The chocolate was delicious.' Henry was touched by the individual chocolate, placed on his pillow when she'd turned down his bed.

'You single. You want more blankets? Keep you warm?'

'No, no I'm just fine, but thank you.'

'Nice sweater,' Jennifer said and gazed at the reindeers racing across Henry's chest. 'You have good day.' Jennifer produced a duster and began to polish the handrail. 'I see you later,' she added.

Henry decided on breakfast in the buffet restaurant, opting for a casual start to the day and as he ascended the stairs, his spirits lifted. He was *so* looking forward to the voyage ahead which promised so much, not only the excursions but also the magic of the Arctic. The little town of Molde would be the first stop, where daylight was already fleeting, then further north into the deepening darkness of the polar night. The chances of witnessing the aurora borealis were high, and Henry could hardly contain his anticipation as he steadied himself against the sudden sea swell beneath the ship, pausing to grab hold of the balustrade.

A woman in a velour tracksuit with bright pink hair passed him, heading down the stairs. 'Brace yourself,' she called out, 'wind's up, and later we're in for a rollercoaster ride!'

But Henry shook his head as he continued upward. 'This is no more than a slight swell,' he muttered. Paying no heed to the forecast in the *Daily Times*, Henry made his way through the ship and went in search of his first breakfast on the *Emerald Dream*.

* * *

In her Ocean View cabin, 2617, on Coral Deck Two, Joy had woken as dawn broke, and despite the comfort of her cabin, she'd been unable to get back to sleep. Wrapping her dressing gown tightly, she opened the blind, allowing light to flood in through the picture window. The morning outside looked grey, and the dark North Sea heaved under a brooding sky.

Through habit, when Tom booked the cruise, he'd

opted for a mid-range cabin, and though not as luxurious as those on upper decks, Joy welcomed its location. The middle of the ship would offer a smoother sail should the seas become rough. Not that she suffered from sea sickness, quite the opposite in fact. She found the waves soothing and whenever previous cruises had met with turbulent weather, she'd enjoyed a bumpy ride. Unlike Tom, who, in the Bay of Biscay, had taken to his bed where his complexion turned a worrying shade of grey, and he didn't emerge until they reached calmer waters.

Joy shook her head to disperse the memory.

Picking up a copy of the *Daily Times*, she studied the day's itinerary and wondered what Tom would have liked to do. She knew he would have enjoyed the destination presentation, keen to learn about the tours ashore. Always ready to try something new, perhaps he'd have joined in with Killer Darts, whatever that might be . . .

Resting back on her pillows, Joy closed her eyes and thought of the previous evening when she'd ventured to the Triton Lounge after dinner. Despite preferring an early night, Susan's words had drummed in Joy's ears, insisting that she join in.

Arriving early to find a quiet spot, Joy positioned herself on a comfortable chair at the end of a row in the balcony area. As the theatre filled, she ordered sparkling water from a steward, and while she waited, Joy studied the audience.

Sitting below, in the middle of the front row on the main floor, she could see Barbara and Kenneth. Barbara held a fluted glass in her hand, and as she spoke to the person beside her, she waved it around. Joy wondered if Barbara was making a point, perhaps extolling the virtue of the fine wine or describing the benefit of their personalised fjord cruise the following day. Kenneth meanwhile appeared to be dozing, his head falling forward to rest on his chest. Joy hoped his hairpiece was secure and didn't slide onto his lap.

To one side, she caught sight of Leticia, resplendent and impossible to miss in her glorious red gown. With practised ease, she assisted Jim into a seat while chatting happily with everyone within her radius. Joy admired the sheer force of Leticia's presence and remembered that Leticia had told them at dinner that she was a nurse. Joy sensed that the kindly woman had excelled in her caring career.

There had been no sign of Henry in the packed theatre, but he'd be impossible to spot with his silver-grey hair blending seamlessly into a sea of similar heads. Joy had enjoyed his company at dinner. Although quiet and unassuming, Henry had contributed to the conversation despite Kenneth's occasional snide remarks.

The show wasn't to Joy's liking. She considered the content by Taffy Taylor, the comedian, somewhat sexist. Consisting mostly of mother-in-law humour, his jokes felt inappropriate, and the act laboured. But the audience had clearly enjoyed the entertainment, and Kenneth took to his feet to applaud when Taffy took his curtain call.

Opening her eyes and returning to her copy of the *Daily Times*, Joy saw that the show that evening was named *Colours*. It was described as a magical world seen through an artist's paintbox, showcasing song and dance. She decided that *Colours* was more to her taste. But what to do in the meantime as the sea day stretched ahead?

Joy was tempted to settle with her book. In the comfort of her cabin, she wouldn't have to socialise, but the bestseller she'd brought wasn't hitting the spot and she found it challenging to engage. Time passed, and despite Joy flicking through the channels on the TV, nothing caught her attention.

It was no good. Joy knew she had to get dressed and join the day's activities. By now, Tom would have planned the day, having completed three brisk walks around the promenade deck, working up an appetite for his breakfast. If she'd enabled Wi-Fi, Joy knew that Susan would be calling to ensure that she was up and about.

'Come on, Joy Bradley. Pull yourself together,' she mumbled as she reluctantly rose, steadying herself as the ship occasionally swayed.

In the bathroom, she looked into a mirror and saw that her cheeks were hollowed and the eyes that stared back appeared tired, her expression forlorn. Joy shrugged. The mirror reflected a stranger's face but what did it matter how she looked? Her glow had faded a long time ago, like sunlight leaving a room. On the other hand, Susan, was striking. Her daughter had inherited the best of both parents. With her mother's sculptured features and her father's charm, the result was effortless beauty. Joy sometimes wondered if Susan felt any pressure from her looks, but her daughter had the arrogance of one who took such a gift for granted. In her job as a tough-talking prosecuting lawyer, she was the confident queen of her own successful world.

Joy wondered if she'd ever been that assured herself. During her career as a domestic science teacher, she'd taught generations of students self-sufficiency, but now, the woman who'd educated others in managing their lives no longer knew what to do with her own.

Joy smoothed moisturiser into her skin. She could see that the lines were fine, the skin soft and, thankfully, belied her age. Despite feeling ancient some days, she knew that she really wasn't that old. For years she'd told her students that you were as old as your mindset, reminding them that fifteen-year-olds often acted like fifty and vice versa. Life was as young as you made it, but these days that sentiment felt hard to embrace.

Joy dressed in navy trousers, adding a cream cashmere sweater and matching scarf. Slipping into soft leather loafers, she brushed her hair and, with a last glance at her reflection, picked up her cabin card then headed out of her room.

Joy stood by the lift and acknowledged a couple waiting to ascend to the buffet restaurant. As the doors opened the ship suddenly rocked and the couple held onto each other as they lurched into the lift.

'It feels like the sea is doing the samba today,' the man said, 'do you think it will get worse?'

'Like everything else, these waves pass,' Joy replied. But as they reached the upper floor and stepped into the foyer of the buffet restaurant, another swell hit the ship.

'Good gracious,' the man exclaimed as he staggered sideways, knocking into a fruit sculpture. 'Apologies,' he said, 'blame the swell not the spirits.'

Joy braced herself against the wall as they watched apples and pears tumble to the floor. Turning to the couple, she shrugged, 'At least it wasn't a chocolate fountain.'

Chapter Five

In the motion of the ocean, may the sea be your strength.

'Good morning, everyone! This is Simon, your cruise director, and I'm hoping you've all enjoyed a restful night and are now waking to the bracing sea air as we sail towards Norway. Whether you are a seasoned cruiser or setting sail for the first time, we are thrilled to have you with us.'

Simon's cheerful voice echoed through the ship's public address system, reaching passengers in cabins, corridors, and public rooms. In the buffet restaurant, amidst the chink of crockery and cutlery, diners paused mid-bite to listen, their breakfast momentarily forgotten as Simon's jolly tones brought the day to life.

'We have a full programme onboard today,' Simon continued, 'and for those participating in our Killer Darts, may I remind you that it's the only activity where it's permissible to throw something sharp, so try not to stab other competitors.' Simon paused. 'Only joking, of course!' he quickly added with a chuckle. 'The book club meeting will be held in the Botanical Room, and those chapter chasers amongst you will be pleased to hear that today's book for discussion is *The Sinking of the Titanic*.'

Several diners stared at each other, their expressions a mixture of concern.

'Well, that sounds ominous,' a woman was heard to say, while another wondered if it was wise to read a novel with such . . . depth.

'For the Women's Institute ladies who booked the cruise through the magazine *WI Life*, we've added a meetup for you today,' Simon informed, 'and this gathering will take place shortly, in the Ocean Bar at ten-thirty.'

In the buffet restaurant at her table for one, Joy listened to Simon as she buttered a slice of toast. She wondered if the bar would be open so early in the day and if cocktails and wine would replace the ladies' tea and cake. A former Women's Institute member, she'd always enjoyed the activities and contemplated joining the meeting.

Simon's enthusiasm continued as he explained that there was an art class in the Emerald Art Studio and an additional Christmas quiz in the Deck Café at two o'clock where complimentary mulled wine would be served. Joy noticed several pensioners reach for pens to make a note of the quiz time. With complimentary drinks there was sure to be a stampede.

Simon concluded by mentioning that as the ship sailed further north, the weather might get a little bit bumpy and advised passengers to be careful when moving about the ship.

'Now, everyone, on behalf of Captain Lindholm, and all the crew,' Simon almost sang as he ended his announcement, 'please be sure that you have a wonderful day aboard the amazing *Emerald Dream*.'

Joy, with Susan's orders ringing in her ears, determined to motivate herself and decided that her day would begin with a walk around the ship. She'd start at the top and work her way down. When a steward offered more coffee, Joy politely declined and, pushing back her chair, she left the restaurant to take the stairs to the Sports Deck.

It was too cold to head outside, so Joy amused herself by pausing in the Observatory, where several passengers had already bagged the best seats to spend the morning gazing out to sea. A couple of heads were dipped, and as she moved away, Joy heard the soft, rhythmic purr of an elderly man enjoying a nap.

Next, she saw that the sports courts were deserted, but when Joy stopped by the Emerald Art Studio, she noticed a woman setting up easels and arranging brushes in pots.

'Are you joining us?' the woman called out.

She wore a paint-splattered smock, and her vibrant red hair was fluffed out like a halo. Her eyes were dramatically lined with vivid green kohl and an empty cigarette holder perched between the fingers of one raised hand, as she paused to stare at the newcomer. Jo saw that the artist's gypsy-style dress flowed from her smock to the floor and skimmed her toenails, which were painted a sparkling blue.

'Lucinda Green,' the woman continued before Joy could reply. 'I'm famous. Don't miss the opportunity to learn from the best.' She placed the cigarette holder in her mouth and pouted.

'Well, I hadn't planned . . .'

'Well, you should. Don't dawdle the day away.' Lucinda turned on her espadrilles and, ignoring Joy, moved to an easel.

Startled, Joy decided that a morning with Lucinda, though informative, might not be *entirely* what she'd planned. The woman was like a walking theatre production, and Joy had no desire to participate in Lucinda's first act. The Lido Deck beckoned, and heading down the stairs, she passed a well-equipped fitness centre where an instructor, smart in logoed tracksuit, asked if she'd like to join the morning circuit training.

'Er, not today, thank you,' Joy replied and hurried on.

A wonderful aroma of eucalyptus and lavender drifted along the corridor, and Joy realised she was almost at the Atlantis Spa. Deeply inhaling, she remembered the exorbitant cost of treatments from the *Emerald Dream* brochure, but feeling drawn to the spa like a gentle embrace, Joy decided that during the cruise, she might treat herself.

A man wearing a towel wrapped around his waist came out of a changing room. His naked, corpulent torso was pale, and as he passed Joy on his way to the pool, his sliders slapped against the tiled floor.

'Don't be late for Kyle's Frost & Flex,' the man said. 'He's excellent, I worked out with him in the Med.'

'Ah, thank you, I'll make a note of his classes,' Joy nodded.

'You'll need to get your kit off if you don't want to miss it . . .'

Joy had no intention of getting her kit off or flexing any part of her body that might be susceptible to frostbite. But as she approached the indoor pool on the covered Lido Deck, she saw that the class was a hit. A determined crowd of hardcore passengers, already stripped off and unfazed by the chill, appeared eager and ready for the start of the session.

Joy found a seat, and when a steward approached, she ordered a latte.

Suddenly, the door by the side of the bar was thrown open, and music exploded across the deck as 'Eye of the Tiger' blasted out. As though entering a boxing ring for a world title fight, a man in brief shorts and a cape that billowed about him jogged towards the pool.

The Frost & Flex class began to clap excitedly, and Joy noticed one or two participants swaying perilously close to the pool's edge. The man raised his hand, and the music stopped. Then, with a dramatic sweep of his arms, he tossed his cape to one side.

'Morning luvvies!' he said. 'Welcome to Frost & Flex!'

Kyle, the fitness instructor, walked around the pool, high fiving everyone in turn, as a lady with bright orange hair in a skirted swimsuit lost her balance and toppled sideways into it.

'Grab a noodle, Nora!' Kyle called out and tossed a flotation aid into the water. 'We don't want you drowning before we get started.'

Mid-sip of her latte, Joy noted that Kyle, tall, blonde, and handsome, was familiar with passengers from previous cruises, and encouraged everyone to enter the water. At the deep end, a man paused, preparing to dive. He wore a swimming cap, and Joy recognised Kenneth from the previous evening. His chest hair was as thick as his conker-coloured rug.

I hope your toupee is tucked in tight! Joy thought as Kenneth belly-flopped into the pool, knocking into Nora and sending a tsunami of water over guests enjoying morning coffee at tables nearby.

Joy identified Barbara beneath a fur hat and matching

45

jacket. As water splashed across the pages of Barbara's book, she turned with an irritated glare in the direction of her husband. Picking up a wine glass, Barbara took a large gulp then ordered another and, shaking the pages of her dampened paperback, continued to read.

'Now, Kenneth!' Kyle called out. 'We're not ready for synchronised swimming just yet. Give Nora a hand and bring her back to the surface.'

Joy stared as a spluttering Nora was pulled from the pool.

Finishing her coffee, Joy saw Leticia waving from a jacuzzi. 'Joy! Come and join us, it's divine in here.'

Joy made her way to the jacuzzi where Leticia sat in the steamy water with Jim alongside. 'I haven't got my swimsuit,' Joy said and stared at the rising bubbles.

'That's a shame; the water is lovely, isn't it, Jim?' Leticia raised her hand to his face and stroked gently. In return, Jim kissed her fingers.

'Did you sleep well?' Joy asked.

'Like logs, didn't we, Jim?' Leticia smiled lazily at her husband, then turned to Joy, 'Did you?'

'Not really, but it doesn't matter, I never sleep much these days.'

'I'm a good listener if you ever want to talk about your husband,' Leticia said softly.

Startled, Joy was taken aback. Leticia had peered straight into Joy's subconscious, naming aloud the one subject Joy never expected anyone to mention.

'Only if you feel comfortable, of course,' Leticia smiled.

No one ever asked Joy about Tom anymore. People

46

avoided the subject, as though her husband's death was something best left untouched. Joy knew it was discomfort or fear of saying the wrong thing. Or perhaps it was the thought that conversation might stir up aching memories, and people didn't know how to deal with Joy's pain. Neighbours often crossed the street or darted away to avoid Joy, unaware their reaction only worsened things.

Death could be so alienating.

Even Susan swerved the subject of her father's death, suggesting that the trauma had passed, and it was time to move on. But here, in the most unusual circumstances, was a woman who appeared to have a sixth sense. Joy had never mentioned Tom, but Leticia, her face softening, seemed to understand. Joy stared at Leticia and an unspoken sign passed between them when Leticia reached out, her fingers brushing Joy's arm, squeezing gently in solidarity.

'This jacuzzi is so good, but I think we may have had enough.' Leticia studied Jim's skin, which appeared slightly prune-like. 'Time to get dressed.'

Joy stood back, her eyes wide, as Leticia rose from the water like a goddess emerging from the deep. Voluptuous in a jewelled and sparkling swimsuit, water cascaded down her gleaming body. With the grace of an athlete, she placed her hands beneath Jim's shoulders and gently lifted him from the jacuzzi and helped him walk towards his chair.

'Pass me a couple of towels,' Leticia called out as she carefully placed one foot slowly in front of the other while linking Jim's arm, determined not to slip.

Joy reached for a stack of blue and white guest towels and handed two to Leticia.

'Perfect, thanks,' Leticia told Joy as she dabbed Jim's skin gently. 'We'll hopefully see you later. Perhaps you'll join us for the Christmas quiz?'

'I'd like that,' Joy said, surprising herself with her prompt reply.

The ship suddenly swayed as it encountered a swell of waves and Joy watched Leticia steady herself while she manoeuvred Jim away. Guests nearby turned as one, as Leticia's swimsuit sparkled and she moved gracefully in an almost choreographed motion to the waves outside.

Behind Joy, the pool deck buzzed as Kyle exercised in time to the music. Wearing a headset, he called out commands. 'Splash like your ex is watching!' he yelled.

Perched on the edge of the pool, gripping her foam noodle, Nora kicked the water, then paused to glance skyward, her smile almost serene.

'Oh, I hope he is,' Nora shouted. 'Especially as I'm having so much fun.'

Kyle continued to strut and dance, encouraging his class, and for a moment, everything seemed to blur as Joy painfully thought of Tom. The deep smell of chlorine, tinged with the eucalyptus, still hung in the air, but the space beside her was empty, a constant reminder that she was alone.

With one last glance at the party in the pool, Joy turned and walked away. Waiting by the lift to descend to her cabin, she remembered Leticia's invitation to the Christmas quiz.

I must make the effort, Joy thought, and with a sigh, stepped inside.

Chapter Six

No journey is as great as one on the open sea.

Henry always enjoyed his first meal of the day and after a breakfast of fresh fruit, followed by poached eggs with bacon, he made his way through the ship taking note of the activities taking place. Sea days were busy onboard and there was a buzz as passengers gathered for events that included bridge, art and dance lessons. Passing the Lido Deck he saw passengers by the pool in swimming gear, many spreadeagled on sunbeds as a fitness instructor in brief shorts and wearing a cape, collected flotation aids from around the deck before disappearing through a door at the side of the bar.

It must have been a very active class, Henry thought as he noted a woman with bright orange hair, shrouded in a hooded dry-robe, already asleep on an upright chair.

In the atrium, Henry paused to watch a string quartet set up for their mid-morning performance of classical music. He wandered on until he came to the busy Bookmark Café and chose a book from the photography section. He looked forward to reading it as soon as he found a peaceful spot. Remembering the quiet of the Botanical Room, Henry made his way there and soon found a comfortable seat.

The walls of the wide windowed room were decorated with leafy fronds and climbing vines and Henry admired several tall palms beside a display of jasmine. *Wildlife Photography: From Snapshots to Great Shots* lay on Henry's knee and, turning the pages, he began to read.

Nearby and gathered around a long table, the book club meeting was in progress and as their discussion began, Henry was unable to concentrate. He recalled Simon's earlier announcement that the chosen title for the meeting was *The Sinking of the Titanic*. Now, a discussion between two members was becoming heated and Henry looked up.

'You've got it all wrong,' a woman said, 'there were protocols to follow. You can't just chuck folk into lifeboats willy-nilly. There had to be an order for who went first.'

Henry saw that the speaker, a rake-thin woman of considerable height, appeared to be the book club's self-appointed leader.

'It was a class issue, Judy,' a man replied, folding his arms tightly across his chest. 'They let the wealthy sail off while the rest of the passengers in steerage were locked down and left to freeze and drown. I wouldn't be surprised if you would be one to push past everyone in an emergency,' he added.

'I think that comment is out of order.' The woman, Judy, glared and shifted in her seat.

'Has anyone watched the movie?' The man turned to the others. 'It was a cracking film. Kate Winslet's corset was so tight I needed oxygen to watch.'

A lady wearing a lavender shawl that matched her hair spoke out. 'I watched the film and cried when DiCaprio went under,' she sighed, 'he was so handsome.'

'I cry when my tea goes cold,' Judy snapped, tossing her head back and shaking her thick grey curls, 'but given the difference of opinion, shall we choose an alternative novel?'

Henry returned to his book, but opinions flared loudly, and unable to concentrate, he decided to find an alternative place to sit.

In the Ocean Bar, two smiling ladies, their silver hair neatly styled and wearing identical cardigans and slacks, gave a friendly wave from a far corner. Returning the greeting, Henry thought they must be sisters, their resemblance so alike, but otherwise, he saw that the room was deserted. Deciding to stay, he barely noticed the ship's sway as he looked out of the panoramic windows where a container ship appeared on the horizon, its vast grey shape a contrast against the watery blue sky.

Henry ordered coffee and shortbread, and turning back to his book, began to enjoy the peace. The coffee was rich, and the shortbread buttery. Soon, he was happily lost in images of wild animals and birds photographed in their natural habitats. His fingers paused on the glossy pages and his mind marvelled at the clarity. Henry wished he could replicate the composition and the photographer's keen eye. Despite his passion, he knew that his own pictures would never be this good.

Suddenly, the door flew open, and there was a flurry of florals and pearls. 'This way!' a woman called out, and Henry recognised Judy from the book club.

The ladies of the Women's Institute had arrived, and the calm atmosphere Henry had sought was drowned by the gaggling group as they filled the room. The sisters in the corner joined in as the meeting began.

Surrounded by craft bags, knitting, and notebooks, Henry slumped in his chair, wishing he could disappear. No wonder the room had been empty! *Fellow travellers, beware . . . the Women's Institute gets everywhere!*

Reaching out to finish his coffee, Henry closed his book and prepared to slip away. But first, he needed to sign his bill. He scanned the room anxiously. Unfortunately, the steward was now swamped with orders, and Henry couldn't escape.

With introductions complete, the ladies launched into their latest national campaign on environmental sustainability. Carbon emissions and plastic waste were hot topics, and one woman declared clingfilm to be the cause of moral decay, while another insisted sandwich wrappers should be banned nationwide.

'My husband should be banned,' sighed the lady in the lavender shawl. 'His emissions are one of the biggest causes of climate change.' She took a sip of sweet sherry while heads nodded in sympathy.

The door crept open again, and Henry saw Joy nervously scan the busy room. Spotting Henry, who felt like a man cornered by lions, Joy looked as though she was about to flee, then changed her mind and made her way towards him.

'How's it going?' she whispered and crouched down beside him.

'I feel trapped and am regretting wearing synthetic fibre socks,' Henry muttered.

'Your sweater is pure wool, so I wouldn't be too worried.'

'It's a gift from my friend Audrey,' Henry said, 'and I'm not sure she'd approve of this debate.' He knew that old-school Audrey wouldn't know an eco-friendly alternative if it struck her in the face.

'So, you're planning an escape?'

'I would if I could, but I've got to sign the bill, and the steward is neck-deep in orders.'

'Here's a trade,' Joy, said, still crouching, 'give up your seat, and I'll sort the bill out.'

'I couldn't possibly let you . . .' Henry began.

But Judy had seen Henry and called out: 'I say, the gentleman in the middle, this is a *women's* meeting so either pipe down or leave the room.'

'So much for equality,' Henry muttered. 'See you on the other side,' he whispered to Joy, and grabbing his book, rose, and made his exit.

Reaching the atrium, Henry puffed out a breath, checked his watch, and decided that to celebrate his escape, a drink was in order. Despite the early hour, he made his way to the bar.

* * *

'Had a good morning?' Leticia asked Joy when they met up that afternoon for the Christmas quiz. Jim, wearing a snowman jumper, sat alongside in his chair, polishing his glasses. The horns on Leticia's reindeer headband wobbled as she patted a seat.

As Joy sat down, she stared at the Christmas puddings that decorated Leticia's woolly chest. Her emerald-green velvet skirt clung to her hips and was embroidered with sequins. Joy pushed up the cuffs of her beige sweater, removed her scarf, and thought how dull she must once again appear next to Leticia's festive vision.

'What have you been up to?' Leticia asked.

Joy explained that tensions had run high at the Women's Institute meetup when a member from Melton Mowbray suggested that everyone should eat lentils and grow their own beans to eliminate greenhouse gases.

'How was that received?' Leticia asked.

'She was told by her friend that as she drove a diesel vehicle, she was in no position to voice an opinion on such matters, and should consider going electric,' Joy replied and remembered that knitting needles had poised mid-knit before Judy, fearing an escalation of tempers, suggested that in the spirit of the organisation, a few verses of 'Jerusalem' were in order.

'Things calmed down following the anthem,' Joy said, 'and after a round of sherry, blankets for the Red Cross and crocheted cot covers for African babies were discussed. Thankfully, the meeting ended happily.'

'I've never been a Women's Institute member, but it sounds like a lot of fun,' Leticia replied.

'It's a few years since I went to meetings, but I remember that I enjoyed them and it could get lively, but tea and cake generally smoothed things out.'

Leticia's brow arched. 'Why did you stop going to meetings?'

Joy hesitated, her gaze flicking away. 'Things came up at home,' she said dismissively, and brushed a loose strand of hair behind her ear.

Leticia told Joy they'd enjoyed a delicious roast lunch

in the restaurant. 'Our servers, Jhamille and Ryan asked where you were,' Leticia said. 'They hope we'll all be back together for dinner.'

'I had a snack in the buffet.'

Leticia gave her a knowing smile. 'Things will get better as you get to know everyone,' she said.

Once again, Joy found herself struck by Leticia's uncanny intuition.

'How's your quizzing?' Jim chipped in. With his glasses perched on his nose, he shifted in his chair to reach for the sheet of paper and an accompanying pencil.

'I'm probably not going to contribute much, but I'll try,' Joy said.

She thought of the Sudoku games she played to fill the empty hours at home. The puzzle didn't require anything more taxing than logic. Crosswords she'd left to Tom, who always retreated behind a closed door in his study to complete the puzzle in his daily newspaper.

Sitting opposite Jim, Joy saw that his posture was slightly distorted, and she wondered if he was uncomfortable as she watched Leticia reach for a magazine to allow him a firm surface to rest his paper.

'Oh look, here's Henry,' Leticia said and waved.

Henry returned the wave and, as he approached, appeared mellow. 'I've been in the sports bar,' he began. 'Several football fans are hoping to watch a game, but there seems to be a problem with the satellite signal,' he explained. 'I had a couple of pints and came away before they started a riot.' He looked at Joy. 'It was quite lively. A bit like the Women's Institute meeting.'

'Grab a seat, we need another brain to join our team,' Leticia said and shuffled chairs. 'I like your sweater; you look very Nordic.'

Henry looked down and smoothed the wool over his chest. 'It was a gift from my friend Audrey,' he said, 'she thought it would be ideal for this cruise.'

'Clever Audrey, it's perfect.'

'Let me get you a drink,' Henry said to Joy. 'I owe you for getting me out of a tight spot this morning, and Jim and Leticia, what will you have?'

'There's complimentary mulled wine; shall we start with that?' Leticia asked, and everyone nodded.

As the lounge began to fill, and with drinks on the way, Jim sorted a name for their team, and Santa's Little Helpers were soon ready for the quiz. The sound of 'Jingle Bells' playing softly in the background and twinkling fairy lights gave a festive feel as guests formed groups and settled around tables.

A member of the *Emerald Dream* entertainment team appeared. Straightening his Santa hat and flipping open the quiz sheet on his clipboard, he picked up a mic and began speaking. 'Greetings and welcome!' he addressed the crowded room. 'My name is Amit, and I'm your Christmas quiz master.'

Amit paused to look at the faces gazing back. Most guests had entered into the spirit of things and wore festive jumpers while one man modelled a Christmas tree-shaped hat, and another balanced a snowman-shaped beret on his head.

'On your tables, you will find paper for your answers, so please appoint a leader and a name for your team,'

Amit continued as heads dipped, and discussions began. 'Remember, no phones.'

'You'd need a lottery win to buy the ship's Wi-Fi package for your phone,' someone piped up.

Outside, the sea had grown choppy, but as the ship rose and fell with the waves, guests sipped their mulled wine and scarcely took notice.

'Whoops!' Amit faltered as a swell almost sent him sideways, but regaining his balance, he launched into the first question. 'An easy one to commence the proceedings. Is everyone ready?'

'Born ready!' came a chorus from the corner where Rudolph's Rowdy Sailors were poised.

'Question one. What natural phenomenon is commonly known as the Northern Lights?' Amit asked.

'Mother Nature is showing off her new LED system,' a Rowdy Sailor called out.

'Write your answer down,' Amit chided.

'It's the aurora borealis,' Henry whispered to his team. 'Sorry, I shouldn't jump in,' he apologised. 'I'm sure you all know that.'

'Jump in all you like,' Leticia said as Jim scribbled the answer.

'I can't wait to see the Lights as we get further north,' Henry said. 'It will be a highlight of my holiday.'

'You can't guarantee a sighting,' Jim commented, 'but I agree, the Lights will be a highlight for me too.'

'Question two,' Amit continued. 'What name is given to the indigenous people of Arctic Scandinavia known for herding reindeer?'

'Sámi,' Santa's Little Helpers all mouthed and Jim noted the answer.

'Now for a popular tradition.' Amit consulted his clipboard. 'What beverage is traditionally served warm and spiced in many Nordic Christmas celebrations?'

'It's Glögg,' Joy whispered. Suddenly, she was transported back to her domestic science classroom, where she taught practical cookery and cultural knowledge of traditional European cuisine. The spiced mulled drink named Glögg perfectly matched Pepparkakor, the Swedish ginger biscuits the class had been making.

'And for an extra point, can you name three of the ingredients in the beverage?' Amit asked.

Joy nodded. 'Apple juice, cardamom, cinnamon, cloves, orange peel, raisins, almonds, and ginger,' she explained, ticking the list off on her fingers.

'Well done, Joy.' Jim grinned as he filled in the answer. 'Amit might double the points for all those ingredients.'

'Next, a geography question.' Amit looked at his notes. 'Which ocean is Christmas Island located in?'

Sitting towards the front, the Wrinkled Elves began to argue while the Noel-It-Alls looked smug alongside.

'I think it's the Indian Ocean.' Henry cupped a hand over his mouth so the Quizmas Crackers at the next table couldn't hear.

Amit continued, and Henry answered most of the questions for Santa's Little Helpers. Amit repeated several questions for those who needed more time, then collected everyone's answers. 'Now, please take a break while I work out which team is the winner of today's champagne prize.'

Servers appeared with more mulled wine, weaving amongst the tables while guests sat back to relax and chat. When Amit returned, conversation halted and a hush rippled across the room as all eyes turned to him.

'It has been a close-run contest,' Amit began. He slowly shuffled his papers, adding to the rising tension. 'But we have an outright winning team.'

'Get on with it!' someone called out from the far side of the room.

When Joy looked up, she recognised Kenneth sitting beside Barbara and four guests who had made up a team named the Festive Foreign Office.

'In third place,' Amit said, 'we have . . . the Wrinkled Elves!'

A cheer went up from the Elves, and there was applause as the eldest elf tottered over to Amit and was presented with a box of chocolates.

'Our runners up today,' Amit continued, 'with only one point nudging them into second place . . . are Santa's Little Helpers!'

Henry leaped to his feet and high-fived Jim as Leticia gave Joy a hug. Amit held out a bottle of prosecco and invited Henry to come forward to receive their prize.

'Did your grandma knit your jumper?' Kenneth called out as Henry held the prize high, and his sweater rose. 'It's so tight that even the reindeer are asking for more space.'

Henry froze. With the bottle in his hand, his smile faltered, and tugging his sweater over his tummy, he returned to his seat.

'It takes a fine figure of a man to carry off such a magnificent sweater,' Leticia said to Henry, 'and without your extensive knowledge, we would never have come second. Clever Henry.'

Amit announced the winner, and to boisterous cheers from the Festive Foreign Office team members, Kenneth accepted the prize on their behalf.

Tapping his forehead, he winked at the audience as he gripped the bottle of champagne. 'Good job the old brain is still sharp,' he said, 'otherwise I might have ended up wearing Henry's jumper!'

Barbara could be heard laughing and Joy's eyes narrowed as Kenneth, grinning widely, strode back to his seat. She wondered if he was always so rude and knew that she'd find it difficult to dine with the couple that evening.

Leticia reached out to pat Joy's hand as though acknowledging her thoughts. Henry, meanwhile, politely clapped, but his smile was tight, his gaze lingering on Kenneth for a moment too long, and Joy knew that the comment had stung. She remembered Henry mentioning that the sweater was a present from his friend Audrey, and she hoped that it wouldn't put him off wearing the gift.

But as her thoughts settled, Joy reflected that Henry had mentioned Audrey more than once. Last night, at dinner, she'd assumed Henry was single, but maybe Audrey wasn't just a friend with good taste in sweaters, maybe she was a *special* friend and held a place in Henry's heart.

The ship rolled as the guests began to disperse. Concerned that Jim was tired, Leticia said their goodbyes and headed to their cabin. Alone with Henry, Joy suddenly felt self-conscious and said she, too, must be on her way.

'I'll see you at dinner,' Henry said as Joy pushed back her chair.

Joy thought of Kenneth and Barbara. It was probably too late to escape from the shared table for the evening meal, and she didn't want to appear rude to Henry.

'Wouldn't miss it,' Joy said with a smile that she hoped looked more enthusiastic than it felt, and moving swiftly through the room, she began to rehearse small talk.

Anything to stop Kenneth making remarks that might ruin the evening again.

Chapter Seven

We are all wanderers on this earth, especially at sea.

'Good morning, everyone!' Simon's sing-song voice boomed through the ship's public address system the following morning as the *Emerald Dream* docked at her first port of call. Joy, who'd been restless throughout the night, was jolted from her sleep. Lifting her arm from beneath the cosy duvet, she glanced at her watch and considered seven o'clock rather early for Simon to address the passengers, especially as many would be weary, having had little sleep.

The sea had been unforgiving as they sailed north.

It churned violently in the night with waves crashing with relentless regularity as the wind howled, and every gust felt like a vicious assault. Many guests were confined to their cabins, unable to move around, too nervous to venture out for fear of falling. The decks had been closed as the sea surged, battering the ship's sides and making the hull shudder. When it came, sleep was uneasy, and even the most seasoned travellers found themselves lying still, some unwell, waiting for the storm to pass. But it did pass, and as dawn rose, calm waters came, and the *Emerald Dream* sailed on towards Norway.

Now, Joy sat up as Simon continued.

'Today's port is the lovely town of Molde,' he said, 'and it is pronounced "Mohl-duh." When you disembark, if you want to greet the local folk, you can say, "Hei" and to thank them it's "tusen takk".'

Joy thought it unlikely that she'd be lapsing into Norwegian. It was common knowledge that at least ninety-five per cent of the population of Norway spoke English, having been taught from an early age in school.

'Don't forget, if you're staying onboard today, you can ease those aches and pains with our Atlantis Spa Specials, and if all that salt air is too much for your hair, come and have a deep conditioning treatment with our salon staff.' Simon chuckled. 'Love is in the hair!' he added.

Simon then explained the procedures for disembarking and reminded the guests that the temperature outside was below zero, with snow predicted, and to wrap up warmly. He concluded by wishing those heading out on trips a wonderful day. 'Don't forget,' Simon added, 'with so many new experiences today, you can store them in your memory bank for the days when you no longer can.'

The cruise director also informed guests that a raffle ticket would be left in their cabin later that day along with the *Daily News*. 'Keep hold of your ticket because it is your free entry for the captain's Gala Raffle and the winner will be announced on the last night of the cruise.'

When Simon had finished, Joy swung her legs over the side of the bed. Her immediate concern was to dig out her thermals and ensure she was prepared for the excursion to the Atlantic Ocean Road. As she stepped into the shower and let hot water pound against her skin, Joy thought about the previous evening.

The sea swell that they'd been experiencing all day had built into a storm by early evening, and the dining room that would normally be bustling had thinned to less than half its usual occupancy. With each sway of the ship, stewards moved carefully, balancing dishes on laden trays with the poise of tightrope walkers as they battled to serve the guests.

Leticia and Jim were already seated when Joy arrived.

'You made it!' Leticia grinned. 'Well done.'

Joy grabbed her seat and carefully sat down. 'It *is* a bit choppy,' she said. 'Are you both coping?'

'Nothing will keep Jim and me away from a plate of fine food,' Leticia laughed. 'Oh, and of course, with a little bit of help too.' She pushed up the cuff of her silky blouse to display acupressure bands on both wrists, and dipping her head, she pointed behind each ear. 'These motion patches are lifesavers.'

'I'm so lucky that I don't suffer from seasickness,' Joy said as Jhamille greeted everyone and placed a napkin on Joy's knee. Turning, she thanked him.

'Your friends won't be joining you,' Jhamille said as he held a glass pitcher. 'Mr and Mrs Montgomery Jones have ordered a light meal in their suite.'

Joy's eyes widened. 'Oh, that's a shame,' she said. Her relief felt as soothing as warm sunlight on cold skin, and the thought of dining without Kenneth's smug remarks loosened muscles in Joy's body that she hadn't realised were tense.

Jhamille leaned in. 'Seasick, like many,' he whispered and poured iced water into Joy's glass.

Before she had time to turn to Leticia to comment on Kenneth and Barbara's ailment, Henry teetered to the table. Clutching his photography book, he still wore his reindeer jumper, and thanked Jhamille, who assisted Henry to his seat.

'Sorry, I haven't changed,' Henry said. 'I decided that finding my cabin involved too much motion, so I stayed put in the Bookmark Café, which is within staggering distance of the dining room.'

'You look a little pale, if you don't mind me mentioning it,' Leticia said. She dug into her bag to produce a supply of bands and patches, urging Henry to put them on. 'Here, these will help. In the meantime, sip some water and nibble on bread.' She pushed a basket of warm rolls towards him.

Leticia's sickness aids helped and Henry soon rallied to tuck into a delicious dinner while explaining his admiration for the Vikings, who sailed these waters centuries ago.

'My Year Nine students once staged a mock raid on the school,' Henry said and was animated as he described how they'd made sackcloth clothing and horned helmets from papier mâché, terrifying everyone in the vicinity. 'I taught them to understand that despite being generally perceived as outlaws, the Norse warriors were hunters and fishermen who embarked on their voyages to help them survive harsh winters at home.'

Jim poured wine for everyone. 'How satisfying to bring history to life, your students must have enjoyed your lessons,' he said.

'Re-enactment helped get the facts across,' Henry admitted. 'They loved being plunderers, and I dressed up as a Viking chieftain in faux-fur cloak, plastic axe, and a fake beard. It itched like mad, as I remember.'

'Do you still have it?' Jim laughed.

'No, those days are gone, but I think Audrey kept hold of the cloak and occasionally wears it.'

As Joy listened to Henry explain how students had absorbed his teachings, she wondered what Audrey, Henry's friend, was like. Obviously intelligent, she'd have the same interests as Henry and was a woman who wore faux fur. Joy pictured Audrey wrapped in a cloud of confidence, the decadent faux-fur the colour of chocolate, and her hair perfectly coiffed, not a strand out of place.

'What's the Althing?' Leticia asked.

'It was the world's first parliamentary system.' Henry became animated again. 'Created by the Vikings, who had their own laws, despite being a brutal race.'

'Sounds like the IT team I worked with.' Jim smiled dryly.

'Even without any written law, there was a system of government,' Henry continued as Jhamille cleared away the main course. Henry looked out at the darkened windows when the ship lurched yet again. 'If we were living in the ninth century, this sea would be teaming with longships,' he said, a whimsical smile on his lips. 'Well, perhaps not so many in this weather. But enough of me, what about everyone else's career?'

Leticia spooned gelato and licked her lips. She told them that she'd been a nurse at St Thomas' Hospital in London, where she'd met Jim. 'I was working on a children's ward and Jim was a frequent visitor,' she explained.

Leticia turned, sidelining her own story to ask Joy about her working life.

Joy sensed Leticia wanted to steer away from her own career. But not wishing to disclose too much about herself, Joy reluctantly picked up the conversation. 'I loved teaching,' she slowly began, 'there's something so rewarding about watching a child kneading dough, their eyes wide as they watch it rise, then the magic of baking and tasting it. Especially when they thought it came ready-made and pre-packed.'

'Didn't domestic science, as it was, include other subjects?' Jim asked.

'Yes, I taught sewing too.'

As Joy thought about her life in the classroom, her shoulders relaxed and for a moment she was at ease. She could almost hear the grind of sewing machines as her pupils, heads down in concentration, stitched items that included aprons and tea towels.

'My job title evolved to home economics teacher.' Joy smiled. 'The head insisted that it wasn't just about cooking and cleaning, but life skills and independence too. Tom used to laugh and say I knew little about either.'

She paused and placed her dessert spoon on her plate, and the clink was louder than expected in the sudden hush. There it was. She'd mentioned Tom. Now, everyone would change the subject and glance away, pretending not to have heard.

'How powerful.' Jim nodded earnestly. 'You taught the next generation confidence and how to take care of themselves.'

Leticia leaned in. 'But I'm sure that Tom was very proud of you,' she said softly. There was warmth in her deep, dark eyes. 'Why don't you tell us about him?'

'Yes, do,' Henry urged, resting his elbows on the table, his dessert forgotten.

Joy reached out to fiddle with the stem of her wine glass. 'Well,' she began, 'Tom was the manager of a box-making company. Their main products were boxes for cakes, especially wedding cakes, and he sold to all the major manufacturers.'

'Did he design the boxes?' Jim asked.

'Oh, yes, he was head of design and sales, as well as managing the company.'

'He must have been very skilled.'

'He was. There wasn't a thing you could teach him about the machinery on the factory floor or design and the demands of the customer.' Joy paused. 'It was a very stressful job, and he worked terribly long hours.'

'Did you manage to take holidays?' Henry asked.

'Yes, Tom made sure that we had at least two weeks away, every year, while our daughter enjoyed visiting Tom's sister, who lived in London. Susan loves the city and bright lights.'

'Did you visit anywhere in particular?' Leticia asked. She nodded as Jhamille hovered, a bottle of wine in his hand.

'We went on cruises; it was Tom's passion.'

'How wonderful.' Leticia raised her glass.

'Yes, even in the days when cruising was quite elitist, we saved hard to take the trips.'

'Isn't it great that cruising is accessible for everyone now?' Leticia commented.

Henry was staring at Joy. 'And you're still cruising,' he said.

Joy took a sip of wine, then carefully placed her glass down and moved her hands to her lap. 'This cruise,' she began, her voice edged with fragility, 'was meant to be for our fortieth wedding anniversary.'

The table fell still.

'Tom wanted to see the fjords at Christmas. We were married on Christmas Eve you see, and he said it would be the perfect celebration.'

'What happened?' Leticia asked, her tone soft.

'We were cruising in the Greek Islands. It had been a lazy day at sea, and after dinner, Tom said he was tired and would have an early night.' Joy paused. 'I stayed up a little longer, and he was already asleep when I came to the cabin. He looked so relaxed, like he always did after a day beside the pool and a glass of wine or two.' She swallowed, then continued. 'I got into bed and fell asleep, but when I got up in the morning . . .'

A silence followed, but no one rushed in to fill it.

'The doctor said it was his heart. He described it as a catastrophic cardiac arrest. It was very quick.'

Leticia reached out to squeeze Joy's hand. 'If there is any kindness in death,' she said, 'I suppose that was it. How brave you are to talk about it.'

'I think you're very brave to come on this cruise,' Henry added.

Jim reached for his wine. 'To Tom,' he said.

As Joy fiddled with the stem of her glass, she watched Henry and Leticia raise their glasses, 'To Tom,' they said and toasted the absent passenger too.

The silence after the toast seemed heavy, as though weighted by the missing presence of Tom, while the sea outside shifted darkly, reminding the guests that life moved forward.

Joy's smile flickered, 'I suppose we're both on this journey after all, only Tom's took him further than mine. To the journeys we never finish . . .' she whispered.

Letting the toast hang, unfinished, the others nodded.

Leticia raised her glass and, catching Joy's eye, said, 'To the journey you're about to begin.'

Chapter Eight

Live without excuses and chart your
course with no regret.

In their comfortable suite, Leticia rummaged through the drawers in their bedroom, searching for the thermal underwear she'd purchased for the cruise. Jim, on the other hand, was already dressed and ready for the day. His expression was serious as he sat by the window, reading the *Daily Times*. He wore his favourite sweater, a thick Shetland wool with an intricate cable stitch that Leticia had lovingly knitted for the trip.

'I enjoyed the show last night,' Jim said.

'Fabulous entertainment,' Leticia replied, 'so clever to theme dance with colourful song titles and costumes.' As she pushed a pair of Bounce Buster Support Briefs to one side, Leticia thought of the talented troupe who'd entertained the audience as they performed to songs that reflected their routine. 'Purple Rain', 'Yellow Submarine', 'Black is Black' and 'Goldfinger' to name but a few.

'I'm glad we're not going on the snowshoe walk today,'

Jim said, 'it's a four-hour hike over uneven ground with no facilities.' He studied the page. 'No good for us, my darling, but I expect the participants will enjoy the "snow-covered landscapes, unique flora and fauna, and tales of centuries-old local traditions"', Jim quoted, 'and no doubt a lunch will be thrown in with authentic dishes from the Molde region.'

Leticia smiled. She stood in her bra and knickers, having located long thermal leggings and a matching top. 'Now, should I wear two layers of these, or just the one?' she asked.

'Well . . .' Jim turned to study his wife, 'as we will be on a coach, then a ferry and finally a train, I think you can play it safe with just one layer underneath. You know you get overheated.'

'Fair comment,' Leticia said. She dug her toes into the thick fabric and tugged the garment over her legs.

'Steady now,' Jim grinned, 'you'll get me going in that sexy outfit.'

'Sexy?' Leticia raised her eyebrows as she reached for the top. 'Jim, it's thermal undies, not lacey lingerie.'

Jim smiled as Leticia pulled the vest over her head.

'Lucky for you, I didn't pack the fleecy knickers covered in snowmen,' she mumbled through the fabric, 'or you'd be unstoppable.'

Jim held up his hands in mock surrender as he watched Leticia manipulate her full breasts into place. When her head appeared, the braids were dislodged and covered her face, and they both burst into laughter.

'Phew, that was hard work,' Leticia said as she zipped

up her fleece-lined trousers and wriggled her body. 'I'll need aircon on the coach despite the temperature outside.'

In the bathroom, Leticia stood by the his-and-her sinks and organised her hair under a snood, then began applying her makeup. As she worked, she thought of the forthcoming excursion. Assisting Jim onto the coach, the ferry, and finally the train would be challenging. But as she applied eyeliner, Leticia knew they were both determined that Jim's illness wouldn't stop him from enjoying his bucket list while he could still walk, even for a short distance.

This trip had been one of the items on that list.

Metastatic spinal cord compression was a bitch of an illness to beat, and a battle that Leticia knew Jim wouldn't win. She pursed her lips to apply gloss and remembered the shock of learning that despite having treated Jim's prostate cancer, the disease had spread to his spine, causing problems with mobility. As the condition worsened, in Jim's case, ultimately it would lead to paralysis and death. Now, things were stable but not without problems, and Leticia knew Jim would deteriorate when The Beast, as they called it, returned.

As if the man hadn't had more than enough grief in his life, she thought as she moved away from the mirror.

Smoothing her top over her hips, Leticia remembered the night before and the dinner conversation when Henry enquired about her job. Henry seemed such a decent sort of man, but Leticia hadn't wanted to dim the tone of the evening by relating their history and, of course, how she and Jim had met. There was a time and place for everything, and some memories were too sacred to be casually discussed.

Now, as she readied herself for the day, she remembered how Jim had rested his hand on her knee as they listened to Joy talk about Tom. Leticia had chosen not to speak of her own long working days at the hospital, to the backdrop hum of machines and the little girl she'd cared for in intensive care. The little girl with too small limbs and eyes too wise for her years. A single father sat beside her every day, hollow with exhaustion, clinging to hope as he held his daughter's tiny hand, willing her to live.

The father was Jim. The child was named Grace, and Grace's mother had died in childbirth.

Strange things happen in hospitals, especially at night when the corridors are quiet, and the rhythmic beeping of monitors is soothing. Grief walks through the wards openly, but there are times when much-needed kindness can be found. Jim had responded to Leticia's kindness, and she made time for him long after Grace had gone.

Now, as Leticia stood in the doorway and stared at Jim as he read the *Daily Times*, she thought that there had been no rush or drama in their developing relationship. Just two people, who'd been brought together in unbearable circumstances. It wasn't a lightning strike. Their love, a healing of a different kind, came quietly and steadily, and Leticia had never looked back. Jim was her world, he was her rock, and she knew that she'd love him unconditionally, always and forever. The modest, intelligent man, who ran one of the most successful IT companies in the country, had the sense to sell up as his condition worsened, and now they had the freedom to travel and do as they please.

'I'm ready!' Leticia sang out. She placed her hands in

the air and, moving her hips suggestively, began to groove through their spacious suite until she came to Jim's side. 'Hi sexy,' she cooed, running her fingers through his hair and planting kisses all over his face. 'Are you ready for the Rauma Railway Rock?'

'Oh, how I love you,' Jim breathed as he returned Leticia's kisses. 'Take me anywhere you want to go.'

'Well, if we don't get a wriggle on, we'll miss the coach, and with limited daylight hours we need to get going.' Leticia grinned and, taking Jim's hands, helped him to his feet.

With love oozing between them Leticia carefully led Jim to the door, where his wheelchair, piled high with outerwear, was waiting.

'Let's go and chase some fjords,' Leticia said as she gently guided Jim. 'I can't wait to see where this wonderful day will take us.'

* * *

For the Montgomery Joneses, the wonderful day hadn't started as well as it had for Jim and Leticia. After a fitful evening of seasickness, like no other sickness the well-travelled couple had experienced, they'd spent a restless night tossing and turning on their king-sized bed, praying that the sea would calm and sleep become possible. When sleep finally took over, they were woken abruptly by Simon's voice booming through their suite.

'What the hell!' Kenneth shouted out as Simon began his morning greeting. 'It's the middle of the bloody night!'

Pulling herself into an upright position, Barbara peeled off her eye mask and blinked, then focused on the clock by the bed with one open eye. 'Buggeration!' she said. 'It's getting late, and we must have breakfast before our trip.'

Swinging her legs slowly and placing a bed-socked foot gingerly on the deep carpet pile, Barbara tested the floor level before she stood up. 'All fine, Kenny, the sea is calm, you can rise.'

Barbara stared at her husband and sighed. His eyes were closed, and he appeared to be sleeping, despite Simon droning on about the delights of Molde to be had that day.

'Come on.' Barbara reached out to shake Kenneth's leg. 'We've docked. The ship is in Molde, get up!'

'Mohl-duh,' Kenneth mumbled.

Barbara made her way to the bathroom. She was determined to get first dibs at her ablutions before Kenneth polluted the air. As she opened the door, she sighed.

Kenneth's spare toupee lay beside the sink. It reminded her of a small, bedraggled animal that had been abandoned and left to wither. No wonder the housekeeper had been hysterical when she'd arrived to turn down the room on their first evening at sea. They'd been lucky that they hadn't been charged for a visit by the ship's pest control, and it had taken several euros to calm the housekeeper down and convince her not to repeat what she'd seen, as Barbara explained to the horrified woman that the 'unidentifiable creature' was none other than Kenneth's hairpiece.

Barbara washed her face and reached for a towel. Holding it against her face, she wrinkled her nose in disgust. Kenneth's dreadful aftershave clung to the fabric; the spicy aroma was overpowering and made her eyes water. She was sorely tempted to tip the entire bottle into the sink, but knowing that it was his favourite, Barbara restrained herself.

Now, she could hear Kenneth moving about. Good, he was up, and she didn't have to raise the dead after the dreadful night they'd experienced. Barbara had forgotten to pack anti-sickness meds, and Kenneth had been none too pleased that they had needed to call out a medic during the night to administer medication to them both.

'Could pay for a new hip for the cost of these tablets,' he'd complained.

Thank God the tablets had worked and calmed things down, Barbara wearily thought as she scrubbed her teeth. But it was a pity that the same couldn't be said for the terrible sea swell that had kept them awake all night.

Barbara picked up the toupee with two fingers and opened the bathroom door to see Kenneth waiting on the other side.

'Hei! All ship-shape and tidy, old girl?' he asked.

'Don't forget this,' Barbara said.

'Tusen takk.' Kenneth nodded and snatched the offending hairpiece.

Barbara sighed. Kenneth could be such a tosser at times. She objected to being called 'old girl' and was sure that the many women whom he chose to address in that manner felt the same way too.

Wandering through their lounge, Barbara was about to style her hair when she noticed a note had been pushed under the door. Stooping, she studied the handwritten envelope.

Ripping it open, Barbara read the contents, feeling her face grow hot as she realised that the exclusive excursion that they'd booked for the day had been cancelled, due to unforeseen circumstances. A replacement excursion had been reserved for them. The note read:

We trust that you will accept our sincere apologies for the inconvenience.

Enjoy an interesting and rewarding day out with other passengers on the Atlantic Road Trip. The coach will leave at 9.30am.

'Atlantic Road Trip! A coach?' Barbara gasped. 'And it's leaving at nine-thirty? Kenny will have a fit!'

Fumbling for her vanity bag, Barbara extracted a small flask of brandy and took a large gulp. Moving back to the bathroom, she tentatively tapped on the door.

'Kenny?' Barbara whispered. 'Sweetheart? There's been a change of plan . . .'

Chapter Nine

*Driving the Atlantic Ocean Road feels like
flying over the sea.*

Joy dressed warmly for her excursion and after a brief
wait in the Triton Lounge with other passengers, she'd
followed instructions to disembark and join coach number
eight, which would be waiting beyond the port's gates. A
huddle of chattering guests descended the stairs, quilted
and booted, many wearing scarves and bobbble-hats, and
pompoms bounced with every careful step. Coats rustled
and boots clomped as they trudged through security.

Outside it was still dark and Joy soon found herself
joining a queue to board the coach.

'Hei!' said a female guide, ticking Joy's name off a list.
'My name is Ingrid. Please take a seat.'

As the coach door hissed open, Joy wondered who she'd
sit next to. She climbed the steps and, to her surprise, saw
that the first row of seats was occupied by Kenneth and
Barbara. Joy wondered what had happened to their private
boat trip to the fjords and was tempted to stop and ask the

couple. But noting that Barbara wore her fur hat pulled low over her face, her expression a scowl as she stared straight ahead, Joy decided against it. Kenneth, looking glum too, was winter-ready in a bright yellow cagoule with a thick fleece collar. A trapper hat covered his head, the ear flaps snug against his cheeks. Both gripped walking poles folded across their knees and pointedly ignored the other passengers joining the excursion.

Halfway down the aisle, Joy found a seat. As she eased her coat off and bundled it onto her lap, a woman stood beside her.

'You're a WI member,' the woman said, 'I saw you at the meeting. Is anyone sitting here?'

'Yes, I was and er . . . no.' Joy felt a flutter of panic. Was she in the wrong seat?

'Judy Carrington,' the woman announced and sat down.

'Joy Bradley, hello again.'

'I see the Montgomery Joneses have hogged the front of the coach,' Judy remarked, removing her embroidered felt hat and fluffing out her curls with a toss of her head. 'I'd have thought mingling with the common folk would be beneath them.'

'Do you know them?' Joy asked.

'Only from a previous cruise.' Judy sniffed. 'Both a pain in the arse.'

'I thought they'd booked a customised excursion today,' Joy commented.

'The tour guide probably got wind of their reputation and decided to cut their losses.'

'Are they difficult?'

'Worse than difficult. On a Med cruise last summer, there was an incident in Santorini. Something about a private yacht and an irate Greek ambassador.'

'Goodness!' Joy's eyes were wide.

'Seemingly, it ended with Mrs Montgomery Jones, in a hysterical state, banging on about diplomatic immunity. God knows what happened.'

'Today's trip might be quite tame in comparison,' Joy said.

'Indeed,' Judy said and raised her eyebrows.

Judy began to question Joy on her WI membership and told her she was silly to let it lapse. She rattled on about how being a member ensured she had friends, and when she booked holidays through *WI Life* magazine, plenty of company. 'You get a decent discount too,' she added. 'Solo travel has never bothered me. I've travelled everywhere, including Europe and Asia, and I fancy one of those Nile cruises next. I'm not the type to sit at home twiddling my thumbs.'

Joy didn't suspect that Judy sat twiddling anywhere. The confident woman threw herself headlong into conversation with strangers and was soon nattering with the sisters in adjacent seats to them.

Staring out of the window, Joy saw that the sun had risen and the town of Molde was slipping by. She watched a woman wearing a bright pink puffa jacket ride a bicycle, with a dog sitting upright in a basket on the handlebars. People huddled in layered clothing, queued by a bakery window, and Joy imagined the sweet delights inside. Ingrid explained that the town was known as the Town of Roses, and in summer, the parks and gardens overflowed with the sweet-smelling blooms.

Everywhere looked picture-perfect beneath a soft blanket of cloud where peaked roofs were dappled with ice, and buildings, painted yellow and blue, lined the snow-covered road. Ingrid told them that the mountains appearing in the distance were named the Romsdal Alps, and the first part of their journey would involve a one-hour drive before they reached the Atlantic Ocean Road. Joy thought that the wintery scene felt unreal, as though someone had taken a brush and painted the landscape.

Heading westward, the coach drove through a long, dark tunnel that opened to flat farmland and small villages. Joy stared at wooden houses nestling between forested, sloping hills, where the area was deserted, with not a soul about. As Ingrid informed everyone that the coast would soon be in sight again, Joy's eyelids grew heavy. Her thoughts strayed to dinner the previous evening and how she'd spoken about Tom. It hadn't been her intention to be so candid, and feeling anxious that she'd disclosed too much, she'd had a restless night. But now, lack of sleep caught up, and lulled by the motion of the coach and the murmur of Judy's voice, she slipped into a light doze.

A little while later, Joy felt Judy nudge her arm, and as she opened her eyes, she saw that the coach was pulling into a parking area.

'Wake up, you don't want to miss anything,' Judy said and, unfolding her hat from a pocket, thrust her arms into her coat before sliding out of her seat to be first out as the doors opened.

Joy realised that she'd missed Ingrid's commentary and wondered where they were. But when she alighted, she saw that they were alongside a café, built into a wall of steep rock, and as a brisk wind blew and snow clung to their coats, passengers hurried inside. Joy suddenly felt nervous and clutched the strap of her bag, as she scanned faces that hurried by.

When Henry approached, she impulsively called out, 'Hello, are you going to the café?'

'Ah, Joy,' Henry replied. He produced a balaclava and pulled it on. 'I don't fancy the queue for coffee, and there's a short walk I'd like to do.' He wrapped a scarf tightly, then slipped his hands into fleecy gloves.

'Would you mind if I came with you?' Joy asked.

For a moment, she half-hoped that Henry hadn't heard. She'd put him on the spot, but to her relief, Henry smiled.

'Be delighted, normal conversation will be a pleasure,' Henry said, 'I've been stuck on the bus with a woman who said she's an artist and she's been sketching my face for the last hour, as well as providing a running commentary on her bizarre life.' Henry rubbed his chin. 'She told me that I have the jawline of a Greek philosopher and an aura of one who keeps secrets.'

Joy remembered Lucinda Green, the artist she'd encountered at the Emerald Art Studio. 'She sounds quite a character,' Joy said, her nerves easing as they began to walk along the path that followed the coast.

'Mad as a hatter if you ask me, and she kept waving an empty cigarette holder.' Henry shuddered. 'She suggested I pose for her in a life drawing class.'

Joy smiled and thought that Henry had no intention of disrobing for a room full of pensioners wielding charcoal sticks and making eye contact with parts he'd prefer to keep private.

The wind was sharp, and as they rounded the corner of the rock, an icy gust blew up. Joy braced her shoulders and thrust her hands into her pockets. Meanwhile, Henry was fumbling with his camera.

'Look!' Henry called out, the wind tearing the words from his mouth as he pointed.

Joy turned, and her first sight of the Storseisundet Bridge almost took her breath away. The vast steel and stone structure rose from the water like a mythical monster, its curves almost vanishing into the clouds. In a dramatic arc, the steep road seemed to drop dramatically to disappear into the deep abyss of the sea.

'My goodness,' Joy gasped as she held her phone up to capture the image. 'It's magnificent.'

Henry pointed his lens and clicked away, focusing on the bridge. 'More like a work of art than a road, eh?' he called out.

As they walked along a path beside the rocky coastline, Henry explained that the inlets and coves attracted marine wildlife, including birds, seals, and whales, and in good weather it would be a popular spot for fishing as the waters teemed with life.

Henry paused to listen for the distant call of a seabird and, taking his camera, scanned the sea. To his delight, a lone puffin bobbed about, its vivid beak a splash of bright red against the steely grey. Henry focused his lens and was thrilled to witness the bird's black and white plumage, sleek with seawater. As he clicked away, he knew that its small, webbed feet would be paddling for all their might beneath the surface.

When the bird took flight, Henry turned to Joy. 'My friend Audrey will be thrilled when I show her these photographs,' he said. 'I like her to feel as though she's experienced the trip with me.'

When they returned to the café, and stepped into the warm, cosy room, Joy felt relieved that she was accompanied by Henry and didn't have to stand like a wallflower on her own. She'd enjoyed his company and found Henry interesting. Removing her gloves, she felt her phone vibrate and taking it from her pocket she glanced at the screen. It was Susan.

'Coffee?' Henry mouthed.

Joy nodded as she took the call. 'Hello, Susan, how are you?' she said.

'At last, I've finally located you and you haven't jumped overboard.' Susan sounded tense. 'I've been calling for days, why haven't you picked up?'

Joy rolled her eyes. Less than forty-eight hours at sea was hardly days. 'I didn't have a signal,' Joy said.

'For goodness' sake, Mother, will you please buy a Wi-Fi package and stop being so tight? You know that I need to make sure you are coping.'

'I'm coping very well, thank you.' Joy bit her lip. 'You don't need to keep checking on me.'

'On the contrary, I do. You're so introverted these days, I'm sure that you're hardly venturing out of your cabin.'

'Right now, I'm actually in a café on the Atlantic Ocean Road.'

'Oh, well, that's good.' Susan sounded surprised.

Henry returned with coffee and handed Joy a mug. 'It's not too bad, would you like a biscuit?' he asked, producing a packet from his pocket.

'Thank you, Henry. You're very kind.' Joy cupped the phone under her ear and sipped the creamy hot coffee.

'*Henry?*' Susan exclaimed. 'Who's Henry?'

Joy didn't want to embarrass herself by explaining, within earshot of Henry. 'It's lovely to hear from you, Susan, but I really have to go now.' She looked at Henry and shrugged. 'I'll catch you later in the week, take care, dear,' she said and ended the call.

'Everything all right?' Henry asked as he dunked his biscuit.

'My daughter believes I am useless on my own and feels the need to badger me constantly to ensure I'm not confined to my cabin.'

'I'm sure she means well.'

Joy sighed and stared at her coffee. 'Yes,' she said, 'I'm sure she does.' Turning to Henry she asked, 'Did you capture all the photos you wanted?'

'Yes, I think I've got some good shots. I'll put them in an album to share the trip with Audrey. She's unable to travel and misses her holidays to interesting places.'

As they returned to the coach, Joy decided to question Henry. 'You mentioned that Audrey can't travel. Is it her health?'

'Sadly, her health isn't what it was, but it doesn't stop her zest for life. Audrey is a very vibrant personality and involved in many societies, including the Friends of Skipton Castle, the church craft circle, and of course, the U3A.'

'U3A?' Joy asked as she nibbled her gingerbread.

'University of the Third Age,' Henry explained, 'a wonderful organisation for retirees that offers many activities. Audrey co-hosts their creative art classes.' He smiled fondly. 'She still insists on wearing full makeup and lipstick before she goes out each day.'

What Henry didn't mention was that elderly Audrey, fully made up, bore an uncanny resemblance to Bette Davies in *What Ever Happened to Baby Jane?* A sight that never failed to startle the more sensitive students in creative art.

From Henry's description, Joy, however, visualised Audrey quite differently in her faux-fur coat, makeup immaculate, mouth painted a defiant red. Audrey's legs were probably long and stockinged, balanced on high heels that clicked as she walked.

Audrey, Joy thought, was full of surprises.

'But the main reason Audrey doesn't travel far,' Henry continued, 'is because she's broke and doesn't have the funds.'

Joy was curious. 'I'm sorry to hear that about your friend. Er, what caused the financial blip?' she asked, hoping she wasn't prying too much.

'Oh, it was a complete disaster. You hear about being conned out of money when in love, but Audrey fell for it hook, line, and sinker.' Henry shook his head. 'I feel so terribly sorry for her,' he added, still munching on his gingerbread, with a faraway look in his eyes. 'She's such a generous and decent woman.'

Joy nodded. She'd read the stories. Lonely women in later life sending money to supposed army veterans stranded overseas, or suave widowers claiming business troubles before vanishing with their victim's savings. Some men weren't what they seemed, and appearances could lie. Newspapers reported stories of vulnerable women being drawn to a kind voice, a smart uniform, messages that made them feel wanted, and even the idea of being loved. Wise women had been taken in by carefully constructed illusions, falling for someone who never existed. Perhaps Audrey had been one of those rising statistics of catfishing or a romance scam? The poor woman had trusted – and trust, Joy thought, could be the most dangerous thing of all.

But Joy wondered why Henry hadn't offered Audrey financial help. He couldn't be too badly off if he could afford a cruise holiday, and surely his pension was comfortable. But at that moment, Ingrid called everyone back to the coach, and there was no time for further conversation.

Henry reluctantly returned to sit with Lucinda. With everyone's belongings in place, changing seats on the coach was impossible, and as they made their way to the next stop, Joy stared out of the window and reminded herself that she mustn't judge Henry. If Audrey hadn't joined him on the cruise, there would be a reason, and it was kind and thoughtful of him to ensure he kept a visual record for his special friend to enjoy.

The journey along the Atlantic Ocean Road was stunning.

Joy felt suspended between land and sea as the coach negotiated the many twists and turns of the spectacular drive, along the eight-kilometre stretch that connected a series of islands via eight bridges. The rugged, snowy landscape and inky black sea were framed by jagged rocks, and the sky was an ever-changing canvas of grey and blue.

When they slowed and pulled into a steep, narrow road leading to a hill, snow turned to sleet and a stark, steepled building appeared.

Kvernes Stave Church overlooked countryside that fell away to a wide-open fjord.

Ingrid led everyone to trudge over the sodden, snow-covered grass and when they entered the rustic old building, there was a collective shiver as hoods and hats were removed in a damp Mexican wave. It felt colder inside than out, and guests huddled together on pews as Ingrid pointed out the baroque pulpit, an ancient choir screen, and an altarpiece dated 1475.

A local man spoke of the church's history. He played an accordion, then a recorder, and performed Norwegian folk songs. The screeching reedy sound of the latter pierced through the freezing cold air, and Joy noted that the sisters, eyes scrunched and wrapped in blankets, held their fingers to their ears.

As guests left the church and boarded the coach, Joy saw Kenneth and Barbara dozing in their seats. A silver flask lay on Barbara's lap, and Kenneth snored loudly.

Besides Joy, Judy snuggled her hands into her pockets, lowered her head, and closed her eyes. 'Wake me up when we get back to Molde,' she said, and in minutes, like the travellers at the front, she was sound asleep, too.

The snowy countryside flew by, and Joy thought about her return to the ship. She looked forward to a hot shower and speculated on dinner. Later, she might watch another show. Last night's entertainment, *Colours*, in the Triton Lounge, had been excellent. Being on her own wasn't quite as overwhelming as Joy had imagined. She'd expected to feel lost and adrift without a partner, but there was something to be said for moving at her own pace.

To the backdrop of Judy's gentle snores, Joy thought of her retirement. Being at home with Tom had been all-consuming. He was always there. Insistently so. Hovering beside her through every task, every shopping trip and even her quiet moments when sewing. To others, it appeared as devotion, but to Joy, it had another name. Her confidence had drained, and hobbies she'd enjoyed and the interests that gave her pleasure, such as her Women's Institute meetings, had faded from her life as Tom gradually took up more space. Joy missed the woman she once was.

The coach travelled on, and Joy thought of Susan and her insistence that Joy take the cruise. Joy knew that her daughter was right. The holiday was giving her a reason to get up and see what the day might offer, and there was so much to do; she would be foolish not to join in and make memories, even if they were on her own.

If Joy had gone first, she wondered if Tom would have travelled alone, picking up the scattered threads of life and stitching them into something whole again. Joy's memories slipped by like a reel in a film, and she knew that some questions would remain unanswered. Still, after so much solitude, the cruise was just what she needed and with a wistful smile, Joy settled further into her seat and, to the rhythm of the coach, let her thoughts drift away as she lazily watched the wintery world go by.

Chapter Ten

Norwegian nights taste better at sea.

While many passengers enjoyed excursions offshore, Simon's day had been busy onboard as he went about his duties, ensuring the smooth running of the ship. Having checked that there were activities and entertainment for those remaining on board, Simon was confident that guests would be well catered for, with a movie screening, trivia games, a cookery demonstration and plentiful offers of treatments in the Atlantis Spa. He'd also attended the heads of department meeting, where a complaint made earlier by the Montgomery Joneses was raised.

Simon had been surprised to hear that their pre-booked excursion that day, a chartered boat for a private cruise of the fjords, had been cancelled. On investigation, guest services had informed Simon that they had no choice but to cancel as the tour operator had learned of Barbara's behaviour on a previous cruise, during a whale-watching charter in Reykjavik, and refused to take her on the trip. Run by the same company, she'd been blocked, and Simon shuddered to think what their VIP guest had got up to. The alternative suggestion had met with an angry scene as Kenneth and Barbara argued with the staff at the desk.

Wishing to avoid further unpleasantness, Simon had repeated the offer of the Atlantic Ocean Road trip with the compliments of the cruise line, which seemed to pacify the pair.

Earlier that day, Simon had spent time at the poolside bar, with the excuse that he was checking out arrangements for the Martini Experience to be held later. Ordering a coffee, he made himself comfortable.

An exercise class was taking place, and Simon knew that Kyle's *Zumba in the zone – Shake it while you sit!* was popular. Several guests were seated in a circle, on upright chairs, while Kyle, wearing a Lycra leotard and Converse trainers, pivoted in the middle.

'Come on luvvies, this is low impact,' Kyle sang, 'let's all shoulder roll and shimmy!'

Simon studied Kyle's shoulder roll and was impressed as bronzed muscles rippled his upper arms. When the young man began to shimmy, Simon was mesmerised. Kyle's sequinned sweatband glinted in the sunshine beaming through the enclosed roof, and now, his jazz hands were encouraging the guests to thrust forward in a pelvic thrust.

'Careful, Nora, if you thrust too far, you'll end up in the pool again,' Kyle called out.

Simon frowned. He was aware that unless Kyle changed the routine swiftly, Nora would likely end up in the medical facility with a dislocated hip. Her orange hair was plastered to her head, and her furrowed face was wet with perspiration.

'Now, we're all going to do a seated grapevine!' Kyle said, his arm outstretched as he sang along to 'Let's Do the Time Warp Again', then stepped to the right and crossed his left foot behind in a repeated action.

Chairs began to squeak as Sid, a solo traveller from Staines, added a twist to his grapevine, knocking into Nora and sending her water bottle flying.

'Whoops!' Kyle said as he deftly caught it. 'Keep hydrated, mustn't lose your water, Nora!'

'If it were only water, I wouldn't be here,' Nora laughed.

Retrieving the bottle, she took a slug and offered it to Sid, who almost choked as the fiery burn of the forty per cent proof gin hit the back of his throat, causing him to gasp and grip his chest.

'Everything all right, Nora?' Kyle called out as Sid turned puce and Nora banged her fist on his back.

'Tiptop,' she trilled as her new friend recovered. With a sudden gleam in his eye, Sid took her hand, and together, they stood and grape-vined around the deck.

Simon knew he should ask housekeeping to check Nora's room for contraband. Personal alcohol supplies were only allowed on board if purchased from the ship. But Nora, a regular *Emerald Dream* cruiser, had a habit of stashing forbidden bottles in cleverly disguised bags or tucked under layers of her clothing. Simon let it pass. If a little illicit booze made Nora happy, he wouldn't stand in her way.

Kyle was ending the class, and with sharp bursts of his whistle, he encouraged everyone to twist their torsos to the right and then to the left. 'Lift those arms, swivel those hips, and give me one last shimmy,' the instructor called out, and moonwalked towards the bar, where complimentary cocktails awaited the participants.

Simon stared as Nora, leading the charge, thundered towards him. Taking a Frostbite Fizz, she handed one to Sid.

'Hello Nora, are you enjoying yourself?' Simon asked.

'I enjoy all of Kyle's classes,' Nora replied, 'that young man makes my holiday, and I always feel refreshed after a session with him.' She raised her glass.

As he watched Nora take Sid's arm and move to the comfort of the sofa, Simon thought that Nora, gripping her empty 'water' bottle, was not only refreshed but probably three sheets to the wind after her exercise sessions.

Kyle, meanwhile, was tugging a hoodie over his leotard, and when he saw Simon, he hurried to catch him. 'Simon!' Kyle called out. 'It's good to see you, what did you think of my class?'

Simon could feel the heat rising in his face, betraying him even as he forced a cool smile.

'Oh, hello, Kyle. I thought it was great,' Simon said, and fiddling with his tie, he coughed nervously.

The fitness instructor's face was damp, and his hoodie unzipped, and Simon couldn't stop his eyes from straying to Kyle's perfect pecs, then back to his baby blue eyes. He radiated post-workout energy.

'I'm so pleased that you came to watch,' Kyle said with an impish grin. 'It's important to me that I get things right.'

Simon sucked in his stomach and re-fastened the buttons on his jacket. Shifting awkwardly from one foot to the other, he shoved his hands deep in his pockets. 'Y . . . you were great,' he stammered, trying to sound casual and failing. 'I can see that everyone enjoys your classes. Keep up the good work.'

Keep up the good work . . . Simon was mortified! He sounded like a headmaster and felt like a nerd. Keen to high-five or give Kyle's arm an encouraging pat, the moment had passed, and now he felt awkward. *Pull yourself together!* Simon silently scolded himself, his heart pounding, knowing that Kyle, the confident, handsome fitness instructor, would never look at Simon the Teletubby, in anything but a professional way.

But as Simon left the poolside bar, he was unaware that Kyle stood frozen, watching the cruise director with a gaze full of unspoken words. With his stumbles and stammer, Simon hadn't a clue that Kyle's smile lingered long after he turned away.

Now, as the evening began, Simon exchanged pleasantries with the maître d' of the Terrace restaurant, then negotiated through the softly lit tables with the ease of a man who'd walked this route many times before. Pausing to greet guests by name and ask about their day, his megawatt smile was in place as he crouched slightly and laughed at their jokes.

Desserts were being served by the time he got to the Montgomery Joneses' table.

'Good evening, everyone,' Simon spoke warmly, 'and how have we all enjoyed our day?'

'God-awful bus trip,' Kenneth growled as he spooned lemon posset into his mouth. 'We won't be repeating that again, will we, Babs?'

Through a mouthful of chocolate mousse, Barbara said that the excursion was a waste of time. Simon took a step back. He was beginning to regret his visit to table twenty-eight.

Barbara pushed her dessert away, and as she filled her glass with wine, a few drops splashed onto the white cloth, creating a dark red stain. 'Don't know what all the fuss was about on that road trip. We couldn't see a thing,' she slurred, 'far too dark and foggy, and the church was as cold as the grave. We couldn't stay in there and returned to the coach. Someone should have turned on the heating.'

Simon, who'd visited Kvernes Stave Church on a previous cruise, thought Barbara had rather missed the magnificence of the seventeenth-century building, which was rich in cultural heritage.

But Leticia Scott sat forward. 'Such a shame that the Molde Mist ruined your private excursion, causing you to cancel at the last minute,' she said.

Simon was puzzled. He'd never heard of a Molde Mist, but he caught the glint in Leticia's eye and before he could ask, Leticia's husband, Jim, began to nod. 'Terrible thing, the Molde Mist, rolls right in when you least expect it.'

Henry Halliday coughed politely into his beer glass.

'Still, the stress of cancelling your special trip must have been exhausting,' Joy Bradley joined in. 'No wonder you both fell asleep on the coach.'

Simon noticed Joy looked sympathetically towards Kenneth and Barbara.

Kenneth's head jerked up, his hair shifting noticeably and before the guest had time to respond, Simon wished everyone well and turned away.

To his relief, he didn't need to manage the Montgomery Joneses. The diners sharing their table had the couple all figured out.

* * *

The Triton Lounge was steadily filling as the guests from table twenty-eight searched for somewhere to sit. Kenneth and Barbara, as though competing in musical chairs, moved with speed and hurried ahead to secure a front-row spot.

'There's spaces over there,' Leticia said, and pointed out a raised seating area, and together with Jim, Henry, and Joy, she made her way. Once they were settled, a steward took their order for drinks.

Seated between Leticia and Henry, Joy felt a little awkward. It felt too close to be beside Henry, a man she hardly knew. But as the house lights dimmed and a hush fell over the room, she joined in with the ripple of applause as the evening's entertainment began.

A spotlight shone on the stage, and the curtains drew back to reveal the *Emerald Dream*'s resident band, the Oceanaires, who started their act with an instrumental version of 'Moondance'.

A suave man with jet-black hair appeared. He wore a white dinner jacket and introduced himself. 'Welcome to the Miles Donavan show,' he said, 'and we have a fabulous line-up for you tonight!'

As Miles eased into his routine with a medley of popular hits, interspersed with jokes, the *Emerald Dream* dancers glided onto the stage, their sequins catching the lights as they moved in perfect sync. Joy thought of her last cruise with Tom, where Dicky Delaney, the comedian, had entertained them throughout with a hilarious repertoire and endless plugs for his autobiography, a copy of which still lay beside Tom's side of their bed. Miles Donavan had a long way to go to keep up with Dicky's limitless jokes, but Joy was enjoying the show. She glanced at Henry and, to her surprise, noticed his eyes were closed and head tilted to one side.

Cruise ship days could take their toll, especially as the years passed.

Miles's tempo increased at the end of his act, and dancers wore sarong-style skirts and Hawaiian shirts with tropical flowers in their hair.

'You must get to know Soho Joe!' Miles sang and swayed his hips, 'He runs an Espresso, called the House of Bamboo!'

A woman with orange hair leaped to her feet in the central aisle. Nora began to dance with her thumbs inserted in the loops of her belt and encouraged others to join in too. The audience started to sing along with Miles.

> *I'm-a telling you*
> *When you're blue*
> *Well, there's a lot to do*
> *In the House of Bamboo!*

Henry's head jerked up, and he opened his eyes. 'Good Lord! What's happening . . .' he said as Nora sashayed towards him, grabbed his hands, and pulled Henry to his feet.

'You're dancing!' Nora laughed, tugging him up with surprising energy for a woman wearing orthopaedic sandals.

Henry couldn't beat a retreat and reluctantly looped his thumbs in his belt and attempted to line-dance as Nora's chosen guests wove their way through the aisle. As the final chorus swelled, Miles, in the middle of the stage, executed a high kick and fell back into the waiting arms of the dancers who raised him triumphantly to their shoulders. 'In the House of Bamboo!' they sang, and the room erupted.

Clapping their hands and smiling, Nora and her gyrating guests returned to their seats.

Henry quickly sat down as the dancers disappeared, and the curtains closed on the stage. Leticia and Jim leaned forward to congratulate him on his performance.

Joy thought that Henry was a good sport and praised him too. Then, she picked up her bag, thanked everyone for their company, and said it was her bedtime. But as she left the Triton Lounge, Joy couldn't help but wonder if there was more to Henry, the history teacher, and what might his friend Audrey make of his line-dancing antics?

Chapter Eleven

Nerves are the tide within us, they rise and fall,
like the sea lapping the shore.

Henry sat at the desk in his cabin and munched on the chocolate that Jennifer had left on his pillow the evening before. A raffle ticket for the captain's Gala Raffle lay beside his book and he noted that the number was seventy.

'Same as my age,' he murmured and hoped that it was lucky.

Taking a pen and a postcard of the Atlantic Ocean Road that he'd purchased at the coffee shop, he began to write. Audrey loved a colourful postcard dropping onto her doormat, especially from a long-distance location. Beside her chair in her sitting room, she had an old biscuit tin full of faded memories from friends who'd sent her news of their travels with cards showing sun-bleached scenes of faraway cities and snapshots of historical monuments. Stamps from every corner of the globe, and looped handwriting described the destinations, and occasionally, when they were having tea, Audrey opened the tin to share a tale or two with Henry. He knew that these treasures filled her with happy memories from her own days of travel, and during his cruise, he intended to add more to her collection.

Ending his greeting, Henry put down his pen and turned to see a passenger jogging along the deck. The man stopped by Henry's cabin, placed a foot on the steamer chair by Henry's door, and bent his body into knee squats.

'Good morning!' Henry called out and raised his hand to wave, but when he received no reply, he remembered that the doors were mirrored one way.

It was the man Henry had nicknamed Jack Frost. He wore a T-shirt, shorts, and trainers and paused to catch his breath. Henry smiled and slid the door wide open. 'Good morning,' Henry repeated his greeting. 'You're a brave soul,' he added, 'the temperature must be minus many degrees today.'

The man looked up. 'Care to join me for a few lunges? Nothing like crisp arctic air to get the blood pumping.'

Henry noted that the man's skin was pale and almost blue, and several veins pulsed. When he exhaled, the air was misty in the freezing cold. 'Are you sure exercising in such extreme temperatures is good for you?'

'The cold helps maintain my flexibility and with a view like this, I can exercise for longer.'

The ship was cruising through a fjord, and they both turned to stare at ice-capped mountains peeping through the darkened sky. Red-tiled roofs of occasional dwellings, barely visible, dotted the shoreline, where tiny fishing communities were only accessible by boat.

Henry thought that if he was to strip off to plunge his

body into a lunge, he might never get upright again. 'I'm sorry, Jack,' he said, 'I'm not as brave or as fit as you.'

'How did you know my name?' the man appeared puzzled.

'Er, I didn't.' Henry was startled. 'I mean, it's just a lucky guess.' He realised he'd voiced his nickname for the man aloud and was even more surprised that the man was *actually* called Jack.

'You must be psychic.' Jack held out his hand. 'If you ever want to work out, let me know. You can leave a note at my cabin on the Marina Deck, 1904.'

'I'll probably pass but thank you.'

Henry was about to return to his cabin when a sudden splash of colourful cagoules rounded the ship's port side, and a battalion of sprightly passengers came into view.

'That'll be the Deck Mile Club,' Jack said, pausing in his lunges. 'They do this route every day at the same time.'

Henry stared as the group, rosy-cheeked and clad in fleece-lined clothing and warm hats, steadily marched towards him, pounding the promenade deck with rubber-tipped walking poles. Leading the group, Henry recognised Judy, who wore her embroidered felt hat. She waved when she saw Jack, her face suddenly alight.

'Oh Lord, not her again,' Jack said and bowed his head. 'If she gets any closer, I'll have to jump overboard.'

'Has she taken a shine to you?'

'I can't shake her off. She's like a great iceberg and likely to sink me if I let her get close. I bet my route is programmed in her Fitbit.'

'Do you want to hide in my cabin?'

But it was too late. Judy, with her target in sight, closed in.

'Jack!' she said. 'There you are, I've been hoping to see you. You're such an inspiration to the Deck Mile Club.'

Judy towered over Jack, her cheeks flushed and her smile wide. Reaching out her mittened hand, she grabbed his arm and insisted he continue the route with the group.

'See you on the other side!' Jack called out to Henry as Judy moved Jack along.

Henry watched the sprightly parade set off again. But the freezing cold penetrated his sweater, and rubbing his arms, he stepped back to the warmth of his cabin, where he picked up the postcard and re-read his message to Audrey.

Henry said that he hoped she was keeping well and that the flu-like infection she was fighting off when he left had cleared up. He thought about his houseplants and knew he would have a rescue mission on his return. Despite instructions that one light watering would be sufficient in his absence, Audrey considered it her duty to give them a daily dose of feed and water while checking Henry's house. It was a wonder that her own vast urns of ferns and potted palms stayed alive. Tucking the card in his pocket to take to guest services for posting, Henry opened his cabin door.

To his surprise, he almost collided with Jennifer. Flicking her duster, she tucked a strand of hair behind her ear. 'You enjoy cruise?' she asked.

'Yes, thank you, I'm enjoying it enormously.'

'You like chocolate?'

'Very much, thank you for leaving one on my pillow.'

'You want more?' She reached into a box on her housekeeping trolley.

'No, really, I'm fine.'

'Any blankets or extra towels?' Jennifer appeared insistent on helping Henry.

'You provide everything I need and are doing an excellent job.'

Henry attempted to inch his way around her trolley, but Jennifer stood firm. He wondered if he ought to tip her each day but remembered his booking stated an amount would be added to his cabin bill for staff gratuities.

'Some passengers not so friendly.' Jennifer smiled, eyes twinkling.

Henry felt a little flustered. 'Well, good manners cost nothing.'

Jennifer giggled. 'You always travel alone, Mr Henry?'

Mr Henry cleared his throat and tugged the cuff of his sweater. 'Yes, well . . . I er, like the peace and quiet.'

In truth Henry had had more than enough peace and quiet at home. The ship's buzz and being amongst the chatter of strangers and participating in daily activities made him feel part of something again. But Jennifer's unwavering attention was unsettling, and he wasn't sure how to deflect it politely.

'Well, have a good day,' Henry said, and Jennifer stepped aside at last, her expression warm, eyes bright.

'You too, Mr Henry,' she said, her smile lingering.

Moving along the corridor, Henry felt a prickling awareness that Jennifer's gaze followed him, and feeling the need to put distance between them, he stepped up his pace and hurriedly walked away.

Approaching the stairs, Henry remembered that this was a sea day, and as they sailed north towards Tromsø, they were going to be crossing the Arctic Circle that afternoon. He'd read in his *Daily Times* that the Arctic Circle crossing ceremony was a recognised, light-hearted maritime rite of passage, rooted in old sailor traditions. Passengers would be invited to join crew members in marking the milestone event with an enjoyable ritual, and everyone would receive a certificate to commemorate their entry into the Arctic. But first, Henry would have breakfast and then enjoy a talk by Bill Zhang, the astrophotography expert and guest speaker who was hosting 'Chasing and Photographing the Aurora'.

Seated in the buffet restaurant, Henry tucked into poached eggs and bacon and reflected on the cruise. He wasn't sure that he'd repeat the impromptu line-dancing that the effusive Nora had forced him to participate in the previous evening, but otherwise, so far, so good.

From his elevated window table, Henry looked around and noticed Joy walk past. Following a server who was guiding her to a table, she gripped her bag to her side and appeared anxious. Then, as though changing her mind, she suddenly turned and left the restaurant.

Henry wondered if Joy found it challenging to enter a crowded room. Had her confidence been depleted after decades of marriage and unexpectedly ending up alone? Joy had been pleased to see him when they alighted from the coach the previous day. Had she felt like a fish out of water on her first solo excursion? He thought that it took courage to ask if she could join him and he decided he would be more attuned to her feelings if such an occasion arose again.

As he pushed his empty plate to one side and a server

poured more coffee, it occurred to Henry that he liked Joy. It was an odd emotion and not one he'd experienced for a long time. Audrey was his closest friend, and he enjoyed her company; the old lady's sharp wit was entertaining, and their debates stimulating. The friendship for Henry, had been enough in the years since he reluctantly retired.

Now, staring out at the brooding sea and distant horizon, he thought of his past loves and regrets. Henry knew that he should have married. Opportunities had been there, but either he was a coward regarding commitment, or he'd never met the right person to spend the rest of his days with. He wondered if he would have been a good father. Sadly, he'd never know, but generations of young people had passed through his classes, and his supportive role as their tutor had filled the gaping fatherhood gap.

Joy was good company, Henry decided as he folded his napkin, and he'd been delighted to be with her at dinner, the Christmas quiz, and the excursion. But he could tell that she was still grieving for her husband, and any attention he might pay her could be easily misinterpreted. God knows, one read of men searching out vulnerable women for financial gain or hitting on them when they were going through a low ebb.

Actions can be so easily misinterpreted! Dating at Henry's age was a minefield, and not an area he'd venture into again. *Don't be an old fool*, Henry told himself as he pushed back his chair and thanked the steward who'd taken care of him. *Joy may be lovely, but she's strictly out of bounds.*

Friendship? Most certainly.

Romance? Scrub the thought.

Checking his watch, Henry realised he'd need to get a wriggle on to secure a front row seat at Bill Zhang's talk. Henry was keen to witness the Northern Lights and needed to know as much as he could. Wasn't that the reason he'd booked this holiday?

But as Henry made his way through the ship, he couldn't help wondering what Joy had planned for the day.

* * *

Joy's plans for the day had suddenly changed. She'd intended to enjoy a quiet breakfast in the buffet restaurant, but the moment she stepped through the doors and a server offered to guide her to a shared table, the noise and press of bodies was overwhelming and a tightening in her chest sent her pulse racing. Gripping her bag and turning on her heels, Joy blindly hurried from the room, her appetite gone and her confidence in tatters.

As she fumbled with the button to summon a lift, the doors suddenly opened, and Leticia and Jim appeared.

'Joy.' Leticia smiled. 'Good morning.'

'H . . . hello,' Joy gasped, the familiar terror worsening as she realised that she might make a scene. 'I need to . . .'

But Leticia the nurse had already noted the physical signs of distress, and she reached out to take Joy's hand. Pale and visibly shaking, Joy was struggling to catch her breath.

'It's all right,' Leticia said, 'you're safe, I'm with you.'

Leticia turned and whispered to Jim, who nodded understandingly. Placing his hands on the electronic motor button on his chair, he made his way to the restaurant, while Leticia led Joy to a quiet corner and eased her onto a sofa.

'Breathe with me, nice and slow,' she said, 'think of the waves, gently rising and falling.'

Joy closed her eyes and let Leticia's soothing voice take over. At first her chest still fluttered, like a butterfly trapped in a jar. But as she pictured a shoreline and each foamy wave, a rhythm came, and her shaking fingers began to still.

Leticia reached into her bag and took the cap from a fresh bottle of water. 'Have a sip,' she said, her gentle approach calming Joy.

'I'm so sorry,' Joy muttered, reaching for the bottle. 'I don't know what happened, I haven't felt like this for months.'

'It's perfectly understandable,' Leticia said. 'Sometimes being in a crowded place can trigger things.'

'It's a panic attack,' Joy explained. 'It happened often after Tom died, but I thought I'd got over them.' Joy didn't mention that she'd experienced many similar attacks before he died, too. She realised that she was still holding Leticia's hand. It felt warm and comforting, and Joy began to relax.

'Why don't we go to your cabin, and I'll make you a cup of tea? You might want to rest for a little while.'

Joy nodded, and together they stood up.

'I'm so sorry,' Joy said, 'I'm being a terrible nuisance.'

'Of course you're not, we all have our moments,' Leticia said softly.

By the time they reached Joy's cabin, the tightness in her chest had eased and propped up on her bed with a mug of Leticia's sweet tea in her hand, Joy was almost back to normal.

'I'll pop back in a little while,' Leticia said, 'try and rest.'

'You've been very kind,' Joy whispered as the door closed.

Leticia's quiet strength had steadied her, and she felt grateful for the woman's fast action. Perhaps they would become cruise buddies after all.

'Thank you.' And for the first time in a long while, Joy meant it.

Chapter Twelve

*Somewhere beneath the waves, we crossed
a circle we couldn't see.*

Leticia and Jim enjoyed a light lunch on the Lido Deck, chatting with a friendly couple, Peter and Sally from Whitley Bay. The couple had experienced the Rauma Railway excursion the day before and shared stories and compared notes, recalling the breathtaking journey. Together, they relived the train's winding route as it pounded through dark tunnels to emerge in the majestic Romsdalen Valley, surrounded by towering mountains and cascading waterfalls.

'Good to catch up again,' Leticia said, 'perhaps we'll see you on another day out,' she added when Peter took Sally's hand, and they left for Afternoon Melodies in the Observatory.

A steward came to clear the table, and as Jim sipped a beer, Leticia glanced around the deck to see Nora, splashing happily in the pool wearing a pretty skirted swimsuit and swim cap adorned with rubber flowers that bounced above her orange curls. Sid, who'd joined Nora at the previous fitness class, floated on his back, paddling lazy circles around Nora, pausing occasionally to share a refreshing drink from her poolside water bottle. They giggled like teenagers between sips.

Noting the time, Leticia rose. 'I'm going to see if Joy is up to joining us,' she said, planting a kiss on Jim's brow as she made her way.

* * *

Henry was buzzing with excitement as he reached the Lido Deck. Bill Zhang's talk had been fascinating, and he'd learned much about the aurora borealis.

Using an informative PowerPoint presentation, Bill had demonstrated how the aurora comes to life in the sky. 'When the solar wind's streams of charged particles from the sun travel through space and reach Earth, it interacts with the planet's magnetic field.' Bill used a laser pointer on the screen to explain. 'This guides the particles to the polar regions, where they collide with gases in the upper atmosphere, transferring energy, which is then released as light.'

Engrossed in his thoughts as he moved, Henry didn't see Jim, and it was only when Jim called out that Henry stopped and looked around.

'Are you coming to join us?' Jim asked, 'Leticia has gone to get Joy. We're here to watch the crossing of the Arctic Circle ceremony. It will start soon.'

'I'd be delighted,' Henry said.

He sat beside Jim and ordered a beer, clearly in good spirits, then began describing the talk he'd attended, animatedly sharing what he'd learned from the astrophotographer. He'd soaked up the expert insights, and Jim, just as eager to learn more about the aurora borealis, nodded along, listening intently.

'When do you think we'll see it?' Jim asked.

'There's no guarantee, but hopefully further north, and with luck by the time we get to Tromsø. Bill has a channel on Instagram, and you can sign up to his alerts.'

Enabling their Wi-Fi, the two men produced their phones. They began scrolling through Bill Zhang's account, their eyes wide as they studied images of the aurora.

'Sexting while the women are away?' a voice called out, and a shadow loomed.

Startled, Henry and Jim looked up to see Kenneth standing over them.

'Or is it some afternoon delight on the adult sites?' Kenneth took a seat and indicated to Barbara, alongside, to do the same. 'Room for two more?'

'Only if you are interested in images of the aurora borealis,' Henry snapped, 'and not any other exposure as you crudely suggest.'

'Don't get your knickers in a knot, old man.' Kenneth gave Henry a hearty slap on his back. 'I'm only having a joke with you.' He turned to Barbara, who wore her fur hat and a Christmas jumper. 'Be a good girl and find a steward, would you? I'm gasping for a drink.' Removing his cagoule, Kenneth settled himself in. 'I had no idea Improvers Bridge could be so taxing.'

Henry drained his glass and held it up. 'Mine's a pint,' he said, 'Jim will have similar.'

'So, what are you two rascals up to?' Kenneth drummed his fingers on the table and yawned as he looked around the deck.

'We're here to watch the Arctic Circle ceremony,' Henry said as Barbara returned with a steward in tow. In addition to their order, she ordered a bottle of her favourite red.

'Ah, these maritime traditions,' Kenneth mused, 'we've crossed the equator many times, haven't we, Babs?'

'Actually, Kenny, we did it *once* on the Queen Mary sailing to South America,' Barbara snapped. 'I've several photos at home that you'll never live down. King Neptune, you're not.' She snatched the bottle from the steward and filled her glass.

Jim shifted in his seat. He thanked the steward for his beer, then raised his glass to acknowledge Kenneth's round. 'You must be a pollywog,' Jim said.

'I beg your pardon?' Kenneth sat up.

'It's a nautical term for a passenger who crosses the equator for the first time,' Jim explained. 'It's also an old English word for tadpole and an expression the Navy still uses.'

Barbara began to snigger. 'That suits you, Kenny, "pollywog" – I rather like it, Kenneth Montgomery Jones, Pollywog. You always wanted a title.'

'Well, if I am one, then so are you,' Kenneth retorted.

Henry ignored the couple's bickering and gave a wave as Jack strolled by with Judy. Raising one hand to acknowledge Henry, Jack placed the other on Judy's waist and Henry was surprised at Jack's sudden familiarity with her. No longer keeping his distance, the pair now appeared cosied up, and Henry felt quietly pleased to see it. Perhaps the cold was bringing them closer.

Turning to Jim, Henry asked, 'Have *you* crossed the equator?'

'Several times,' Jim replied. 'Leticia and I would be called "shellbacks," an expression for those who've done it before. I'm not sure how often we've cruised the dividing line, but it's many.'

Outdone with equator crossing one-upmanship, Kenneth took his wine and tossed it back.

Jim saw Leticia and Joy approach. 'Hello, both. You're just in time; the ceremony will begin soon.'

Henry stood to make room, and as Joy sat down, he thought that she looked a little peaky. 'Are you feeling all right?' he softly asked.

'Er, thank you, I didn't sleep very well.'

Before Henry could enquire more, music burst out, and a procession began led by Simon, who was wearing a long black hooded robe and a fake frosty beard. He carried a staff made from a mop wrapped in tinsel.

Informing everyone that he was King Boreas, the ancient God of the North Wind, he asked the assembled crowd if any first timers considered themselves worthy of becoming 'Blue Noses'.

'That's the Arctic version of shellbacks,' Jim explained.

'You've got a blue nose, Kenny. I suggest you step up.' Barbara ducked as her husband thrust out a hand to airwave her away.

Suddenly, Simon shouted, 'I call for the captain!'

Heads turned as Captain Lauri Lindholm appeared and began to walk to a podium erected at the side of the pool to stand before King Boreas. Mature, tall, and slim, with waves of dark hair, the captain removed his glasses as he took his position.

'About time he put in an appearance,' Kenneth snidely remarked, 'I was beginning to think the ship was being steered by a rumour.'

'Captain, step forward,' King Boreas said, 'as tradition dictates, no traveller may pass beyond the Arctic Circle without sealing their passage by kissing the fish.'

Two crew members dressed as a mermaid and a pirate, stepped forward. They carried a long silver tray where a large icy cod lay, its milky eyes fixed in a deathly stare, surrounded by crushed ice, kale, and parsley.

'I've kissed worse at Christmas parties!' Kenneth called out and swigged his wine.

'And I kiss worse every morning . . .' Barbara sighed.

'You must prove your worth!' King Boreas held up his staff. 'Kneel and kiss the fish!'

The captain played along, shaking his head and refusing to kneel. Two more crew members, wearing turtle suits, held his shoulders until he crouched down. Passengers, fired up in the spirit of the ceremony, began to chant. 'Kiss the fish! Kiss the fish!'

The captain grimaced, closed his eyes, and puckered his lips. As the fish was thrust towards him, he pecked its cold mouth. But before Captain Lindholm could stagger to his feet, the turtles appeared with a bucket of ice and emptied it over his shoulders.

'You are now a Blue Nose!' King Boreas shouted, and everyone applauded as towels were hastily handed to the sodden Captain.

The turtles nervously moved back, wondering if they'd taken the ice-bucket challenge too far. But Captain Lindholm proved to be a good sport. Wiping his wet face, he retrieved his glasses and held up his towel in triumph. The audience cheered as he took a lap of honour before returning to the Bridge.

Several department heads were introduced and put through the same procedure until it was time for the passengers to join in.

Henry glanced at Jim. 'I will, if you will,' he grinned.

'You're on!' Jim laughed, and grabbing the hem of his fleece and T-shirt, he peeled them over his head.

Henry followed suit, pulling off his sweater and unbuttoning his shirt. Beneath was a thick thermal vest, which he whipped off like a prize-fighter going into battle.

'You'll catch your death,' Barbara mused, one eyebrow raised as she stared at Henry and considered his figure – well-toned for a man of his age.

The sweater landed on Barbara's lap, and she caught it without flinching, calmly smoothing the reindeer pattern across her knees. 'Very festive,' she said, 'I'll look after the reindeers while you join the frostbitten elite.'

Jim moved his chair forward, and with Henry bringing up the rear, the pair laughed like children as they joined the slippery challenge by the side of the pool, acknowledging Jack and Judy, who sat alongside. Jack sported brief trunks, while a shivering Judy wore her felt hat and a long red sarong over her swimsuit.

'This cold activity must suit you,' Henry said to Jack.

'Bring it on, the colder the better,' Jack replied.

'You seem to be getting on very well with Judy,' Henry said as he watched Jack reach out to offer her a towel.

'The woman's a revelation.' Jack grinned. 'She's almost as fit as me, which is saying something. At first, I thought she was chasing me for the sport of it, but she's got stamina and spirit that I didn't see coming, and she's full of passion.' Jack winked, and Henry raised his eyebrow. 'I started out running from her,' Jack continued and looked fondly at Judy, 'and now I can't imagine not running *to* her, if you know what I mean . . .'

Barbara watched Henry and Jim head off. 'Not joining in?' Barbara asked her husband as she poured more wine. 'Once a wimp, always a wimp?'

'Good God, I'm not afraid of a little bit of ice and a slimy old fish,' Kenneth stood up. He looked anxiously around as he removed his upper layer, tucking a vest that had seen better days under his cagoule.

The two turtles, third and fourth engineers from the engine room, were having a high time as they drenched passengers, and the mermaid forced the participants to kiss the fish. Jim and Henry endured the ice bucket challenge and raised their fists in triumph, then high-fived as King Boreas told them they had passed their initiation.

By now, the enthusiasm for the ceremony had reached a fever pitch. The poolside was packed with passengers waiting their turn while onlookers jostled for a good view.

But as Kenneth stepped forward, puffed up with bravado, a look of disgust crossed his face when he leaned in to kiss the fish. He suddenly dodged back, caught his foot, and recoiled on a mound of ice. With arms flailing, he lost his footing, slipped, and vanished with a loud splash into the pool's deep end.

'Where there's blame there's a claim,' Barbara said and shook her head. But when she realised that Kenneth hadn't surfaced, she leaped up, tossing Henry's sweater to the floor.

'HELP! He's drowning!' Barbara screamed, her voice slicing through the chaos.

Nestling in the jacuzzi with Nora, Sid sprang into action and dived headlong into the water. 'I've got him!' Sid called, surfacing with Kenneth in a chokehold and dragging him to the edge.

There was a collective gasp as everyone's gaze turned to the surface of the pool, and Nora shrieked, 'IT'S A RAT!'

She pointed, her eyes wide with horror, and all eyes turned to a strange floating creature. Panic rippled as husbands covered their wives' eyes, and Jim and Henry leaned in for a closer look, while Jack and Judy leaped onto chairs.

'You're never more than three metres from a rat!' Jack said and peered around anxiously, checking the deck for rodent infestation, as Judy trembled and clutched her sarong to her ankles.

At the same time, Leticia and Joy gazed at the disturbing sight of the conker-coloured floating object and the turtles exchanged worried glances. Grabbing King Boreas's staff, the turtles ripped off the tinsel and dunked the mop into the pool to net the offending object.

Leticia turned to Joy and began to giggle.

Barbara, bracing herself with the last of the wine, hiccupped, then finished the drinks remaining on the table and pushed her way to the edge of the pool where Sid's chokehold was causing Kenneth more damage than his drowning.

Grabbing her fur hat, Barbara hurled it frisbee-like to skim across the water. 'Catch it, Kenny!' she shouted, as Kenneth, tearing Sid's hands from his throat, popped up to swiftly retrieve the hat and pull it over his bald head. 'Thanks, old girl!'

'Sh . . . show's over,' Barbara slurred. 'There's nothing to see here.' She waved her hands to disperse the crowd and kicking Henry's sweater to one side, picked up her husband's clothes. The turtles raised the mop, and Barbara unhooked the squelching hair piece and tucked it in a pocket of Kenneth's bright yellow cagoule.

Assisting Kenneth and draping him in towels, Barbara mumbled, 'Good job you've got a spare . . .' Reaching up for his arm she unsteadily guided Kenny from the Lido Deck. 'See yous all at din-dins,' Barbara called out to the wide-eyed group left behind.

'Well, that was fun,' Henry said and stooped down to pick up his sweater. He rubbed at his chest with a towel. 'I never imagined that crossing the Arctic Circle would be so memorable!'

Chapter Thirteen

Steeped in tradition, dining at the captain's
table is more than a meal.

When Joy returned to her cabin after the ceremony on the Lido Deck, she contemplated joining the watercolour class soon to take place in the Emerald Art Studio, where the resident artist, Lucinda Green, was scheduled to instruct a class titled Wildlife Scenes. Joy had enjoyed dabbling in watercolours many years ago and had even taken a residential course one school holiday. She had been proud of her efforts back then and even framed the seaside scenes she painted. Lucinda Green might rekindle the spark and inspire Joy to pick up a brush again.

She recalled Henry's offhand comment about Lucinda favouring life classes, and reversing her decision, Joy wondered what exactly Wildlife Scenes entailed and whether she would walk into a room of reclining nudes instead of prancing deer.

But as Joy removed her scarf and hung up her jacket, her attention was caught by a long cream envelope that lay on her bed. Puzzled, she picked it up and stared at the typed script.

Mrs Joy Bradley – Ocean View Cabin – 2617

Turning it over, she slipped a finger under the light seal and pulled out a sheet of thin cream-coloured card. It was an invitation.

Emerald Dream Dinner Invitation
From Your Captain

Dear Mrs Bradley

Captain Lauri Lindholm would like to invite you
to join him for dinner at his table this evening
at 8pm in the Terrace Restaurant.
Pre-dinner cocktails will be served in the
Triton Lounge at 7.15pm.
RSVP to guest services by 5pm and kindly
pass this invitation to our seating hostess upon
arrival in the Triton Lounge.
We hope to see you there.

It was signed by the captain and the maître d' of the restaurant. Joy stared at the envelope and considered the formal invitation far too grand for someone who'd only packed two sensible dresses, ballet pumps, and a pair of low heels she'd worn for Susan's wedding. Turning the invitation over, she wondered if it was meant for someone else.

There must have been a mix-up. Joy Bradley from Halton-on-Lune, near Lancaster, a retired home economics teacher who lived in a dormer bungalow and was travelling alone, did not merit a place at such an esteemed gathering, and she wondered what Tom would have made of his wife receiving such an invitation.

Probably a joke, she thought with a rueful smile.

As Joy slipped the invitation back into the envelope, she decided to return it immediately. Guest services had obviously made a mistake. But as she stood, the telephone beside her bed began to ring.

'Hello?' Joy was hesitant, wondering if the call was to chase up the invitation.

It was Leticia.

'Hello, Joy, how are you, my dear? I just wanted to check if you needed anything?'

Joy sat down, relieved to hear Leticia's voice. She would agree that the invitation was a mistake and know what to do. 'I'm so glad you called, and yes, thank you, I am feeling fine and don't need anything – there's been no more panic attacks.'

'That's good. So, are you going to go to the painting class Henry mentioned?'

'Well, I'm not sure, something has happened.'

'Oh. Do you want to talk about it?'

Joy picked up the envelope. The luxurious paper felt smooth in her fingers. 'When I got back to my cabin, there was an invitation on my bed . . . I think there has been a mistake.'

'What's the invitation for?' Leticia sounded intrigued.

'It's for me to attend pre-dinner cocktails and then dine at the captain's table.'

'Oh, Joy, how marvellous!'

'Well, no, not really. It can't be for me, and I'm just on my way to hand it back.'

'Wait . . .' Leticia said. 'Slow down before you do anything. Can I come to your cabin now?'

'Yes, but I really don't see . . .' Joy didn't have time to finish, as Leticia declared that she was on her way and promptly hung up.

When Joy answered the door a short while later, Leticia burst in, her exuberance filling the room. With layers of fabric draped on her arm, she carried a leather bag and laid everything carefully on a chair. Joy held out the envelope, and Leticia stared at the thick cream card and read the words.

'But this is wonderful Joy. This is a much sought after invitation.'

'It can't be for me and there's clearly been a mix-up.' She folded her arms across her chest and frowned at Leticia. 'Even if it was, I don't possess anything that I could possibly wear, and I know I'll only embarrass myself.'

Leticia picked up the phone. 'Good afternoon,' she said, when guest services answered. 'I'm calling on behalf of Mrs Joy Bradley, who is staying in an Ocean View cabin, number 2617. She has received the captain's kind invitation to join him for dinner tonight, and this call is to confirm her attendance.' Leticia spoke with confidence. 'Yes, of course, how kind, she's very much looking forward to it.'

Turning to Joy, she smiled. 'All done, cocktails at 7.15pm.'

'Oh, Leticia, I can't go!' Joy wrung her hands then began to twist her wedding ring.

But Leticia reached out and guided Joy to sit on the bed. 'Joy, it's only a dinner, not a royal event,' she spoke softly.

'It's just that I don't fit in. I can't imagine why I've been selected.'

'Fit in?' Leticia narrowed her eyes. 'You'll fit in perfectly. You're Joy Bradley, a fabulous woman who built a career, was a devoted wife, and raised a capable daughter. You didn't just teach your students home economics, Joy, you taught them how to look after themselves and gave them skills that they'll carry for life. I can't imagine that half the folk you'll meet tonight will have achieved so much.'

Leticia paused. 'Do this for yourself, Joy – for you, no one else. Not even for Tom . . .'

Joy's head jerked, and she stared at her new friend.

'His death didn't delete you, Joy. You lost him, but you mustn't lose yourself.'

Joy swallowed hard. Leticia didn't understand. She couldn't. Joy's throat felt tight, and she willed herself not to let a panic attack return. Leticia was kindness wrapped up in bright, bold colours, and Joy didn't want to let her down. How she longed to let her shoulders relax, to sit back, close her eyes, and let out all the emotion she'd bottled up for so long and share her pain with someone else, someone she could trust. But now was neither the time nor the place. If she wasn't going to let Leticia down, she would have to go to this wretched dinner.

'You can't say no to the captain's table, Joy; it would be a crime, and the invitation clearly means that someone out there noticed something in you that you must be too modest to admit.'

'You really think so?'

'I know so.'

'But I've nothing to wear. There's nothing glamorous, only a couple of dresses that I pimp up with scarves and a bit of paste jewellery . . .' Joy shrugged, but her attention was caught by the items Leticia had brought with her.

Leticia saw the shift in Joy's posture, a softening that gave Joy away. 'I can help get you ready. Are you up for it?' she asked.

Joy bit on her lip. 'Okay.' She paused, then nodded. 'Let's do it.'

Leticia clapped her hands and spun around to rifle through the mound of fabrics she'd placed on the chair. 'This is going to be fun!' she said. 'I've brought my bag of tricks and a couple of outfit ideas.' She stopped to study Joy from head to toe. 'Hmm, you've a lovely figure, perfect for what I have in mind. Let's give everyone something to remember.'

Joy hesitated as Leticia asked her to slip out of her trousers and sweater. She wasn't sure if she was excited or terrified of what was to come.

Leticia held up two layers of fabric, one a deep emerald green and the other a midnight blue, and her eyes were mischievous. 'Now,' she said, 'just how fabulous do you want to be?'

* * *

125

When Leticia got back to her cabin, she found Jim sitting by the window, reading a book. As the door opened, he looked up, the corners of his mouth curving into a slow smile as the book slipped from his lap.

The reading light caught the glow of Leticia's face, her dark skin smooth, kind eyes shining. She always took his breath away just by walking into a room. 'Is Cinderella going to the ball?' he asked as Leticia placed her bag down and came towards him.

'Cinderella has become a princess,' Leticia said as she picked up Jim's book and, kissing his forehead, reached for his hand. 'Joy has transformed. I hardly recognised her by the time we'd finished.'

Leticia sat beside Jim and stared out at the darkness and as the ship made headway an icy wind drove flurries of snow onto their balcony. She thought of her emerald-green wraparound dress with its soft, fluid folds. Starting with the bodice, Leticia had crossed the fabric at the front to create a V-shaped neckline and layered it into artful pleats at Joy's slim waist, then knotted it into a flattering bow. The skirt cascaded to the floor, and Leticia took one edge of the fabric, placing it over Joy's shoulder like a sash and securing it with a decorative brooch. Taking styling tools from her bag, she brushed Joy's hair with deft fingers that lifted the weight, pinned it, and finished with a diamanté clip. Next came the makeup, and Leticia added warmth to Joy's skin with foundation and blusher and a glimmering shine to her eyes.

'Just add a hint of gloss on your lips, and you'll dazzle all evening,' Leticia smiled when she stood back to admire her handiwork.

'My goodness, I don't recognise myself,' Joy said as she turned in front of the mirror. She gently stroked her hair and smoothed the gown. 'It's a miracle,' she laughed before glancing down at her bare feet. 'But what about shoes?'

'Your silver ballet pumps will work perfectly.'

Leticia had given Joy strict instructions not to touch her face or hair as she helped her out of the newly modelled gown. She told her to relax and that she'd be back in plenty of time to help her dress before dinner.

'You worked your magic,' Jim said and squeezed Leticia's hand.

Leticia smiled at her husband. *If only I could work some magic on you!* She felt his hand resting in hers, familiar and steady as he looked at her with the loving smile that had deepened during the two decades that they'd been together.

Leticia was vigilant in her care of Jim and constantly looked out for any sign of change or deterioration in his condition. For now, things were stable, but The Beast hovered like an unwelcome guest, waiting to return to Jim's final party. When it returned, it wouldn't knock politely or wait to be invited in. Doctors had told her that when The Beast came back, it would be hungry, and no matter how hard Leticia fought, it was unlikely that she'd weaken its blows.

Her husband's decline would be rapid.

But as they sat quietly, hands entwined, Leticia knew that she would be ready. In the meantime, their lives together were for living, and she would ensure that he lived the best life possible. Jim had suffered too much grief in his life after losing his wife and precious daughter.

'It's a formal night tonight, so we're going to wear our best bib and tucker,' Leticia declared, springing to her feet. 'What would you like me to wear?'

Without waiting for an answer, she moved to the bedroom and reached for a rail of dresses, her fingers dancing along satin, silk, chiffon and sequins. Thank goodness the cruise line offered a generous luggage allowance, for Leticia had packed all her favourites. She held up a midnight blue gown with silver beading. 'This one?' she asked as she stepped towards him.

'It's perfect,' he grinned, 'just like you.'

Leticia blew him a kiss. 'I hope Joy enjoys herself tonight, she seems very nervous,' she said as she held the dress to her body and turned from side to side, watching the fabric shimmering in the light of the cabin. Leticia had an inkling that there was more to Joy than met the eye and hoped that the cruise would help her fledging friend find the confidence she lacked to step into the next stage of her life and enjoy it.

A champagne cork popped, and Leticia turned to see Jim pouring two glasses. 'Shall we toast?' he asked, lifting one towards her.

'How lovely,' Leticia walked over, accepting the glass. 'To what?'

'To you. To the moment. To us.'

Leticia clinked her glass gently against his, the crystal almost singing. 'To us,' she said softly, 'and to Joy and a night full of possibility.'

Chapter Fourteen

At the captain's table, every course arrives with regularity, like the ebb and flow of the sea.

The Triton Lounge was abuzz as guests, dressed in their finest, made their way to enjoy cocktails before dinner. A formal night on the cruise was an opportunity to show off, and elegant gowns and tailored tuxedos were paraded as guests gathered to drink champagne and appreciate the soft notes of a string quartet.

The stage was set for an excellent evening and to Joy's relief, Leticia and Jim escorted her to the lounge so she wouldn't have to make an entrance alone. Senior members of the ship's crew in formal wear greeted guests, and Simon stepped forward to escort Joy to the captain's cocktail party.

'Enjoy yourself,' Leticia whispered as she left Joy and entered the lounge to find seats for herself and Jim.

Joy, meanwhile, was guided to a raised circular banquette, where other invitees were assembled, and introductions made. Joy sat beside a woman from Ireland who stated that she had been at sea for almost a year. Joy soon learned that Lady Eleanor Fitzgerald was eighty-nine and a widow.

'You can call me Lady E,' she said, 'no need for formalities.'

Joy thought that prefacing your name with a title was as formal as it got and unsure of familiarities so soon after meeting, she was reluctant to shorten the name. 'Do you stay on the same ship while you cruise?' she asked, curious to know the routine for one who probably left the packing of multiple cases to her staff.

'Of course, why move from ship to ship when all I need is right here.' Lady Eleanor stifled a yawn.

'Naturally,' Joy agreed and couldn't imagine the cost of such luxury. To stay on a ship for almost a year, one would need to be considerably well off. 'The *Emerald Dream* must have an interesting itinerary?' Joy asked, curious to know where the affluent passenger travelled to.

'I believe so, but I rarely disembark, and this is the second time I've cruised to Norway this month.'

'Still,' Joy continued, 'there's so much to do onboard, and I'm sure you enjoy all the activities?'

'On the contrary, I like the evening entertainment, meals, and formal dinners, but rarely leave my suite. I've everything I need there.'

In her mind, Joy weighed up life at sea, where Lady Eleanor was waited on hand and foot, with kind and friendly staff, as opposed to the life she might lead at home. Her accommodation was the Royal Emerald Suite, the most luxurious on the ship, that consisted of several rooms, an opulent bathroom and a large private balcony.

Curious to know more, Joy soon learned that Lady Eleanor's late husband, Lord Richard Dunmore, of Dunmore

Hall in County Kildare, had been a philanthropist, and they'd met at a garden party in Dublin in 1963.

'He was never interested in cruising,' Lady Eleanor told Joy. 'He preferred staying closer to home and keeping an eye on the estate. When he died last year and our son took over, I decided to indulge my passion, preferring a smaller ship, and have been travelling on the *Emerald Dream* ever since.' Lady Eleanor paused. 'To be perfectly honest, my dear, I miss my darling Richard so much and can't face being at home without him.'

Fascinated by Lady Eleanor, Joy listened intently.

Lord Richard, it transpired, had restored the crumbling inherited Dunmore Estate with its two thousand acres of woodland and farmland. Later, with their son, they turned the main house into a boutique hotel and event business. Keen to charitably support the locals, Lady Eleanor explained that they maintained a substantial holiday property in the grounds, the Dunmore Retreat, for the exclusive use and benefit of the surrounding community, especially those with learning difficulties.

'We still run Dunmore Retreat today, in a trust,' she explained. 'Richard insisted that it be fully staffed and well-equipped, offering respite for the locals, and emotional and educational support whenever appropriate, at no cost to those who make use of the facilities. I've always supported the ethos of this and wish it to continue under our son's guidance,' she added.

Joy nodded, intrigued. It was a charitable concern that she would fully support herself.

'When we married, Richard had a vision to maintain the family fortune,' Lady Eleanor explained. 'Initially, we kept the upper floor of the main house, although there were only sixteen rooms for our use, and since his death, I live in the Dower House. Not that I've spent a great deal of time on the estate, everywhere in Ireland feels so empty without Richard.' Her voice was sad.

Joy considered living accommodation of sixteen rooms palatial, and her three-bedded bungalow wouldn't compare to a sizeable Dower House. As she studied Lady Eleanor and wondered what it might be like to live a life of such privilege, Joy noted her lipstick, a deep red, the kind worn by women who remembered Coty powder and 4711 Eau de Cologne. It had crept onto her front teeth but to mention it would be impolite. Joy was so engrossed with the rouge bouncing up and down on Lady Eleanor's incisors that she didn't notice Captain Lauri Lindholm's approach. When he slipped into the seat beside her, she turned too quickly and almost knocked over his glass.

'Oh, my goodness, I didn't see you,' Joy apologised and felt her cheeks flush. *What a fool!* Seated between a Lady and the captain, and she was all fingers and thumbs.

Captain Lindholm offered a polite smile and held out his hand. 'Good evening, Mrs Bradley,' he said, his Finnish accent low, 'and Lady Eleanor, how are you?'

Lady Eleanor turned her gaze to the captain. 'You startled poor Joy,' she said. 'Be gentle. She might not be used to handsome men dropping in unannounced.'

'We have a presentation for you later,' Captain Lindholm said, 'Lady Eleanor, you are our most travelled passenger this year. But you haven't surpassed a gentleman who sailed with the Diamond Star Line for 949 days.'

'Has he popped his clogs?' Lady Eleanor asked.

'Sadly, he's sailed onto a higher place,' the captain conceded.

'Well, I shall be sailing your seas for some time to come,' Lady Eleanor smiled, 'and I shall expect more than a slip of paper,' she added.

'It is our pleasure to accommodate you and have you on board,' the captain said.

'I shall host a little soirée in my suite on Christmas Eve,' Lady Eleanor said, 'you must all join me.'

Joy stared at the elderly passenger and thought that she seemed weary. She wondered what Lady Eleanor did all day if she didn't join in with the activities. Did she read books or write letters? Or perhaps she daydreamed and rewound memories. But there was a lethargy about Lady Eleanor, a quiet exhaustion, and clearly, she was mourning her husband. Lady Eleanor seemed lost in her own world, and her eyes were dull, no longer watching the glitz and glamour in the Triton Lounge. Maybe she was just tired, Joy thought, and at the latter end of life, bemused by a world without Sir Richard.

No wonder the ship suited her so well.

More guests joined and Joy was introduced to a charming couple from Wakefield, and a former equestrian champion who'd won a gold medal at the Mexico Olympics and greeted Lady Eleanor fondly with a hug.

Old school Margaret was sharp jawed with a nose as elongated as the horses she'd competed on, and a mouthpiece for wit and name-dropping. Joy heard the Olympian mention Princess Anne twice before her first drink was served.

'Dear Margaret,' Lady Eleanor smiled, 'she's such a good friend and companion.'

Another couple sat down and apologised for being late, and then a steward served canapés and more drinks. As everyone chatted, and Joy munched an olive, speared on a plastic sword, she listened to the captain explain the pleasure of overseeing the *Emerald Dream*. 'I do very little,' he modestly shrugged when asked about his duties, 'my staff sail the ship.' There was a polite ripple of laughter as he went on to enlighten the benefits of a smaller cruise line and how he preferred it. 'I dislike the larger floating flats, with thousands of passengers and half as many crew.'

Joy studied the earnest faces as they hung off the captain's words, and as she looked around, she noticed Barbara and Kenneth stroll past the captain's reserved seating area, to make their way to cocktails in the Triton Lounge. They both carried the smug sway of passengers who thought they'd bagged the best suite.

They were mid-gloat when they spotted Joy.

Barbara froze and her jaw suddenly dropped as Joy gave a wave. Kenneth's mouth opened and shut like a fish flailing to wriggle free from a hook. Inwardly, Joy giggled. Here she was, Joy of the sensible slacks and widow's worries, sitting in a VIP booth, beside the captain, a title and an Olympic champion, sipping champagne.

Captain Lindholm offered Joy his arm to escort her to dinner, and Joy felt like royalty as the party moved off. She was sure she heard Barbara give a strangled hiss as she grabbed Kenneth's arm and pivoted on her kitten heels.

Photos were taken in the foyer of the restaurant as the group arrived. Stewards, in their smartest uniform suits, stood to attention and pulled out chairs as the captain's party sat down. Their table was in the centre of the room on a slightly raised platform, and once again, Joy was seated by the captain. As a napkin was unfolded onto her knee, she studied the place card bearing her name in looping gold script, alongside a menu detailing the evening's meal. Appetisers were served and wine poured, and as Joy tasted a delicate millefeuille of goat cheese and microgreens topped with a soft-boiled quail's egg, she looked up.

From their balcony table, the occupants of table number twenty-eight were watching Joy and grinning. Leticia and Jim held their glasses in a toast, and Henry, smart in his dinner suit, gave a thumbs up. Joy felt her heart swell and resisted the urge to blow them all a kiss.

Barbara and Kenneth, meanwhile, turned away.

Following a delicious lobster thermidor, and by the time dessert was served, an exquisite lemon souffle, Joy was glowing. Several glasses of the sommelier's finest wines had settled her nerves. She listened to the captain enlighten everyone about both his working and family life, explaining that he had homes in Finland and Spain. His yacht in the Mediterranean, he admitted with a modest smile, was less a luxury and more a continuation of his love affair with the sea. The cheerful lady from Wakefield asked about his wife, and they discovered that Marja, his second marriage, had been a personal trainer on the cruise ship he once captained while sailing to the Canaries.

'A romance blossomed from the treadmill to Tenerife,' Margaret observed.

'But it was a romance that faded,' the captain remarked dryly, 'she left me for a first officer last year.'

Margaret proceeded to hold court over the main course,

recounting the moment she clinched her Olympic gold medal. Her laugh was loud as she told stories of her time in the saddle.

Simon proved charming and skilled in his job as he steered conversations to bring out the best in his guests, and the two couples, frequent cruisers with the Diamond Star line, spoke fondly of past high-flying careers and well-lived lives.

When it came to Joy's turn to reveal a little of herself, she took a deep breath, then set down her glass and spoke quietly for a few minutes. Eyes studied her with curiosity, or was it admiration? Joy couldn't be sure, but when she finished speaking, she saw the captain raise one eyebrow and nod as though his perception of his dining companion had shifted.

Everyone was relaxed, warmed by excellent food, laughter, and the glow that comes from enjoyable company. Joy smoothed the fabric of her gorgeous gown and silently thanked Leticia for giving her the tools to make the most of the evening. For a moment, she wondered what Tom would think of his wife's single sortie to sit with such esteemed fellow passengers and ultimately feel at ease.

But Joy wouldn't think of Tom now.

She was a woman who'd arrived at the cocktail party almost afraid to be there, but now sat comfortably as though she'd been invited to such events all her life. The evening wasn't over, and she knew that Leticia was hoping she'd meet up to spill the beans and disclose the secrets of the captain's table. But as coffee was served and liqueurs offered, Joy doubted that she'd reveal the revelation that she'd shared.

After all, Joy thought as she looked around at the other guests, *what happens at the captain's table stays at the captain's table!*

Chapter Fifteen

*Sortland – where the sky meets the sea on
the walls of the town.*

After breakfast, Henry started his day sitting by the window of his terrace cabin watching a crew safety drill. Simon's morning message included information that during the drill no action was needed by the passengers, the instructions given over the PA system were for crew only to follow.

'Code Bravo,' Simon announced, 'all crew to proceed to emergency stations and muster as required!'

Henry made himself comfortable as several crew members in high-vis wear and lifejackets mustered at the station in front of his one-way mirrored sliding doors. Unaware that they were being observed, the three engineers flirted with two pretty girls from housekeeping. When a sharp blast of the general emergency signal was heard, it silenced their small talk, and they stiffened into a military posture as the drill began.

As he watched, Henry sipped his coffee and wondered what the day would bring. The ship had docked in Sortland,

and having crossed the Arctic Circle, the sun would no longer rise above the horizon. Within the circle, winter brought a strange phenomenon known as the polar night, and Henry knew that darkness lingered for weeks and even months, broken only by a brief, twilight-like blue light that appeared around midday. It was one of the reasons he'd chosen the cruise: to witness a daytime darkness, unlike anything he could ever experience at home.

Henry intended to join a walking tour. The brochure described Sortland as a charming town known as the Blue City because of its distinct, blue-painted buildings, and he was looking forward to strolling around and learning a little about the Arctic way of life in a place that has a frozen landscape for at least half of the year. Despite the darkness, there were bound to be excellent photo opportunities, and he would ensure he took plenty to share with Audrey.

The crew outside had finished their drill and moved away, and Henry saw that a light snow was falling. Draining his coffee, he slid the door open and took a deep breath of the sharp icy air.

'Morning, Henry!' a voice called out, and he turned to see Jack in his regulation T-shirt and shorts, pounding down the deck.

'Good morning,' Henry replied, and noticed that hot on Jack's heels came the Deck Mile Club with Judy at the helm, arms pumping like pistons.

'You should join us,' Judy barked as they passed. 'Being cosied up in the ship all the time isn't healthy!'

Henry watched them go, their walking boots thudding rhythmically against the decking. As he studied the members, he thought that one or two looked cold and tired and might benefit from being cosied up in the ship, with their feet up and a warming mug of hot chocolate. But with Judy in charge, there was little chance of escape from the morning routine.

Henry moved back into his cabin. There'd be no boot-thumping on the deck for him. His cardiovascular commitment, he decided, would be better spent on his upcoming walk around Sortland, at a leisurely pace. Gathering his things, Henry opened the cabin door and was startled to see Jennifer.

'Good sleep Mr Henry?' she asked, her duster hovering over the brass railing.

'Splendid Jennifer, thank you, and how are you today?'

'I always happy when I see you,' she beamed.

Henry looked down at the woman and thought how pretty she was, with smooth olive skin, bright eyes, and a kindness that lit up her face.

'Thank you,' he said, his smile softening.

Jennifer shrugged and resumed dusting. 'You go sightseeing?' she asked.

'Indeed, I am. I'm going on a guided walk and may even look out for a couple of souvenirs for my friend Audrey.'

'You have friend?' Jennifer's eyes narrowed.

'Yes, my neighbour, she's quite old and doesn't go on holiday anymore.'

'Ah, old neighbour, can't move.' She nodded. 'That is good.'

Henry frowned. 'Not so good for Audrey, but she's had an interesting life.'

'You go enjoy. I'll keep everything nice here for you.' Jennifer reached into her trolley for fresh towels and neatly folded sheets.

Henry buttoned his jacket and began to move away.

'See you later, Mr Henry.'

Henry gave a wave over his shoulder. 'Have a good day!' he called out.

But as he made his way to the Triton Lounge to join the walking tour, Henry was unaware of the smile that tugged at Jennifer's lips and the eyes that lingered before she shook her head, as though chasing away a thought before carrying on with her work.

* * *

Seated in the Triton Lounge, Joy studied a large screen on the stage that listed all the tours about to commence. Many passengers would travel to Vesterålen to experience everyday life in a region whose history spanned from the mid-nineteenth century to the present day. It would include a visit to a herring factory followed by a live music concert. She'd heard all about the tour from Leticia and knew that, together with Jim, they were looking forward to their enjoyable day out. Joy noted that there was a Sámi experience, too, which offered a daytime opportunity to meet a Sámi family and learn about the reindeer herder's way of life. She thought of the tour that she'd booked later in the week. It was for an evening event at a reindeer camp, with the possibility of sightings of the Northern Lights, and although expensive, Joy felt that the cost would be justified, and she was looking forward to it.

The lounge was filling up, and when she saw Barbara and Kenneth enter, Joy sank low in her seat and began to fiddle with the strap on her rucksack, hoping to avoid the couple. But she was too late. Kenneth, with a walking pole in each hand, had seen her and began to make his way over.

'Morning, old girl,' he said, 'off out for the day?'

Joy bristled at his greeting. 'Er, yes, I'm going on the walking tour of Sortland.'

'Bit tame if you ask me.' Kenneth was scornful. 'One can go on a walkabout at home. Babs and I are off on the snowshoe adventure under the polar night, and a midday twilight ice fishing experience. It's not for the faint-hearted,' he added.

As she studied Barbara's pale face and tired eyes, Joy thought that she looked extremely faint-hearted and more suited to a morning relaxing in bed. Had she been burning the midnight oil? Joy wondered how Barbara was going to cope with a torch-lit snowshoe hike through a blackened snowy landscape, and the thrill of blindly casting her line into an Arctic ice hole to wait for a fish to bite. She hoped that Barbara had doubled up on her thermals and that her mood would lift during the drive to the winter camp on the island of Hadseløya.

Kenneth nudged his wife with his elbow. 'We can't wait, can we, Babs? We're both winter sports enthusiasts.'

Barbara scowled and adjusted her fur headgear. Her expression suggested winter sports involved sipping glögg by a roaring fire, not an icy hike, trudging through the snow.

Before Barbara could reply, Henry appeared. 'Morning everyone,' he said cheerfully. 'It's bitingly cold out there, and the forecast is for heavy snow and a thick mist adding to the darkness.'

Joy looked up. 'Morning Henry,' she said. 'Kenneth and Barbara were just telling me how much they're looking forward to their Hadseløya excursion.'

Henry rubbed his hands together and gave a theatrical shiver. 'Well, good luck with that. I'm surprised it hasn't been cancelled, given the impending weather. Dangling worms into Arctic water doesn't appeal to me but do let us know how you find it.'

Barbara's grimace indicated that she'd rather undergo root canal surgery without anaesthetic and was about to open her mouth to speak when Kenneth shot her down.

'What's on your agenda, old boy?' Kenneth asked Henry. He bobbed from one foot to the other, his walking poles poised as though he was about to attempt Mount Everest rather than shuffle over a snowy landscape.

'I'm taking a walking tour of Sortland,' Henry replied. 'It may be less energetic but equally as interesting, I'm sure.' He turned to Joy and asked, 'What are your plans today?'

Joy sat up. 'This old girl is also going on the walking tour, and as I've heard that Sortland is a charming town, I'm looking forward to it.'

'Excellent!' Henry beamed. 'I hear that coffee and cake is included at a café where there's a roaring log fire.'

Joy noted that Barbara's eye twitched. *Coffee*. *Cake*. Henry's words had registered.

'Joy,' Henry rattled on, 'I hope you'll have a few moments to walk with me and share all the details of your dinner at the captain's table. It must have been an interesting experience.' Henry paused. 'I'm sure everyone on the cruise would have traded places with you, wouldn't they, Barbara?'

Barbara's stance stiffened. Taking hold of her husband's arm, Barbara's voice was crisp. 'I didn't realise that they drew names out of a hat for places at the captain's table,' she said, her eyes fixed on Joy. 'Still, I suppose the dining experience was a once-in-a-lifetime opportunity for a schoolteacher.' Lifting her chin, she glanced at the screen on the stage. 'Come on, Kenny, our excursion is being called.'

And with that, Barbara and Kenneth marched off like soldiers going into battle.

Joy and Henry exchanged glances. Joy was trying not to laugh. 'Do you think a walking tour of Sortland is suitable for schoolteachers?'

'Absolutely,' Henry nodded, 'especially for those who've dined at the captain's table.'

* * *

Sortland was every bit as charming as the cruise brochure described. Lenny, their guide, met the passengers as they disembarked. The temperature was several degrees below zero, and Joy was pleased that she'd invested in snow grips for her boots. With ice crunching underneath a fresh layer of snow, her footing was firm, and she walked with confidence. Lenny explained that the weather could change in minutes, and it wasn't long before the mist lifted and through the darkness, they could see the blue-painted buildings looming in the shadows ahead. Their route took them along the fjord before turning into the town. Lamps burned brightly in the main street of Strandgata, which was bustling and lined with shops and boutiques, all offering a range of Norwegian products.

'I rather like these,' Henry said when they stopped in a store selling Christmas items. He held up a tiny pair of Sámi boots, known locally as gállohat footwear, made from reindeer hide and decorated with traditional, colourful stitching. 'Audrey would appreciate these earrings,' he continued. 'She likes unusual objects.'

Joy nodded. The earrings would likely match Audrey's Viking chieftain faux-fur cloak coat. She picked up an oval-shaped bowl and stroked the smooth polished wood. The bowl would make an ideal gift for Susan and fit in well with her minimalist, ultra-modern chic London townhouse kitchen, where acres of sleek cabinetry were created from what appeared to be the entirety of an Amazon forest. Moments later, she stood outside the shop with her purchase neatly wrapped.

The walking group now trudged uphill, and Lenny guided them to a charming church, built in traditional style and painted a soft white that blended into the landscape. With snow falling in flurries, the heavy wooden doors creaked open to reveal a warm glow from suspended pendant lights and the sound of choral music echoing through the peaceful sanctuary.

'This is lovely,' Joy said as she sat beside Henry on a pew and stared at the stained-glass windows. Henry sat quietly beside her and nodded as he, too, looked around at the vaulted ceiling and the flickering flames from multiple beeswax candles.

Joy suddenly felt a sense of calm and she realised that it had been quietly building since Leticia had helped her through the panic attack and insisted that she dine at the captain's table. Like a spring slowly unwinding, Joy's body was beginning to loosen, releasing a tension that had gripped her for far too long. She felt Henry's arm alongside, buried beneath the fabric of his coat and radiating warmth. It gave her comfort here in the sanctity of this little church, far from the uncertainty of the world outside. Joy closed her eyes and thought of Tom.

Would he have enjoyed this holiday? She had an inkling that her husband might have preferred a warm, sunny cruise and would complain about the sunless winter skies, not appreciating the tranquillity and quiet beauty. The tight knot of nerves that had been her constant companion was slowly unwinding, and she was even finding things to smile about. She wondered if she was finally allowing herself to let go and leave the memories behind because the cruise was turning out to be enjoyable and far from the nightmare holiday she'd feared.

'Are you all right?' Henry whispered.

Joy opened her eyes to turn and stare at Henry. His deep blue eyes were focused on her with concern.

'Yes, sorry, I was just having a moment,' she replied.

'That's perfectly fine. We must all have our moments. Sometimes, it's in those moments that we find the strength to keep going.'

'Oh . . .' Joy was lost for words. Had Henry read her mind, and was he aware of her inner turmoil? Like Leticia, did he have a sixth sense that reached beyond what he showed on the surface?

'Shall we go and look at the Christmas trees?' Henry asked, and he waited as Joy gathered her rucksack and wriggled out of the nave seating and into the aisle.

In one corner of the church, three spruce trees stood as a backdrop to a nativity scene. Decorated with pretty lights and a bright star on the highest branch, they highlighted the figures below. Standing beside Henry, Joy felt that she was having another 'moment' and had to resist the sudden urge to reach out and take his hand.

Whatever was the matter with her! She was shocked by her longing and told herself that she hardly knew the man. Yet the desire to touch Henry had been strong.

Leaving the church, they found the snow had stopped as they made their way back down the hill. It lay in a thick, fluffy layer, and Henry reached down to scoop flakes into his hands. Hurrying ahead, he turned and grinned, then hurled a snowball to skim Joy's shoulder. In reply, she leaned down to gather a handful of snow, shaping it quickly between her gloved fingers. As she launched her snowball back at him, a sound she hadn't heard in far too long bubbled up.

Joy was laughing. A genuine, carefree, happy laugh erupted as the delicate white spray hit Henry squarely on his nose, clinging to his skin like a feathery beard. Spluttering, Henry gasped in mock outrage and soon, like children in a play fight, they were ducking and dodging as their snowballs landed.

'Hei!' Lenny called out. 'There's apple cake and coffee at the Scandic café!'

Joy and Henry paused. A guilty look passed between them as a group of children, huddled beneath a streetlight, stared with bemused smiles. Joy brushed the snow from her coat and then touched her cheeks, which were flushed with cold and laughter.

Henry straightened and cleared his throat. 'Apologies,' he said, 'I don't know what came over me, and I suppose we should behave like adults.'

'Absolutely,' Joy responded, fighting to regain her composure. 'I don't know what came over me too.' But as they turned to continue down the hill, Joy knew that whatever had come over her was something she hadn't felt in a very long time. It was the feeling of being truly alive and, of having fun.

Perhaps, just perhaps, she was beginning to live again.

Chapter Sixteen

*Sailing through the Arctic darkness,
one faces the unknown.*

The ship was quiet when Henry and Joy returned and went their separate ways, both agreeing to meet up again at dinner. Henry opened the door to his cabin and noted that Jennifer had arranged a towel in the shape of a penguin and placed it in the middle of his bed.

How clever, Henry thought as he studied the tiny figure, and remembered that penguins were faithful little creatures who thrived in the harshest conditions.

Jennifer had skilfully crafted the shape using a hand towel and face cloths, and he wondered what other guests thought of her efforts. Jennifer went above and beyond to ensure that Henry's cabin was comfortable and tidy. Somewhat different from his home, where, although everything had a place, Henry often misplaced items.

Sitting by the desk, he retrieved his camera and studied the photographs he'd taken. He'd captured a rather excellent shot of giant icicles suspended from a building in the town, and images of the blue-painted buildings in the twilight of mid-day were almost surreal. Streetlamps and Christmas lights glimmered along the busy, snowy streets, casting warm reflections on the ice and snow. Pedestrians in colourful snowsuits added life and vividness to the scene, and Sortland's festive glow looked like a Christmas card coming to life. *Audrey will love these!*

The members of his photography club would be impressed by the beauty of Sortland too. Pleased with his pictures of the church, Henry smiled when Joy appeared on his screen. He noted how the sun caught the gleam of her chestnut hair as she pulled off her hat and shook away the snow from the playful missile he'd launched. Joy was laughing and her eyes crinkled at the corners, while her smile lit up the frame.

Henry paused, his finger hovering over the image.

His thoughts drifted back to the church, to the quiet hush beneath the vaulted ceiling where they'd studied the nativity scene together. How he'd longed at that moment to reach out and take Joy's hand. But, feeling foolish and as uncertain as a schoolboy, he'd resisted the urge. It was unthinkable to make an approach, and Joy would have pushed him away. She was a grieving widow, he reminded himself. But as he studied her face, he lingered. Grief still sat behind her eyes but no longer clung like the shroud that he'd seen when they'd first met at dinner. As the days passed, she'd begun to emerge, and her laugh was music to Henry's ears.

Joy's company was easy, and it was a pleasure to be with her.

Over coffee in the Scandic café, they'd sat by the fire, and she'd told him about her time at the captain's table and the interesting guests she'd met. Henry listened carefully, nodding as Joy spoke of Lady Eleanor and the older woman's endless days at sea, drifting from port to port like a ghost from another era. Being with Joy, conversation flowed effortlessly, and as he did with Audrey, Henry felt that he could be himself without any need to perform or impress. But where Audrey's companionship felt like a warm, comforting cardigan, Joy's wasn't just comfort; it was *possibility*.

Henry hadn't expected to have any romantic feelings again. At seventy, that was absurd. He knew that he was no more than a companion for excursions, and he would be foolish to make a move.

Henry replaced his camera in its case and pushed back his chair. Reaching for the *Daily Times*, he scanned the itinerary for the remainder of the day and saw that there was plenty to do. He toyed with the idea of a Christmas cookery class, where Kransekake, a sweet almond cake, was being demonstrated, then considered a quiz in the Bookmark Café, but his thoughts still strayed to Joy, and he wondered what Audrey would say.

Henry could almost see his friend wagging her finger. *'Life is for living, and our time is short! Don't be a fool and die wondering.'* How many times had Audrey repeated those words when Henry was hesitant. So often, she'd encouraged him to come out of his comfort zone. But despite Audrey's pearls of wisdom, Henry knew that he was unable to express his feelings, and romance with Joy would remain strictly out of bounds.

Henry stood. It was no use sitting in his cabin, and he'd noted that an art class titled Arctic Acrylics would begin mid-afternoon. Taking heed of Audrey's words, he decided that he'd step out of his comfort zone and head to the Emerald Art Studio to brave Lucinda Green. He'd never attempted to paint, and perhaps it was time that he did.

But first, he'd grab a bite to eat in the buffet restaurant.

Moving to a mirror, Henry tugged on his collar and straightened his sweater. 'Who knows?' he asked his reflection. 'I might be a budding Lowry or even paint like Picasso.'

As he moved past the penguin, he gave the little bird a wave. 'Hold the fort until I return with a masterpiece,' Henry called out, then shook his head, chuckling softly.

He was talking to towel sculptures now!

* * *

Leticia and Jim had enjoyed their excursion to Vesterålen, and both felt as though they'd stepped back in time as their guide explained the history of a region rich with Sámi heritage. There was something about the area that held Leticia as she stood on the snow, listening for sounds in the almost silent, dark landscape. By a boathouse, she was enchanted by a line of drying fish, and the winter rhythm of Norwegian life went on behind the walls of the red-roofed houses that they passed. Jim chatted with fellow passengers about how summers in Vesterålen had permanent daylight, and in winter, the polar night went on for months.

They'd sat hand in hand in the Royal Triton Hall, their fingers entwined as local musicians played. The notes danced through the hall's exquisite acoustics and Leticia remembered turning to Jim, her eyes shining. A wave of emotion welled, and she felt a fierce gratitude for the man she loved. She'd wanted to hold onto the moment, to capture the shape of his smile and the adoration in his eyes and freeze frame his face forever. Tears pricked her eyes. Loving Jim was the most beautiful thing she'd ever known. No words were required. It was a magical moment that they both felt, and one that Leticia would treasure.

Now, Leticia sat in the Emerald Art Studio.

Jim was resting in their suite and, having been inspired by the thriving arts scene in Vesterålen earlier, Leticia had decided to try her hand at Arctic Acrylics. It would be pleasing to paint something as a reminder of the cruise and take home a memory. Leticia knew she wasn't an artist, but it might be fun to try.

The windows of the studio were wide, framing the tranquil sea. The ship wouldn't leave Sortland until early evening, giving passengers on longer excursions plenty of time to enjoy their day. Leticia had arrived early and chosen a seat in the middle of the room, where easels surrounded her, and a scent of paint and turpentine hung in the air. She stared at a table scattered with palettes and jars of water, where someone had laid out brushes in a haphazard fashion.

'All on your own?' a voice rang out, and a halo of vivid red hair sprang into the room.

Lucinda Green's thick green eyeliner appeared to have missed the mark, giving her a reptilian look. She wore well-worn dungarees over a thin white vest, the straps of the bib casually unfastened and hanging loose. It was clear to

Leticia that Lucinda had chosen to forgo a bra and didn't care who noticed. She held a cigarette holder in one hand and removed a short stub, tucking it casually in a pocket.

'Blasted rules,' Lucinda mumbled. 'One can't have a fag inside, and I've been up on deck. Almost froze my tits off.' She tapped the cigarette holder on a table and, reaching into her vest, tucked it neatly beneath one breast. 'The old pencil test,' Lucinda said, catching Leticia's curious look. 'Back in the school dorms, amongst body-conscious teenage girls, it was the ultimate benchmark. If the pencil fell to the floor, it meant your chest was still defying gravity,' she gave a nonchalant shrug. 'Sadly, I made peace with gravity years ago and could probably get a whole case of the buggers under there now.' She placed her hands on her sagging breasts, shoving them upwards.

Leticia thought that a decent bra would eliminate the problem but decided to keep her thoughts to herself.

'Grab an apron while you wait,' Lucinda instructed, then turned to busy herself, placing a canvas on each easel.

The room began to fill, and budding artists entered, taking their seats with nods and smiles to each other. Leticia was delighted to see Joy hesitantly standing in the doorway, and she waved to beckon her over. 'You're here!' Leticia smiled. 'Have you done much painting?'

Joy placed her bag down and inched onto a chair at a nearby easel. 'I've dabbled in watercolours, but that was a long time ago.'

Suddenly, Lucinda clapped her hands. 'That's enough gossiping,' she called out, 'we're here to work, not chatter like fishwives.' She showed the class where to gather paint and brushes and, instructing them to watch her work, she began.

'I want you to imagine the silence of fresh snow,' she said as her brush touched the canvas. 'Think of pale blue light suffusing the mountains.' As she daubed paint, she explained how to block in the land, the sky, and the snow. 'This is Norway in winter. Feel how it looks and let your imagination run free.'

There was a polite cough in the doorway, and Henry appeared. 'Apologies,' he muttered as he stepped into the room and slid onto a seat. 'Lunch lingered longer than I calculated.'

Lucinda walked over to Henry and glared at the new arrival, wagging her brush. 'We're not interested in your dietary habits, and if you turn up late again, you'll be barred.' She hoisted her left breast, smoothed her vest, and almost blinded Henry with a cotton-covered nipple as she turned.

Leticia and Joy exchanged amused glances and when Lucinda's back was turned, Leticia gave Henry a double thumbs up.

'Use broad strokes, not too tidy, and don't worry about the detail yet. But remember, acrylic paint dries fast, so trust your instincts.'

Lucinda instructed everyone to begin, telling them that, in between assisting them, she would pause to add to her own work and explain the techniques she was using.

An hour passed, and the room was silent with quiet concentration, broken only by the sound of the clink of water jars and the gentle rasp of brushes stroking canvas.

Lucinda wandered around, her cigarette holder clenched

between her teeth as she issued advice, both cruel and kind. Returning to her own easel, she demonstrated the method of adding a line of dark pines and a red cabin far away in the distance. 'Snow isn't just white,' she said, 'and it is soft. Use grey or violet in the shadows to capture the mood.' She stood back to study her work before telling the class to continue.

Standing by Henry's easel, Lucinda pursed her lips. 'It's not a bloody postcard to mail home to your mother,' she rudely commented. 'You're overthinking it. Be a bit wild!'

As Lucinda moved away, she missed Henry's one-finger salute, unaware that he'd deliberately focused his painting on being postcard perfect, knowing that Audrey would love it.

Another hour passed, and when stewards appeared with refreshments, Lucinda concluded the class. 'Well, you've all had a go,' she said, 'and some of it isn't bad, but I doubt that many of you will want to take your efforts home.'

'I rather think that's for us to decide,' Henry piped up.

But Lucinda merely shrugged, and turning to the table where the stewards had placed laden trays, she picked up a glass of wine. 'None of the tea and cake nonsense in here,' she said. 'If anyone fancies a livener, help yourselves.'

Chairs scraped back as the artists dived towards the drinks, almost knocking over easels, such was their haste.

'Ah, that's hit the spot,' a silver-haired woman sighed as she guzzled a glass of Chardonnay 'I'm sure I'd paint better after a drink.'

Lucinda raised her glass. 'Indeed, Picasso drank absinthe and look where that led him.'

In minutes, the class had transformed, and as everyone admired each other's work, the room took on a new energy.

'I think my mountains are having an identity crisis,' Leticia said as she stared at pillow-like blobs of paint on her unfinished work.

'My fjord is slipping off the canvas,' Henry added and sipped an excellent malt whisky.

'Climate change,' Leticia nodded. 'It's a melting glacier, very contemporary.'

They both agreed that Joy's fishing village nestling on the edge of a fjord was excellent.

Across the room, guests gathered around one man's painting, where bold, indistinguishable purple sprawled across the space. 'The Northern Lights,' he declared proudly, with the confidence of a man committed to his vision.

'Ah, yes . . .' someone murmured, as puzzled eyes looked on. 'Very interpretive.'

'A splendid abstract,' Lucinda cut in, swigging her third glass of wine. 'Nature is wild, just like this painting.'

Drinks and compliments flowed, and Lucinda turned on a backing track of a medley of popular seventies and eighties songs. 'To art!' she declared. Her face, more splattered than her palette, appeared like a Jackson Pollock and grabbing hold of Henry's hands, Lucinda began to dance.

The class cheered, and Henry downed his whisky. Remembering her earlier advice to be a bit wild, he carefully sidestepped Lucinda's liberated breasts and joined in.

'What a great class, and Henry is such a good sport,' Leticia said to Joy as she stood alongside, swaying her hips to the music and clapping her hands.

Joy was still watching Henry. 'Yes, he is,' she said softly, almost to herself.

'There seems to be more to our Henry than meets the eye,' Leticia added with a knowing smile. While she began to dance, Leticia glanced at her friend and saw that Joy's gaze lingered on Henry, her expression wistful.

At that moment, Leticia wondered if Joy's heart was beginning to loosen. She crossed her fingers and hoped that, between the two, there might be more than friendship.

Even if neither of them quite realised it yet.

Chapter Seventeen

The best part of any voyage isn't the destination; it's the company you keep on the journey.

Dinner that evening was good-humoured, with the artists still buoyed up from their impromptu boozy painting party and the chaotic whirlwind that was Lucinda. Leticia recounted the scene in colourful detail to those at table twenty-eight who'd missed all the fun, and Jim, Kenneth, and Barbara were all wide-eyed.

'Lucinda had finished the wine and was on her third cigarette when Simon appeared,' Leticia recounted, as their appetisers were served. 'He gently suggested that Lucinda save her cigarettes for when the ship was in port.' Leticia smiled at Jhamille, who hovered with her prosecco. 'He told her that onshore, she was welcome to disembark and smoke to her heart's content.'

'Apparently, she'd disabled the smoke alarms in the art studio,' Henry added as he tucked into a towering shrimp cocktail.

'Simon didn't want to upset the guests and to be fair, we

were still rocking out moves to the seventies tunes,' Leticia explained. 'But I heard him tell Lucinda that smoking was against the rules and he was tired of telling her off.'

Henry chuckled. 'That was all very well, but Lucinda had flung herself over a bench and lay back as though posing for a painting. She scoffed at Simon's polite request and declared that he was nothing more than a "deck detective", and couldn't a girl have just a *little* bit of fun?'

'I hope Lucinda's days at sea don't come to an end,' Leticia concluded. 'I thought she was entertaining and a great art tutor.'

'The woman is off her head, if you ask me,' Kenneth rudely added.

'No one was asking you,' Barbara snapped, secretly wishing that she had joined the art class and met the wine-guzzling artist herself.

Henry turned to Kenneth. 'How was your day?' he asked.

'Oh splendid, splendid.' Kenneth assured. 'Naturally exhausting for some, but for Babs and me, it was exhilarating. There's nothing like the crunch of ice underfoot as you hike up a twilight-lit mountain track. Excellent exercise and a true Arctic adventure!' he exclaimed and raised his glass.

Leticia thought Barbara looked sceptical and wondered if the only crunch of ice she'd experienced was cubes dropping into her cocktail glass when they returned to the ship.

'Did you enjoy the ice fishing and catch any Arctic char?' Henry pursued.

Kenneth was now on a roll, and as he spoke, he topped up his glass. 'Sitting by lantern light, on a thick slab of ice that groans every so often, you realise that the tiny round holes before you are a window into the dangerous world below.'

'But did you catch any fish?' Leticia asked.

'Well, those little devils are elusive, but I soon had a few tugs on my line and was netting them like a cat pouncing on a mouse.' He thoughtfully swirled his glass. 'But of course, you haven't lived until you've battled a twelve-pound brown trout in the shadow of the Andes with nothing but a bamboo rod.'

Struggling to recall Kenneth's fishing experiences and wondering if his sudden poetic turn of phrase was something he had read in a wildlife magazine, Barbara studied her husband, her fork paused on its journey to her mouth, eyebrows raised.

'All in all, the most expensive excursion of the day was worth every penny,' Kenneth bragged. He was oblivious to Barbara's audible sigh and had forgotten her comment as they left the coach, that she'd hated every minute and had never felt so cold.

At that moment, Margaret, the former equestrian champion, made her way to their table.

'I say, it's Joy, isn't it? I thought I recognised you, especially as you wore such a stunning gown for the captain's dinner last night.' Gripping the back of Joy's chair, she leaned in and whispered loud enough for everyone to hear. 'The captain is divorced, you know,' she gave Joy a gentle nudge, 'and stranger things have happened on a cruise.'

160

Joy smiled and introduced the newcomer. 'Everyone, this is Margaret.'

'Cracking night wasn't it, such entertaining and enlightening company,' Margaret continued, 'and I have to say that none of us had any idea. You really outshone us all.'

All eyes turned to Joy, who suddenly appeared self-conscious.

'Oh, no,' Joy spoke up, 'you were the star of the show with your equestrian achievements, and it was a pleasure to be in your company.' Joy swiftly diverted the conversation from herself. 'This lady is an Olympic gold medallist.'

Margaret dismissed the comment with a wave of her hand. Searching their faces, she recognised Kenneth and Barbara from the snowshoe and ice fishing excursion earlier that day.

Barbara, who'd sat up straight when she heard that the captain was single, didn't say a word. But the slight arch of her brow and the thoughtful sip of her wine suggested that she'd quietly filed the information away.

'Hello again,' Margaret said, 'bit of a rumpus with your hole today.' She gave a nod to Barbara. 'Our guide thought you were a magician pulling out a quart of Grey Goose while everyone else caught char.' Margaret laughed. 'I thought it was a shame they confiscated it, though; the Norwegians are quite strict about alcohol out of hours and away from a licensed bar.'

Barbara's face burned, and she glared at Margaret. Bored senseless by fishing and frozen to the bone, Barbara had taken out her illicit vodka and dangled it in her ice hole, banking on the science that alcohol doesn't freeze. Her plan had gone well until the guide caught her red-handed mid-swig and told her off.

Now, attempting to salvage her dignity, Barbara sat upright and tapped her nails on the table to ensure her dazzling diamond rings caught the light.

But Margaret was oblivious to Barbara's show of wealth. 'Shame about the weather too, and the excursion being cut short. We didn't even get any money back.' Margaret slapped Kenneth playfully on his back. 'Despite your protests,' she said with a grin, 'you told them exactly what you thought!'

Barbara closed her eyes, willing away the memory of Kenneth bickering with the guide. The old fool made such a spectacle of himself at times.

'Anyway, mustn't keep you,' Margaret said cheerfully and turned to leave. 'Don't forget Joy, cocktails and canapés in Lady Eleanor's suite on Christmas Eve, for her soirée. Her ladyship rather took a shine to you.'

Barbara felt a fresh arrow of humiliation shoot through her carefully guarded pride. *Lady Eleanor?* Barbara stared resentfully at Joy. The titled woman had been topping Barbara's must-meet list and so far, she'd failed to engage.

'*You* know Lady Eleanor Fitzgerald?' Barbara glared at Joy.

'She's a charming lady but doesn't join in with many activities other than socialising for dinner with the captain and enjoying the evening entertainment,' Joy politely enlightened Barbara.

Leticia turned to Joy with a glint in her eye. 'And you've been invited to her soirée on Christmas Eve, Joy, how fabulous. You simply must go and then report back to tell us all about the Royal Emerald Suite. It's the finest accommodation in the fleet and I'd love to know.' She paused, then added with honeyed sweetness, 'Wouldn't you love to know too, Barbara?'

Barbara's face stiffened. She had been out-suite-ed and out-soirée-ed. The Dream Suite that she shared with Kenneth, despite its opulence, paled when compared to Lady Eleanor's accommodation and Barbara would flog her last diamond for an invite to the soirée.

Kenneth, sensing his wife's distress, reached for her glass. 'Top up, old girl?' he asked.

* * *

Henry picked up the conversation and was soon engrossed in a cheerful account of his walking tour of Sortland and describing the merits of the town.

As Henry spoke, Leticia studied Joy.

The woman was like a butterfly, slowly emerging from its chrysalis. Gone were the anxious glances, and Joy seemed lighter now. With no more panic attacks to speak of, it was clear that the cruise was suiting her. Her face glowed as she listened to Henry, laughing gently when he described their snowball fight.

A colourful silk scarf lay on Joy's shoulders, which brightened her modest navy dress. With delicately applied makeup, Leticia thought that Joy looked elegant and poised, and it was clear that she'd enjoyed her time with Henry that day. As she watched their easy rapport, Leticia wondered, yet again, where things were going. Stranger things happened at their time of life, especially at sea, where the confines of a ship often made for the most unexpected connections.

But there was something that puzzled Leticia. Margaret's offhand comment that Joy had 'outshone' them all lingered. Beneath the sensible clothes and modest appearance, was there more to Joy than she let on? Leticia's eyes narrowed and she wondered if more was to come.

After all, the sea had a habit of revealing things, and while they were on the cruise, if it did, Leticia hoped that she'd be there to watch it all unfold.

* * *

After dinner, guests gathered in the Triton Lounge, where the *Emerald Dream* string quartet entertained the audience with their fusion of classical and contemporary tunes. Stepping onto the stage, the musicians began their performance with a graceful medley, and familiar songs from beloved musicals such as *West Side Story*, *South Pacific*, and *The Sound of Music* floated through the auditorium. A gentle hum rippled as guests, filled with nostalgia, quietly sang along.

Barbara sat beside her husband in the centre of the front row. Kenneth had dozed off, his chin resting on his chest and hair flopping over his face. Although she hoped that no one had noticed, Barbara couldn't entirely blame him. Kenneth was exhausted from playing the part of a rugged adventurer all day and then overindulging at dinner. Glancing sideways, Barbara hoped that his gentle snores wouldn't swell and compete with the musicians, but everyone was away with *The Sound of Music* and even Julie Andrews might have forgiven Kenneth for not joining in with 'Edelweiss'.

When there was a break in the music, Barbara thought about Joy, her dismay growing and bubbling away like an itch she couldn't scratch. It had been her intention from the beginning of the cruise to befriend Lady Eleanor. The woman had a title and enough pedigree to elevate Barbara's standing at the Ladies Circle and golf club back home, and Barbara had already rehearsed the stories she would share. From drinks in Lady Eleanor's suite and chumminess over canapés and, hopefully, a photo or two casually displayed on her phone and shown to girlfriends while waiting to tee off: *'My best friend Lady Eleanor and I . . .'*

But Joy had upstaged her, and Barbara could barely hide her frustration. Not only had Joy received an invitation to the captain's table but now she was on Lady Eleanor's guest list! How had Barbara been so overlooked? She'd sent two invitations, via guest services, to Lady Eleanor, asking her to join them for cocktails in their suite, but there had been no reply. Not even a polite decline.

Barbara seethed beneath her diamonds as the music started up again.

As they approached the end of their show, the trio explained that they would play a piece entitled 'The Prodigal Son'. The haunting melody from the Philippines began with a single mournful note and as the lament played, Barbara suddenly felt a stab of sadness.

The cruise was not going as she'd planned.

Used to being Lady Bountiful in her own environment, Barbara couldn't help but feel that she was constantly being outshone. Despite her diamonds and show of wealth, she was being eclipsed by personalities onboard who had no right to outshine her. Take Joy, for example, Barbara thought as the trio continued their sad lament. The woman, a mere schoolteacher, was somehow beginning to take centre stage. People seemed genuinely charmed by her, and it was infuriating. Barbara wondered if the grieving widow was a deliberate act, a ruse to wriggle her way to the captain's table and befriend Lady Eleanor for some ulterior motive – perhaps Joy fancied her chances with the eligible captain?

And what was all the intrigue mentioned by Margaret's offhand remark about Joy having 'outshone' them all? The phrase had lodged in Barbara's mind like a splinter. Something didn't sit right, she thought as she raised her hands to applaud the trio, ensuring that her diamonds caught the light.

As the entertainment finished with a rousing tune and everyone clapped along, Barbara caressed her necklace. Something had to be done. If Joy, the so-called grieving widow, was playing a game, Barbara would not be relegated to the wings. She intended to join in, and one thing was for sure. Barbara would win.

Kenneth suddenly jolted awake and appeared bemused, blinking furiously. 'What . . . where . . .' he mumbled, his voice thick with confusion as he violently shook his head and looked around.

Barbara shot out a hand to steady him, fearing that his toupee might at any moment land at the trio's feet. 'It's all right, Kenny dear,' she cooed, 'you were having a little nap. Nothing to worry about, I'm here.' She subtly nudged his hairpiece back into place, and Kenneth gave a grunt of approval as he slowly came back into the room.

Barbara made a mental note to limit his wine consumption at dinner tomorrow. A couple of glasses of red and certainly no brandy. She needed her husband compos mentis if she was to regain her status on this ship. It was bad enough being upstaged by a schoolteacher, and now she had Kenneth snoring through the entertainment with his wretched hairpiece threatening a solo act.

No! Barbara vowed as she rose and took Kenneth's arm to help him to his feet. From tomorrow, they would both be on form and, more importantly, sober. Barbara had a sabotage to plan. She tugged on the straps of her sequined top, ensuring plenty of cleavage, and lifted her chin proudly as they made their way from the lounge.

The game, Barbara decided, was on.

Chapter Eighteen

*Gliding gently through winter's fjords, the ship whispers
secrets to the silent snowy world.*

The *Emerald Dream* glided gracefully into the fjords south
of Tromsø, the next port of call, which would be reached
by late afternoon. Captain Lindholm took to the PA and
assured passengers of a smooth voyage ahead, adding that
there would be a pause mid-fjord at midday, to allow everyone to soak in the beauty of the Norwegian winter landscape
reflected in the mystical blue twilight at that time of day.

On the promenade deck, the Deck Mile Club were out
for their morning routine. Jack and Judy now took charge
together, the pair guiding the group confidently past early
risers who stood by the rails to let them pass. It was clear
to all that a closeness had begun between the two that went
beyond the daily exercise.

'Best foot forward!' Judy instructed, pausing to gather
any stragglers at the back who'd taken the liberty of
pausing during the walk to catch their breath. 'Plenty of
time for dilly-dallying once your heart rate recovers. Let's

move!' She clapped twice, then spun on her heel to power off again with Jack, leaving no room for resistance.

Henry was in his cabin when the Deck Mile Club appeared outside. Opening the sliding door, he heard Judy issuing instructions. With a full day ahead on the ship, he knew she would also be asserting her authority at the book club, and, if they'd scheduled another meeting, God help the Women's Institute members too. Judy would oversee both, whether they liked it or not.

He waited for the group to pass, then taking in the icy air, Henry's breath formed soft clouds as he exhaled. The fjord was silent save for the low hum of the ship's engine, and time seemed to suspend itself, the stillness thrilling as he absorbed the grandeur of what he imagined beyond the darkness. Henry felt like a mere speck of humanity in the shadow of something ancient and vast. If the mountains could speak, what centuries of stories they would whisper to the historian over the water? Fascinating tales carved out of stone and not written down on parchment.

Henry remembered Audrey's tales of Norse folklore and fables of trolls lurking in the mountains. It was easy to see how such myths took root in such a mysterious landscape. Henry didn't believe in trolls, but in that moment, he felt a shiver of wonder and thought that anything was possible.

'Mr Henry!' Startled, Henry turned to see Jennifer at the doorway of his cabin. She held up her hand and waved. 'You get cold out there,' Jennifer called out, 'put coat on!' She reached into the wardrobe for his jacket and scarf.

Realising that Jennifer was about to tidy his cabin, Henry had no wish to get in her way. Nor did he intend to engage in conversation; their chats were starting to feel a little too familiar.

'Splendid,' Henry said and stepped forward to place his arms in the jacket sleeves as Jennifer tucked the scarf carefully around his neck.

'You take pictures?'

'Er, no . . .' Henry was hesitant. 'It's too dark, and I can't take any photographs for Audrey until there's some light at midday.'

Jennifer scowled. Before Henry had time to move, she swivelled around, whipped out a phone from her apron pocket and took a selfie of them both. 'You send Miss Audrey our picture,' she said, 'better than silly mountains.'

Jennifer held up her phone, and Henry realised that she wanted to exchange numbers. Flustered, he patted his pockets. 'I don't have my mobile . . . and I should let you get on.' Before she could respond, he turned on his heel and, with a vague wave, quickly moved off to hurry along the promenade deck.

'See you later, Mr Henry,' Jennifer called after him.

Henry thought he caught a trace of amusement in Jennifer's voice. Puzzled, he checked the buttons of his coat, adjusted his scarf, then ran his fingers through his windblown hair. 'All in order,' he muttered and opened the door to the forward deck where a number of passengers, including the Deck Mile Club, had begun a floodlit game of shuffleboard.

But the moment he stepped forward, Henry looked down, then froze and uttered a curse. 'Hellfire,' he hissed.

Henry was still wearing his slippers.

* * *

170

Joy sat in her cabin, her head tilted slightly as she studied her painting from Lucinda's art class. *It's quite good!* She felt a quiet satisfaction. There was something gratifying about this small creation that she would take home as a keepsake, a reminder that this cruise had given her something of herself. Tracing a finger over the hardened surface of the acrylic paint, she realised that Lucinda had been clever to suggest violets and greys to shadow the mountains, colours that captured not just the mood, but a sense of serenity woven into the landscape scene. Joy looked forward to finding a place to display the painting at home, knowing that it would stay there for as long as she wished.

She set the painting carefully to one side and then picked up the *Daily Times*. The schedule was packed with activities for the day, but it was the evening excursion which she'd pre-booked that caught her eye.

A cruise highlight, it was hellishly expensive, but the cost would hopefully be worth it. An Evening with the Sámis promised a warm welcome from a local reindeer-herding family, and Joy couldn't wait to soak up the culture and meet their stock of over one hundred and fifty reindeer. But first, a whole day at sea stretched ahead.

After six days on the ship, Joy was beginning to feel the tight knot of tension she carried start to loosen. Thank goodness she hadn't had a reoccurrence of her panic attack. The ship had become a sanctuary where she felt her burdens ease. She'd been helped by a newly formed friendship with Leticia and was beginning to hope that they might stay in touch after the cruise had ended. Henry, too, was proving to be great company, and perhaps, Joy admitted to herself, something more than that. She was surprised to realise that she found him attractive, not in a dashing, movie-star sort of way, but something more enduring. There was kindness in his manner, the way he was interested in what she had to say, and Henry had a definite twinkle in his eye. Joy couldn't remember when she felt this sort of pull. She must have done with Tom, but that was decades ago, a faded memory from pages of another life.

But then there was Audrey. Henry's friend and the woman he spoke so fondly of with a tenderness that needed no explanation. Joy was sure that Audrey would be counting the days until Henry returned. Besides, it wasn't as if Henry had shown the slightest interest in Joy.

Not in that way.

Joy sighed and thought of Susan and yet more calls. She'd reluctantly given in to the Wi-Fi package, if only to ease Susan's fears that Joy hadn't jumped overboard. Now, with the connection open, Susan had access to her mother and made sure to check in relentlessly. Not that Joy always picked up. Susan had been her daddy's girl, and their closeness often made Joy feel like an outsider. But she was grateful for her daughter's concern. It reminded her that she wouldn't be entirely alone when she returned, and the calls and occasional visits would continue, keeping their fragile family bond alive.

There was a loud knock, and Joy turned. 'Coming!' she called out.

A representative from guest services stood in the doorway and handed Joy an envelope. 'A message for you, Mrs Bradley,' they said.

Puzzled, Joy went to her bed and sat down to read it. She stared at the envelope, letting her fingertips drift over the writing, lingering on the letters. Sliding her finger under the flap, she pulled out a sheet of duck-egg blue paper, its edges trimmed in soft gold. A crest of a rearing stag encircled by the wording: Dunmore Hall, County Kildare. As Joy studied the elegant looping script, she realised that it was an invitation from Lady Eleanor.

'Good heavens,' Joy exclaimed, 'I've had more invitations in two days than I've received in a year.'

Lady Eleanor wrote that it had been a pleasure to meet Joy at the captain's table and that she would very much like the chance to become better acquainted. Would Joy consider joining her for a small Christmas Eve soirée in the Royal Emerald Suite? A plus-one was most welcome.

So, it was official. Margaret had been right. Lady Eleanor genuinely wanted Joy's company. A smile crept across Joy's lips, but moments later, panic set in. What on earth was she going to wear? She couldn't possibly ask Leticia to lend a gown again. Nothing she owned felt remotely worthy of such an event. But then, Joy remembered that there was an exclusive boutique onboard where one could book a consultation with a personal stylist. Joy couldn't imagine the cost of such an experience, but with a whole day at sea, wouldn't it be fun to make an appointment and see if there might be anything remotely suitable for a schoolteacher from Lancaster to wear?

Before she could change her mind, Joy picked up the phone on her desk.

'Hello?' she said nervously. 'I'd like to be connected to the boutique . . .'

* * *

Barbara was in her element. It was the Ocean Cocktail Party day – an exclusive affair for guests who were members of the *Emerald Dream* Platinum Club. The cruise line made a point of entertaining its highest spenders, ensuring that their loyalty remained as sparkling as the champagne served at the mid-morning event. Barbara stepped onto the red carpet of the Observatory Bar and swept in, gliding ahead with effortless poise, barely glancing back as Kenneth trailed in her slipstream, dutifully bringing up the rear.

Greeting familiar faces from previous cruises, Barbara air kissed and cooed civilities.

Earlier that morning, she'd treated herself to a coral-coloured, knee-length cocktail dress from the ship's exclusive boutique. The dress was tight on her tummy and thighs, and she'd had to squeeze into a pair of Spandex support shorts to enable the zip to fasten. Decorated at the neck with tiny jewels, the dress had cost a bomb, but Barbara didn't care. This was her stage, and she intended to shine.

Kenneth had bravely remarked that there had been no need to break the bank, especially as she already had a whole closet of perfectly suitable outfits. With his usual lack of tact, he'd added that the dress was too tight, and given her short stature, she looked like a space hopper and ought to ask for a refund. He was rewarded with a sharp elbow to the ribs.

Looking dapper in his official uniform, Simon joined the party and announced that Captain Lindholm had been delayed but still hoped to join them. Barbara's smile faltered. But she recovered quickly, expressing her disappointment with a gracious, 'Oh, that's a shame. Kenny and I were so looking forward to catching up with the captain, weren't we, Kenny?'

Kenneth, midway through his second glass of champagne, gave a startled grunt when his wife's elbow nudged sharply into his side. 'Such a shame,' he mumbled, and promptly drained his glass.

But Barbara sensed an opportunity and reached out to lightly stroke Simon's arm. 'We haven't received our invitation to the captain's table yet,' she said with a practised smile. 'I know it's just an oversight and there will be places at the next captain's table. I'm sure a resourceful fellow like you can rectify this mistake.'

Simon was saved by the timely arrival of Leticia and Jim. 'Ah,' he greeted them, 'Mr and Mrs Scott, welcome!'

Jim was having a difficult day and was confined to his chair, carefully manoeuvring it with his handheld control. Despite his discomfort, he smiled at Simon and held out his hand. 'Thank you for all your assistance, Simon. Everything you do for us is sincerely appreciated.'

Simon's chest puffed out, and he shook Jim's hand. The Scotts were a wonderful couple, and he wanted to ensure their cruise was the best that it could be. 'It's my pleasure,' Simon beamed, 'and everything is arranged for this evening's excursion for your visit to the Sámi reindeer-herding family.' Knowing that Jim would be unable to manage the uphill walk in thick snow, Simon had organised a complimentary snowmobile.

'What a coincidence!' Barbara trilled. 'Kenny and I are on the same excursion. We'll all have to stick together when we meet the reindeer.'

Leticia and Jim offered polite smiles.

Barbara, sensing an opportunity to undermine Joy and begin her sabotage plan, slipped her hand lightly through Leticia's arm and leaned in with a conspiratorial whisper. 'I wanted to ask what you thought about our grieving widow?' she murmured, eyes narrowing. 'I heard her husband left her with nothing, and I can't imagine what she's done to afford a cruise like this . . .' Her voice dropped to a spiteful undertone. 'I think she's playing us all, and we need to keep an eye on her. Do you suppose she's making a play for the captain?'

Leticia stared at Barbara. She was lost for words and momentarily speechless, but before she could find a suitable reply, Barbara pressed on.

'All this nonsense about having an invitation to Lady Eleanor's soirée – if only Lady Eleanor knew the truth about Joy!' Her voice dripped with faux concern.

Before Leticia could ask what exactly Barbara was implying, Simon announced, 'If everyone would care to step into the Observatory Viewing Room, Bill Zhang, our very own astrophotography expert, is ready to meet you all with signed copies of his book, and to give an exclusive insight into the stars and possible sightings of the Northern Lights tonight.'

Barbara saw that Leticia hesitated, though was unaware that Leticia was toying with a response to put Barbara in her place. But Jim had reached out to take his wife's hand, clearly excited to meet Bill Zhang.

Barbara sighed. The galaxy could wait and who needed a copy of the most boring book one could place on their coffee table? She would hang back and catch the captain.

The corner of her mouth curled into a smug smile as Barbara watched Leticia and Jim move away. It was working. A few carefully chosen words, albeit fictitious, a hint of fabricated gossip and Barbara's concerns were voiced, and soon, whispers about Joy would begin and take on a life of their own. Barbara was planting the seeds that would take root and spread, and the schoolteacher would be put firmly in her place. Smirking, Barbara leaned over to reach for a glass of champagne.

A small celebration, for now.

But as she stretched out, Barbara felt the seam on her dress slowly give way, releasing the overstretched fabric. Barbara froze. Her Spandex support shorts burst out of the seam as the dress lost the battle. With as much dignity as she could muster and grateful that the room had emptied, she looked anxiously around for her husband.

But Kenneth, keen to go stargazing, had followed the other guests.

With a flaming red face, Barbara searched around. She snatched a napkin from the table, but it barely covered the bulge of flesh escaping from her dress. *Damn!* Not only had she had a wardrobe malfunction, but now she would miss the captain. Gritting her teeth, Barbara was tempted to lash out and kick a chair, but as her eyes scanned the room, she saw a newly opened bottle of champagne and grabbed it.

With no alternative and needing to deal with the disaster, Barbara let out a groan of frustration and hurried back to her suite.

Chapter Nineteen

Our destiny isn't written in the stars, but dances
like the aurora in the light we hold within.

When Henry returned to his cabin after an enthusiastic game of shuffleboard in his slippers, he saw that Jennifer had created a dog, shaped out of hand towels. The little animal sat upright on Henry's bed, bearing a chocolate in each paw. Admiring Jennifer's creativity but grateful that she wasn't lingering by his door, he sat down to remove his sodden slippers and rub life back into his frozen feet.

There was a full programme of activities today, and he was keen to head to the Triton Lounge to listen to the guest speaker, Aren Nydegaard Øvreid, who was hosting an engaging talk on how Norwegian farmers thrive in today's world. Henry felt sure that Audrey would be interested to hear all about Aren's talk, and he intended to take notes.

Remembering that he was going on an excursion when the ship arrived in Tromsø, Henry dug out his cold weather clothes. Moving the towelling dog to one side, he laid the thermal items on the bed.

'All set for tonight, Fido.' He nodded, unwrapped a chocolate, and popped it in his mouth.

With a last look at his cabin and checking that he was wearing the correct footwear this time, Henry tucked his cabin card into his pocket and headed out of his room.

* * *

Joy slowly stepped out of the changing room in the ship's exclusive boutique and stood before a full-length mirror. Wearing her fourth change of clothing, she stared at the dress she was wearing and decided that the assistant who'd chosen it was right. The dress, a soft coral colour, flattered her chestnut hair, and the tiny jewels at the neck caught the light when she moved like ripples on water.

Initially, Joy had stood stiffly during her consultation, arms tucked against her chest, as the personal shopper asked about the event. The woman moved with ease, selecting gowns in soft fabrics that felt luxurious against Joy's skin. Resistant to colour, Joy had gravitated to the safety of darker shades, but when the coral dress was suggested, she'd hesitated, then, with gentle encouragement, given in.

'We only had two of these dresses in stock, and fortunately, you are slim enough to wear this one and show it off perfectly,' the assistant said as she fastened the zip, gliding it smoothly over Joy's hips.

Now, she could barely recognise her reflection. The dress skimmed Joy's tummy and flowed gracefully to her knees, catching the light in a way that enhanced her skin tone.

Her arms, usually hidden, were flatteringly exposed under transparent sleeves to the elbow.

'We have shoes that will match,' the assistant said and held out a pair of satin courts, 'and a clutch bag too.'

As Joy signed the bill that would be charged to her account, she hardly noticed the amount. She knew that she'd never spent so much on an outfit and, for a moment, wondered what Tom would say.

'I'll have the items delivered to your cabin,' the assistant smiled, 'and I hope that you enjoy your Christmas party, Mrs Bradley. I can assure you that you will be the belle of the ball.'

* * *

A little while later, Joy sat in the Ocean Bar. After joining in with a rousing rendition of 'Jerusalem', she settled into her seat for the afternoon meeting of the Women's Institute ladies. Judy took charge, declaring that the topic to be discussed was entitled Navigating Life's Journeys at Sea and Ashore.

Judy suggested that cruising was a metaphorical voyage, mirroring the journey women undertake throughout life. Joy thought that the meeting was interesting, with ladies sharing stories of reinvention in later years, and steered by Judy, reflections on their personal growth.

A member of Latham & District WI explained that she'd taken up pole dancing at sixty, which had significantly enhanced her personal growth, improving her confidence and core strength. Her husband especially enjoyed her routine with a feather boa, she added.

Members were impressed, until she admitted that the pole, an adapted rotary clothesline, had collapsed and she'd broken her hip. Those still knitting paused, needles poised and heads bobbing sympathetically.

'How admirable that you came out of your comfort zone, despite your later years,' Judy said and led a round of applause. But despite Judy's well-meaning sentiment, the door to transformation hadn't swung open for everyone, and Joy noticed that a significant portion of Judy's audience had nodded off to sleep.

'Too much suet pudding at lunch,' murmured a woman beside Joy, barely pausing in her knitting as she shaped the crown of a bobble hat. 'Always a mistake to hold these meetings mid-afternoon,' she added, tilting her head to the silver-haired sisters in matching cardigans, who were snoring softly.

Joy felt her mobile vibrate in her pocket. Glancing at the screen, she saw it was Susan calling. Unwilling to answer during the meeting, she slipped the phone into her bag. Susan was probably keen to know if Joy intended going on the excursion that evening. She'd mentioned to her daughter how much she was looking forward to visiting the Sámi camp and feeding the reindeer.

'Be very careful, Mother,' Susan had warned. 'Reindeer have sharp horns, and if you upset them, you could easily fall and break something. At your age, it could be fatal. I think you should stay put on the ship.'

Joy wondered how many angry reindeer Susan came across in leafy Ladbroke Grove and had no intention of following her orders. As the meeting continued, she closed her eyes and imagined the gorgeous animals that she would engage with. The soft fur, their gentle breath. She thought of the fascinating talk that the Sámi family would share and the warm glow of the campfire. In that moment, feeling content and relaxed, Joy sank into the shared stillness with her WI sisters and, closing her eyes, took advantage of a power nap too.

* * *

When Kenneth returned to his suite, the first thing he noticed was the dress that Barbara had been wearing flung to one side on a sofa. It lay beside a suspicious item that was big and beige and crumpled. Stepping carefully, he placed his signed copy of Bill Zhang's book on the coffee table and looked around.

Where's Babs? His wife had deserted him at the Ocean Cocktail Party, and she'd missed all the fun. Bill had conducted a fascinating lecture on wavelengths and solar winds. However, Kenneth noticed that several ladies, uninterested in atmospheric science and the shimmering lights, had returned to the bar.

'Babs, darling? Where are you?' he called out.

As he peered around the bedroom door, Kenneth tripped over Barbara's shoes, almost knotting his feet in her discarded tights.

'In. The. Bath,' Barbara retorted.

Attuned to his wife's moods and fearing that all wasn't well, Kenneth followed the scent of Jo Malone's Pear & Freesia bubble bath.

'Everything all right, my dearest?' Kenneth tentatively asked as he stepped into the bathroom.

182

'No. It. Bloody. Well. Isn't!' Barbara snapped.

She sat in the steaming bath, her skin flushed a deep, angry red, and Kenneth thought she resembled a lobster, slowly boiling alive. He noticed a glass upended on the mat alongside an empty champagne bottle.

'I'll leave you to enjoy your soak . . .' Kenneth attempted to retreat.

'KENNY!' Barbara yelled. 'You HAVE to get an invitation to the captain's table and Lady Eleanor's soirée!'

Kenneth raised his hands in a placating gesture and twiddled his bow tie, searching desperately for a diversion. 'I'm sure all that will soon fall into place, Babs, but don't forget the event tonight. You're going to love the Sámi excursion; just think, you can dress up in all your expensive furs, and we might even get to see the aurora borealis!' Kenneth drew breath. 'There's no need for fancy parties,' he added.

With her eyes closed, Barbara sank back into the steaming water and contemplated going under. Drowning could be a welcome release from her dull-witted husband. Would he ever truly grasp what she longed for from life? Status and social standing were everything, and during this cruise, Barbara intended to claim her rightful place, not have some wretched schoolteacher stealing the limelight from under her kitten-heeled feet.

'You relax and enjoy your bath, my darling,' Kenneth soothed, stepping away. 'I'll warm your fluffy robe and slippers, and you can have a little nap before we set off with the Sámis.'

With a deep sigh, Barbara gripped the side of the bath. Kenneth would never understand. Puffing out her

183

cheeks and closing her eyes, she dipped her head and disappeared under the water.

* * *

Simon lingered after the Ocean Cocktail Party ended. He thanked Bill Zhang for his fascinating talk and tucked a copy of the guest speaker's book under his arm. It was good to have a souvenir from each cruise, and Simon's apartment at home was full of interesting artefacts and objects. He reached into his pocket and touched the smooth amulet of kohl that he'd picked up from a bustling market bazaar in Egypt. Shaped like a heart and engraved with strange symbols, the stallholder had assured Simon that carrying or gifting kohl attracts passion and deepens emotional connection in one's search for their soulmate.

To date, the amulet hadn't worked, but Simon remained hopeful.

The captain arrived late and hadn't lingered at the party. He wasn't keen on social events, despite them being a part of his job description. Simon was relieved that the dreadful Barbara Montgomery Jones had left by the time the captain arrived, and he hadn't been forced to make an introduction. There was always a difficult guest on each cruise, and Mrs M ticked all the boxes.

Simon was looking forward to the evening. With many of the guests treating themselves to An Evening with the Sámis, he'd decided that he would take advantage of his complimentary pass and join the group. Simon loved reindeer and had visited Lapland countless times. Despite having experienced similar excursions before, Simon looked forward to meeting with Matti, the head of the Sámi family, who was always entertaining and welcoming to *Emerald Dream* crew members.

But Simon's real reason for joining the tour was personal.

On special occasions, senior crew members had their names drawn out of a hat. As a treat, the successful participant was allowed to go on an excursion. Knowing that it was Kyle's birthday that day and the treat was An Evening with the Sámis, Simon had manipulated the draw and announced that birthday boy Kyle was the winner.

As he made his way through the ship and back to his office, Simon visualised Kyle all dressed up for the evening. Wrapped in a soft, fur-lined coat to keep his athletic body warm against the cold, Kyle would drape a soft woollen scarf around his neck. The image of his easy smile and cute boyish grin flashed in Simon's mind and as he thought of Kyle's undeniably handsome face, his heart skipped a beat.

For Simon, Kyle was the perfect partner to keep a man warm on a cold Arctic night. But as he opened his office door and stared at a daunting stack of paperwork, he knew that deep down, Kyle would never see him romantically in the way that he wished. No matter how often Simon rubbed his amulet in Kyle's presence, hoping for a spark to ignite, it was clear that Kyle didn't feel the same quiet longing when they met, nor did his heart lurch at the slightest touch. He was kind, friendly, and good at his job, and surely had someone waiting for him back home.

Kyle was a beautiful fantasy. An unreachable dream. And sometimes, despite the saying, Simon believed that dreams rarely came true.

Chapter Twenty

Reindeer move like whispers across the snow.
Graceful and silent, they are living threads
in the tapestry of Arctic magic.

The guests who left the Triton Lounge with instructions on how to join the departing coaches for An Evening with the Sámis were in a jovial mood. After a relaxing day at sea, they stepped ashore ready to embrace the evening as everyone found the correct transport, and the party set off. As Joy boarded, she noticed that Barbara and Kenneth were seated at the front, having bagged the best seats on the coach again. Barbara, bundled in fur and avoiding eye contact, stared pointedly out of the window.

Making her way, Joy heard someone shout her name and turned to see Henry wedged behind two boarding couples, his head leaned to one side to catch her attention. As he stepped onto the coach, he called, 'Save me a seat!'

Joy felt a tiny ripple of pleasure that he'd singled her out. Halfway down the aisle, she spotted an empty seat and, removing her coat, she placed it on the rack above and then sat down by the window.

As Henry caught up with Joy, he looked relieved. 'I hope you don't mind?'

Joy was more than happy that Henry had joined her. The nerves she'd felt about visiting the Sámi camp alone vanished almost instantly. 'I'm delighted,' she replied.

The coach departed, and the guide explained that the journey was approximately forty minutes long, taking them from Tromsø to travel through the countryside until they reached their destination. Outside, the sky was black, and there was little to see as the city lights faded, giving way to the shadowy silhouettes of trees and snow-covered hills gliding by in the darkness. Henry asked how Joy had spent her day and listened with interest as she explained her astonishment at receiving Lady Eleanor's invitation, her worry over what to wear, and then her description of finding a new dress in the ship's boutique.

'I think you're very wise. One needs to feel comfortable at such an event, and if the gown does the trick, then it's a sound investment.'

Henry understood her dilemma and Joy felt pleased by his response. It was, she suspected, precisely the kind of support Tom would never have offered. He would have told her to wear the navy outfit. It was a practical, reliable dress and, therefore, should be worn. But then again, would the invitation have been extended if Tom had been with her?

Joy set aside thoughts of Tom and turned to Henry, who was telling her about his day. He described his 'slipper' incident, alluding to Jennifer, the lady who tidied his cabin, and Joy wasn't sure if he was amused or mildly traumatised. Henry then went on to explain that he'd sat through a stupefying lecture on how Norwegian farmers might thrive today. A talk, he explained, that was so dry it could have been harvested for hay.

'That bad?' Joy asked.

'Worse,' Henry admitted. 'The speaker, Aren, came onto the stage in a traditional embroidered costume consisting of a jacket, vest, and breeches, and I sat back, hoping for something that included the history of farming over the centuries to the present day.' He folded his arms and smiled. 'But instead, the talk was more *Farmer Wants a Wife*, followed by how the government should supply free Wi-Fi and provide a generous subsidy.'

'In that order?' Joy smiled.

'Actually, I think the wife came last.'

Joy giggled. 'Did the talk improve?'

'Hardly,' Henry replied with a wry smile. 'After seventy-eight slides, each more mind-numbing than the last, I started to realise that I was the only one still awake in the room.'

Joy nodded sympathetically. 'I'm sorry it was so dull. It was probably on a par with the Women's Institute gathering, where, I hate to admit, I too nodded off to sleep.'

Comfortable in the other's company, the journey flew by, and the coach soon rumbled onto a winding uphill road to a snow-covered stop. As the doors swung open, an icy chill swept in, and everyone reached for their outerwear.

Waiting to greet them was Matti, their Sámi host.

Dressed in a traditional gákti, the rich reds and blues of his jacket and trousers were embroidered with detailed

188

patterns that spoke of his heritage and tribe. Beneath his fur-lined cap, his rugged face was smiling.

'Velkommen!' Matti called out in his rich melodic voice, 'Welcome to our home.'

* * *

On a smaller coach, Simon sat opposite Leticia and Jim, and to his delight, Kyle boarded and chose the seat next to him. As he made himself comfortable, Kyle placed a plastic box on the table that separated them from Leticia and Jim and proceeded to produce paper napkins.

'One of my friends in the kitchen made these for my birthday,' he said and removed the lid. 'They're called Fiskekaker bites, mini fishcakes, and they're delicious. Do try one.'

Simon reached in and had to agree that the tiny salmon nibbles were tasty, with a crisp outside and a hint of spiced dill. He wondered if Kyle had a *special* friend in the kitchen and if they'd supplied the contraband as, officially, chefs weren't allowed to hand out food. But as he bit into the mouth-watering morsel, he decided that some rules could be overlooked.

'Happy birthday, Kyle.' Leticia smiled. 'We'll toast your special day with a Fiskekaker.'

'Many happy returns,' Jim joined in. 'I hope you've been celebrating.'

Kyle explained that he'd been busy all day with fitness classes and a personal training session for a couple who were keen to stay fit despite their later years. 'Nora and Sid are solo travellers but they've got together on the cruise.'

'How lovely for them,' Leticia said.

'Yes, it's great when we see guests chumming up during their holiday,' Kyle replied, his face lighting up. 'Lots of singletons find their way to each other. One minute they're watching a show in the Triton Lounge and the next they're inseparable.'

Leticia chuckled. 'Cruise Cupid strikes.'

'Exactly,' Kyle said, 'bracing air, fine food, lovely locations – it's a matchmaking service at sea!' He threw a glance at Simon.

Simon shuffled in his seat and, with a nervous cough, diverted the conversation. 'It was fortuitous that your name came out of the draw,' he said. 'The evening ahead will be memorable.'

'I'm thrilled to come on this trip.' Kyle grinned, his face lighting up. 'I have the best job in the world, travelling to so many different destinations, and now, here I am on a Christmas cruise in the Arctic with snow, mountains, fjords and, best of all, I'm about to meet a herd of reindeer.' Kyle's enthusiasm was infectious as he kept up a constant chatter. He offered Leticia and Jim a private meditation session, insisting that it would help them align their Arctic energy. 'You'll love it,' he said brightly, 'I can teach you how to breathe out any stress.'

'Leticia has plenty of energy for both of us, but I'm game for a session as long as I don't have to sit cross-legged,' Jim laughed.

Their coach, equipped for passengers with mobility issues, arrived at their destination, where a beaming Matti stepped forward. 'Velkommen!' he called out as the doors opened.

Simon and Leticia assisted Jim, who wore a fur-lined parka coat and matching bomber hat which he pulled low over his ears, and soon, the couple were seated comfortably in the waiting snowmobile. Matti informed them that the other guests were currently ascending the path to the camp.

'See you at the top,' Kyle smiled and waved as the snowmobile set off. He adjusted the hood of his coat, the fur trim framing his face, and as he wriggled his fingers into warm gloves, turned to Simon. 'Looks a bit steep. Shall we race?'

Simon wondered if Kyle was taking a hallucinatory drug and suddenly saw Simon as an athlete. He hadn't raced anywhere since coming last in the egg and spoon contest at junior school.

Zipping his coat over his bulging tummy and thrusting a hand into his pocket where his fingers sought out his Egyptian amulet, Simon wondered how to reply. 'I really don't think . . .' he began but paused when he saw that Kyle was laughing.

'Only joking,' Kyle said, 'but be careful on the ice. Why don't we go slowly, together.'

To Simon's surprise, Kyle tucked his arm into his own to steady them and gave him a reassuring squeeze. 'Let's enjoy the walk. There's no need to rush.'

Relieved and slightly surprised by Kyle's thoughtfulness, Simon nodded, and they began their ascent side-by-side, crunching through the thick snow, the crisp Arctic air filling Simon's overworked lungs.

'Do you think we'll see the Northern Lights?' Kyle asked. 'It would make my birthday *and* my Christmas,' he added.

Simon paused to catch his breath. 'Bill Zhang predicted too much cloud this evening, but you never know. It might lift and surprise us.'

'Is it true that if you wish on the aurora borealis, your wish will come true?' Kyle asked.

'Well, that's a lovely thought, but I think it's more legend than fact,' Simon replied as they set off again. 'I know that the Sámi people regard the aurora with respect and believe that it is connected to spirits in some way.'

'Well, if we see it, I shall take a chance and make a birthday wish.' Kyle's voice, though light, was sincere.

Simon felt the amulet nestling solidly in his gloved fingers. He glanced at his companion and saw something hopeful in his expression, earnest and almost childlike, as though he genuinely dreamed of the possibility of wishes coming true.

But Simon didn't. Dreams were for sleep and wishes for wells. Still, he smiled and, rubbing the amulet harder, said, 'Then I'll make one too, it can't hurt to try.'

As they trudged, the puffy clouds in the sky overhead suddenly began to thin, and a narrow streak of deepening blue, highlighted by a faint glow, slowly appeared.

Kyle stopped and, looking up at the sky, gripped Simon's arm. 'Is that . . . ?' he whispered.

'I think it is,' Simon murmured, his eyes wide with wonder as ribbons of green and violet suddenly danced between the disappearing clouds.

They stood in silence as the aurora began to unfurl.

Simon closed his eyes and made his wish. When he opened them again, Kyle nudged him gently. 'I hope that whatever you wish for, it will soon come true.'

Simon took a deep breath. He turned to stare into Kyle's blue eyes. 'Me too,' he whispered, 'me too.'

'You said that the evening would be memorable,' Kyle said softly.

But as Simon gripped his amulet and stared at the incredible lights in the night sky, neither man had any notion of just how memorable the evening would be.

* * *

In the reindeer camp at the top of the hill, excitement buzzed amongst the guests, as many had just witnessed their first glimpse of the Northern Lights. But, as Bill Zhang had predicted, the cloud cover thickened, and the ribbons of green and gold, which had been momentarily brilliant, faded, much to everyone's dismay. However, any disappointment soon vanished when Matti stepped forward and clapped his hands.

'Are you ready to meet the true stars of the Arctic?' he asked.

Heads turned to the clanging sound of gates swinging open, and to everyone's delight, a herd of reindeer trotted into the clearing.

'Take a bucket and fill it with pellets, but be sure to hold it in outstretched arms,' he warned as the soft-eyed creatures surrounded the guests and, knowing that food was imminent, began to nuzzle and bump into bodies.

'I say!' Kenneth shouted as his bucket was upended by a boisterous young reindeer. He was suddenly surrounded by the hungry creatures who piled in to scoop up the pellets scattered on the ground. 'Babs! Help!' Kenneth called out as he was butted in his bottom while another sniffed his pockets with a snort of warm breath.

Losing his footing, Kenneth stumbled to the ground, where a reindeer bit into Kenneth's trapper hat and shook it like a terrier with a chew. Unfortunately for Kenneth, the reindeer's grip snatched the toupee with the hat, and Kenneth yelped as it landed unceremoniously on the snow.

'Babs, *please* help!' he cried out, with one hand covering his bald head while he frantically searched for his wife as the reindeer, losing interest, pranced off to find another food-filled bucket.

'Man up, Kenny!' Barbara retorted as she reached down to retrieve the offending objects and return them to her husband. Then, stroking a Bambi-like reindeer, Barbara was thoughtful as she said, 'They're rather cute,' and ran her gloved fingers over the soft fur, wondering if a coat made of reindeer might be stylish. But soon bored with fondling smelly reindeer, and regretting drinking too much before they'd set off, Barbara wandered away in search of a bathroom before her bladder burst.

Observing the incident and seated on the snowmobile, Jim laughed as he held out his bucket. Leticia stood alongside, stroking the bulky frame of the bull that was gobbling up Jim's pellets. 'His coat is almost white,' Leticia said as she admired the magnificent male.

Jim nodded. 'It's a brown-grey colour in summer and lighter in winter,' he said.

'But he's not got any antlers?' Leticia was curious as she ran her fingers over the knobbly lumps on the reindeer's head.

'Matti says that males lose their antlers in winter, when the mating season is over. Females shed their antlers after calving in spring.'

'So, are you telling me that Santa's Rudolph and his reindeers, who all have magnificent antlers, are possibly female?' Leticia laughed.

'I suppose they might be, which means that Santa's sleigh is probably pulled by a team of strong, determined women.'

'Well, that figures,' Leticia said, 'it takes a woman to navigate the globe overnight and deliver billions of Christmas gifts to children.'

* * *

With the reindeer herd contentedly fed, guests followed the glow of a line of lanterns that led to a Sámi lavvu. The large, tent-like structure was made from a covering of reindeer hides stitched together and stretched over a framework of wooden poles. In the centre of the lavvu, a fire burned, the smoke escaping from an opening in the top.

'It's lovely and warm in here,' Joy said as she removed her coat and sat down on an extended bench. 'Is this where a Sámi family live?'

Henry sat beside her, and as he stared into the flames, he rubbed his hands together. 'It is,' he replied, remembering the guidebook he'd studied. 'The fire isn't just for heat, but for cooking too, and the lavvu is portable. It's perfect for a nomadic Sámi tribe as it allows them to move with their herds across the tundra.'

Food was served, and Joy was cautious as she stared at the deep dish of stew placed before her. 'Is this what I think it is?' she asked Henry.

'Yes,' he nodded, 'try not to think about it because I have to say, it's absolutely delicious.' Henry spooned a piece of reindeer meat and tucked in.

But Joy was hesitant, and her spoon hovered mid-air. 'I don't know if I can,' she said, 'they were licking my mittens only moments ago.'

'This one wasn't.' Henry forked a chunk of potato with the reindeer meat.

Steeling herself, Joy took a tiny bite. 'Actually,' she said, her eyebrows lifting, 'that's quite tasty.'

Henry grinned. 'Served with a thick gravy, guilt tastes surprisingly good.'

The meal was topped off with apple cake and almond cream, and when plates were cleared away, Matti took to the centre of the lavvu and stood beside the fire. The guests became silent as he began to speak.

Matti told tales of his family, their seasonal migration, and their bond with the herd. Reindeers were everything to the Sámis, he explained, from providing food, clothing and tools, every part of the animal was used. The creatures were the Sámis' partner in survival.

Joy was fascinated to learn that the knee of Matti's traditional trousers was made of a reindeer knee, and the sections of his jacket were stitched pieces of reindeer hide. Henry nodded his respect as Matti told how his ancestors could 'smell' an approaching storm and track lost reindeer in white-out conditions.

Matti ended the evening by performing a traditional joik, sang a cappella: a haunting song that had been passed down through generations of Sámis. The guests were spellbound as they listened to his raw, deeply emotional voice. When he finished singing, there was a momentary silence as though the ghosts of Matti's ancestors were lingering in the shadows of the flickering flames of the fire.

Then, slowly, one by one, the guests began to clap, and as the applause rose, Joy felt tears in her eyes. She suddenly felt emotional, as though all the anguish of everything that had gone before had loosened its grip. The joik had unlocked something, and now, as guests left the lavvu, her tears fell softly.

When Henry's fingers curled into her own, she let them. When he dabbed at her eyes with his handkerchief, she smiled. As he helped her into her coat and tucked the scarf at her neck, she let him take her hand and lead her back to the coach. And when he settled her into her seat and placed his arm around her shoulders, she lay her head on his chest and closed her eyes.

As the coach began its journey back to the ship, snow started to fall in soft, silent flakes against the windowpane. Joy heard the hum of the engine and felt the steady beat of Henry's heart against her cheek, and for the first time in as long as she could remember, Joy didn't think about what she'd lost with Tom.

Instead, she was thinking about what she might have found with Henry.

Chapter Twenty-One

Where silent stars watch over silent seas, Christmas drifts in on an Arctic breeze . . .

Christmas Eve, and after a lie-in, Leticia had decided that they would enjoy a leisurely brunch in their suite. Anxious that Jim might have overdone things the day before, she wanted to start the day quietly, with no busy buffet restaurant, nor bustling dining room. Instead, she'd arranged for warm pastries, savoury sausages, and softly scrambled eggs, all delivered impeccably under silver domes and placed on a table by their balcony.

Pouring them both a glass of champagne, Leticia winked. 'For medicinal purposes,' she said, 'and a toast to the love of my life.' She placed a hand on Jim's shoulder and leaned in to rest her cheek against his. 'And as it's Christmas, I won't fight you for the last sausage.'

Leticia wore a onesie, festively patterned with snowflakes and Christmas trees, and as Jim's eyes followed her, she danced around the table, singing 'Santa Baby' off-key. Her braids billowed out as she moved.

'You're as bright as the Northern Lights.' Jim grinned and raised his glass to his cavorting wife. 'I know visiting Norway is part of our bucket list . . . but this trip is mostly about our precious time together.'

Leticia plopped down beside him. She'd thought he'd be tired from the late evening the night before, but the light in his eyes suggested otherwise. Jim's smile was one of happiness, and he radiated an energy she hadn't seen for a while.

'I enjoy every moment together, my darling, no matter where we are,' Leticia said, kissing Jim's cheek, then added, 'and I think the silent disco last night suited you.'

Arriving back on the ship after their evening with the reindeer, they'd headed to the silent disco. Wearing headphones tuned to music of their choice, they'd moved around the dance floor, long past midnight, with Jim guiding his wheelchair energetically through his rock and roll moves and Leticia twirling with abandon to Motown.

'I almost imagined that I was on my feet and dancing right beside you,' Jim said softly.

'Seated or standing, you have better rhythm than me.' Leticia laughed. 'Now don't move, I have something for you.' She went to the bedroom and reappeared with a parcel tied with red ribbon. 'Happy Christmas,' she whispered, kissing Jim again.

He carefully unwrapped a solid silver pen and a leather journal, on which his initials were inscribed in gold. On the first page, Leticia had written,

Commit all the beautiful memories we're making together, on these pages xx

199

'It's perfect,' Jim smiled. Reaching into his pocket, he produced a velvet-covered box.

Leticia gasped when she opened it, and Jim slipped a stunning ice diamond ring onto her finger. 'It looks like a frozen snowflake,' she whispered.

'To remind you of our Arctic cruise,' Jim said, 'now and always.'

Leticia stared at her husband, drinking in the love shining in his eyes, and her throat tightened.

Holding her hand, his voice was soft, 'Let the ring be your *always* . . . for the days when I no longer will be.'

Instinctively, Leticia wanted to tell Jim not to say such things, but honesty had always been their pact, both knowing that his days were numbered. She held his hand a little tighter and smiled bravely. Truth, even the hardest kind, wouldn't dim what they had.

'I'm never going to take it off,' she announced.

'You'll wear it even when you're gardening?'

'Especially then.' Leticia held her hand high to admire the glittering stone. 'Even when it's covered with muddy soil, I shall feel like the Queen of the Arctic.' She gave Jim a lingering kiss, then busied herself insisting that they tuck into their brunch.

As Leticia enjoyed the delicious food, her mind drifted back to the evening before. She remembered, as their coach was preparing to leave for the ship, seeing Joy and Henry walking arm in arm.

'Do you think Joy and Henry are getting together?' she asked, her eyes bright with curiosity.

'They seemed very cosy from where I was sitting,' Jim replied.

'I have a feeling there is more to Joy than she's letting on.'

Jim chuckled. 'Well, if anyone can prise out secrets, it's you.'

'I don't mean in a sinister way,' Leticia continued. 'I'll leave that to Barbara's malicious mind. That woman has a poisonous tongue. But there's something about Joy that I can't quite put my finger on, and my instinct tells me . . .' She paused, searching for the words, 'Whatever it might be, it's waiting for the right moment to reveal itself.'

'No doubt,' Jim concurred, 'but in the meantime we're here in Tromsø, and what have you got planned for the day?'

'Well, if you're up to it, we'll take the courtesy coach into town for a little Christmas shopping and a visit to the Arctic Cathedral.'

'Sounds perfect,' Jim agreed. He reached out with his fork, 'Now about that last sausage . . .'

* * *

At eleven-thirty on Christmas Eve morning, Barbara was in the Ice Bar in Tromsø, sitting on a polar bear's knee. At minus six degrees in the room, the ice-sculptured creature was as cold as Kenneth's eyes as he stared at his wife in disbelief. He should have known that stepping into this tourist trap so early was a massive mistake.

Taking a taxi to the centre of Tromsø, to avoid mingling with passengers on the ship's courtesy coach, Kenneth had intended to enjoy a wander around the marina, where the snow was thick and lights from the magnificent Arctic Cathedral could be seen twinkling against the polar night sky. But within moments of placing their walking boots on the heated pavement, Barbara had spotted Tromsø's famous Ice Bar.

'Oh, look!' she'd exclaimed. 'We must go and see the ice sculptures.'

Now, he was deeply regretting the diversion.

'Babs, darling,' Kenneth began, and flicked his wrist to check the time, 'you're on your fourth Frosty Cocktail, don't you think you should ease up?'

'Not at these prices . . .' Barbara slurred, clutching her ice cup, encased in its plastic cone. She swirled the ruby-red contents as though it might reveal answers. 'Daylight robbery,' she muttered. 'Seven hundred kroner for a couple of mugs of berry juice.'

'Sweetie, that berry-like liqueur is fifty per cent alcohol, which even for you, is a bit much before noon.'

'Oh, bogof, Kenny,' Barbara muttered.

'Yes, buy-one-get-one-free might be appealing, but after two rounds, I think you should call it a day.'

Barbara glared at Kenneth. She was contemplating calling it a day on her marriage, after his inability to secure their place at the captain's dinner table and Lady Eleanor's Christmas Eve soirée. The lack of an invite was ruining her cruise, and despite the Frosty Cocktails, Barbara's mood wasn't improving. Dressed in a long rubber cape with a vast hood, courtesy of the Ice Bar, which provided such items to protect patrons' clothing from frost, Barbara regretted donning the outfit to cover her precious furs and reckoned that if she carried a broomstick she would be mistaken for a witch.

Kenneth, having waved a cape aside, was frozen to the bone in his waterproof cagoule. He thought that his wife resembled the Grim Reaper and was tempted to tell her so, but noting her icy expression, he decided that he valued his life too much and smiled faintly, subconsciously willing Barbara not to drink any more.

Kenneth looked around and wondered which was the best route to ease his wife out of the bar. The frozen corridors, under blue LED lights, led to other themed rooms, and despite cheery Christmas lanterns, the maze-like rooms appeared more like prison cells and were daunting to navigate. Barbara began to sway on her polar bear perch and Kenneth extended his hand with exaggerated cheer. 'How about a spot of lunch?' he asked brightly.

'I want an invitation . . .' Barbara slammed her empty cone down, splintering the ice in the plastic cup.

'Yes, dear, all sorted, just as soon as we find our way out of here.'

Kenneth took her hand and yanked Barbara to her feet. As her body slumped, he slid her awkwardly away from her seat. Her hood flopped forward, covering Barbara's face and as they shuffled past a group of wide-eyed Americans, a Texan drawl boomed out, 'Hey, y'all! I swear, there *really are* trolls in Norway.'

Kenneth resisted the urge to punch the Texan on the nose. But, as his outstretched arm would barely reach the man's Stetson, he settled for a cold glare before steering Barbara away, her hood shielding further humiliation as they stumbled through the Frozen Crypt, which adjoined the Black Ice Tomb, then into the Icebound Catacombs to the exit.

Once outside and with Barbara's outerwear returned to reception, Kenneth breathed deeply with relief. He straightened his wife's fur coat and hat. 'Now, dear,' he said, and searched around for a taxi, 'a nice buffet-style meal with a variety of hearty dishes, is just what we need on a cold day like today.'

'What I need . . . is an invitation . . .' Barbara's eyes were glassy, but her theme remained the same.

'Not that old chestnut again.' Kenneth sighed as a taxi pulled up and he manipulated her into the warmth of the cosy cab.

'Hei,' the driver said, 'where to?'

Kenneth stared at Barbara and decided that a restaurant was too risky and gave instructions to the driver to head back to the ship. For the time being, Barbara would be best off in the safety of their suite. In the meantime, unless he wanted a war with his wife when she sobered up, Kenneth *had* to find a way to gatecrash Lady Eleanor's soirée.

But, unbeknown to Kenneth, his wife had already devised a plan . . .

* * *

Christmas Eve – the day of Joy's wedding anniversary, and the reason for her cruise. If Tom had lived to see this day, they would be together, stepping quietly through the heavy wooden doors of the Arctic Cathedral with the cold crisp air of Tromsø fading behind them.

Instead, as Joy entered, she stood alone. With her shoulders taut, a weight seemed to press down as she heard organ music that Tom loved, rich and resonant, swelling into every corner of the vast space. Joy was aware of the empty space beside her and the absence of an arm linking her own. The thought should have saddened her, but instead it left her curiously confused, tilting between sorrow and a guilty lightness.

Once inside, she strolled into the silence of the place of worship and stared at the architecture. Light and shadow interplayed across stark white walls, and when her fingers brushed lightly against a wooden pew, she decided to sit and contemplate the immensity of the building surrounding her. Soaring triangular panels of aluminium rose like shards of ice, and, as it always did when she thought of his death, the absence of Tom weighed heavily. Would he have enjoyed this experience on the day that celebrated four decades of marriage?

Coloured light from a glass mosaic cast soft blues and reds across the polished floor, and biting down on her lip, Joy refused to let thoughts of Tom cloud her day. After all, it was Christmas Eve, and tonight she was going to Lady Eleanor's soirée.

But then she thought of Henry.

What to do about Henry? He was the unexpected rock who'd silently comforted her when she was filled with emotion during Matti's song. Joy had held herself together through so much, for so long, and although she didn't understand the words, Matti's voice was so raw and full of aching beauty that something had unravelled within her.

As though he understood her silent pain, Henry hadn't said a word; he didn't press or question. But he'd helped her to the coach and, with his arm around her shoulders, was a comfort throughout the journey, an anchor in the dark. Once back on the ship, Joy suddenly felt exposed. She'd let her guard down and leaned into someone she barely knew. What must Henry think of her, so incapable of holding herself together and crumbling pathetically during a song? Avoiding his eyes, Joy had muttered a quick thanks and hurried away to her cabin, her thoughts churning.

Now, as she sat in the beautiful cathedral, Joy stared at her hands. It wasn't just the song or the emotion it had stirred; it was the way Henry had simply been there when she needed him. And that scared her more than anything, because Joy knew that the people who stayed were the ones who could hurt you most.

But why was she thinking of Henry? Audrey was back in Skipton, no doubt waiting by the phone for Henry's call. With Audrey in the wings, Joy had no right to let her thoughts further fantasise about friendship with a man she hardly knew.

She was about to stand and make her way out when a hand lightly touched her shoulder. It was Leticia. 'Room for a little one?' Leticia asked and indicated to Jim that she was going to have a chat with Joy. Jim nodded and pointed to the glass mosaic behind the altar, then propelled his chair forward, smoothly down the aisle.

'So, how are you?' Leticia asked and arranged herself on the pew. 'If I'm not mistaken, today would have been your fortieth wedding anniversary?'

With a flicker of discomfort, Joy turned towards her, surprised that Leticia had remembered.

'Would you like to talk about Tom?' Leticia's voice was soft, her eyes full of kindness.

For a moment, Joy hesitated. 'Actually, I'd rather not.' Joy clasped her hands and lowered her gaze.

'Is it still too painful?' Leticia asked.

'Yes,' Joy replied, almost in a whisper. 'At times.'

Leticia gave a slight nod and reached out to pat Joy's knee. 'Well, my dear, I'm a good listener, if you ever feel ready.'

Joy's mind flicked back to Leticia's words by the jacuzzi, days earlier. *I'd like you to tell me about your husband, when we get a moment to ourselves.*

Could Leticia sense something? Was she psychic, or just incredibly perceptive? Suddenly, Joy wanted to pour her heart out and felt the dam about to break. The fear, the guilt, the story she hadn't told anyone. But not here. Not in this sacred place.

Instead, Joy straightened her spine, smoothed her coat, and asked with a practised smile, 'Did you have a good evening?'

'Yes, the reindeer were magical, weren't they?' Leticia giggled. 'Especially when a reindeer butted Kenneth and he lost his comb-over companion.' Leticia shook her head. 'I know I shouldn't laugh, but it *was* very amusing.'

'I'm afraid I missed that.'

'Perhaps your thoughts were elsewhere?' Leticia raised an eyebrow. 'I saw you with Henry and watched how he looked at you. You both looked very cosy together.'

'Er . . . well, he is a very kind man,' Joy faltered.

'Is he becoming more than just a cruise buddy?'

'Oh, heavens, no . . . I couldn't possibly think of him in that way . . .' Joy stumbled over her words.

But Leticia wasn't fooled. 'Why not?' she asked. 'Wouldn't Tom want you to be happy?'

Joy stared straight ahead. Once again, she wondered how much she could share with Leticia. Would talking about Tom bring back memories? On today of all days, their wedding anniversary. But as Joy thought of Henry, she had an urge to confide. Feelings she hadn't thought possible were spinning in her head despite knowing that they'd never be reciprocated.

As though reading her mind, Leticia continued. 'I can tell that you like Henry, and he is clearly smitten with you.'

'I don't know what I feel,' Joy said quietly, and the words tasted like a lie.

Leticia waited and didn't press.

'It's not that simple,' Joy began. 'Henry has someone. You may have heard him mention Audrey.'

'*Audrey? Are you sure?*' Leticia was puzzled. 'Does he talk about Audrey the way he looks at you?'

Joy flinched. She tried not to think about the way Henry looked at her, but she knew it was more than just wanting to be her friend. His glances and how he'd held her. His hurt look last night, when she'd muttered her thanks and hurried away. 'Maybe he's just being kind,' Joy said.

'Or maybe you've both found something neither of you expected?'

'Oh, I don't know, I'm just being silly and I'm far too old to fall in love.'

Leticia reached out and took Joy's hand. 'My dear, you are never too old to fall in love.'

'But Audrey is waiting for him, back home . . .'

'And what's waiting *for you*, Joy?'

Joy couldn't answer. She thought of the dormer bungalow. The ghostly rooms, the garden she'd neglected.

'Don't talk yourself out of something just because it isn't in the script, Joy. Take each day as it comes, and if you enjoy your time with Henry, make the most of it.' Leticia squeezed her hand. 'You have an invite for a plus one tonight for the soirée in Lady Eleanor's suite. Why not ask Henry?'

'But . . . I couldn't,' Joy hesitated, 'I'm sure he wouldn't want to . . .'

'Stop it,' Leticia laughed. She took her phone from her pocket and tapped in a number.

'What are you doing?' Joy asked.

'I'm leaving a message with guest services.'

'But . . .'

'Hello,' Leticia began when her call was answered, 'I'm Mrs Joy Bradley in an Ocean View cabin, number 2617, and I'd like to leave a message for Mr Henry Halliday, who is staying in a Terrace Cabin on the promenade deck.'

Joy's eyes widened in alarm. 'No, please . . .'

But Leticia had a mischievous grin. 'Yes, that's right, please ask him if he'd like to accompany me to Lady Eleanor's party tonight and to meet me in the Ocean Bar at six-thirty.'

'You're outrageous,' Joy lowered her voice. She was conscious of being in a church, receiving several disapproving glances, as Leticia returned the phone to her bag.

'Well, it's done, so no more dithering. What are you going to wear?'

Joy sat back. It was no use. Leticia had forced the situation, and now, she must go along with the ride. 'I spent a couple of hours in the ship's boutique, and I have a new dress.'

Leticia punched the air. 'Hurrah!' she mouthed.

'But what if it's all a mistake?'

'Then you'll enjoy a few drinks, and a good look at the finest suite in the fleet and have plenty to tell me in the morning.'

Jim had made his way back to them, with a questioning smile, and Leticia, maintaining her cheerful composure, told him they were ready to leave. She touched Joy's arm. 'Come on, Cinderella, let's get you back to the ship and ready for the ball.'

Joy glanced down at her sturdy walking boots, fleece lined trousers and sensible winter coat. She was hardly Cinderella, but the thought of the new dress and the party, the soft clink of glasses and, with any luck, Henry waiting for her, gave her an excited feeling.

As they stepped out into the bright light and made their way to the coach, Joy's evening lay ahead, and she wrapped her coat a little tighter. She didn't know what might happen or even if Henry would accept. But somewhere beneath her uncertainty there was a bubble of excitement in her chest.

Joy Bradley was going to a posh party. Who knew what might happen next!

Chapter Twenty-Two

Aboard the Emerald Dream, *the waves whisper, the chandeliers glisten, and every toast starts a new story.*

Henry sat on his bed and stared at the telephone. For the tenth time in as many minutes, he pressed the button to replay the message left earlier by guest services. Joy Bradley had invited him to be her plus one at Lady Eleanor's soirée, and he was to meet her in the Ocean Bar at six-thirty.

When he'd booked the Arctic cruise for Christmas, he'd imagined an enjoyable festive escape, in contrast to Christmas in Skipton, where Henry attended the camera club's Christmas Eve buffet, which was a dutiful and staid affair. He always spent Christmas Day with Audrey and enjoyed preparing the meal, following it with his finest plum pudding before settling down to the King's Speech, a tin of Quality Street and a nap, to the sound of Audrey's knitting needles clicking away. The cruise was quite a contrast, and so far, the entertainment had been lively, the food deliciously prepared by someone else, and the conversations with lovely folk like Leticia and Jim a delightful change.

But he'd never anticipated being invited to an elegant party by a woman like Joy.

Joy had slipped into his world like a soft light breaking through his grey skies. Now, here he was, dressed formally and brushing lint from his jacket, wondering if this trip might turn into something far more interesting than talks about Norwegian farming and puffin watching. Henry wondered what Audrey would make of it but knew that she'd be delighted and would encourage her neighbour.

Go and have an adventure, Henry Halliday, before it's too late!

Henry felt like it was the first day of a new school term. His fingers fidgeted and he straightened his cufflinks for the umpteenth time then smoothed his hair. He wasn't used to this kind of anticipation and swallowed hard, feeling like a teenager in the first flush of a crush. For all his later-life careful planning, this was new territory, and he didn't want to mess things up. Joy was a lovely woman, and it was clear that she was still navigating the stages of grief.

What kind of grief he wasn't quite sure.

She rarely spoke of her late husband. Perhaps, like Henry, she was also mourning the loss of purpose that retirement brought, or maybe the ache of facing life on her own. Last night, they'd shared something significant as they listened to Matti's song. But when they returned to the ship, she'd hurried away so quickly that Henry thought he'd done something wrong.

But here he was, with the minutes slipping by, and Joy

would be waiting to meet him. Shaking away his confusion, Henry stood. He patted his pockets and took one last look at his reflection.

'You'll do,' he muttered and, dimming the lights in his cabin, moved to open the door.

'Good evening, Mr Henry!' Jennifer almost fell into the room, her eyes sparkling with mischief. 'You all dressed up,' she said, noting Henry's smart appearance. 'You sit with captain tonight?'

'Good Lord, no,' Henry chuckled, 'but I have been invited to a cocktail party with a friend.'

'Friend . . . what friend?' Jennifer frowned, her eyes narrowing.

'I'd better be on my way,' Henry said and side-stepped into the corridor. 'Thank you for checking my room and have a good evening.'

'I make room nice for you,' Jennifer called after him.

Henry paused. 'I appreciate that, Jennifer, you're very kind,' he said softly.

And with the excitement of the evening awaiting him, Henry turned and made his way to the Ocean Bar.

* * *

Joy wasn't used to standing in a bar on her own and decided to order a drink to calm her nerves. As she sipped the crisp prosecco, she glanced towards the entrance, wondering if Henry would appear. Golden garlands were strung throughout the room, and a pretty Christmas tree stood in one corner. To one side of a small dance area, a pianist played a soft rendition of 'Have Yourself a Merry Little Christmas', the notes delicate amidst occasional bursts of laughter from guests gathering for the evening.

Joy smoothed the skirt of her dress and touched the jewelled edge of the bodice. Leticia had helped Joy get ready, and as she finished sweeping her hair into a chignon at the nape of her neck, she fastened it with a silver comb and told her that she looked amazing. Joy hardly recognised herself when she checked her reflection in a mirror. The shoes and bag matched perfectly, and the dress hugged her waist before flowing softly to her knees; the coral colour catching the light and shimmering like a delicate dusting of snow. Joy remembered a special occasion when she'd longed for something new, but at Tom's insistence, the navy had been rolled out again. Despite smiling politely and playing the part, she'd felt herself disappear into the background when, in her heart, she'd wanted to shine in her own light on that notable day. Whatever would Tom have thought about this outfit, worn on their wedding anniversary? The thought lingered, and she shook her head to chase it away. If Tom were still here, she would never have worn a dress like this, nor styled her hair and painted her lips as she had tonight.

But now, on Christmas Eve on a cruise ship, her dress felt just right, and as she finished her drink, she turned to steal a glimpse of herself in the mirror behind the bar.

A tap on her shoulder made Joy jump.

'Joy?'

There he was. Henry, looking resplendent in his dinner suit.

'You look . . .' Henry hesitated, then laughed. 'Wow!'

Joy felt heat rise from her neck, but she managed a smile. 'You look very . . . good too.' She wanted to say handsome but bit back the word. In truth, Joy hardly recognised Henry from his academic attire of tweed jacket, brogues, and his comfy reindeer sweater. Tonight, he looked entirely different. Elegant in a suit that was perfectly cut, the red pocket hankie a bold touch, and his thick hair neatly groomed.

'I wasn't sure that you'd come,' Joy said as the low hum of music wrapped around them.

'I'm very honoured that you've asked me.'

'Actually, I wasn't sure if I should go myself, but Leticia said I'd regret it if I didn't.'

'And do you?'

'Not yet.'

Henry laughed, and the tension between them eased.

'Leticia asked if we'd like to join them for dinner later,' Joy said. 'She's booked a table in the speciality restaurant.'

'In Malabar?' Henry asked. 'I'd love to try the food there.'

'Yes, it's said to be delicious.'

'But first, the cocktail party.' Henry smiled. 'Shall we?' He held out his arm with a flourish.

Joy hesitated, then took it, and as they moved through the ship, her nerves eased, and she no longer felt like fading into the background.

* * *

Henry felt ten feet tall with Joy on his arm as they approached the top deck where Lady Eleanor's suite was located. He was relieved that he'd invested in a new formal suit and hoped that he did Joy justice. She looked so lovely in her coral-coloured dress and moved with such quiet grace that he couldn't help but glance at her every few steps, as if to reassure himself that she was beside him.

A steward stood at the entrance to the Royal Emerald Suite and greeted the couple as Joy showed her invitation. Inside they were welcomed with cocktails and Henry's eyes were wide as he stared at the sheer grandeur before him. The suite was breathtaking and reminded Henry of a drawing room in a stately home, certainly not accommodation one would expect to find on a ship. In the centre, a chandelier glimmered above a parquet floor, the grain of dark walnut polished to a mirror-like gleam. Floor-to-ceiling windows wrapped around the curved edge of an outside flood-lit deck, offering a glorious view of the Arctic world beyond.

'My goodness, there's a fire,' Joy exclaimed and stopped to admire realistic flames dancing over synthetic logs. They moved towards velvet armchairs and long sofas in shades of deep green and gold, where a string quartet were assembled beside a grand piano. 'Just look at the artwork,' she added as they gazed at walls lined with huge abstract images in striking, vibrant colours, 'this is like something out of a dream.'

'I'm not sure what this is,' Henry commented as he studied a pile of empty rusting herring tins, stacked and welded together on a plinth of blue glass.

Joy leaned in and read a label. 'It's called *Echoes of the Fishwives* – an installation by Lucinda Green.'

'I don't think Tracey Emin has anything to worry about,' Henry muttered.

'Joy!'

Henry and Joy turned as Lady Eleanor came towards them. Elegant in a calf-length silver shift dress adorned with a diamond brooch, her shoulder-length silver hair was held back with a velvet band and again, Joy noticed bright red lipstick staining her teeth as she smiled.

'I see you're admiring the art,' Lady Eleanor said. 'I like to indulge the artist,' she added, holding out her hand. 'And you must be Henry.'

As he acknowledged their host Henry wondered how she knew his name but realised that guest services covered every detail.

'I'm so glad that you could join us,' Lady Eleanor said, 'I was delighted to meet the lovely Joy at the captain's table and long to hear more about her amazing contribution to education.'

Puzzled, Henry glanced at Joy and saw that she appeared self-conscious.

But Lady Eleanor continued. 'My dear, please don't look so embarrassed. Your revelation at the captain's table was marvellous and I've been researching you too. I'm so impressed by your dedication. It's no wonder that you were awarded the MBE.'

Henry blinked, certain he'd misheard. 'You have an MBE?' he asked.

Joy's cheeks flushed a deeper shade than her dress, and she looked down at her glass. 'It's nothing, really,' she murmured.

Lady Eleanor smiled. 'Nonsense,' she said. 'You were instrumental in developing a curriculum that innovated and modernised home economics at a county level, mentoring student teachers, and helping to shape future education in your field.'

'Well, it *was* only in Lancashire . . .' Joy gave a modest shrug.

'That's not to mention your outreach work,' Lady Eleanor continued, undeterred. 'I've read that you organised funding for healthy eating initiatives, set up cookery classes in underprivileged areas, and even authored resources tailored for students with special educational needs. That kind of impact goes far beyond the county lines, my dear.'

Henry stared at Joy, but she seemed suddenly fascinated by the bubbles rising in her champagne. He felt his heart swell with pride. This quiet remarkable woman, who had never boasted and had downplayed any accomplishment, had achieved so much.

And he hadn't had the faintest idea.

'We have much in common, Joy,' Lady Eleanor continued, 'you know all about my trust in Ireland and your legacy, like mine, will last long after our days are done.' She turned as Margaret joined them. 'Hello, dear,' she said to the Olympian, 'you remember Joy? And this is Henry.'

'Splendid to see you again Joy, and pleased to see you here, Henry.' Margaret wore a long floaty scarf around her neck and, flicking it to one side, gave Henry a hearty slap on his back. The glass in his hand wobbled, almost spilling the contents. 'Good man! You've landed a gem there.' Margaret nodded towards Joy. 'She's an MBE don't you know?'

'Now, I do know,' Henry smiled.

But before their conversation could continue, Lucinda Green waltzed into their circle, her diaphanous gown, almost transparent, an explosion of paint-splattered purple tulle, billowing around her. She held her cigarette holder in one hand and had tucked an oversized paintbrush through her updo.

'Hello Lucinda, dear.' Lady Eleanor smiled warmly, as Lucinda covered her ladyship's rouged cheeks in kisses. 'Do you know everyone?'

'You must be the mysterious Mr Henry,' Lucinda said, eyeing Henry and gripping the cigarette holder between her teeth. 'We wondered who you were when your name popped up on the guest list, but I recognise you now from my art class.' She raised a heavily painted eyebrow. 'I hope you're more interesting than your painting,' she rudely added.

Henry opened his mouth to speak but wasn't sure what to say. Lucinda appeared to be naked beneath her gown, and he was having difficulty keeping his focus at eye level.

Lucinda beamed. 'Speechless already, that won't last long.' Turning to the art on the walls, she swept out an arm. 'Do you like my paintings? Lady Eleanor is my biggest fan.' Lucinda stroked Lady Eleanor's arm then snapped her fingers to a passing steward and scooped up a glass of champagne. 'I'm taking commissions, do come and see me in my studio.' Draining her glass, she looked around for the steward again and moved away.

Henry suddenly understood how, despite her outrageous behaviour, Lucinda managed to keep her job on the ship.

With Lady Eleanor as her patron, the usual rules wouldn't apply, and Lucinda could get away with near mutiny. Her position was secured by protection from someone untouchable, and Lucinda brought colour and theatre into the old lady's life.

'Oh look, we have more guests,' Lady Eleanor announced, and everyone turned to see Simon lead a couple into the room. 'Over here, Simon!' she called out.

Bringing up the rear, his hair polished and smooth, wearing a Union Jack bow tie and waistcoat beneath his dinner jacket, Kenneth's expression was smug as he led Barbara towards them.

'You must be the Montgomery Joneses.' Lady Eleanor smiled. 'Dear Simon has told me so much about you both and insisted that you join us.' She extended her hand to Barbara, the diamonds on her wrist catching the chandelier's light. 'Welcome to my modest little soirée . . .'

* * *

No one watching Simon would have noticed the tension in his shoulders, nor his discomfort beneath his immaculate uniform jacket, as he stepped forward, smiling and acknowledging Lady Eleanor.

But behind the polished exterior, his brain seethed as Barbara's face flashed before him. It was a sharp reminder of her earlier visit to his office, brandishing the phone in her hand, wearing her cruel little smile. She hadn't needed to speak as she turned the screen towards him and watched the colour drain from his face as she made her terms clear.

If only he'd secured the bathroom door at the Sámi camp. If only Kyle hadn't chosen that moment, to Simon's shock and surprise, to pull Simon into the narrow space where Kyle had pressed him against the icy cold tiles and fiercely kissed him.

It had been brief and clumsy, fuelled by adrenaline and the thrill of secrecy. Hands, hot breath, the rustle of discarded clothing . . . And then, just as Simon had let go, he'd heard the unmistakable creak of the outer door. But it was too late. The flash of Barbara's camera was swift, before she disappeared into the dark.

The wretched woman had blackmailed her way into the party and unless he wanted the compromising images displayed all over the ship and forwarded to head office, Simon would have to make sure that the Montgomery Joneses were welcomed to the soirée and seated at the captain's table for the Christmas meal.

* * *

Barbara's smile broadened and she almost dropped into a curtsy as she took Lady Eleanor's limp hand. She briefly noted the glint of the dazzling diamonds on the old lady's wrist, and a quick calculation told Barbara that their worth far outshone her own entire jewellery collection, which was considerable.

'Charmed,' Barbara said. 'Do meet my husband, Kenneth.'

'How patriotic,' Lady Eleanor said as she stared at Kenneth's red, white, and blue waistcoat. 'But the cruise line no longer holds British Gala Nights.'

'Such a shame,' Kenneth said, turning to his wife, 'Babs and I like nothing more than belting out "Land of Hope and Glory" and flying the flag.'

'That may be so, but that doesn't really resonate with non-British guests, does it, dear?' Lady Eleanor dismissed, 'Colonial-era anthems are terribly outdated,' she added.

Barbara gritted her teeth and resisted the urge to kick Kenneth in the shin. But Lady Eleanor had turned to Joy and Henry and was busy making introductions.

'We've met.' Barbara forced a tight smile. Her eyes dropped to Joy's dress, and suddenly, her stomach churned. The schoolteacher was wearing *the* dress! The very one that Barbara had burst out of.

'I like your dress,' Joy said kindly. 'Did you get it from the ship's boutique? I thought I saw something similar when I was browsing.'

'Yes,' Lady Eleanor joined in, 'navy is so flattering on a fuller figure.'

Barbara's grip tightened around her glass. The assistant had insisted the dress would be perfect for the cocktail party, with a low-cut bodice, an empire waist, and a full skirt that bypassed any seams. Barbara had reluctantly agreed, hoping to elevate it with her diamonds. But now, as she stared at Joy, who wore the coral confection effortlessly, Barbara realised that she'd been totally upstaged. Worse still, the assistant had flatly refused to credit the damaged dress when Barbara had tried to return it.

'I'm so thrilled to have an MBE in the room,' Lady Eleanor ploughed on.

Kenneth sensed Barbara's mood and felt the need to

lighten the conversation. 'Ah, those awards,' he chuckled, 'they hand them out willy-nilly these days, eh, Babs?' He smiled at his wife. 'An old boy in our village has one and we all say he Mostly Blagged Everything . . .'

Barbara closed her eyes and hoped that the parquet flooring would part and swallow Kenneth into the bowels of the ship. 'Oh, Lady Eleanor, please ignore him. Kenny likes a little joke.' She fluttered her eyelashes and playfully punched her husband's arm. 'Do tell us who has achieved such worthy recognition?' Her eyes strayed beyond Joy and Henry as she cast her glance around the room.

'But it's Joy.' Lady Eleanor raised her eyebrows. 'Didn't you know?'

'J . . . Joy?' Barbara spat out the name. 'Er . . . well, how marvellous,' she stuttered.

But Lady Eleanor appeared tired, and she gently touched Joy's arm. 'Do excuse me, my dear, I need to sit down, but please help yourselves to more drinks and canapés and of course, enjoy the music.'

Barbara begrudgingly noted the warm exchange, and as Lady Eleanor moved away, she flung her empty glass out to Kenneth for a refill. She was damned if she'd ask the schoolteacher what miraculous doings had credited her with such an honour. She was about to move away and mingle when Margaret cantered across the room to join the group, landing at Barbara's side.

'I say, would you believe it – SNAP!' Margaret yelled and everyone turned. 'We're like Tweedledum and Tweedledee!'

Barbara froze. The room had silenced, and there was a mild ripple of laughter.

Margaret was wearing the same dress and was oblivious to the catastrophe she'd just detonated. The same deep navy that Barbara had only agreed to purchase after being assured by two boutique assistants that it was exclusive.

'You wear it well, despite being so short,' Margaret bulldozed on, 'and there's something about navy that hides all the bumps.'

Kenneth appeared with Barbara's refill, and grabbing the glass, she half-drained it. Margaret turned to Joy and Henry and was now engaged in conversation.

Barbara narrowed her eyes and searched around the room for Simon. She had another request that he needed to fulfil. Mentally remembering the names of the assistants who'd sold her the navy dress, Barbara vowed they would find themselves unemployed by morning!

Chapter Twenty-Three

Though the sea surrounds us, the spirit of a Christmas cruise brings us home.

Christmas Day in the Arctic and the *Emerald Dream* set a southerly course to make its way to the next stop in the port of Ålesund. Guests awoke to a warm and cheerful greeting over the PA from Captain Lindholm, on the Bridge.

'Merry Christmas everyone, and on behalf of myself and the entire crew, I wish you all a happy and enjoyable Christmas Day.' The captain's tone was almost melodic. 'This voyage may find you far from home, but you are sailing amongst friends, and we are honoured to share this special time with you.'

He continued to inform everyone that the day would be spent at sea where the sea state was slight with a Force Four moderate breeze.

Passing the intercom briefing to Simon, the captain signed off and the cruise director highlighted the day's activities that would include a champagne breakfast, carol singers in the lounges and a lavish Christmas meal, not forgetting an appearance by Santa Claus on the Lido Deck. Tonight's entertainment in the Triton Lounge would be The Emerald Dream Crew Show.

'Join our crew for heart-warming, contemporary and traditional performances,' Simon explained. 'And don't forget everyone,' Simon reminded cheerfully, 'join the crew in your festive finest and celebrate Christmas Day in style!'

Seated at his desk in his office following his announcement, Simon's tone changed. He wasn't having the best start to his Christmas Day and his festive finest fell far short of the jovial effect he'd hoped to create. The sequinned waistcoat that the ship's wardrobe supervisor had unearthed felt far too tight, and the red velvet blazer, paired with black satin-sheen trousers, suggested circus ringmaster more than Christmas cruise director. He pulled on the lapels, willing them to meet, when Penny, his assistant, knocked on the door.

'Come in,' Simon called out, sounding as weary as he already felt.

Dressed as an elf in green velvet, Penny looked adorable. 'I've just had a message from Mrs Montgomery Jones that she'd like to see you,' she said, 'and she's on her way down.'

'Oh damn,' Simon cursed and pushed back his chair. 'Please keep that dreadful woman away from me.'

'She says you've arranged for them to sit at the captain's table today?' Penny held a clipboard in her hand and appeared puzzled. 'But I don't have them on the list.'

Simon shook his head. 'You'll have to make room, or we'll never hear the end of it.' Inwardly, he knew that if Barbara didn't get her way, the outcome would be too career-destroying to think about. 'Just don't put her next to the captain,' he added.

'No problem, I'll juggle the seating plan.' Penny nodded. 'By the way, you look very . . . festive,' she giggled.

'Festive humiliation,' Simon muttered, tugging at his velvet cuffs, 'I just need a top hat and a striped tent.'

As he navigated his way through the ship, Simon took care to steer clear of Barbara, knowing that she would soon be preening and bragging about her invitation to anyone unlucky enough to be within earshot. With practised ease, he offered warm greetings to passengers who'd risen early to make the most of the champagne breakfast, many of whom were wearing Santa hats and Christmas jumpers. Stopping occasionally to exchange Christmas pleasantries with those dressed in more colourful seasonal attire, Simon plastered on a smile when his outfit drew amused comments.

Reaching the Lido Deck, he took a seat in the adjoining bar and ordered a coffee. He dug into his pocket where his amulet nestled and let his fingers rub gently over the engraved symbols. Nearby, energetic guests were waiting for Kyle's early class named Jingle Bell Rock & Stretch. He noted that Nora, her orange hair pulled into a sharp ponytail, wore a close-fitting tunic and had sewn baubles onto the bodice, which bounced as she moved. Sid meanwhile, had donned leggings that highlighted his varicose veins. Wrinkled at the knee, they reminded Simon of gnarled tree roots.

Music suddenly burst through the speakers, and everyone turned to see Kyle, riding an inflatable reindeer, jog across the deck. 'Morning, gang!' he called out as Michael Bublé crooned that it was 'beginning to look a lot like Christmas'.

Simon blinked and rubbed his eyes. Was Kyle really wearing a gold lamé leotard, pointed elf shoes and matching hat?

As everyone began their stretches, Kyle dismounted.

'Lengthen those limbs!' he called out and began to strut around the class, reaching out to ease the elderly passengers into positions they hadn't performed since they were in high school. 'Wings like an angel, Nora,' he encouraged as he raised Nora's arms into a wide arc. 'Release that tension, babes.'

Kyle turned to Sid and ran his knuckles up and down the older man's spine.

Sid's eyes popped, and Simon felt sure he heard something crack.

A little while later, Kyle led the class in a chorus of, Slade's 'Merry Xmas Everybody'. Instructing them to speed walk in a conga around the pool, he slipped away and made his way over to Simon.

'Everything all right?' Kyle whispered.

The golden glare of Kyle's torso and too-tight tube-like outfit was almost too much for Simon, and he longed to reach out and pull the fitness instructor into an embrace. 'Everything is fine,' he softly replied.

'No repercussions? We're not about to be exposed?' Kyle tapped a foot up and down, and the bell on his pixie shoe jingled.

Simon thought that Kyle would be exposed to a police

indecency raid if he were wearing his outfit anywhere but the ship, but the passengers seemed to like the young man's revealing clothes. 'It's all in hand, no further damage, the price has been paid,' Simon reassured.

'Thank goodness,' Kyle let out a deep breath. 'We'll have to be more careful next time.' With a cheeky wink, Kyle pursed his lips into a teasing pout, then pirouetted and moved away.

Next time? Simon felt his heart thump.

He murmured a thank you to the server as a fresh cup of coffee was placed before him, then absently ran his fingers over the heart-shaped amulet. A private smile tugged at Simon's lips.

Maybe, just maybe, his search for a soulmate wasn't in vain.

* * *

The *Emerald Dream* sailed slowly through the fjords, and in their suite, Leticia and Jim nestled against the pillows in their king-sized bed and stared out of the window to the dark mysterious world outside.

'It's so surreal,' Leticia reached for Jim's warm hand.

'A perfect Christmas morning,' Jim replied.

'Mmm . . .' Leticia nodded, enjoying the quiet beauty of the moment.

'When the time comes, promise me you won't grieve for too long.' Jim squeezed Leticia's hand. 'You have so much life ahead of you and I want you to make the most of every day.'

Leticia rested her head on Jim's shoulder, and he shifted gently to wrap an arm around her. His embrace was so familiar yet didn't feel the same. Jim's frame was leaner and his grip softer, as though the illness had been stealing him away by degrees. Leticia ached for the strong, agile man who'd once swept her into his arms without effort and hid the sorrow that rose at how fragile he felt against her now. It struck her how easily they spoke of his illness, and she was grateful for that ease. It would be simple for her to shush him and insist that life would go on as usual.

But Leticia knew better. There was no normal, and when The Beast returned, its power would be beyond her reach. All she could do then would be to ease Jim's pain and make his remaining days as gentle as possible. She was aware of the extra effort it took at times. As his strength ebbed, frustration would flicker, brief but unmistakable, like clouds passing across a once clear sky.

'Promise me, no treatment,' Jim said softly. 'We've discussed this. No hospitals or false hope.'

Leticia edged closer and kissed his cheek. 'You got it, my darling. Just me and you.'

She knew it would be cruel to deny his wishes, no matter how much she wanted him to cling to every day of life. But the image of his baby daughter, Grace, lying small and still in a stark hospital cot, surrounded by the sterile silence of death, was carved into both their memories, and it was too raw to forget. Leticia knew what she had to do, and Jim would leave Leticia in the comfort of their home.

He hugged her closer, and they lay quietly, both accepting the truth that their time was running out, yet grateful to each other for the mutual understanding that came with their deep love.

There was a knock on the door, and Leticia sat up. Room service had arrived with their breakfast. Swinging her legs out of bed, she adjusted the straps of her silk negligee and stood.

'I much prefer your lovely gown to your Christmas onesie,' Jim laughed as he watched his wife sashay across the room.

Leticia wriggled her bottom suggestively.

She opened the door to a smiling steward who entered the suite wheeling a trolley laden with fresh fruit, pastries, orange juice, and a chilled bottle of champagne. Leticia wished the steward a happy Christmas and thanked him with a generous gratuity. She placed the trolley beside their bed, and after assisting Jim into a comfortable position, poured the champagne.

'A toast,' she said brightly, 'to Christmas.'

They clinked glasses, and their eyes met.

'To us,' Jim whispered, 'let's hold on to happiness for as long as it lets us.' His gaze lingered lovingly. 'Happy Christmas my darling, Leticia.'

* * *

Henry was in the buffet restaurant and despite hoping that he'd catch sight of Joy to share a table, the restaurant manager had cheerfully seated him with Nora and Sid, and he'd felt it churlish to decline. Over a second helping of crunchy granola, Nora suggested that Henry join them for

Kyle's early-morning fitness sessions. 'It's not too late,' she said brightly, 'and you'll feel the benefit by the end of the cruise.'

'Not if you belly-flop into the pool while doing the conga,' Sid muttered and rubbed his sore tummy.

'You needed waking up,' Nora laughed.

Nora was wearing a bright red dress with a candy cane pattern and wore reindeer antlers on her head. Sid's Santa hat sat low on his forehead and came complete with a fluffy white beard.

'Damn thing is tickling,' Sid grumbled, wrinkling his nose.

Henry smiled politely as Nora told him that the previous evening, the pair had narrowly missed first prize at the midnight Christmas trivia quiz.

Sid, chewing on a slice of toast, shook his head. 'How the devil would we know what year "White Christmas" was released?' he said solemnly, brushing crumbs from his beard. 'We might have guessed that posh couple, the Montgomery Joneses, would know. Probably a guess, but they stole it from us.'

'The answer was 1942, Bing Crosby,' Nora nodded.

'The year Barbara was born, no doubt,' Sid sniped.

'Don't let Her Highness hear you,' Nora chuckled, 'she swears she's not a day over fifty.'

'Aye and I'm twenty-one,' Sid grinned.

Between crunching her granola, Nora shook her head. 'That Barbara isn't a very nice person,' she said. 'She was bad-mouthing one of the guests, but I wouldn't join in.'

Henry kept his silence, unwilling to be drawn into

anything that involved Barbara – unaware that the guest at the heart of her gossip was Joy.

'Come on, Henry,' Nora insisted, 'it's Christmas, fill your boots.' She reached for a bottle of champagne and poured.

Henry raised his glass, but his eyes flicked towards the entrance, still hoping to see Joy. As he sipped the champagne, he thought back to their evening and felt his shoulders slump.

The cocktail party had been thoroughly enjoyable, and as they made polite conversation, they mingled with the guests in the room. At one point during the evening, Lucinda took to the centre of the room and regaled everyone with a poem she'd written about art in the Arctic, which began with the line,

'The Arctic is the spirit's way of painting the Earth,
with brushes of silence and palettes of mirth . . .'

She'd waved her cigarette holder for emphasis, and as the light caught her dress, Henry remembered several guests averting their eyes. Lucinda's breasts shimmered through the sheer tulle, swaying from side to side, reminding him of the metronome on Audrey's piano. At the end of Lucinda's performance, there was a polite ripple of applause before she sauntered to the bar.

As the party wound down, Henry and Joy looked for Lady Eleanor to thank her but were told by Margaret that their host had retired.

'Too much for the old gal,' Margaret said. 'She's knackered and has retired to her stable . . .' Margaret lowered her voice and confided. 'Between you and me, she's like a thoroughbred, entertaining, temperamental, and prone to bolting.' Margaret moved away, her floaty scarf fluttering behind her like a saddle blanket caught in the breeze.

Henry and Joy left the party and headed to the Malabar restaurant, where Leticia and Jim welcomed them. They wanted to know all about the party and were delirious with delight when Henry told them that Joy was an MBE.

'You dark horse.' Jim grinned.

'I knew there was more to you.' Leticia laughed and reached out to pat Joy's arm. 'You've been holding out on us.'

Joy appeared embarrassed. She blushed as she tucked a loose strand of hair behind her ear. Henry's gaze took in the soft pink that spread across her cheeks and the way her eyes darted away. He thought that Joy looked impossibly delicate, and in that instant, he couldn't help but think how lovely she was. Joy's shyness and the tiniest flicker of self-consciousness made her more captivating than any words could.

Jim raised his glass in a toast, 'To Joy, our undercover MBE.'

The meal was delicious, and Henry enjoyed his starter of flaky fish, wrapped in banana leaves and subtly spiced. His prawn moilee was so tasty that he exclaimed he must remember to ask for the recipe for silky coconut milk, flavoured with chillies and ginger, and served with ghee rice. He told them that Audrey loved to try new recipes, and he felt sure that she'd enjoy such a dish.

They were sipping mint tea when an announcement came.

A gentle chime was followed by Simon's voice on the PA, informing the guests that the Northern Lights were visible off the starboard side, and Bill Zhang was on the observation deck and urged everyone to join him.

With boyish excitement, Henry leaped up. 'I must see them,' he said. 'Audrey will never forgive me if I don't report back in detail and take lots of photos.'

'Do go ahead,' Joy had said, smiling politely at his enthusiasm. 'I'll need a coat and will join you up there.'

'More champers?'

Nora's voice jolted Henry now, and placing his fingers over his glass, he declined.

'Me and Sid are off for a couple's Christmas massage,' Nora said. 'The early session with Kyle has hit Sid's lumbago like a fandango.' Taking Sid's hand, she stood. 'Happy Christmas!'

As Sid hobbled to his feet, he gave Henry a wink as the pair moved away.

Henry sighed. There was no sign of Joy in the restaurant, and in the end, she hadn't joined him on the observatory deck last night. It was a shame, because the aurora borealis had been breathtaking. A shimmering wave of vibrant blues and greens rippling across the sky, and the photographs he'd taken were spectacular. *Audrey will be so impressed*, he thought.

He hoped Joy wasn't unwell but hesitated to call. Would it seem too forward? Too presumptuous? Henry weaved through the festive bustle of the ship as carollers sang 'Joy to the World!'

At the mention of her name, he frowned.

Henry had always been hopeless with women, as Audrey often reminded him, either too eager or too cautious and never striking the right note. Still, they'd all agreed to dine together at their table in the Terrace Restaurant for Christmas lunch, and as he pictured Jim and Leticia dressed for the occasion, Henry crossed his fingers and hoped that Joy would be there too.

Chapter Twenty-Four

The secret at sea to living the life of your dreams, is to start living the life of your dreams.

Joy sat in her cabin and placed her book to one side. Turning to a mirror, she stared at her reflection. The smile she'd worn all through the previous evening had inwardly faded the moment Henry mentioned Audrey during dinner with Leticia and Jim. Despite enjoying every moment of his company, she knew that his heart was elsewhere. Henry spoke of Audrey often and with a softness that told Joy everything she needed to know. Whoever the woman was, Joy could only hope she understood how fortunate she was to have the affection of such a kind and endearing man.

With a sigh, she began to prepare herself for the Christmas lunch, knowing that Henry would be at their table, surrounded by crackers and Christmas cheer. How would she manage to be herself and relax, feeling comfortable in his company? Sleep had offered no escape, and all through a restless night, Joy's dreams had been filled with glimpses of his smile, and the deep sense of safety and warmth in his presence.

How she longed to rest her weary head on his shoulder again.

This is ridiculous! Joy suddenly snapped to and reached for a brush to stroke firmly through her hair. She was acting like a teenager and couldn't understand how someone could occupy so much space in her heart, so quickly, and after so little time. Did she crave affection *that* badly? Was Joy so starved of love that any kind word from Henry felt like sunlight on her skin?

'Stop it!' Joy said out loud. She told herself that she was far too old to have feelings of this nature and must put all thoughts of a relationship with Henry aside. If he really knew her, she thought, as she brushed for the umpteenth time, she doubted that he'd want to be in her company.

Rising, she went to her wardrobe to find something suitable for Christmas Day. But when her mobile rang, Joy paused.

'Hello, Mum!' Susan trilled. 'Just thought I'd call to wish you a happy Christmas, since you've clearly forgotten my number.'

Joy sighed and sank onto the edge of her bed. Susan had been at the sherry; her voice had a lilting slur. 'Hello, dear, are you having a lovely day?' Joy asked.

'Yes, still sweating away over the hot stove. I've never stopped and am expecting the in-laws at any moment.' Susan's voice was heavy. 'There's so much to do, and it would have been good to have you here.'

Joy was tempted to remind her daughter that it was she

who'd insisted that her mother come on the cruise, but she refrained. Susan was playing hostess, and the irony wasn't lost on Joy. She'd spent more years than she cared to remember working hard over Christmas lunch for Susan and her extended family of Hugh's parents, her brothers and sisters-in-law and their hordes of offspring. Joy couldn't ever remember a thank you.

'Well, it sounds as though you're going to have a lovely house full,' Joy said kindly.

She knew that Susan, who'd never wanted to have children and barely tolerated them, would be horrified by the arrival of toddlers with sticky fingers and loud voices, leaving smudges and crumbs all over her cream-toned designer interior. The thought of ice-cream on her velvet cushions or toys scratching polished wooden surfaces would have Susan emptying the barrel of sherry by midday. But husband, Hugh, also a lawyer, who Susan worshipped, was the apple of his family's eye. Hugh loved having their house filled with his family and if Hugh said, 'We're hosting Christmas,' Susan plastered on a smile, poured another drink, and ordered everything in from Fortnum's.

'I'm sure it's not too tedious to reheat and arrange nicely on platters,' Joy commented on Susan's trick of having it all pre-made and delivered.

At least Joy didn't have to explain the method behind perfectly prepared sprouts, honey-glazed parsnips, or how to stuff and roast a succulent turkey. Susan had never shown any interest in cooking, not even as a child. Joy often wondered if Susan deliberately rebuffed her mother's talents, as if acknowledging them would mean conceding

239

some unspoken, generational rivalry. Growing up, Susan had always been demanding and self-absorbed, showing no curiosity about Joy's career or accomplishments. Joy suspected the roots of it ran deeper. Perhaps a quiet loyalty to her father, who had never offered Joy praise either. Could valuing her mother, even in the smallest way, feel like a betrayal of that bond?

Who knew? Joy thought as she pasted a smile and listened to her daughter complain about the absurd pressure of Christmas.

'At least you're spared all of this,' Susan said with a theatrical sigh. 'You must feel like Lady Bountiful being waited on twenty-four-seven.'

Joy heard the faint chink of a bottle and wondered how much sherry Susan had put away. 'Yes,' Joy said evenly. 'I'm fortunate.'

'Have you made any friends?' Susan asked, 'I hope you're keeping away from that H . . . Henry,' she hiccupped.

'You've no need to worry, dear.'

'Well, I must dash, can't stay here chatting when there's a massive meal to serve up. Have a good Christmas, Mum. Toodle-oo!'

'Toodle-oo . . .' Joy echoed.

As the call ended, she glanced at her watch. 'Goodness,' she murmured. She'd idled the day away, and it was almost time for the Christmas meal.

Crossing the cabin, she reached into the wardrobe and pulled a hanger from the rail. The garment, an impulse purchase as she was about to leave the boutique, shimmered faintly. She'd intended to return it. It was too bold, and

Joy knew that Susan would shake her head and frown, and Tom would turn in his grave.

But why shouldn't she wear it? Joy thought as she stared at the soft fabric, Tom was gone, and Susan was a zillion miles away. With a swift motion, she held it against herself and could almost hear Leticia whisper permission.

'Then I will . . .' Joy gave her reflection a firm nod and began to change. 'After all, it's Christmas Day.'

* * *

Henry was dithering. He didn't like to dither and much preferred decisive action. In his teaching years, there were no grey areas; his lessons had clean lines and solid instructions. In retirement, his life was structured around regular social activities and a predictable routine. But as the days of the cruise passed, he found himself faltering and not following the pattern he'd expected. The planned lectures, attendance at activities, and the things he'd intended to experience had, at times, gone out the window.

And the reason for that was Joy.

Henry paced around his cabin until he stopped by the doors to the deck. Leaving the polar night of Tromsø behind, the ship was sailing into a world where daylight lingered briefly, stretching from around ten in the morning until three in the afternoon.

He held a mug of tea and stared out at the vast white mountains that looked like soft meringues floating on a dish of cold blue glass. It had been years since anyone had unsettled him in this way, and even then, he'd soon sorted

241

himself out. Now, Joy was complicating everything, and he felt completely disarmed. Was it wrong to have feelings at his age and for these to happen so quickly? Surely, he was past all of this.

Henry looked out at the endless fjord and remembered their moments. Closeness at the Sámi evening, shared laughter at the soirée, glances that lingered, and silences that felt safe. Now he felt confused. Yesterday, as he seemed to step closer, Joy had stepped away. Had he said something to upset her, or had he said too much? One explanation, he reasoned, might be that she was still mourning Tom, and her hesitation wasn't about Henry at all but how she carefully navigated this new world without the man who had shared it with her for so long.

He wished he could discuss his feelings with Audrey and wondered if he might call her, but it was Christmas Day, and he knew that she would be living it up. In Henry's absence, Audrey had bought forward her annual festive event and was hosting a Misfits & Mulled Wine party surrounded by her merry gang of LGBTQ pensioners. The rainbow wrinklies enjoyed re-enacting scenes from *It's a Wonderful Life* and judging who looked best in sequins. Audrey made much of the occasion that Henry had looked forward to in the past.

No, Henry decided. He couldn't possibly trouble Audrey with his dilemma.

As he continued to take in the majesty of the mountains, he sensed that Joy was holding back, almost as though she were afraid. Her humility was humbling, and he was blown away by her MBE. She'd achieved so much professionally yet was so unassuming. Joy hardly mentioned her personal life, and Henry knew little of it. Was there something else that she was hiding?

An announcement sounded, and Simon's voice could be heard, informing passengers that in the brief daylight, they were about to sail past the Seven Sisters, a range of steep peaks, shrouded in folklore. Henry placed his mug down, picked up his camera, and slid the door open. Stepping onto the promenade deck, he leaned on the railings and listened to the legendary tale as he gazed at the seven magnificent snow-covered mountains.

Condensing the story, Simon explained that seven beautiful troll sisters, determined to escape their overprotective father, had set off on a moonlit night. But as dawn broke, they were caught by the light, and in an instant turned to stone, forever frozen into the mountain range that guests could see today. Taking his camera, Henry adjusted his lens and focused on a panoramic image.

Perfect! Audrey would love that shot.

He was about to take another photo when the sound of pounding boots alerted him on the starboard side. Later than usual for their daily laps, Jack and Judy were striding purposefully towards him, their expressions set. In their wake, a pack of determined Deck Milers came hot on their heels, Santa hats bouncing, legs striding and arms pumping, like athletes visualising a victory.

'Eyes right!' Judy yelled, momentarily allowing everyone a glimpse of the towering mountains.

Unwilling to get involved, Henry hastened back to his cabin. Closing the door behind him, he turned when he heard an overattentive knock rattle the door.

'Mr Henry!'

It was Jennifer. Henry froze and contemplated bolting back onto the deck, but the choice of being caught up in a sea of cagoules and brisk-footed hikers lost out to his kindly housekeeper.

'Coming,' he called out.

Jennifer stood in the doorway. She wore a poinsettia bloom tucked behind one ear, and on her earlobes, tiny bells tinkled. 'Happy Christmas, Mr Henry!' Jennifer's smile was as wide as a harbour on a bright summer day. 'I got you gift,' she beamed, and produced a card.

Henry stared at a hand-drawn and brightly painted picture of a Filipino nipa hut nestled under lush green palm trees, the fronds swaying in the twilight sky. Star-shaped lanterns hung from bamboo poles, and two children dressed in traditional Filipino barong, their beautiful little faces alight, reached for colourful bibingka cakes from a wooden table.

Inscribed neatly across the top of the card, like a string of festive bunting, Henry read the words, Happy Christmas, Mr Henry.

'Jennifer,' he whispered, 'it's beautiful.'

'You like?' Her pretty face beamed. 'I make for you.'

'You painted this?'

'Yeah, my hobby.'

'And the children?' Henry's fingers traced the charming faces of the boy and girl.

'My beh-bees.'

Henry noticed the absence of adults in the painting and couldn't help but ask. 'And their father?'

244

'No dada.' Jennifer cast her eyes down.

'Oh, my dear . . .' Henry was lost for words. He instinctively knew it was wrong to accept a gift from a staff member, but her kindness made it impossible to refuse, and he felt an unexpected swell of gratitude. 'But who takes care of your beh-bees?'

'Nanay, my mama. She old, but . . .' Jennifer shrugged.

'I will treasure your gift,' Henry said. 'It will have a place in my home each Christmas.'

'Jennifer!'

His housekeeper suddenly turned. 'My boss,' she said. 'I gotta go.'

Henry closed the door quietly. Despite his gratitude for Jennifer's thoughtful gift, he couldn't help but feel relieved that she was called away. The mental image of Jennifer and her children bustling into his life made him shudder. Goodness, had he encouraged her? He considered this with a troubled frown and instinctively knew that he had to tread carefully.

'You are hopeless with the female sex!' Henry berated himself.

He checked his watch and realised that he needed to get a move on. Bill Zhang was hosting a talk in the Mermaid Theatre about the coronal aurora, which Henry very much wanted to hear, and this would be followed by Henry's attendance at table twenty-eight for the lavish Christmas meal.

Undecided what to wear and trying not to dwell on the hope that Joy would be at the meal too, Henry moved into action. 'Enough dithering!' he admonished himself.

Chapter Twenty-Five

The sea stirs slow, the Arctic winds blow, as Christmas
cruisers gently go . . .

In their Dream Suite, the Montgomery Joneses were preparing for the highlight of their cruise, and Barbara sat at her dressing table holding a thin, cream-coloured card. A beatific smile lit up her face as her fingers touched the lettering for the umpteenth time while she gazed at the printed words. Kenneth, lying alongside, stretched full length on their king-sized bed, yawned as he peered over his reading glasses to study his wife.

'For goodness' sake, Babs, put the damn thing down. Anyone would think it was a love letter from George Clooney, from the way you're swooning over that invitation.'

'In my mind, Kenny dear, it might as well be,' Barbara sighed happily, 'I've waited all week to get this.'

'I told you it would arrive,' Kenneth said and peered at his fingernails. Reaching for a file, he began to neaten a rough edge. 'The captain was just waiting for the right occasion, and you couldn't have anything finer than the formal Christmas meal.'

Barbara turned slowly to look at her husband, who was more stupid than she thought. Did he really have no idea that his wife had engineered the invitation through stealth and careful negotiation?

She stared at the man whom she married decades ago.

Barbara often wondered if he truly knew her, or if he ever had. Kenneth had turned a blind eye to her 'dalliances' over the years, as she had of his. Barbara had been discreet with a golf club pro in Zurich, unlike Kenneth, whose clumsy lingering glances over waitresses half his age were irritating to say the least. But nothing was as humiliating as his affair with the yoga instructor in Hong Kong, which had put his back out for the best part of a year. Long ago, they had settled on an arrangement that included mutual tolerance, but if truth be told, despite his air of arrogance, misplaced contentment, and total reliance on his wife, Barbara still had some feeling for the silly old devil, and she knew that he felt the same. When the chips were down, Kenny didn't flinch. He always stood by her side, through thick and thin, and that counted for a lot. When she accidentally had too much to drink or made a social faux pas, he defended her honour with a loyalty that touched her.

She studied him now and sighed as he flicked the nail file to the floor, closed his eyes, and fiddled with the waistband of an appalling pair of underpants that he refused to part with. His toupee was lopsided and in need of a good comb, and his once proud body that had given in to good living, appeared flabby and mottled in the bright cabin lights.

'Time to find your trousers, dear,' Barbara said gently, 'and we should dress to impress.'

Turning back to the mirror, she adjusted her sequinned top and eased on her diamonds. She leaned in to study her face, adding a touch more blusher and highlighter to her cheeks. As she fluttered her eyelashes, she saw the determination in her eyes. Polished and poised, Barbara was perfect, as she reached for a jewelled headband and secured it in place.

Shuffling about behind her, Kenneth had begun to dress. 'Not the Union Jack!' she called out.

Kenneth muttered to himself then set about replacing the waistcoat, peering into the wardrobe to dig out a bright scarlet cummerbund.

Barbara reached up to straighten Kenneth's matching bow tie, and as her little fingers poked and tugged, she nodded. So often she'd coached him through multiple charity dinners, and many formal occasions, and today, Barbara prayed that he would behave and do her proud.

Taking his arm, Barbara turned to the mirror and smiled. 'Showtime, darling,' she said. 'The captain's Christmas table awaits!'

* * *

Joy closed her cabin door and decided to take a circuitous route as she made her way through the ship to the restaurant, soaking in the Christmas cheer. Twinkling lights guided her, and a faint medley of carols and festive songs played from performers strategically placed in cocktail bars and lounges. Crew members were jovial, with Santa hats and smiles, and passengers paused to take photos by glittering trees and snowy displays. Gripped in her hand, Joy held a carrier containing small gifts that she'd wrapped for her table companions, and when she reached the threshold of the Terrace Restaurant, she paused to smooth her dress and straighten her shoulders.

'Mrs Bradley,' the maître d' came forward. 'Happy Christmas! Allow me to escort you.'

As Joy entered the softly lit room, her steps slowed as she approached table twenty-eight. She blinked once, then again.

Leticia, looking beautiful in bright emerald-green, raised both hands and waved. At the same time, Henry, resplendent in his formal wear, stood up the moment he saw Joy. Jim, with Leticia's assistance, raised himself courteously and smiled his welcome.

To Joy's amazement, on either side of Henry sat Lady Eleanor and Margaret, who both grinned in greeting.

'But where are . . .' Joy began.

'Barbara and Kenneth?' Margaret called out. 'They've got their bums on plush seats and blagged a place at the captain's table,' she grinned. 'Lady Eleanor and I should be down there, but we've swapped places. Fait accompli!'

Margaret didn't mention that after Barbara had accosted her with spiteful gossip about Joy, she had been only too happy to put the dreadful little woman in her place, warning that if Barbara hoped to gain any favour with Lady Eleanor, she must first stop her malicious tongue or Margaret would see to it that any chance of a relationship with Lady Eleanor was derailed entirely.

All eyes peered over the upper tier to stare down at the elevated table in the centre of the room below, where a party of ten smartly dressed guests and senior crew circled the captain. As though sensing the stares, Barbara's bejewelled head shot up. Having switched place cards, she was seated next to the captain. She wriggled to get closer then, with a smug smile towards her former table companions, raised her glass and gave a wave.

Jhamille pulled out a chair for Joy, and Margaret's voice boomed out. 'Settle your rear in the saddle and we can get the party started.'

'Gorgeous gown,' Leticia whispered as Joy sat beside her. 'Gold is a perfect choice for Christmas Day.'

'I wondered if it was too much,' Joy confided, 'and almost took it back.'

'You can never have too much glam.' Leticia patted Joy's hand, then held up her finger to flash her new ring.

'Wow, that's stunning,' Joy said as she studied the beautiful ice diamond that gleamed against Leticia's dark skin. 'It looks fabulous on you.'

'Divine dress, my dear,' Lady Eleanor commented from Joy's left. Her smile was wide, and a bold red sweep of rouge lipstick clung to her teeth, undetected by her Ladyship, but impossible to miss.

'A toast!' Margaret announced. 'To Christmas at sea and glorious company!'

Glass clinked and laughter bubbled as Margaret told a horsey story about an over-keen Olympian who was so inebriated they'd mounted the wrong horse and performed an entire routine on a disqualified animal. 'He still scored higher than he did in Tokyo, such a shame he was banned,' she grinned.

Joy sipped her champagne and avoided Henry's glance. Catching his eye made her chest tighten, and in her heart, a tug-of-war pulled between longing and loyalty, between the past she'd shared with Tom and the unexpected attraction to someone new. The feeling was almost painful. Could it be right to let herself feel for another so soon after loss? But then she remembered Audrey, a constant presence in the background, and knew that there was no room for anything more. Joy bit on her lip. She must bury her feelings! Having made up her mind, she straightened her back and, smiling at happy faces all around her, began to look forward to the meal.

Leticia distributed gifts, and everyone opened the neatly wrapped parcels. They oohed and aahed at the pretty Christmas baubles depicting a miniature *Emerald Dream* ship that could be hung on a tree.

Joy reached into her bag and produced her parcels too. 'Only a small keepsake,' she said, as she handed the gifts out, 'something to record memories of this cruise.'

'But this is lovely,' Lady Eleanor exclaimed as she opened a notebook, the cover an arty design of the route of their cruise as it sailed through the Arctic. 'I must show it to Lucinda; it might inspire an abstract piece of art.'

Joy remembered Lucinda's rusting herring tin installation and wondered what the eccentric artist might create.

Their meal commenced with lobster medallions served with citrus butter on microgreens, accompanied by a pink peppercorn drizzle. As they ate, Henry mentioned the talk he'd attended earlier. Jim was intrigued by Henry's explanation of the coronal aurora, which, he'd learned from Bill Zhang, is one of the rarest and most breathtaking types of auroral displays.

'It must be spectacular,' Henry said, 'and a dream come true for the one per cent of aurora chasers who are fortunate to have seen it.'

A porcini soup followed, and as everyone tucked in, Lady Eleanor was questioned on the cruises she'd enjoyed most.

'At this moment, my dears, it is this one.' She carefully tilted her plate in the old-fashioned way to scoop her soup from the opposite side of the bowl. 'Getting older teaches one to live in the moment. My Christmas gift is being given time, which I know is running out, so I value it more. Every minute I have is worth a hundred.'

'That's a lovely sentiment,' Leticia commented softly and reached for Jim's hand.

As their plates were cleared, Joy looked up. For a moment, she saw that Henry was staring at her.

'Being alive at my age is a privilege,' Lady Eleanor continued, 'you people mustn't waste a moment doing things that don't please. Embrace life with both hands and breathe it in.'

Joy digested the words and, as their eyes met, knew that Henry had too. His gaze lingered with kindness and warmth, and she longed to reach out across the table and wrap his fingers in hers. But Audrey, the wretched Audrey, sat like a ghost on her shoulder, and Joy tore her eyes away.

Before the main course arrived, they pulled their crackers with theatrical pops, then donned paper crowns and took turns to read aloud the silly jokes. From the menu, Joy chose the turkey ballotine, which was served with chestnut stuffing and cranberry-orange relish, while Leticia tucked into the seared Arctic salmon, and everyone else picked the Christmas tasting plate, featuring turkey, beef, and pheasant. The restaurant's sommelier hovered, and Lady Eleanor insisted that at her expense, he match each course with the finest wine.

Traditional Christmas pudding followed, dramatically flamed with brandy by Jhamille and Ryan, before the maître d' wheeled a trolley to the table, piled high with international cheeses. By the time coffee, liqueurs, petit fours, and hand-dipped truffles were served, the guests patted their stomachs and leaned back in their chairs.

'Good heavens,' Leticia sighed, 'I don't think I could possibly eat another morsel.'

'I'm certainly saddled with a few extra pounds.' Margaret unbuttoned the looped belt on her dress.

'It was a splendid meal and company,' Henry added.

'My dears, you have all made my Christmas Day very special,' Lady Eleanor said as she reached for her clutch bag, 'but now I shall leave you and retire for a nap before the crew show this evening.'

Jhamille and Ryan rushed forward to help Lady Eleanor from her seat, and the maître d' extended his arm to escort her from the restaurant.

'I might have forty winks myself,' Margaret said, 'I shan't be requiring a nosebag for the rest of the day.' Unsteadily rising and moving away, guests heard the cry of 'Tallyho!' as Margaret trotted through the tables and made her way out.

'Well, that just leaves the four of us,' Leticia grinned, 'and as Santa will be visiting the Lido Deck shortly, shall we all head up there?'

For a moment, Joy and Henry hesitated, their eyes meeting across the debris of the meal and half-drunk wine glasses. They could sense the other's uncertainty, and the weight of things unsaid. But Henry rose and offered his arm to Joy, and she took it.

Jim adjusted the controls of his chair, then straightened his paper crown. 'Lead the way, Leticia,' he was heard to say. 'Christmas Day is a time of goodwill, and it just gets better and better.'

* * *

On the captain's table, goodwill was thin on the ground and for Barbara, the day couldn't get any worse. It had begun with Kenneth mistaking Captain Lindholm for a steward as they were seated at the table and insisting that he fetch a wine list. Kenneth casually assumed that the man in the dress uniform was there to serve.

Barbara's cheeks burned, and she wondered if her husband was deliberately being thick-headed, as she heard the captain politely tell Kenneth that wine was already chosen and paired to each course. Kenneth, blissfully unaware of his blunder, flicked out his napkin and told the lady to his right that if the captain was on wine duty, he hoped he was better at pouring drinks than navigating the ship. 'It was a rough old ride the other night,' Kenneth laughed.

'Oh, my husband likes to tease.' Barbara gave a girlish

giggle. 'Always having a joke or two. Please pay no attention.'

But it was difficult for the guests to pay no attention when Kenneth, who'd once done a day's sailing course in Kefalonia, began to argue with the captain about their route. Taking a pen from his breast pocket, he reached for a linen napkin and drew a map.

'If you'd taken the fjord split earlier today, and missed the Seven Sisters, we'd have been forty minutes ahead.' Kenneth stared at his squiggles and nodded.

Barbara sank lower in her seat. Kenneth was too far away for her little legs to kick out at his shins, and with the captain's gaze fixed icily on her husband, she was beginning to wish that she could disappear back to table twenty-eight.

Beside her, Simon, smart in his uniform, sat with his head tilted to catch the discussion which had taken a sharp turn. His eyes flicked between the captain, who was drumming his fingers on the table, and Kenneth's oblivious grin. Turning to Barbara, Simon asked, 'And how are you enjoying yourself, so far?'

Barbara's eyes narrowed and she reached for her wine, but before she could retort, Simon intervened and turned to the guests to switch the conversation to the evening show.

'I do hope you all experience the entertainment tonight,' Simon said. 'Crew members have spent hours practising to provide a performance worthy of Christmas Day.'

To Barbara's relief, guests began to question the captain about his career at sea. As the main course progressed, they learned that he'd started his working life on cross-channel ferries and when the Diamond Star Cruise Line bought two new ships, he signed up and worked his way through the ranks. The gentlemen were interested to know that the *Emerald Dream* cruised at fifteen nautical miles per hour and could travel up to twenty-five and currently, was one of the fastest cruise ships in the world. A lady asked if he'd experienced anything unusual during his cruises, and the captain told a story about finding a man in a rowing boat, in the middle of the Atlantic, travelling from France to the Caribbean.

'I asked if he needed anything and he just wanted water, so we supplied forty litres, and he rowed away.'

When asked if anyone had ever jumped overboard, Kenneth chipped in. 'No one on a cruise full of oldies like this is capable of getting their leg over the railing,' he guffawed, 'think of the dislocations!'

Barbara sipped her drink and prayed that he wouldn't launch into another ridiculous joke. By the time desserts were served, Kenneth was pie-eyed and plastered, and knocked over a glass of red wine, which splashed across the captain's pristine white jacket.

'Sorry, old boy.' Kenneth dismissed the incident with a wave of his hand as stewards rushed to assist. 'Don't fuss,' he snapped.

Barbara wanted to crawl away and, tugging on Simon's sleeve, she whispered, *'Do something!'*

'A little too late, I fear,' Simon remarked, but he pushed back his chair and went towards Kenneth. 'Why don't we take a breather? Let's leave the ladies to enjoy the captain's company over Christmas pudding.'

Kenneth, tilting his empty glass, read Simon's comments as an invitation to the bar and, with a nod of his head, which loosened his toupee and almost sent it sliding into his neighbour's brandy sauce, he rose unsteadily. 'Drinks are on me!' he called out to the captain as Simon took his arm and led him away.

Barbara didn't flinch and was porcelain calm. She felt duty-bound to apologise for her husband's behaviour, but it was beyond Barbara to debase herself with apologies. She had the captain to herself and was going to seize the opportunity over dessert, cheese, and coffee.

'Don't mind Kenny,' she said. 'His blood pressure medication is strong and doesn't mix with spirits, but as it's Christmas, I'm sure you'll all forgive me that I allowed him a drop or two.' Barbara looked at the remaining guests and smiled sweetly. 'And now that the entertainment has taken an intermission, might I ask how everyone is enjoying the cruise?' She reached out and placed her diamond-decked fingers on the captain's sleeve. 'With our immensely capable captain at the helm, it's no wonder that this ship runs as smoothly as it does.'

Back on form, Barbara sailed through the rest of the meal.

She noted a flicker of appreciation in the captain's eyes and perhaps even a touch more than that, as he leaned in slightly whenever she spoke and nodded with a lingering smile. He was attentive now, asking follow-up questions to her comments and laughing warmly at her witticisms. Ever the tactician, Barbara responded with girlish giggles. Inwardly, she thought how gullible some men were. A little bit of flattery, a hint of cleavage and a flutter of one's eyelashes, and he'd be eating out of her hand.

She steered the conversation carefully, guiding it away from Kenneth's earlier chaos, and back towards the captain, keeping him in the spotlight. Convinced that he was charmed, Barbara was quietly delighted. Serene as a swan on the surface, Barbara paddled furiously, knowing that when everyone drifted away, she would return to her suite ready to face the storm that was brewing. Kenny had gone too far this time, and she was ready to kill him, not with fists or fury but with far more devastating means. Kenny might play the fool, but she wasn't joining in with the game and would make her blundering lump of a husband realise that she meant business.

When coffee was served, Barbara turned to the captain with a sugary smile, her fingers brushing his jacket again. 'Let me pass you a truffle,' she asked, 'or are you sweet enough?'

Chapter Twenty-Six

You better watch out . . . Santa Claus
is sailing into town . . .

The Lido Deck was buzzing with guests, full of their Christmas meal and plenty of cheer as they settled into seats around the swimming pool to await the arrival of Santa Claus. The domed ceiling above the pool was laced with colourful lanterns, a sharp contrast to the darkened sky outside. It was cool on the deck and many guests indulged, as stewards circled with trays, balancing steaming mugs of mulled wine and marshmallow-topped hot chocolate.

Henry found a table suitable to accommodate Jim and hastened to pull out chairs for Leticia and Joy before reaching for blankets from a neatly folded stack. As they settled the blankets around shoulders and knees to await Santa's arrival, Nora and Sid appeared and stood at the side of the pool. Suited and capped and ready for a swim, the couple held hands and plunged in.

'Are you joining us?' Sid called out as he turned on his back and floated by.

'It's lovely and warm,' Nora added. Her orange hair was tucked under an explosion of rubber flowers. As she swam, Henry was reminded of a tropical bird that had crash-landed on the water.

'I think I would sink like a stone after that meal,' Leticia replied and patted her tummy.

'It was rather good, wasn't it?' Henry agreed.

Jim began to discuss the merits of the meal and the company they'd enjoyed, and as he spoke, Henry's attention drifted. Surreptitiously, he watched Joy, taking in how lovely she looked in her glamorous gold gown. The shimmering fabric caught the light, complementing the rich chestnut waves of her hair. Despite her polite smile, Henry sensed that she was holding back when he'd chatted during the meal, and he wished that he could talk to her and break down the wall that had risen between them. He wondered what Audrey would tell him to do but knew that she would bark out instructions to act like a man, take the lead, and push forward.

Henry wasn't sure if he was ready for that. He wanted to push forward but was worried about trying too hard and couldn't risk the fragile connection they'd made. For now, as they sat waiting for Santa, he knew that he would have to find the right moment and hope that Joy's wall might eventually tumble down.

Before it was too late, and the cruise ended.

Stirred from his thoughts, Henry turned as Simon appeared and stood beside Jim. After escorting Kenneth to his suite to sleep off his excesses, Simon had changed into his festive outfit again, and greeting the guests, commented, 'I thought it was only children who got excited about Santa. You all look as though you've just spotted him surging through the sky.'

'It's the magic of Christmas,' Leticia replied, 'you're never too old to act like a child.'

Before Simon could reply, music sounded, and all eyes turned to look to the side of the pool, where several crew members, dressed as elves, began to appear, singing 'Santa Claus is Coming to Town!'

A sleigh, carried by four fluffy reindeer, burst across the Lido Deck and resplendent in a long red cloak fur-trimmed to match his hat, Santa sat astride a huge sack, jingling a large brass bell.

'Ho ho ho!' he called out as the reindeer staggered under the weight of the sleigh, their antlers akimbo and tangled in a string of fairy lights.

'The reindeer remind me of bears,' Henry commented, his head thoughtfully on one side as he studied them.

'Wardrobe had to improvise with *Jungle Book* costumes,' Simon hastily explained.

'Santa looks extremely fit,' Leticia added and noted the slim lines of his coat that moulded to his body.

Santa made several laps around the pool, and the elves encouraged guests to join in with the Christmas songs before the reindeer, knees buckling with exhaustion, brought the sleigh to a stop by the bar.

'Who wants to see what's in my sack?' Santa called out.

Guests gasped, but many moved forward, as, without warning, Santa leaped onto the bar and, in one grand sweeping motion, ripped off his cloak and threw it theatrically to the floor.

Simon closed his eyes. Already, he was calculating the number of complaints that would land on his desk before showtime.

Kyle, wearing nothing more than red sequinned budgie-smugglers and scarlet Converse trainers trimmed with white fur, adjusted his beard and straightened his hat before reaching into his sack to retrieve parcels that he hurled into the crowd with the gusto of a man launching T-shirts at a pop concert.

'Who's been good all year?' Kyle called out as Sid leaped from the pool, soaking two silver-haired sisters, and reached up to catch a gift.

'Watch your lumbago!' Nora yelled as she too scrambled from the deep end, determined to snag a gift of her own.

As Wham! sang out 'Last Christmas', Simon wondered if it was a sign. If he didn't do something to stop the mayhem, there was little doubt that this Christmas at sea would be *his* last.

Pressing hastily forward, he made his way through the crowd.

'Here comes the ring master!' Sid called out.

'Time for Santa to get back in his sleigh,' Simon said and indicated to an elf to recover the cloak. Dodging several soggy seniors and an inflatable snowman, he clapped his hands together to spur the reindeer into life. 'Santa has a lot more visits to make,' he said.

Kyle had one hand on his hip and distributed candy canes, and as he lifted his beard, he flashed Simon a dazzling smile. 'Just spreading a little Christmas cheer, babes,' he called down.

'You've gone too far,' Simon hissed. 'If the captain hears about this, we'll both be working at Butlins next year.'

Kyle pulled a face, and as Sid helped him down from the bar, Nora offered Simon a swig of her hip flask. He reluctantly declined.

The music had swelled, and with the reindeer recovered, Kyle wrapped himself in his cloak and, to a round of applause, disappeared from the deck.

Back at Henry's table, Simon was hoping to see that things had calmed down, but his eyes soon widened when he saw that Henry, encouraged by Jim, had taken hold of Leticia and Joy's hands and, together with the elves, joined Sid and Nora, who were leading a conga line around the jacuzzis.

Turning to Jim, Simon sighed.

'If you can't beat them, why not join them?' Jim asked. 'I would if I could,' he added with a grin.

Glancing again at the riotous group, Simon shrugged. 'Oh, why not?' he said. 'To hell with it.' And casting off his doubts, Simon stepped forward to grab hold of Nora and surrender himself to the fun.

* * *

By the time the meal ended, with Kenneth dispatched from the table and the captain suitably charmed, Barbara's blood pressure had settled, and she was feeling pleasantly serene. The captain's invited guests had begun to disperse when one lady, whose rope of emeralds were as large as olives, caught Barbara's arm.

'Do you think Kenneth might be in the early stages of cognitive decline?' she asked quietly. 'My own husband became quite aggressive when that awful illness took hold. Perhaps it's worth looking into?'

Barbara fought an urge to laugh the comment away. The only cognitive decline in Kenneth was when he'd forgotten where he'd hidden his brandy. But she managed a gracious smile and thanked the woman for her concern, with as much feeling as she could falsely muster.

With the guests moving away, Barbara seized the opportunity to hold back and catch the captain on his own. 'Captain,' she said, 'I must thank you for your company.'

Captain Lindholm smiled politely. 'The pleasure was mine. You brought a welcome calm to the conversation.'

Barbara let that hang for a beat, before fluttering her eyes, her expression coy. 'Kenneth and I, we've been married a long time and as you can see, he's becoming . . . *difficult*.' She moved a little closer and lowered her voice. 'I'm not used to unburdening myself to a handsome captain who has his hand firmly on the rudder.'

Captain Lindholm looked nervous and frowned.

'But, if I am to be perfectly frank, a woman can find herself very alone in a *difficult* relationship and when on the open sea, she might wonder what it would feel like to indulge in a little *diversion*.'

The captain's eyes widened, but before he had time to reply, a steward politely informed him that he was wanted on the Bridge.

Moments later, Barbara slipped her keycard into the lock of her suite, a smug smile played on her lips. The seed was sown, and she felt certain an invitation to the captain's quarters would find its way to her before the cruise was through. All it needed was the right nudge, and after all, it had happened before.

Tossing her bag on a sofa, Barbara unclipped her diamonds and thought fondly of sultry Caribbean moments aboard a similar ship, wrapped in the arms of a handsome Jamaican first officer, while Kenny, full of rum punch, dozed contentedly on a sundeck.

'Babs! Is that you?'

Barbara rolled her eyes. She'd been hoping to find her husband asleep and out for the count for the rest of the day.

'Babs, darling, there you are . . .'

Kenneth stood in the bedroom doorway. Stripped of his formal wear, he now sported a monogrammed dressing gown, the belt loose and doing little to conceal the soft fold of stomach that sagged over the waistband of the atrocious underpants Barbara detested.

Barbara glared, her eyes icy.

'I'm not going to be speaking to you for some time,' she began crisply, 'so listen carefully.' Barbara crossed her arms. 'You made a complete ass of yourself over the meal and embarrassed me *terribly*. I don't want anything to do with you for the rest of the day. Your behaviour is inexcusable.'

'I suppose a bonk is out of the question?' Kenneth leered, and his fingers trailed suggestively.

The ice bucket, when it landed, caught Kenneth off-guard and before he had time to duck, the heavy object caught his forehead, sending his toupee flying.

'I say!' he yelled, holding his head, 'that's a bit rich . . .'

But Kenneth, seeing stars, staggered back to the bed.

Barbara reached down and with the tip of her fingers, pinched the offensive toupee. She walked to the balcony and calmly slid back the glass door, and with a swift flick of her wrist, hurled the object into the night. It caught the wind, sailed over the railing and somersaulted once before vanishing into the black swell below. Without pausing to consider her actions, Barbara turned on her heel and marched to the bathroom and seized toupee-two. Her face curled into a vicious sneer as the second toupee arced into the air and joined its fallen twin in the churning sea.

'That will teach you,' she muttered.

* * *

Simon was back in his office, seated at his desk, where Penny had kindly placed a cafetiére of coffee beside him and now poured a hot, steaming mug.

'Thought you could do with this,' she said, 'there are a few things to deal with before you head off to host the crew show.'

Simon sighed. He was exhausted from his exertions in the conga line. The line, led by Sid, had snaked away from the Lido Deck through the hushed elegance of the Observatory Bar, where guests from the higher-priced suites were quietly enjoying their complimentary Yule Mule cocktails, nestled in leather armchairs beneath twinkling fairy lights.

They hadn't taken kindly to being interrupted by a

sweaty conga line. Deciding to make a sharp exit, Simon had untangled himself from Nora's grip and hurried past frozen expressions of disbelief as Sid, still in his Speedos, chanted 'Loosen up, it's Christmas!' and twirled a string of tinsel like a lasso over several dipped heads.

'Unfortunately, we've received one or two complaints...' Penny let the words hang as she unloaded a thick wad of paper on Simon's desk.

As Simon read a note from Patrick and Celia from Godalming, he wondered if the cruise was unravelling. This wasn't in the brochure, and we were appalled by Santa's nudity on the day our Lord was born...

Another was marked, 'Formal Complaint' by Muriel and Derek from Cheltenham. My husband and I are deeply disturbed to see Santa gyrating in a manner unbecoming of the season... Margaret added that this sort of behaviour could only lead to moral collapse and wasn't something they thought would be included in their upgrade.

An indignant woman occupying a Dream Suite complained that she hadn't paid thousands of pounds to see a man's nipples and partially clad nether region bouncing about on a bar while she was having a hot chocolate.

'Are there many more like this?' Simon looked up at Penny.

''Fraid so, but there's good news too.' She held out another sheet of paper.

Simon held his breath and read on.

Finally, some Christmas spirit! Kyle had us crying with laughter. More, please! Cabin 2310, Beryl & Mandy (Book Club).

'Then there's this one . . .' Penny ploughed on.

Best Christmas ever! Haven't laughed so hard since Judy leaped on a table thinking there was a rat in the pool. Jack & Judy, the Deck Mile Club.

'Well, that balances things out a bit,' Simon said, and wondered how soon he should be handing out complimentary bottles of champagne to the complainers.

'You need to get ready,' Penny said and pointed to the clock on the office wall. 'The stage manager says one of the engine room dancers has twisted his ankle and he isn't sure if the Backroom Boys routine can go on.'

'Hell! Well, I'm not standing in for him.' Simon cursed and imagined himself in a tight boiler suit split to the waist as he fumbled the steps to the Village People's 'YMCA'. He tried to remember the lyrics and vowed that this young man wasn't 'going to feel down' and wouldn't be 'picking himself up from the ground'.

As Penny reached the door, she turned. 'Oh, and there is a message from the captain saying that if you ever put him beside Barbara Montgomery Jones again, he'll make sure you end up scrubbing the decks until the cruise is over . . .'

Chapter Twenty-Seven

*When the curtains rise at Christmas, let
the crew entertain you!*

'Ladies and gentlemen, welcome to this very special evening. Our very own crew Christmas show!' Simon stood on the stage in the Triton Theatre and addressed the packed house.

In a circular box to one side, Lady Eleanor sat with her invited guests: Margaret, Lucinda, Henry, Joy, Leticia, and Jim. 'Shouldn't he be gender neutral when greeting us?' Lady Eleanor asked loudly. She looked around then returned her attention to the stage.

'The crew members that you see tonight have been rehearsing relentlessly to put this show together for you,' Simon continued, 'and along with Captain Lindholm and all the team, we ask you to sit back, relax and let the magic of Christmas come alive right here, on the *Emerald Dream* stage!'

Joy, sitting beside Leticia, found her eyes wandering to a couple in the front row. She couldn't be sure but had an inkling that she recognised the man with a large sticking plaster on his forehead, almost covering his bald head.

She gave Leticia a gentle nudge and whispered, 'Is that Kenneth?'

Leticia, whose view was partially obscured, followed Joy's gaze as the lights dimmed. 'Well, if the dazzling jewels on the woman next to him are anything to go by, that's definitely Barbara.'

'Do you think he's had an accident?' Joy was concerned.

But before Leticia had time to reply, the band struck up and the curtains parted to reveal the *Emerald Dream* dancers glide onto the stage as Miles Donavan burst into song. Feathers and sequins caught the light as Miles rocked to 'Holly Jolly Christmas'. When he gave his rendition of the Hawaiian Christmas song, 'Mele Kalikimaka', a team of ladies from the kitchens, hula'd across the stage. As they performed the ancient dance, barefoot and wearing grass skirts, they carried leis that they gracefully threw into the audience.

Next came enchanting Thai dancers.

The restaurant staff wore glittering silk costumes of golds and reds with flame-like headdresses. As they moved, every flick of the wrist or dip of the shoulder carried a mystical story of a dance as old as time. The audience sat in a reverent hush as they followed the slow, hypnotic steps, the bells at the dancer's ankles chiming softly.

'Simply marvellous!' Margaret called out and, holding her fingers to her lips, blew a whistle so loud it woke Lucinda, who'd been snoring in the seat beside her.

The dancers pressed their hands together and bowed their heads, eyes smiling as they left the stage to enthusiastic applause.

'Esteemed guests!' Simon said into his microphone as he

returned to the stage. The steward waiting on Lady Eleanor's party had given him a tip-off, and Simon was determined to be more inclusive. 'Friends and fellow travellers,' he continued with a nod to the occupants of the circular box. 'It gives me such pleasure to introduce our next act. Will you please give a big *Emerald Dream* welcome to the crew from the engine room . . . The Backroom Boys!'

The lights went out, and a moment of suspense rippled through the audience.

Then, suddenly . . . BOOM! A driving beat kicked in from the band. Under bright spotlights, dancing down the aisles to the stage, ten smiling men in high-vis overalls and steel-toe boots held their hands aloft, clapping to the rhythm as 'Macho Man' by the Village People began. The audience watched with delight as the engine room boys, hips swinging and hard hats held high, launched into their routine.

When the music changed to 'YMCA', several guests were on their feet, shaping their arms into the letters of the song. One of the dancers, supported on a crutch with a heavily bandaged ankle, stepped forward to shrug off the top of his overalls and, bare-chested, began to shimmy in a routine that would make a Vegas showgirl proud.

At the side of the stage, Simon surveyed through half-lidded eyes, vowing that he should have vetted the performance. As he scanned the audience, which included several elderly guests enthusiastically attempting to mimic the moves, he sighed. It was only a matter of time before the medical team earned their wages.

* * *

Henry was enjoying himself. He'd had a wonderful day, with a first-class Christmas meal and company that had been delightful. To his surprise, even the conga on the Lido Deck had been absurdly good fun, and, other than Audrey's Mulled Wine & Misfits party, he couldn't remember the last time he'd let his hair down so much.

As he sat through the crew Christmas show, he was enthralled. Those wonderful staff members who worked tirelessly throughout the ship had given up their time to rehearse their acts for the guests, and the result was unexpectedly magical. There was happiness in every step, laughter in every misstep and a sincerity that no professional company could match, and Henry clapped as hard as he could. When Simon announced that they were in for a treat, the Triton Theatre fell into an expectant hush.

The stage was dark, and a rustle could be heard. When a single spotlight came on, Jennifer stepped up to the microphone, her trembling hands clasped together. Dressed simply in a traditional soft green gown, her eyes darted nervously, and she gave a nod, then opened her mouth and began to sing.

When her voice emerged, it was clear and achingly beautiful.

Henry was spell-bound. His housekeeper, whom he knew for her kindness and warm smile, was singing in soft lilting tones that carried across the theatre like a lullaby on the wind. He stared at the little woman as she made a rocking motion with her arms as though soothing a baby to sleep. Singing at first in Tagalog, her native language, she gently shifted into English and told a story of a mother whispering dreams to her child of a better life and holding onto hopes from oceans away. Tears sprang to his eyes as he remembered the card that she'd made for him, and he thought of every spare cent she earned, that she must send home to enable her children to eat and attend school.

Jennifer's voice held everyone captive. When she sang of lighting a candle for her children, in the final verse, there wasn't a dry eye.

Henry, with a lump in his throat, fumbled for a handkerchief, and when the last note faded, there was silence. Guests were in awe of what had been witnessed. Jennifer bowed low, and an ovation broke like a tidal wave, with applause that brought the house down.

Henry dabbed at his eyes, and as he watched Jennifer step off the stage, he realised that this unassuming little woman had reached into the hearts of strangers and reminded them, despite all their indulgences and privilege, of something so deeply real.

* * *

Joy was on her feet beside Leticia when the Backroom Boys finished their act. They both beamed as they applauded the entertaining engineers, and as Leticia sat down, she tapped Joy's arm. 'Yes, I think you're right, it *is* Kenneth in the front row, and he seems to have hurt his forehead, but why he's wearing a lei on top of his head is anyone's guess.'

When a woman stepped onto the stage and began a heartfelt Filipino lament, Joy realised that it was Jennifer, Henry's housekeeper. She turned her head to catch his eye. Henry was sitting three seats away beside Lucinda, whose head had dropped onto her chest, the slow rise of her shoulders suggesting she was sound asleep. But as Joy watched Henry, she saw tears glistening on his cheeks. He was crying and completely caught up in the beauty of Jennifer's song.

Joy blinked. Soft, warm, kind Henry was dabbing at his cheeks with a handkerchief, his expression unguarded. The tenderness in his expression touched something in Joy. She knew that there was more behind his gentle steadiness, and had she not seen him let down his hair today during the conga on the Lido Deck? Even she had gone along with the fun. But seeing him quietly weeping in a darkened theatre, filled her again with an aching fondness, and she longed, once more, to reach out and take his hand. The man didn't hesitate to show such emotion, and Joy found herself blinking back tears of her own.

Joy turned back to the show, but she didn't see Simon return to the stage, nor hear him introduce the final act. For too long, she'd let her own hesitation dominate her life, tiptoeing around others and doubting her future. But here, today, on Christmas Day, as the cast returned, alongside the captain and his officers for the finale, Joy decided that the time had come to talk to Leticia.

Tomorrow she would confide.

Joy wasn't sure where to start or even what to say, but she was suddenly certain of one thing. It was time to stop waiting for the rest of her life to truly begin.

Chapter Twenty-Eight

We were strangers at sea, until your secret reached me . . .

'Good morning, everyone, today's port of call is Ålesund, which promises a captivating blend of history, nature, and adventure for those going ashore.' Simon's cheery voice rang out throughout the ship as guests rose and prepared for the day. 'There is a gentle breeze outside and the temperature is minus two but sunny, so do wrap up,' he advised. 'Boxing Day festivities will continue onboard for those not disembarking, but I know that many of you are keen to discover this gorgeous little town.'

Joy stood in her bathroom, staring into the mirror as she listened to Simon and scrubbed her teeth. When he signed off, Simon wished all guests, regardless of their background, identity, or belief, a joyous day, whatever their activity. She couldn't help but smile and wondered if a little bird had whispered Lady Eleanor's inclusivity suggestions to the cruise director.

Sitting down to brush her hair, Joy thought of the previous evening, after the crew show, when those guests who'd not retired to bed, dispersed for late-night drinks, a silent disco or the showing of Christmas movies. Bill Zhang had made a sudden announcement that there was a chance that the Northern Lights might soon be seen, and within moments, word spread like wildfire as many grabbed warm outer clothing and made their way to the top deck.

Joy lost her show companions after returning to her cabin for her coat and stood alone, her breath clouding the icy air as she looked up at the vast Arctic sky. All around, cameras clicked, and voices whispered excitedly as a faint green streak rippled above.

Like a delicate brushstroke of light, she remembered that it had glowed softly at first before gathering strength to twist and dance boldly across the sky. More streaks appeared, shimmering in pale greens tinged with violet and vibrant slashes of electric blue.

'It looks like smoke,' a man murmured, and Joy noted that he was wearing pyjamas beneath a fur-lined parka.

'Or a twist of silk . . .' a woman in a padded ski suit whispered, her breath catching the cold air.

Joy stood, captivated as she stared, and fascinated by the night sky coming alive. *So, this is the aurora borealis!* But as fast as the lights had appeared, they vanished, melting back into the night.

Now, as she sat in her cabin and readied herself for the day, Joy checked her phone and forwarded a couple of images to Susan. She doubted that her daughter would be interested in the Northern Lights, and she might be surprised to see her mother wearing a flattering gold coloured dress. But Susan would be recovering from the excesses of Christmas Day and was likely to be nursing a headache. She would barely glance at her phone other than to have her cleaner on speed dial, ready to triple the usual hours, the moment Hugh's family departed.

The phone on the desk rang, and Joy reached out. 'Hello?'

'Hello, sweetie, sorry we lost you last night, it was chaotic on deck, wasn't it?' Leticia's voice was like warm, syrupy honey.

'Yes, but weren't the lights wonderful?'

'I'll say, hope you took lots of photos, Jim is up to his ears editing a zillion of me photobombing and trying to get a look in while the lights took all his attention.' Leticia chuckled. 'But the reason I'm calling is that Jim wants to go to another talk by Bill Zhang, and Henry is going with him. I wondered if you'd like to have a wander around Ålesund with me instead?'

'Yes, please.'

'Shall we meet up after breakfast by the cruise terminal? It's only a short walk into town.'

'I'll see you there,' Joy said. 'Ålesund is known for its art nouveau buildings, and I've heard that it's like stepping into a pretty postcard.'

'Then let's go and find out,' Leticia replied.

Joy made a coffee and munched on a cereal bar, and as she dressed, she wondered where Henry had got to last night. She hoped that he'd managed to see the lights. Joy hadn't had a moment alone with him all day, but it hadn't diminished the pleasure of the company, especially when they let their hair down and did the conga around the ship. As Joy reached for her thermal vest and fleecy top, she remembered that Lady Eleanor had been a marvellous table guest. To their surprise, she told everyone that she'd decided to leave the ship at the end of the cruise and return to Ireland to throw a party on New Year's Eve.

'I want you all to come and won't take no for an answer.' Lady Eleanor was forceful, 'There is plenty of accommodation and you'll enjoy the Irish craic. I'll call my son and have it all arranged.'

Joy wondered what Susan would have to say about that.

To counteract Hugh's stuffy family Christmas, her daughter threw a Boxing Day party at home in Ladbroke Grove to a room full of their neighbours and overgroomed lawyer colleagues, most of whom charged by the millisecond and only ever smiled when they were serving a subpoena. Had Joy not set sail on the cruise, Susan would have expected Joy to be there, as usual, *to assist with the catering*. Susan's code for Joy to wait on them all, hand and foot.

As she styled her hair, Joy remembered that throughout the Christmas Day meal, Margaret had kept them entertained with tales of her travels and horsey escapades, delivered with the assurance of someone who'd once corrected the Queen on her bridle technique.

'In Helsinki,' Margaret announced over lunch, 'I was freezing my tits off in a paddock, when my stirrup leather snapped and I flew over my mare's neck like a champagne cork. Landed in a snowdrift beside a Finnish colonel, who thought I was an avalanche.'

Joy wondered how Margaret and Irish craic would blend at the New Year's Eve party and decided that it was a party she wouldn't miss. Being on the cruise, Joy was relieved not to be at Susan's Boxing Day party, her daughter could serve her own canapés and would be pouring her own drinks this year.

Fastening her coat and hitching her cross-body bag, Joy picked up her cabin card and made her way out of the ship.

* * *

In the Mermaid Theatre, Henry and Jim were waiting for Bill Zhang's talk to begin. It was a more intimate gathering than before, with only a scattering of guests dotted amongst the rows. Henry thought that many might be sleeping off the excesses of Christmas Day or heading out to Ålesund, something he fancied himself a little later.

As the lights dimmed and a screen flickered into life, Bill Zhang stepped onto the stage and launched into another fascinating lecture on the mystical wonder of the Northern Lights. To Henry's delight, Bill included Norse mythology, explaining that it was believed the lights were reflections of Valkyries' armour, before discussing Sámi beliefs and how those communities saw the lights as the souls of the dead.

'In Inuit folklore,' Jim commented later as they sat having coffee in the Bookmark Café, 'many indigenous people think sightings of the lights are tied to good fortune.'

'That's interesting,' Henry mused and bit into a shortbread.

'So, how are you enjoying the cruise?' Jim asked.

'It's been great, more enjoyable than I thought, to be perfectly honest. The onboard entertainment is excellent and has exceeded my expectations, and the excursions have been memorable.'

'You seem to be getting along well with Joy.'

Henry hesitated. Was now the time to talk about his feelings?

Jim sensed Henry's pause. 'Look,' he said, 'Leticia is the most perceptive woman I have ever met, and she's very impressed with Joy.'

'Yes,' Henry agreed, 'me too.'

'And she can tell that Joy likes you, even I can see that.' Jim finished his coffee and leaned in. 'Henry, if you feel something, don't overthink it, my friend. I know that my days are very limited, and if I could snatch more than the moments I might have left with Leticia, I would move heaven and earth to do so. I can promise you that life is too short,' Jim touched Henry's arm lightly, 'and so is this cruise.'

Henry looked at Jim and, for a moment, was filled with shame. The man who sat before him was living with a terminal illness yet spoke without bitterness and with such courage.

There was a pause between them, broken only by the hum of conversation from a book club meeting nearby.

'Is there someone else?' Jim asked, 'You often mention a woman named Audrey.'

'*Audrey?*' Henry appeared puzzled.

'Yes,' Jim folded his arms. 'You talk about sending her photos and remembering to tell her about the places and things that you've seen.'

Henry grinned and shook his head. 'Good heavens, I must have given the wrong impression.' He leaned back, still smiling. 'My dear fellow, Audrey is my neighbour, an eighty-three-year-old lesbian, with a wit sharp enough to cut glass and a heart of pure gold.'

Jim burst out laughing, throwing back his head with such force that several members of the book club turned to scowl.

'In fact,' Henry continued, undeterred, 'Audrey's constantly nagging me to find myself a good woman. But I'd rather accepted that all that sort of thing had passed me by.'

'Until recently.' Jim raised an eyebrow.

'Until recently.' Henry nodded.

'Good man.' Jim lifted his cup in a mock toast. 'Come out of your comfort zone, before it's too late.'

Henry smiled faintly and for a second, he thought Audrey was speaking through Jim.

'Why not ask Joy to have dinner with you tonight, away from our usual table, just the two of you?' Jim suggested. 'You've nothing to lose after all.'

'That is an excellent idea.' Henry nodded as though approving the suggestion. 'But there is another matter,' Henry pressed on, 'and it's a little delicate. I would appreciate your expertise and help.'

'You have my full attention,' Jim replied. 'I'm listening.'

* * *

Barbara had barely slept. She'd spent most of the night with a pillow clamped around her ears, trying in vain to block out Kenny's pacing and wailing, before finally succumbing and taking something to knock herself out. As a result, she'd overslept and was bleary-eyed when she went to guest services mid-morning to ask if there were any messages.

There weren't. *Rats!* She'd been hoping for a hint from the captain that he might be up for a little *diversion*, but she reasoned, the day was young.

Bundled in her furs and boots, Barbara decided to get some fresh air and clear her head by taking a walk around Ålesund. Anything to get away from her husband whom she was still refusing to speak to. Kenny, meanwhile, was beside himself with anguish. First the horror of discovering that his toupee was missing, then the devastation of finding out that it had been hurled into the sea along with his backup, toupee-two.

'You should have realised that your little stunt at the captain's table would have consequences,' Barbara had snapped, reluctantly breaking her vow of silence when Kenny threatened to fling himself into the sea after his hairpieces. 'Now man up and sort yourself out.'

To add to her embarrassment, as though making a point, the previous evening he'd pasted the biggest sticking plaster he could find over a measly bump on his forehead and when a Hawaiian dancer threw a lei into the audience, Kenny insisted on fashioning it in a ridiculous covering over his bald head.

'He really is the limit!' Barbara huffed as she thrust her hands into her pockets, kicking at the snow, and made her way through the charming streets of the art nouveau town. 'Well Kenny, can entertain himself,' she mumbled and imagined her husband prostrate on their bed all day. 'I'm going to have a little *me-time*.'

Boxing Day in Ålesund was calm and with many shops and businesses closed, the streets were quiet except for a few locals. One or two touristy shops were open to entice cruise passengers but as church bells chimed in the distance, Barbara was oblivious. She'd heard that a former chemist shop would be open, serving coffee and cakes. Having hardly eaten a morsel at dinner as she sat beside the captain, she would treat herself to the largest slice of cake she could find.

Glancing at her watch, Barbara reckoned she had at least two hours to spare. She'd booked an anti-ageing facial in the ship's Atlantis Spa that afternoon and fully intended to relax and pamper herself. Noting that she was near the waterfront, she stood and looked around. Within seconds she'd located the building described by guest services. With its graceful curves and intricate stonework, carved swan motifs stood proudly above the door.

'Perfect!' Barbara murmured, and placing each fur-clad foot deliberately on the path, made her way inside.

* * *

Joy's cheeks were pink, and her fingers cold as she held a guidebook and stood with Leticia at the summit of the Fjellstua Viewpoint. Having tackled the four hundred and eighteen steps to reach the top, they were rewarded with a panoramic view of Ålesund's islands and fjords, scattered like a necklace on the dark, glassy water.

'Wow,' Leticia exclaimed, puffing out a breath, and enjoying the few hours of daylight that the journey now allowed. 'It was worth every single step to witness this.' She raised her phone and began to take photos. 'I must send these to Jim.'

'A terrible fire in 1904 destroyed the town, and twelve thousand people lost their homes,' Joy read from the book. 'Apparently Kaiser Wilhelm II sent the first recovery ship with supplies and followed this with humanitarian aid, including materials and money.'

'Good old Kaiser Bill, but how did the fire start?'

'It started in the herring factory, although no one seems to know how.'

'Hmm, lots of fishy products and oil might have sparked it.'

'It says here that there was a gale-force storm which whipped flames across the rooftops and into the wooden buildings, and at that time all the town's buildings were made of wood.'

'How devastating.' Leticia drew in her breath as she stared at the buildings spread out below.

Joy read on. 'The fire brigade couldn't manoeuvre through the narrow streets, and it soon got out of control.'

'Many people must have lost their lives.' Leticia shook her head.

'Well, despite everyone losing their homes, only one person died.'

'But that's a miracle.'

'Absolutely,' Joy agreed and placed her book in her bag. 'But as you can see, it was rebuilt in stone and plaster, which gives the art nouveau feel to all the buildings.'

'Shall we head down and have a look at some of them?' Leticia tightened the scarf at her neck and tugged on her bobble hat.

'And perhaps find somewhere for a coffee.'

As they'd made their way up the steps, Leticia had spoken

quietly about Jim's illness, how the couple coped and how they had prepared themselves for what was to come. As they descended, Joy asked Leticia how the couple had met and when Leticia explained how she'd nursed Jim's sick child, Joy paused and reached out to touch Leticia's arm.

'Grace died?' Joy was shocked.

Leticia nodded, her expression softening. 'Yes. Her mother died during childbirth, and Grace . . . well, she never really recovered. There were complications. The doctors tried everything, including surgery and round-the-clock care. Still, it was too much for her tiny body.' She tucked Joy's arm through her own and began to walk again. 'I was a surgical nurse on the NICU, the neonatal intensive care unit.'

'Leticia, how on earth did you cope?' Joy's voice was hushed.

'I coped because in a job like that you have to,' she said with a small, knowing smile. 'You're trained to hold yourself together. And maybe . . . maybe because I was never blessed with children of my own in my first, very difficult marriage. Caring for them, those fragile little lives, became my blessing from God.'

'And Jim?'

'Oh, my goodness, he was a mess.' Leticia shook her head at the memory. 'That clever, capable man had lost his wife and child, his world and his faith, and I'm afraid he fell apart.'

'But you helped him?' Joy asked gently.

'Yes,' Leticia said, pausing. 'And he helped me. Learning to love again wasn't easy for either of us, but when it came,

,it grew into something we couldn't stop. Despite all the grief and loss, we found our path to happiness once more.'

Joy nodded, falling into step beside Leticia. 'But learning about Jim's illness must have been shocking.'

Leticia gazed out over the water, where the sunlight caught the clouds and reflected them onto the surface like a perfect mirror beneath a brilliant blue sky. 'The Beast takes no prisoners,' she said quietly. 'I often wondered if the pain of his loss trigged his symptoms and they lay dormant. I know doctors who say stress of such a tragedy, can eventually, many years later, trigger the terrible disease.'

'I've heard that can happen.'

'But my clever man kept his business going, and when we learned of what he was facing with the diagnosis, he sold it for a considerable sum. We made a promise to each other that we'd make the most of the time we had left.'

Leticia gave her slow smile and thought of the large amount that Jim had anonymously donated to the hospital where Grace and his wife had died, in the hope that future research would help families and no parent or child would be lost in the way they had been.

They'd reached the foot of the steps and walked briskly through the prettily painted storybook buildings and into the town. 'Oh, look,' Joy said and pointed to a stone building 'That must be the old chemist shop. According to the guidebook the carved swan motifs above the door are a symbol of healing.'

'And now it's a museum and coffee shop.' Leticia grinned. 'Let's hope they have lots of cake!'

Chapter Twenty-Nine

Sailing through the fjords as they whisper
their timeless secrets . . .

Joy and Leticia found a cosy corner table in the café of the chemist shop museum and ordered coffee and cake. On their way in they'd admired the apothecary's polished wooden cabinets lined with glass jars and antique bottles from a bygone era. A huge brass scale stood on a counter alongside souvenirs of art nouveau tiles, fridge magnets, notebooks, and coloured prints of the town.

'I can almost smell ancient herbal remedies and tinctures,' Leticia said as she stirred her latte. 'It seems to seep from the oak panelling.'

'This was the first house to be rebuilt after the fire,' Joy said. She took an enamelled handled fork and sectioned a fat slice of a fluffy meringue cake, topped with almonds. Rich vanilla custard oozed from the filling. 'The chemist rented out the second floor and was the wealthiest man in the town. I believe there's a large safe where he secured his money, somewhere in the building.'

As they settled in, a man suddenly darted across the room and vanished around the corner where more tables were situated. His trapper hat was pulled low, almost covering his eyes, and he didn't notice the two women.

'Wasn't that Kenneth?' Joy whispered.

They both froze as voices floated in from the adjacent room, the conversation clear despite the distance.

'Babs, old bean! I knew I'd find you in here, your sweet tooth always gets the better of you and this is the only place open.'

'Go. Away. Kenny.'

'I thought you weren't speaking to me?'

'I'm not.' Barbara's voice sound muffled, as though a piece of cake had wedged in her mouth.

'Well, I'm here to tell you that despite your vicious cruelty, I fixed my unpleasant problem that you created. You needn't think that it will ruin the rest of my cruise.'

'Bully. For. You.'

'Hah! Got you! You can't help yourself.'

'Sod. Off.'

'There's no need to be like that . . .'

There was a crashing sound as though a chair was being thrown across the floor and a moment later, Kenneth reappeared and dashed from the café.

'What do you think his unpleasant problem is?' Joy asked, trying to keep a straight face. 'Do you think they might sell something in here to help him?'

'I'm not sure if they stock Viagra or hair restorer.' Leticia grinned.

'Look out, Barbara's coming . . .' Joy sat up and brushed crumbs from her lips.

Shaking out her hat, Barbara turned when Leticia called out a greeting. She quickly tucked the fur over her flattened hair and forced a smile. Her sour expression indicated that she was far from pleased to see the schoolteacher, but Margaret's threat of ruining any hope Barbara had of cultivating Lady Eleanor's favour had reined in her campaign to discredit Joy.

'Hello, you two, I see you're carb-loading again after your indulgences yesterday.' Barbara nodded towards the cake-laden plates.

'Just like you.' Leticia smiled sweetly, pointing to a piece of meringue clinging to the fur at Barbara's bosom.

'How was the captain's table?' Joy asked.

'Marvellous.' Barbara pigeon-puffed her ample chest and cooed, 'Captain Lindholm and I are such good friends and he's such a charming man. You saw I was seated right beside him?'

'Yes, just like Joy,' Leticia replied.

Barbara's eyes narrowed. 'Well, I mustn't keep you, you have a lot to get through before the ship sails,' she added staring at their cake.

'We're looking forward to having your company at our table tonight,' Leticia called out. 'Kenneth too!'

As Barbara glided away, Joy turned to Leticia. 'Are we *really*?'

'I suppose not, but I wanted to talk to you about that. I know a way that you can avoid it.'

'Do tell.'

'Have dinner with Henry.'

'Sorry?'

289

'Book a table for the two of you, why not try the French restaurant, it would be very romantic.'

'Romantic?'

Leticia set her fork down, her eyes steady on Joy. 'Joy, isn't it about time you stopped pretending that Henry is just an acquaintance and nothing more than a friend?'

'But . . .'

'No buts. I've seen the way you look at each other. Heavens, after everything we've discussed today how time is too short and we should live in the moment, like Jim and I, don't you think you should do the same?'

'Leticia . . .' Joy searched for the right words. 'But what about Audrey? Henry has a partner at home and although I'm sure he has feelings for me, I am not going to come between them.'

'Are you *sure* about that?'

'Yes, he talks about her often.'

'Then why hasn't she come on the cruise, especially at Christmas?'

'I've no idea, perhaps she's infirm.'

'Well, you'll never know if you don't ask him.'

'I suppose I could . . .'

'I suppose you *will*!' Leticia was adamant. 'Unless there's another reason why you hold back?' she asked softly.

Joy pushed her empty plate away. It was now or never. The taboo subject that she bottled up. Was it finally time to expose it and release the anxiety that had crippled Joy for years?

Leticia gently stroked Joy's hand. 'I'm going to order

another coffee,' she said, 'and when I come back, I want you to tell me all about it.'

* * *

'Everyone thought that Tom was wonderful,' Joy began. 'He had a way of lighting up a room and always knew what to say to make people feel special. You would have liked him,' she added, slowly stirring the coffee Leticia had placed before her.

'Go on,' Leticia encouraged.

'But behind closed doors . . .' Joy paused, 'Tom chipped away at me, bit by bit, until I was broken. If I'd gained a promotion, he'd say, "Don't let it go to your head, it's big enough. You only got it because there was no one else."'

She stared at Leticia with a weary sadness.

'Sometimes it was the little things that hurt more than most. I used to love painting with watercolours, and I remember a series of seaside scenes that I was proud of. One day, he came home from work and made a bonfire of them in the garden. He said they were too pathetic to display.'

'That's not a little thing,' Leticia said and squeezed Joy's hand.

'Or he would have a cruel look in his eyes and ask who I'd slept with to earn the promotion.' Joy laughed, but it was hollow. 'At first I thought he was joking . . .' She gripped a napkin and twisted it in her fingers. 'But then he got crueller. He never hit me where anyone could see.'

'Oh, my dear . . .'

'I never told anyone about his abuse. My parents were dead, and Susan adored him. Tom was her hero, and I didn't want to take that away from her.'

'What about your friends?'

'Tom made sure there were none. Other than work, he never let me out of his sight. I'd built a career, but he made me feel like I was worthless.'

'But you ran a team, mentored others, and even got an MBE?' Leticia's eyes were wide.

Joy gave a dismissive shrug. 'I felt inadequate beside him, as if any light that fell on me was somehow stolen from him. He made me feel as though the honour of the MBE didn't matter. Even for the ceremony, he wouldn't let me buy a new outfit and said my old navy dress would do. I felt like my achievement was an inconvenience to him.'

'Why didn't you leave him?'

'I led a double life at work and home. It's not easy when your partner controls all the money, and by the time I wanted to leave, he'd made me feel like I was lucky that he'd stayed with me.' Joy's voice cracked. 'And the worst part was that I started to believe him.'

Joy was silent and cradled her cup. She paused to sip her drink and, with a shaky smile, looked up at Leticia. 'When Tom died, people were kind, and his colleagues were sorry for my loss.'

'And you?'

'I . . . I wasn't sorry; I was glad and relieved. But then I felt guilty for feeling that way, crushed by it all because no one knew. No one was truly aware of the man I lived with; they only saw the public performing side of Tom.'

Leticia took a deep breath, and her grip on Joy's hand tightened. Exhaling slowly, she began to speak. 'Thank you for telling me,' she said gently. 'I knew something was troubling you from the first time I met you, but I had no idea what. I am truly sorry that you've had to go through all of this. And that you've gone through it alone.' Leticia paused and looked Joy in the eye. 'I wish there was someone that you'd felt safe enough to talk to,' she continued.

'B . . . but if Tom had found out . . .' Joy stuttered.

Leticia stroked Joy's hand. 'I understand, there would have been consequences.' She saw Joy nod. 'But *you* were never the problem. He dimmed your light because he couldn't handle how brightly you shined. He lied to you about your worth, and his fear surfaced by way of control.'

Leticia let the words settle.

'And your guilt? Well, that's playing tricks on you and shouldn't ever be a burden you carry. You didn't fail Tom. He failed you. In every single way that mattered.' Leticia's eyes were damp. 'I won't let you carry this weight any longer.' She smiled. 'Joy, my darling girl, you have survived. You've survived something that tried to erase you, and you're still here. Still beautiful Joy, still kind, still amazing and still truly wonderful and good.'

Joy pushed her chair back, and as Leticia stood and wrapped Joy in a hug, the two women rocked gently. 'Don't let the past spoil your future.' Leticia whispered.

After a few minutes she pulled away and held Joy at arm's length. 'Do you remember that I asked you if we could be cruise buddies?'

Joy nodded.

'You never answered me.'

Joy gave a soft, tearful laugh. 'Yes, of course, yes.' She wiped her cheek with her fingers and smiled. 'I just didn't know how much I needed one until now.'

Leticia's eyes were gentle. 'Good. Because, unlike that rotter you were married to, I'm not going anywhere,' she grinned.

Like bobbing boats on a silent sea, the two women nodded. And in that moment Joy knew that her new cruise buddy would be beside her for life.

Chapter Thirty

A dinner at sea, turns a meal into a memory . . .

The Arctic sun hung low in the sky, casting long dark shadows over the art nouveau buildings when Henry made his way back to the ship. His afternoon walk had been interesting, both peaceful and rewarding, especially his climb to the Fjellstua Viewpoint where he spent time taking in the sweeping panorama that included terrific views of the *Emerald Dream*, sitting stately in the harbour. The snowy peaks and glittering water were paradise for a photographer, and Henry knew that Audrey would be fascinated by the images. He hoped that in some small way she'd feel as though she'd been here too.

Making his way back to the ship, Henry breathed in the lingering scent of roasted almonds from a nearby stand as seagulls soared above, their cries an echo in the icy air. He was greeted in the embarkation area by a smiling steward handing out hot chocolate, which soon warmed Henry's chilled body.

Making his way, Henry stopped briefly at guest

services to ask an assistant to deliver a message. As he approached his cabin, he noticed Jennifer emerging, a feather duster in one hand, and her housekeeping trolley neatly arranged.

'Hello, Mr Henry,' she said, flashing a beaming smile. 'You had good day?'

'Yes, thank you, Jennifer, Ålesund is a lovely town.' He paused, hesitating before meeting her eyes. 'But I wanted to tell you that you were magical on the stage last night. I have never witnessed such a beautiful song, sung so poignantly and with such feeling. It was very moving.'

'Poig . . .?' Jennifer's brow furrowed. 'What is this?'

'Poignant,' he clarified, 'I mean to say that you were marvellous.'

A moment passed, then her eyes widened in delight. 'Oh, Mr Henry, you like me!'

Henry froze.

'I knew it,' she held her hands to her chest. 'I felt your eyes when I sang.'

'Oh . . . oh no,' Henry stammered and felt his face flush. 'I mean, yes, you are very talented . . .'

'You gentleman.' Coquettishly, Jennifer dipped her head and lowered her eyes.

Henry suddenly stepped back and banged into the wall, his eyes darting to his door. 'Yes, well, I must press on and let you finish your rounds,' he muttered with a strained smile, and fumbled for his keycard, thrusting it forward.

Side-stepping around the trolley, Henry sighed with relief as he almost fell into the room. But as the door began to close, he paused. Jennifer, the wheels of her trolley echoing as she pushed it away, was happily humming the song that she'd sung the night before.

'Oh, Lord, what a mess you made of that!' Henry told himself as he ripped off his Barbour and threw it on the bed. But as he placed his camera case down, he noticed an envelope propped up on the desk. Mr Henry Halliday. Pulling on the seal, Henry's fingers revealed a message on a guest services card.

It was from Joy. Asking if he'd like to join her for dinner and if so, perhaps he'd book a table in the French restaurant for eight o'clock?

Henry blinked at the message. Then blinked again.

He punched the air, then clutched the note to his chest. Doing a full spin and almost knocking over a reading lamp, Henry launched himself on Jennifer's perfectly made bed, scattering a heart-shaped towel that Jennifer had placed on his pillows.

'Wait,' Henry sat up. 'Focus and book the dinner reservation.'

As he flipped through his information booklet to find the number for the restaurant, Henry imagined white tablecloths and flickering candles. The phone clicked as the call connected.

'Bonjour,' he said, hoping to sound confident.

And in moments, Henry Halliday, retired history teacher from Skipton, proceeded to make the most important dinner reservation of his later life.

* * *

297

Joy sat in her cabin, smiling to herself as she read the message delivered by guest services. Henry had invited her to dinner, and their messages must have crossed. She held the card to her chest and imagined him finding her note and booking the table at that moment.

For the first time in years, Joy felt a fluttering nervousness. Not the tight anxiety of fear or dread, with the shadow of Tom lurking, ready to step in and burst her bubble, but a light feeling of happy anticipation. Something good might be happening! The only fly in the ointment was Audrey, but Leticia had made a fair point. If Henry and Audrey were in a serious relationship, surely, she would be on the ship with him, even with infirmities. Jim managed to travel with his wheelchair, despite the discomfort of his condition. When something mattered enough, one made it work.

Joy's attention was diverted when her mobile rang. It was Susan.

'Hello, dear,' Joy said, 'I thought you'd be enjoying your party.'

There was a pause, and when Susan spoke, her voice sounded slurred. 'Mother,' she groaned, 'it's a disaster, *a social apocalypse . . .*'

'Good heavens.' Joy straightened in her seat. 'What on earth has happened?'

'The lawyers are fighting.'

'Fighting?'

'Yes, over a bloody cheeseboard.'

'How did the cheeseboard get blood on it?'

'Nooo . . .' Susan sighed, and Joy imagined her daughter rolling her brilliant blue eyes.

'Over some nonsense about there being lashings of port in the stilton,' Susan ranted. 'I didn't know Hugh had been feeding it for weeks, and Carl from corporate law, who's been on the wagon for forty-two days and missed his AA meeting over Christmas, is accusing Hugh of deliberately getting him pissed.'

'Surely Hugh wouldn't do that.' Joy wondered how much impregnated Stilton Carl had consumed if he was plastered on port.

'God knows,' Susan snivelled. 'Sandra, Carl's wife, is sobbing in the downstairs loo and Millicent from number twelve is trying to coax her out.'

'Where are you?'

'In the ensuite,' Susan miserably replied.

'Perhaps you should stay there until it's all calmed down,' Joy advised.

'But the house is such a mess! There's Caerphilly all over the carpet and the Stinking Bishop has ruined my Christmas cloth.' Susan gave a half-hiccupped sob.

'I didn't know you'd invited a bishop?'

'Mother!' Susan yelled.

Joy stifled a laugh. Susan's call was merely to remind her mother that no one was cleaning up the cheesy mess. *Thank God I'm more than a thousand miles away!* Joy thought.

'And by the way, what the hell were you wearing on Christmas Day?' Susan's tone was sharp. 'Do you really think it is suitable for someone your age to look like they've fallen off the top of the tree?'

'You didn't like the gold dress?'

'Like? It was terrible, and goodness knows what Daddy would have said. You looked ridiculous, like mutton dressed as lamb.'

Joy felt her blood pressure rising.

'Well, "Daddy" isn't here to criticise my wardrobe, nor is he here to tell me not to have too much to drink and join a conga line around the ship.'

'What did you say? My m . . . mother in a conga line?'

Joy paused, letting the words settle before wondering whether to fire her final arrow. But having loosened her bow, the words poured out.

'Neither can he stop me having dinner with a very charming man named Henry, and if I have too much to drink again, I shall probably have mad, passionate, unrestrained sex with him all night too.'

'MOTHER!'

Joy heard a thud, as though Susan had collapsed on the floor.

'I must dash, dear, there's a peek-a-boo set of lingerie in the ship's boutique that I want to snap up before I get dressed for the evening.'

'M . . . MOTHER!'

'You'd best go and sort out Carl and the Stinking Bishop. Good luck, dear.'

Joy disconnected the call.

With a quiet giggle, Joy made her way to the bathroom. She knew she shouldn't have taunted Susan, but really, after years of bending to Susan's every whim, standing up for herself suddenly felt empowering. Of course, she had no intention of sleeping with Henry, nor of purchasing a peek-a-boo bra, and as she removed her watch, she noted the time. Two lovely, luxurious hours to herself. Now to get ready, Joy thought, reaching for a bottle of perfume and releasing the light floral fragrance all over her skin.

Dinner at eight with Henry . . . and Joy simply couldn't wait!

* * *

In her Dream Suite, Barbara was also preparing for dinner. Another lavish meal awaited in honour of Boxing Day but instead of dining at the captain's table, she and Kenneth would be back on table twenty-eight. Leaning into the magnifying mirror in the bathroom, Barbara examined her face with professional scrutiny. The age-defying facial had worked wonders. The seaweed-based products recommended by the spa-beautician had clearly done their job and her skin appeared firmer and positively radiant.

'I look at least five years younger,' she murmured, tilting her chin for effect.

Barbara was pleased that she'd indulged, and acting on the beautician's enthusiastic advice, had treated herself to a luxury beauty bag brimming with seaweed infused creams and serums that had cost an arm and a leg.

'No need for Kenny to know,' Barbara murmured as she began to apply makeup and thought about her outfit for the evening.

Wandering into their bedroom, Barbara halted in dismay at the sight of Kenneth sprawled across the bed, fast asleep, naked but for his baggy pants. With an exasperated sigh, she marched over and shook his foot.

'Wake up!' she barked. 'You need to get dressed for dinner and I'm absolutely gasping for a decent drink.'

A short while later, Barbara was ready. Dressed in a floor-length evening dress, strategically supported by her Spandex support shorts to keep her tummy in check, Barbara's diamonds caught the light with every movement and her freshly styled hair shone.

From the bathroom, she could hear the shower running and the occasional muffled grunt from Kenneth. *Thank God*, she thought, *at last he's making an effort*. She decided that if her husband kept his behaviour toned down, she would end her vow of silence and begin speaking to him again.

'Kenny!' she called out. 'I'm going ahead, I'll see you in the cocktail bar.'

'Lovely jubbly, Babs!' he replied. 'Line up a large one for me and I promise to be good.'

Without her husband peering over her shoulder, Barbara was secretly pleased to be heading out on her own and felt that there would be a message from the captain. Something discreet, possibly handwritten, waiting for her at guest services.

Lifting her chin, she made her way with the confidence of a woman who knew the power of cosmetic surgery, diamonds and perfectly applied lipstick. Whatever the evening ahead held, Barbara was ready for it.

* * *

Leticia and Jim were also ready for the evening. They were making their way to the restaurant for the Boxing Day meal. Knowing that Henry and Joy wouldn't be joining them, Leticia had called Lady Eleanor and Margaret to ask if they would like to dine with them again, feeling duty-bound to explain that Barbara and Kenneth would no doubt be at the table too.

Lady Eleanor's reply had been warm. 'Dear Leticia, you and Jim made such good company, and with Henry and Joy away, a little solidarity wouldn't go amiss. I'm sure we can buffer ourselves against Kenneth's anecdotes and survive to enjoy the evening.'

Margaret accepted in a flash. 'Don't worry, Leticia, I can always remind Kenneth that conversation is a two-way affair. Hope springs eternal!' she added.

With the four of them comfortably seated and Jhamille and Ryan attentively seeing to their needs, glasses of champagne were poured as they waited for Barbara and Kenneth's arrival.

'I've spoken to my son, and everything is arranged for a New Year's Eve party at the Dower House,' Lady Eleanor said, turning to Leticia and Jim. She had a warm smile for Jhamille as she accepted her glass. 'You'll have accommodation at the Dunmore Hall Boutique Hotel. It's part of our estate in County Kildare, and I truly can't wait to return home now. It will be a joy to have a celebration to look forward to.'

There was a noticeable change in Lady Eleanor that hadn't been there before. Gone was the weariness of someone passing away their time at sea. The idea of returning to the Dower House seemed to have stirred her as though her lethargy following Sir Richard's death was passing.

'Are you looking forward to going home?' Leticia asked.

Lady Eleanor's gaze rested on Leticia, 'It's time, my dear,' she said. 'I must face up to the fact that Richard won't be there. I need to create new memories in my home, and a party will be the perfect way to kick start them.' She raised her glass, 'Here's to stepping back into my own world.'

Heads turned as Barbara joined the party. 'Sorry I'm late,' she said. With no message for her from the captain, Barbara's expression was disgruntled. 'No Joy or Henry tonight?' she asked, and as she looked at the company, her face lit up. 'Lady Eleanor and Margaret . . .'

'Nope,' Margaret replied. 'The pair of them have gone AWOL, but we won't be gossiping about them,' she shot a warning glance at Barbara, 'so you'll just have to put up with us.'

'Oh, what a terrible shame.' Barbara, taking heed of Margaret's comment, could hardly disguise her delight as Jhamille flicked out her napkin. 'I mean that we won't have their company,' she added, clearly delighted by the replacement guests. A flush of satisfaction coloured her cheeks.

Margaret raised an eyebrow, and Lady Eleanor gave a gracious nod.

'No, Kenneth, tonight?' Jim asked.

'He had an important call and will be along presently,' Barbara lied, silently cursing her husband for not arriving on her arm. She took a sip of champagne and attempted to appear calm, but her kitten-heeled feet tapped anxiously beneath the table.

Leticia was extolling the delights of Ålesund and describing her earlier walk with Joy, and everyone's attention was diverted. No one noticed that Kenneth had ambled into the restaurant, one hand in his pocket, the other waving to guests as he passed.

When a sixth sense made Barbara look up, her glass almost slid through her fingers, and her jaw dropped.

The fool has completely lost his marbles and parted ways with his sanity . . . Barbara stared aghast at her husband.

Kenneth beamed as he sat down, wearing an unmistakable troll wig, clearly a gift shop purchase. It was perched on the top of his head. Despite his handiwork with Barbara's nail scissors, orangey-conker-coloured tufts stuck out at odd angles, and an uneven fringe wobbled as he moved.

'Good evening, everyone,' Kenneth said grandly, as though nothing were amiss.

As he sat next to Barbara, Lady Eleanor pressed a handkerchief to her lips, and Margaret coughed loudly into her napkin. Tactically looking away, Jim and Leticia studied a wine list.

Barbara didn't flinch. To her credit, she smiled at Kenneth with a haunted calm. 'There you are, darling,' she said sweetly, patting the seat beside her. 'You've made quite an entrance.'

Kenneth took his place and whispered, 'I think it gives me an air of Viking mystery.'

Too stunned to reply, Barbara looked away.

The meal continued, at times with a forced politeness as the dinner guests found it impossible not to steal a glance at Kenneth. Eventually, Margaret, reaching for the butter, leaned towards him. 'Is the hairstyle inspired by local folklore?' she asked.

'Ah, you noticed,' Kenneth said proudly. 'I had it styled in Ålesund,' he said as though the hair of the wig was his own. 'I told the stylist I wanted something with ancestral gravitas.'

'Well, you've certainly achieved *something*. Congratulations on your bravery. Last time I saw a head of hair like that it was on Fergus, my Shetland pony,' Margaret smiled, 'just after he caught it on an electric fence.'

By the time desserts arrived, Kenneth's wig had begun to droop to the left. Barbara, who'd calmed her anger with a bottle of Sauvignon, thought that he looked like a garden gnome caught in a gale. To make matters worse, her skin had begun to itch, and as she glanced anxiously in her compact mirror, she saw that bright red blotches were blooming across her face.

'Are you all right?' Leticia asked kindly.

'Perfectly,' Barbara said and snapped the compact closed. 'Just a touch of earlier sea breezes, which are very bracing on the pores.' She touched her skin, which felt as though it had been dipped in a deep-fat fryer.

Kenneth squinted and leaned in closer. 'I say, Babs, you look like you've been stung by a swarm of bees.'

Barbara stared at him. She must be allergic to the seaweed infused products that the beautician had used on her skin.

Her face burned. The wig. Her hypersensitive reaction. Together they were the complete irrevocable humiliation. She rose stiffly and pushed back her chair. 'I think I need a little bit of air,' she said, her voice tight, and without waiting for Kenneth to join her, walked somewhat unsteadily towards the exit.

'I've got some aloe vera lotion in my cabin,' Leticia offered, already folding her napkin. 'It might help soothe her skin.' She kissed the top of Jim's head and followed Barbara.

''Allo Vera?' Kenneth grinned brightly and looked around the table. 'Who's she?'

There was a moment of silence. Then, with a sigh, Margaret picked up her wine glass and muttered softly, 'Poor old Babs . . .'

Chapter Thirty-One

When the aurora kisses the sea, love
rises with the light . . .

Three hours into their departure from Ålesund, the *Emerald Dream* left Norway and the magnificent mountains, bathed in darkened skies, as the captain set sail through the North Sea on her homeward journey to Newcastle. Inside the French restaurant, the icy world outside felt far away as candles flickered, and the raw tones of Édith Piaf's 'La Vie en Rose' drifted from a speaker.

Henry sat on a red leather banquette in the corner, perfectly positioned with a clear view of the room's entrance. He fiddled with the edge of his shirt cuff, then adjusted his tie for the umpteenth time, and checked his watch. He'd arrived fifteen minutes early, wanting to be there first so Joy wouldn't have to walk in on her own. But every minute stretched unbearably as he patiently waited.

On the dot of eight o'clock, Joy entered the room wearing her gold-coloured dress, and as he stood to greet her, Henry caught his breath. The low hum of surrounding conversation and the soft chink of cutlery seemed to fade as she smiled and came towards him.

'Henry, you're here,' she said.

Her dress caught the light of the candles, casting a shimmer across the walls and he thought how lovely she looked, as Audrey's voice whispered in his ear. *Don't mess it up!*

They made themselves comfortable and decided on wine, and a server placed a little dish with tiny cheese puffs before them. 'These are delicious,' Joy said as she licked her fingers and pushed the plate towards Henry. 'Now, tell me, how was your day?'

As wine was poured, they both spoke of Ålesund and how much they'd enjoyed wandering around the pretty art nouveau town. Henry sipped from a demitasse cup, and as a velvety vichyssoise, drizzled with truffle oil, melted in his mouth, he summoned his courage.

'Joy,' he began, 'I'm so glad that you decided to join me tonight and what a coincidence that our messages crossed.' Tentatively, he smiled, and his fingers reached to touch hers. 'What I am trying to say is that I really enjoy your company and am so glad that I've met you, and I wondered, if . . . when the cruise ends . . . we might meet up?'

Joy moved her fingers away. 'Lady Eleanor has invited us both to Ireland for the New Year, and I am certainly going to go,' she replied.

'Yes, me too, but perhaps we could get together . . .' Henry trailed off, noticing that Joy's gaze was fixed on the tablecloth, and she didn't meet his eye.

'Henry,' she said suddenly, 'I need you to be completely honest with me.'

'But of course . . .' he replied, sitting up straighter.

'Please, just tell me what Audrey means to you. Are you in a relationship with her?' The words tumbled out.

'S . . . sorry, did you say *Audrey*?' Henry frowned, genuinely baffled.

'Yes, you talk about her all the time.' Joy's eyes finally met his.

Henry blinked, then let out a surprised laugh. 'That is the second time someone has asked me about Audrey today. Oh, Joy, Audrey is eighty-three, a retired art teacher, and my friend, a very dear woman who lives next door to me. Most importantly, she is a proud lesbian who sadly got financially ripped off by a lover and cannot afford to travel these days.' He took a breath. 'She is *extremely* opinionated, drinks a great deal of gin, and is a fascinating soul whom I feel sure you would adore.'

Henry felt Joy stare, her expression momentarily frozen. He thought that she was about to speak and held up his hand.

'To conclude, I take photos and make notes because she enjoys reliving my holidays.' He paused. 'Did you really think that I was dating my octogenarian neighbour, who thrashes me at chess, beats me at Scrabble, and invariably drinks me under the table?'

He saw Joy blush as she shook her head. 'I feel so silly,' she quietly whispered.

Henry reached out and took her hand in his, and this time she didn't pull away. 'Please don't', he said. 'Audry will be delighted to know that she's been mistaken for my lover, she'll dine out on that with her rainbow wrinklies for weeks.'

They stared at each other and both began to laugh.

Their meal was served, and as the candles glowed, any tension melted away like ice in a summer drink. For the first time since he'd met Joy and she'd quietly slipped into his heart, Henry felt everything ease into place.

* * *

Joy felt herself blush when it became painfully clear that Audrey was no more than a friend. Feeling foolish, she let Henry take her hand and his touch, his voice, and the easy kindness in his eyes melted away her uncertainties, and she realised that she'd like to meet Audrey and her rainbow wrinklies.

Their meal progressed from one delicious course to the next and as Joy tucked into a delicate king crab salad, laced with fennel, apple and lemon vinaigrette, she took a sip of chilled Chablis and let out a soft sigh. 'This is so good,' she murmured.

Henry offered his pan-seared halibut. 'Wait till you try this,' he said, gently sliding his plate towards her, and as Joy took a bite she smiled as the delicious champagne sauce, dotted with Arctic herbs, combined with the succulent fish.

They laughed at the other's jokes and listened to each other's stories and any tension between them finally gave way. Conversation flowed easily as they talked about the eclectic cast of passengers they'd met on board and how they hoped that Leticia and Jim would become good friends of theirs. Henry described the Deck Mile Club and how he'd managed to avoid Jack and Judy's insistence that he join them, while Joy remembered the Women's Institute meetings and how she'd struggled to stay awake.

'I wonder if Lucinda will be at the New Year's Eve party,' Henry mused and thought of the eccentric artist with mild dread.

'Oh, I think that's a given. Lady Eleanor is very taken with her and when she leaves the ship, it wouldn't surprise me if Lucinda did too.'

'I don't know if Ireland is ready for Lucinda.' Henry frowned. 'She told me that my aura was beige.'

'Well, she is rather colourful in comparison.' Joy smiled.

Over dessert, Joy talked of her teaching work and in turn Henry spoke about his days coaching history and how he loved encouraging his students. When the cheese board arrived, Joy looked across the table towards Henry, who was studying the trio of French cheeses, and realised that she hadn't once mentioned Tom, and Henry had instinctively known not to ask.

There was time for that much later.

One day she would tell this lovely man, who had somehow stolen her heart, that her marriage hadn't been the story it appeared to be. But for now, Joy understood that some secrets were best kept quietly in the background, waiting for the right moment to be spoken.

If they ever need to be spoken about at all.

* * *

312

After dinner, to work off the richness of the meal, Henry and Joy decided to take a short walk, if the wind didn't prove too wild. 'We're in the North Sea now and it will probably get quite rough as we journey south,' Henry said. 'I have a spare coat and my cabin is closest, and it leads out to the promenade deck,' he added.

Joy happily accepted, and after admiring his cabin and the mirrored doors that conveniently slid back to the deck, she let Henry wrap her in an oversized coat, and they stepped into the cold night air. Taking hold of his arm, she nestled against him as the wind nipped at their faces, and they strolled side-by-side.

'I'm surprised Jack and Judy aren't pounding the boards,' Henry commented, 'but know for certain that they'll be out here in the morning come what may.'

It was surprisingly clear, and as they stopped to look up, any clouds parted, and the stars appeared studded like diamonds in the dark sky. Suddenly, without warning, a flash of colour erupted, and a sweeping curtain of green, tinged with violet shimmered against the inky black sky. Joy gasped, her hand gripping Henry's as a symphony of purple and gold danced above them, and the aurora's light gently kissed the sea.

'It's like a glowing dome,' Henry whispered as white light suddenly burst outward, 'and it appears to be coming down to us . . . Joy, I do believe this is the coronal aurora!' He was breathless as he stared wide-eyed at the rare sight.

'My goodness, it's so beautiful.' Joy was dazed, spellbound in the moment.

'Just like you.' Henry turned and tilted her face gently towards him.

Joy stared in wonder, while Henry's eyes held a soft intensity, steady and full of hope. When his lips found hers, Joy leaned into him, her hand curling against his chest, feeling the rhythmic beat of his heart beneath her fingertips, and her own pulse quickened as their kiss deepened.

Overhead, the Northern Lights danced in graceful arcs, casting waves of purple and green across their skin as though the aurora itself had given its blessing, as their world finally aligned.

Joy followed without a word when Henry reached for her hand and led her gently to the warmth of his cabin. For in that moment, Joy knew, with absolute certainty, that she was exactly where she wanted to be.

Chapter Thirty-Two

The sea stays behind but the memories sail on forever . . .

On the final day, the weather was pleasantly calm as the *Emerald Dream* glided through the steely waters of the North Sea, her bow pointed southwest towards Newcastle. Seagulls wheeled lazily in the breeze that blew through the decks as early morning risers prepared for the day.

In Henry's cabin, Henry and Joy ordered breakfast. As they sat by the window looking out, both grinned as the Deck Mile Club made its final round, led by Jack and Judy, who were hand-in-hand as they marched determinedly ahead, setting a brisk pace that left many fleece-covered walkers struggling to keep up.

In their suite, Leticia and Jim were in bed. Leticia, snuggled in her onesie, cuddled cosily next to Jim as they studied a new brochure and planned their next cruise.

As a weak sun shone through the panoramic windows of the Royal Emerald Suite, Margaret sipped a coffee while seated comfortably beside Lady Eleanor. Feeling tired from all her exertions, Lady Eleanor reclined, propped up in her bed. Margaret held a copy of *Horse & Hound* and read aloud a product review for a saddle that claimed to cushion one's rear like a cloud. Dismissing it as more of a medieval torture device, Margaret turned the page and moved on.

In the lounge area of Lady Eleanor's suite, Lucinda settled into a sofa, a cigarette holder gripped firmly between her teeth. Her eyes were fixed on a brochure of Dunmore Hall Boutique Hotel, where, in her mind's eye, she was already the artist in residence, paintbrush poised, bathed in the glow of Irish sunlight spilling across a lofty studio, dancing on the rich antique oak panels. Her gracious mentor, Lady Eleanor, was going to allow Lucinda to lose herself in her creative world, tutoring the wealthy clientele who would finance Lucinda's space. From now on, she could bloom and dream without limits.

* * *

The Lido Deck was busy as Simon made his morning round. Kyle's Back to Britain Booty Blast was about to begin and proved popular amongst the more energetic passengers. An enthusiastic display of Lycra and fleece-covered flesh stood waiting for their instructor, many beginning to stretch out arms and legs with solemn determination. Simon noted Sid and Nora in matching neon headbands. He smiled as Nora touched her toes in her leopard-print leggings, encouraging Sid, who grumbled to his new partner that he hadn't touched his toes since England won the World Cup.

Simon turned as he saw the door by the café half open, and a hand peeked out, beckoning Simon in. 'Morning, sweetie,' Kyle whispered as he pulled Simon into a darkened service space and planted a kiss on his lips.

Simon stroked the amulet in his pocket and felt a ripple of pleasure as he returned the kiss. At the end of the cruise, he would disembark for two weeks' leave and, as luck would have it, his subtle manipulation of the ship's rota meant that Kyle would be joining him too. Fourteen days of good old northern hospitality beckoned, with nights out planned on Manchester's Canal Street where glitter clung to every surface, cocktails flowed in every bar, and nobody blinked at two grown men singing Kylie duets all evening.

Simon pictured his mother's face when he turned up for his Sunday roast in Salford, with Kyle on his arm, and knew she would be thrilled. He smiled as he imagined her voice. *'By heck, our Simon, about time you settled down, and this one seems like a lovely lad.'*

'Did you get hold of the pictures?' Kyle cut through Simon's thoughts. 'I don't like the thought of that witch of a woman leaving the ship with them still on her phone.' He lowered his tone. 'She could drop a bomb whenever she feels like it.'

Simon nodded grimly. Kyle was right. Barbara Montgomery Jones wasn't just a gossip; she was dangerous and had a smartphone full of ammunition. And that ammunition needed to be destroyed. He'd already decided that somehow, he had to get hold of her phone.

'I'll think of something,' Simon said with confidence he didn't feel. In truth, he hadn't a clue what to do. 'You better get out there, they're baying for your blood.' Simon gave

Kyle a reassuring hug, then headed back out to the deck, where Nora led a chorus of '*Why are we waiting?*'

Suddenly, to whoops and cheers, Kyle appeared with the flourish of a West End finale and strode onto the deck in metallic shorts and a matching vest. 'All right, my glacier-busting-babes!' he called out. 'Let's thaw those joints and tighten those glutes!'

And as the Lido Deck became the most energetic dance floor south of the Arctic Circle, Simon continued with his morning preamble.

* * *

In the Atlantis Spa, serene panpipe music caressed the eucalyptus-scented air and a faint burble from a decorative fountain could be heard as Simon stepped into the reception area. He was keen to replenish his supply of tinted moisturiser, especially as he was due on stage that afternoon for An Audience with the Captain, and Simon wanted to look his best.

Before he could reach the desk, a small, monk-like figure barged past and slammed a designer tote bag on the counter. 'I demand to speak to the manager!' the figure shouted and removed a smaller bag of Atlantis Spa skincare products.

Simon winced and took a cautious step back to hide behind a large potted palm. He recognised the voice with cut-glass vowels. It was Barbara Montgomery Jones, shrouded in a hooded towelling robe.

'I spent a fortune in here with the aim of looking younger,' she yelled, when the manager appeared, her voice

318

echoing angrily throughout the spa, 'not to emerge looking like a bloody beetroot with hives!'

Heads turned, and a woman relaxing in a mud mask, dropped her magazine.

Barbara dug into the bag to clutch a jar of anti-ageing seaweed-infused cream and held it up as though it were radioactive. 'I asked for rejuvenation, not inflammation!'

The spa manager spoke soothing words and with a click of her manicured fingers, summoned a therapist to guide Barbara into a treatment room to see what might be done.

As Barbara continued to rant, Simon saw his moment.

Her bag, gaping open, was perched on the reception desk. With everyone fixated on the drama, Simon slid out from behind the plant, and moved to the counter, his body shielding the bag, and as he pretended to study a list of treatments, he slipped his hand neatly in. *Bingo!* His fingers found her phone, while Barbara, still in full indignant mode, was being swept into the treatment area.

Simon sidestepped into a vacant bathroom and stared at the screen of Barbara's phone.

Passcode. But would it work?

Earlier, Simon had checked Barbara's passport on file and memorised her date of birth. Was the woman likely to be that stupid? He tapped in the numbers and held his breath. YES! Simon almost punched the air. There was a god, and it *had* worked!

Within seconds, Simon accessed Barbara's photo stream. He deleted the incriminating images and, just to be sure, wiped them from her cloud backup as well. Quickly returning to reception, he carefully returned the phone just as the manager reappeared.

'I think the lady forgot something,' Simon said smoothly, holding out the bag.

The manager rolled her eyes and leaned in. 'That woman . . .' she whispered and took Barbara's bag.

Minutes later, Simon, with his tinted moisturiser replenished, left the spa. As he reached halfway to the stairwell, he tapped out a text for Kyle.

Code Red. Mission Accomplished!

* * *

Jennifer moved quickly through the corridor as she pushed her housekeeping trolley towards Henry's room. The door hanger indicated that the room was ready to be made up, and using her housekeeping keycard, she stepped in. In the bathroom, she wiped down every surface and polished the chrome fixtures until they gleamed. She was surprised to see that Henry had used all the toiletries, including the shampoos and body lotion.

'First time, Mr Henry,' Jennifer muttered, knowing that shower gel had been his only choice throughout his cruise.

She took care to fold the toilet paper end into a neat triangle and finally, with practised hands, smoothed a fresh set of towels into place. Jennifer was methodical and always noted the slightest hint of a fingerprint on a glass or a hair on a surface, anticipating details that the fussiest guest might notice. Checking the minibar, Jennifer was puzzled once again. The miniature bottles of wine had been emptied for the first time during Henry's stay. On his hospitality tray, all the coffee had gone.

Mr Henry had had a party by himself, she thought as she began to strip the bed.

But it was as Jennifer folded the used linens that she suddenly caught an unusual scent. It was light and floral and unlike anything she'd smelled in Henry's room before. Holding the sheet to her face, she closed her eyes and suddenly everything became clear.

Mr Henry had not been alone last night.

A cold knot tightened in her stomach, and Jennifer's hands began to tremble as betrayal burned in her eyes. The room suddenly felt suffocating, and Jennifer's heart pounded against her ribs. She had to get out of there, to get away, back to the cabin she shared with three others, to lie on her bunk, draw her curtain around her, and take in the realisation that she hadn't captured Mr Henry's heart.

Choking back tears, she reached for fresh sheets and snapped them over the mattress. Arranging the pillows to fluff them with a series of punches, she proceeded to hurriedly vacuum the carpet and finally, spray a light citrus mist in the air.

Before leaving, Jennifer opened the wardrobe door and reached for Henry's reindeer jumper. Hugging it to her face, she let her tears flow as Henry's smell engulfed her. Then, folding the fabric, she placed it back and with a deep sigh that wracked her little body, Jennifer left the room with her memories of Henry locked inside.

Chapter Thirty-Three

Sail each day as though it's your last voyage.

The meal at lunchtime on table twenty-eight was another happy affair and Lady Eleanor had made the effort to rise and join her new friends. Together with Margaret, she sat beside Leticia and Jim, and was pleased to see that Henry and Joy were there too.

'You two look like love birds,' the old lady said with a knowing smile and a twinkle in her eye, as Henry exchanged glances with Joy.

'I take it you had a lovely evening?' Leticia whispered to Joy as everyone discussed their activities for the final day.

'Couldn't have gone better,' Joy replied, 'I can't tell you how happy I am.'

'Bottle that feeling, my dear, and keep it close, you deserve it.'

Kenneth, arriving late to the table, and uncharacteristically polite, informed the group that Barbara, regrettably, wouldn't be joining them. He thanked Leticia for her kindness in offering a lotion for his wife's skin condition and added that the

Atlantis Spa management had been exceptionally attentive. Barbara was receiving treatment and hoped to rejoin them all later. Remarkably, Kenneth looked somewhat improved. His hairpiece had lost its tufty troll-like appearance and sat neatly in place, smoothed down to a respectable sheen.

Lady Eleanor hoped that everyone would be heading to the Emerald Art Studio, where Lucinda was holding an exclusive exhibition of the work she had completed during the cruise. 'It is an opportunity for you to own a treasured piece and a lasting reminder of your holiday,' she added.

'I rather liked my painting that Lucinda inspired in class,' Joy said and thought of her fishing village in acrylics that would look lovely on her dining room wall.

None of the guests were quite sure how Lucinda's wild and whacky artwork could possibly resemble memories of the cruise, but once in their living rooms, they agreed that the pieces would be conversation starters for visitors, to kickstart stories of Arctic adventures. Even Henry decided that he would head up to the studio later to see if there was anything suitable to take home for Audrey.

Margaret said that she was looking forward to An Audience with the Captain, which would take place in the Triton Lounge after dinner and hoped that Captain Lindholm would enlighten them, and they would discover what it took to captain the *Emerald Dream* and sail around the world. Plans were made for the afternoon ahead and the group drifted apart, their curiosity stirred, each wondering what secrets the captain might share later that night.

* * *

323

With passengers making the most of their final hours on the ship, Henry and Jim had taken themselves off to Bill Zhang's last talk. Both were keen to see the guest speaker's most popular photos of the aurora borealis and the stories behind them. Leticia, insistent that the masseur avoid any seaweed-infused products, was enjoying a full-body massage in the Atlantis Spa.

Joy, after stopping by the Mermaid Theatre to listen to a concert entitled, *Music of the Homeland* decided that she wasn't in the mood for Grieg's Norway and would prefer something less wistful. She was about to head to the Bookmark Café, where the Women's Institute members were holding their final meeting, when the phone in her pocket rang.

It was Susan, and feeling guilty from their last conversation, Joy decided to wait to take the call in her cabin, where she could concentrate on her daughter's demands.

'Why didn't you answer straight away?' Susan cut in with no preliminaries when Joy called her back.

'Sorry, I was walking around the ship.'

'Walking or wandering around in a fog? Honestly, Mother, I do worry about you, I'm sure you've been overdoing your iron tonic.'

Joy sighed. Would Susan never let up? 'Did you manage to sort out your Stinking Bishop?' she asked.

'Yes, no thanks to you, but my cleaner came up with a solution.'

'I hope you're paying them overtime,' Joy said dryly, fully aware that Susan regarded working in her designer-inspired home as a privilege, one that never justified more than the minimum wage, even on a bank holiday.

Ignoring her mother, Susan went on. 'Your cruise ends tomorrow, and as you'll be going straight home, I just wanted to let you know that Hugh and I are taking a New Year break and heading out to the slopes in St Moritz for the skiing. The snow is pristine at this time of year.'

Joy heard Susan yawn before she continued.

'So, I won't be seeing you for a while, but I wanted to ask if you'd like to come to us for a visit in February?'

Joy knew that Susan would be wiping the snow off her boots in St Moritz faster than Hugh could say 'Glühwein' and would spend more time enjoying the après-ski than any exertions on the slopes. She was also aware that February was Susan's month for spring cleaning her immaculate house and unwilling to be roped in for hard-core scrubbing, Joy decided to nip the invite in the bud.

'Actually, dear,' Joy began, 'I'm rather glad you caught me before you go away because I wanted to let you know that I shall be in Ireland for the New Year.'

'Ireland?'

'Yes, I've been invited to celebrate as a guest of Lady Dunmore.'

'*What? Lady Dunmore?* B . . . but where will you stay?'

'I believe we're being accommodated in a hotel on the Dunmore Estate.'

'You can't mean Dunmore Boutique Hotel in County Kildare?' Susan was aghast, as though she'd just heard a salacious scandal.

'Yes, that's the place, is it nice?'

'NICE?' Susan shouted. 'It's the most exclusive hotel in

Ireland, Hugh and I have always . . .' She paused, realising that she'd been outdone.

'Wanted to stay there?' Joy completed the sentence. 'Well, we'll be sure to let you know what it's like.'

'But, who's "we"?' Susan sounded suspicious.

'Oh, didn't I mention it? Henry and I will be sharing a room.'

'Mother, I really think that you need to sit down and consider all this foolishness. You can't go gallivanting off with a man you don't know.'

'Oh, my dear, but I can, and it isn't as if I don't know him, intimacy has a way of revealing things a great deal about a person.'

'Pleeeease!' Susan was horrified.

'Well, you did ask . . .'

'But, what about the house, my inheritance? This man is obviously after your money.'

'Hardly, he has plenty of his own, and I intend to spend every penny of your inheritance. After all, you and Hugh do very nicely.'

'I need to speak to Hugh,' Susan spluttered, 'I think we should drive up to Newcastle tomorrow . . .'

'I wouldn't hear of it. Now don't fuss. Go and enjoy a lovely alpine break and perhaps, if Henry and I are not away ourselves, you can come and visit *us* in February.'

Joy scrunched her face up as Susan launched into a full-blown tirade, peppered with a string of expletives.

'Susan, I am going to cut the call now, I'm heading out to dinner and debating what to wear. Maybe that gold number again, what do you think?'

'I think you've completely lost your mind,' Susan snapped, and before Joy could offer a response, the line went dead.

Joy shook her head. Her daughter would get over it, and if truth be told, Joy knew that all of this must have come as a shock. Her mousey, stay-at-home mum, who'd waited on Susan all her life, had broken out of her domestic cocoon and was heading into the unexpected.

Joy was about to step into the shower when Simon's cheerful voice sounded through the cabin. 'Hello again, fellow travellers,' he began, 'this is a gentle reminder that your cases will need to be outside your cabin door tonight before midnight. We will arrive in Newcastle just before sunrise.'

Simon went on to inform the passengers that the outside temperature was now seven degrees with a moderate breeze and a slight sea state. He reminded guests that he looked forward to hosting An Audience with the Captain later that evening and hoped to see everyone there.

Joy paused. How quickly this cruise had passed. Christmas was over, and in the time that she'd spent at sea, her life had suddenly changed. She thought of Henry and the happiness that they'd found and knew that she must seize the day. For years, she'd paid the unhappy price of compromise and regret. But now, she understood that each day was *the* day to watch the dawn rise, to paint every picture, and to walk hand in hand, without looking back.

And Tom would no longer haunt her.

* * *

In their Dream Suite, Barbara lay stretched across the bed, a silk sleep mask over her eyes. She'd spent the entire day in the Atlantis Spa and, having threatened to sue the company, had been pampered to within an inch of her perfectly polished existence. To her relief, the calming creams had toned down her blotches. With a full refund on the seaweed products, she had a complimentary case of marine creams, serums, and bank-breaking beauty merchandise tucked under her arm when she finally came away, and it hadn't been necessary to contact Simon and apply pressure.

But mysteriously, the photos she'd taken, which contained incriminating evidence against the cruise director, had disappeared from her phone, and it was a puzzle that Barbara couldn't solve.

Kenneth, another puzzle, was nowhere to be seen, and Barbara sincerely hoped that he wasn't causing more mischief. They were due at dinner in less than an hour, and she'd be damned if she missed both the meal and the entertainment that followed. Barbara's determination to win over the captain had, for the moment, eclipsed any thoughts of maligning Joy, especially after Margaret's curt rebuke. Yet, with no word from the captain, Barbara remained distinctly miffed. Still with a face like a pockmarked planet, she'd have been in no position to entertain even the most discreet rendezvous.

She heard the door open and, lifting her mask, blinked in surprise as Kenneth stepped in, partly obscured by an enormous bouquet of flowers.

'Babs, my darling old girl, your Kenny says he's sorry.'

Taken aback, Barbara stared at her husband. To her surprise, he'd made quite an effort, and the rug on his head looked half-decent. He no longer resembled a startled troll. Dressed smartly and smelling faintly of a scent she didn't recognise, he stood there beaming.

'What have you done?' she spoke sharply. 'And what's that smell?'

'I've been to the ship's barber, and he's tidied me up,' Kenneth stepped forward, 'and I've replaced the aftershave you hated with a new one.'

Barbara narrowed her eyes.

'It's sandalwood, the barber said you'd love it.'

'Sandalwood doesn't cover up bad behaviour.'

'I know,' he said, inching closer. 'I've even ironed my own shirt.'

'You haven't ever ironed a shirt.'

'Indeed,' Kenneth said and held up a bandaged finger.

Barbara was trying to hold onto her indignation, but the beautiful bouquet, the tidied hair, and the clean-shaven Kenny were slowly wearing her down.

'Well, this doesn't mean that you're off the hook,' she said and sitting up, swung her legs over the side of the bed. 'But you can pour me a drink.'

Kenneth's grin was broad. 'Fizz or gin?'

'Surprise me, just don't spill it on the rug.' Lifting her mask, Barbara tossed it aside and added, 'Including the one on your head.'

Chapter Thirty-Four

*The cruise may be ending but the next
journey is just beginning.*

Dinner on the final night of the Arctic cruise was an informal affair with the dress code relaxed, and as Henry stepped out of the shower and laid out his clothes, he paused for a moment and considered the reindeer jumper. Deciding that it was too casual, he opted for a smart shirt and jacket. As he dressed, he realised he was stepping into a chapter of life he'd never anticipated. So much had shifted over the past ten days as his feelings for Joy grew steadily, then in the last twenty-four hours exploded. Henry had never felt this way before, and he was astounded by how good he felt. Suddenly, he had the wind beneath his elderly wings and was flying in a wonderful direction, soaring into something new with Joy, with a mutual longing they both wanted to embrace.

Henry couldn't imagine a day without her now and knew that she felt the same. There was a special kind of pleasure in falling in love in later life and knowing that it was returned. He wondered if the magic of the aurora borealis had brought them together. *Was it destiny written in the Northern Lights?* For under that curtain of celestial light, their love hadn't just flickered. It had blazed.

'Goodness, I'm coming over all poetic.' Henry smiled as he straightened his collar and grinned at his reflection. 'Whatever would Audrey say?' But in his heart, he knew that his friend would be delighted that he had, in her words, finally found a good woman.

Henry was sure that Joy's marriage had been troubled. Common sense told him that much. She never spoke of Tom, deftly sidestepping probing questions. At first, Henry had taken it for grief, but now he sensed something more profound, more complicated. One day, he felt certain she would tell him the truth of it, in her own time. Until then, he would ask nothing more than she was willing to give, but from now on, he would do everything in his power to ensure that their days together felt safe and were filled with the happiness Henry thought she had long been denied.

As Henry dimmed the lights in his cabin, he noticed the absence of the usual towel sculpture on his bed. In fact, he hadn't seen Jennifer all day. A flicker of concern crossed his mind. Perhaps the housekeeper was unwell.

He opened the drawer at his desk and pulled out an envelope. Inside was a card wishing Jennifer a happy New Year alongside two neatly handwritten sheets of company stationery. He found himself wondering if New Year celebrations in the Philippines were as lively as they would be in Ireland, with fireworks and the kind of revelries he eagerly anticipated in a few days. How sad that Jennifer wouldn't be at home with her family, but instead, at

331

sea, working hard to ensure the comfort of a new set of passengers.

Taking a pen, he wrote her name on the envelope and left it propped up on a book on the desk, where he knew she would find it.

'Happy New Year, Jennifer,' Henry whispered as he left the room, 'to you *and* your family.'

* * *

Jennifer lingered in the alcove at the end of Henry's corridor. She watched him leave his cabin and disappear down the hallway towards the lifts. When he was gone, she let out a sigh, then tightened her grip on her trolley and began to wheel it slowly forward. Her heart felt heavy, and she was filled with a sadness she couldn't explain. Mr Henry, the older guest travelling alone, had been unusually kind and warm.

Jennifer was used to being invisible. Most guests barely acknowledged her, and some not at all. But Mr Henry was so courteous and interested in her life, and Jennifer had dared to hope, just a little, that he might be different. Perhaps there would be a connection between them that might lift her from the achingly long days and months she spent far from her beloved family.

But Mr Henry had let her down, and his affections lay elsewhere.

Placing her trolley by the door, Jennifer reached for a stack of fresh towels and made her way into his room. She would do her duty and make everything as nice as could be, after all, it was her job to ensure that the guests had everything they needed. Straightening the bed, she plumped up the pillows and placed a chocolate on each one. Perhaps his lady friend had a sweet tooth. She sighed, and reaching into a pocket, added two more.

As Jennifer turned to close the curtains and dust the desk, she noticed an envelope propped against a book. Frowning, she studied the handwritten name and realised it was for her. Sitting down, she carefully undid the seal before removing a colourful card with a wintery scene, then smiled when she read the handwritten words on the inside.

Maligayang Bagong Taon!

Henry had found a translation for Happy New Year, and inside he'd written a note thanking Jennifer for her kindness, and that he hoped the enclosed would in some small way make her life a little easier going forward. A handful of hundred-euro notes fell onto her lap alongside two pages of notepaper.

As Jennifer began to read, tears welled in her eyes and her breath caught. She shook her head and tried to make sense of what she was seeing. Her fingers trembled as she scanned the lines to be sure she hadn't misunderstood. As the stillness of the room engulfed her, she closed her eyes and pressed the note to her chest.

'Oh, Mr Henry,' Jennifer whispered, 'what have you done . . .'

* * *

Dressed in their finery despite the informal dress code, Barbara and Kenneth, buoyed by several drinks in their suite, promenaded through the ship. Barbara's diamonds dazzled as she flashed a smile at guests, offering nods as they made their way to dinner, like royalty on a grand tour. Kenneth gave a cheerful wave to a passing couple he didn't know, while Barbara clicked her kitten heels as though moving across a stage. Kenneth wasn't quite back in her good books, but he'd been granted visiting rights, and the show must go on, she reminded herself. She would play the part, at least until something more diverting came along.

As they passed the desk at guest services, a voice called out. 'Mrs Montgomery Jones, there's a message for you!'

Barbara paused. If it was the message she'd been expecting, how could she keep it from Kenneth?

'Come on, Babs,' Kenneth urged, 'don't keep them waiting.'

Before Barbara had a chance to intervene, Kenneth stepped forward and took the envelope from the young crew member's outstretched hand. Barbara attempted to snatch it away, but her husband was too quick.

'Allow me,' he said smoothly in a tone that made Barbara's stomach tighten.

She lunged to grab it, but Kenneth stepped away. He tore the envelope open and read on. 'Well, how intriguing,' Kenneth said, his eyes cast down as he handed her the opened note.

'Kenny, I can explain . . .' Barbara's heart thudded as she took it, already forming excuses. Then her eyes darted over the note.

Once.

Then twice.

A pause. Barbara's lips parted, 'Oh, I'm . . .' she faltered.

'It's all right, Babs,' Kenneth said with a shrug. 'Not what you were expecting?'

She looked up at him, stunned, not with guilt but with disbelief.

Printed on official stationery, the short note read:

Congratulations! Mr & Mrs Montgomery Jones

You are the grand prize winners of the captain's Gala Raffle

On behalf of all the crew on the Emerald Dream, we hope you enjoy your hamper!

Barbara blinked.

'You thought it was from the captain, didn't you?' Kenneth asked, his eyes dark.

Barbara said nothing.

Offering his arm, Kenneth stepped forward. 'Don't worry, Babs, I knew all along. We know each other too well.'

Barbara's cheeks were flushed as she took his arm. 'Kenny . . . I'm sorry,' she whispered.

'Shall we?' he asked and led her away from the desk. 'We don't want to keep our table waiting. After all,' he added, 'we're both winners tonight.'

* * *

In the Triton Lounge, there wasn't a spare seat when Simon, in his smartest uniform, stepped onto the centre of the stage.

335

'Good evening, friends and fellow travellers,' he began and looked out at the expectant faces. 'On behalf of myself, Captain Lindholm and all the crew of the *Emerald Dream*, we hope that you've had an unforgettable holiday. I can hardly believe that we're at the end of it already.' He dug into his pocket and pulled out a card. 'But before we part ways, this is the moment many have been waiting for, and I'm about to announce the winner of the captain's Gala Raffle, which was drawn earlier today.'

There was a shuffle as guests dug into their pockets to retrieve their raffle numbers.

Simon held up a card. 'The grand prize winners of a magnificent hamper are . . . . Kenneth and Barbara Montgomery Jones!'

Simon looked around for the lucky winners and gritted his teeth. He silently cursed his own handiwork as Kenneth and Barbara paraded triumphantly up the aisle. The whole fiasco, with Simon's subtle manipulation of the draw, had been designed to keep the Montgomery Joneses happy and to send them ashore with smiles instead of complaints. He watched them relish their unearned glory and congratulating them both, Simon thought of more deserving winners. But sadly, he'd had to engineer that the prize inevitably went to the ship's most persistent complainers.

There was a polite ripple of applause and a lukewarm reception as Kenneth and Barbara gave a wave and returned to their seats. 'She thinks she's royalty!' Nora was heard to call out.

Ever the professional, Simon continued. 'If the lucky winners would like to return to the stage after the show, there will be a photograph with Captain Lindholm.'

Tucking the card back in his pocket, he continued by saying that it had been a pleasure sailing with everyone, and he hoped that guests had made many memories of their time on the Arctic cruise. 'We hope to see you all on another voyage soon. But now, please put your hands together for An Audience with the Captain!'

Captain Lindholm appeared in the wings and strolled onto the stage, where two chairs surrounded a small table.

* * *

Lady Eleanor, with Margaret by her side, was seated next to Joy, and as Simon and the captain settled, Joy whispered, 'Will you miss this?'

'No, my dear, it's time I went home, I feel that I need to connect with Richard if only in a spiritual sense.'

Lady Eleanor sighed, her gaze drifting into the distance. To Joy, she seemed suddenly weary; the earlier sparkle at the thought of returning home had quite vanished. Before Joy could inquire further, however, the event commenced.

Captain Lindholm opened by discussing the *Emerald Dream*, sharing her tonnage and technical details of her engines. He entertained everyone with amusing facts and informed guests that they had consumed 39,000 eggs during the trip and 500 kilos of cheese.

Simon patted his tummy and quipped, 'Not all the cheese ended up in my sandwiches.'

When asked about cruise ships polluting the oceans, the captain explained the latest environmental regulations and how the Diamond Star Line ensured full compliance, and that one day the ship would be completely carbon neutral. He acknowledged accountability, stating that the captain's decisions are final. If something were to go wrong, it is the captain who would be held legally responsible.

During audience questions, Kenneth asked the captain about the most unusual sea creatures he'd ever encountered.

The captain grinned. 'Submarines,' he replied, prompting a round of laughter. Another guest wanted the captain's opinion on the social aspects of cruising, particularly when thousands of passengers descended from large ships onto small islands.

'I hope that it becomes regulated,' Captain Lindholm replied. 'Ideally to just one ship per day.'

Margaret stood up and called out, 'Have you ever lost someone at sea?'

The captain replied that thankfully, he hadn't, then paused, 'Although I did once have a passenger claim her husband was missing, but it turned out he was in another cabin, with someone else's wife.'

Simon concluded the evening by asking the captain if he would do it all again.

Captain Lindholm slowly nodded. 'In a heartbeat,' he said. 'The sea is magical and mysterious, she humbles you and once cast in her spell, you realise that she is the gateway to all things on Earth. I have the best job in the world, and for that, I am truly grateful.'

There was a brief pause as everyone absorbed his words, then, as if sensing the close of a wonderful journey, loud applause filled the room in an unspoken farewell to the shared adventure.

A crew member appeared, carrying a hamper, and Simon beckoned Barbara and Kenneth to the stage for photos with Captain Lindholm.

Guests began to disperse, and Joy, taking Henry's hand, smiled and said how enjoyable the evening had been. They turned to bid goodbye to Lady Eleanor and walked with her to the foyer, while Margaret went on ahead. Joy noticed that Lady Eleanor moved slowly, and her faltering steps seemed unsteady.

'Can I help you?' Joy held out her hand. 'Are you feeling unwell?'

Suddenly, Lady Eleanor's legs gave way, and she crumbled to the floor. Dropping to her knees, Joy wrapped her fingers tightly around the old lady's hand. Guests nearby fell silent and paused, their faces a mixture of worry and unease, unsure of whether to intervene.

Henry rushed to her side. 'Margaret's run to get a medic,' he said, his voice filled with concern.

'Stay with us, Lady Eleanor, help is coming.' Joy's voice was steadier than she felt, and as she spoke, a chill crawled through her spine.

Back in a different room, Joy saw Tom's face and remembered the memory of that Mediterranean morning and hurrying to his side. No one knew fully what she had lived through, and what she had . . . endured.

But shaking her head, Joy blinked the image away. *Not here!*

This wasn't then. This was now.

Joy refocused her attention on Lady Eleanor, willing her to hold on. 'I'm with you and I'm not going to let you go,' she whispered as though her grip would anchor her to life. 'Stay with me, *please* . . .'

Time seemed to stretch, and Joy bent lower, her free hand brushing a strand of silver hair from Lady Eleanor's forehead. She listened and was relieved to hear a shallow breath. 'Breathe with me,' she said softly, 'in and out, that's it.'

'Help is here.' Joy heard Henry's reassuring voice and looked up to see a medic pushing through the gathered crowd. Relief flooded through her, but as she began to rise, the old lady's eyelids fluttered, and her frail grip tightened around Joy's fingers with surprising strength.

'Thank you,' Lady Eleanor whispered, her voice barely audible. 'For staying.'

Joy froze. Something in those two simple words pierced through her.

She couldn't reply and merely nodded as the medic knelt and took over. Stepping back, she felt a ghostly presence brush against her like an icy chill. She shivered, and when she looked up, Leticia was there.

Silent and still, Leticia watched her. Their eyes met, but Leticia didn't speak, and Joy felt her breath catch in her throat. Joy's past had become her present, and Leticia knew.

Somehow, impossibly, she knew.

Chapter Thirty-Five

Goodbye, but not farewell . . .

Leticia stood beside Jim on the balcony of their suite and looked out at the view. The *Emerald Dream* was heading into port, and soon they would arrive in Newcastle. It was a clear sunny morning, and as the ship glided into the mouth of the River Tyne and passed the lighthouse on the end of the pier, Leticia smiled. Beyond the sand dunes of the beach at Little Haven, she glimpsed the *Beach Ladies*, the bronze figures that greeted visitors arriving from the North Sea. She remembered describing the munchkin-like ladies to Jim on the morning that they were due to depart on their Arctic cruise, and now, the ladies were welcoming them back.

People were gathered near the pier, many with raised hands as they watched the *Emerald Dream*, and Leticia smiled and returned the greetings.

What a wonderful cruise this had been!

She leaned into Jim as he slipped his arm around her and thought of the many memories etched in the days and nights, and to her delight, the unexpected gift of a new friendship. As Leticia continued to wave, she thought of Joy and the events of the previous evening.

When Lady Eleanor had gradually regained consciousness, and a medic arrived, Leticia heard her murmur her thanks to Joy, adding the words, '*For staying*'.

At those words, a flicker of fear crossed Joy's face, so quick it might have been missed by anyone close by. But Leticia saw it, and, in an instant, she understood. When their eyes met, the truth passed between them.

The burden Joy was carrying wasn't just grief. It was guilt. And now, Leticia knew why.

Leticia knew the signs, not only as a nurse, but as a woman who had seen too many bear the scars of cruelty behind closed doors. A year ago, when Joy's husband had suffered a heart attack, Leticia now realised that Joy had done nothing.

As Eleanor was assisted by the medics, Leticia took Joy to one side and they sat quietly, as Leticia waited for Joy to speak.

'When I saw Tom, I didn't call for help straight away,' Joy said, her voice barely above a whisper. 'I could have, and I meant to, but when I went into the corridor, I was paralysed and couldn't move. There was a phone in our room, but I had to get out. I don't know how long I stood there before I forced myself to summon medical help. By the time I got back, he'd stopped breathing.' Joy hung her head. 'Tom was horrible to me, Leticia, he made my life a misery. You have no idea.'

Leticia took Joy's hand. 'I do have an idea,' she said, choosing her words with care. 'And I need to tell you something. Not just as a nurse but as your friend. A catastrophic cardiac arrest, the kind the doctors later told you Tom had, is almost always fatal. Even with help, it is unlikely that it would have made a difference.'

Joy looked into Leticia's eyes. 'I've always felt evil for not picking up the phone straight away.'

Leticia wiped a tear from Joy's cheek. 'Maybe he might have lived. Maybe not. But what I am certain of is that he made you feel powerless for so long, and when this happened, you froze. That's not evil, Joy. It's trauma. And you are not to blame.'

Leticia watched as Joy visibly relaxed, as though something in her heart had loosened. 'Let it go, Joy,' Leticia pleaded, 'you don't have to carry this as a sentence for the rest of your life. You've already paid the price.'

* * *

'Almost there,' Leticia said to Jim as she held his hand, and the ship passed the Customs House across the water on the North Shields side.

Further upriver, the scenery changed to the stark beauty of Tyneside's industrial past. They could see towering cranes in the shipyards, standing side by side with old and modern buildings while fishing boats, overshadowed by the *Emerald Dream*, bobbed about nearby.

As the world narrowed from the wide-open sea, Leticia turned to her husband. 'We're home, darling,' she said and kissed his cheek.

'Here's to our next adventure.' Jim smiled, his eyes fixed on the port drawing closer.

Leticia's stomach churned, and her grip on his hand tightened. The doctors had been kind but clear. When The Beast returned, there wouldn't be any more adventures.

But as seagulls swooped and cawed overhead, she remembered the aurora borealis and whispered a prayer that her miracle wish be granted and buy them a little more time. 'Wherever that adventure takes us, I'll always be with you,' she said, blinking back the sting in her eyes.

Jim, still watching the approaching port, placed his arm around her shoulders and squeezed. 'My darling Leticia,' he smiled, 'and that is all I need.'

* * *

In the port terminal, Kenneth searched for a trolley. Laden down with two suit carriers, Barbara's voluminous fur coat and her vanity bag, which weighed as much as a Victorian dressing table, he snatched the last trolley just ahead of a woman in a wheelchair. As the woman cursed, Kenneth, hot and flustered hurried away to catch up with Barbara.

'Why are you dawdling?' Barbara was unimpressed as they waited for the shuttle to transport them to their Range Rover, where the rest of their luggage was already waiting.

'Because I'm carrying half your wardrobe, a mink the size of a sofa, and enough cosmetics to sink the entire ship,' Kenneth puffed. 'Honestly, Babs, you're the limit.'

'You know I don't trust anyone with my valuable things,' Barbara sniffed as Kenneth gave the trolley a shove, narrowly missing his wife's ankles.

Seated and settled in the front of the Range Rover a

little while later, as Kenneth loaded the luggage Barbara stifled a yawn. She wasn't looking forward to going home to Cheshire, where most of her cronies would be wintering in Spain, and with winter weather closing the golf course, there would be no audience to admire her photographs with the captain or listen to her brag about the cruise. The time ahead would drag, stuck in the house with Kenneth.

Barbara needed a new distraction, something to fill the upcoming days.

'All set, old girl, wagons roll!' Kenneth announced as he finally climbed into the vehicle.

Barbara blanched and, for the hundredth time, wished he'd pick something less ageing when addressing her. Glancing sideways, she sighed. He was wearing his trapper hat, at her insistence, and his face was puffed up and red, but she couldn't possibly have him arriving home with a troll wig on his head. God knows what the neighbours would say about that.

As they pulled away from the terminal, Kenneth paused at a junction to allow a Bentley to glide past. In the back sat Lady Eleanor, regal as ever, with Margaret seated beside her.

'Good lord, she's made a rapid recovery,' Kenneth said, giving a cheerful toot of the horn and a hearty wave.

'Must you?' Barbara snapped. She was still smarting from being left off the guest list for Lady Eleanor's New Year's Eve party in Ireland and had no intention of offering so much as a nod. 'It was probably just a fainting fit, her way of vying for attention,' Barbara sniped. 'You know how dramatic gentry can be.'

'I heard the old gal has a dodgy ticker,' Kenneth replied and hit the accelerator.

'Who knows and who cares,' Barbara said and gripped the side of her seat as they hurtled into a stream of heavy traffic.

Heavy rain began to fall as the countryside whizzed by and Barbara remembered the raffle prize they'd won. As described, it *was* very grand and included a generous discount voucher for their next cruise.

'Have you any plans in the next few weeks?' Barbara asked Kenneth, her tone light.

'None that wouldn't include you, my sweetheart.'

'I rather fancy another holiday,' she said, planting the idea, 'and the Caribbean would be delightful at this time of year.'

'Couldn't we use that voucher towards another cruise?' Kenneth suggested.

Barbara smiled. He'd taken the bait. 'Exactly what I was thinking,' she said, adjusting her chair, to lie back. In moments, Barbara was dreaming of cocktails, calypso, and a sultry Caribbean cruise.

And who knew? Maybe there would be a more compliant captain, or even a first officer or two . . .

* * *

In the Mermaid Theatre, Henry sat with his luggage beside him, waiting to disembark. Passengers in the lower decks were called by the colour of their luggage tags, and he hoped that his turn would come soon. Joy had already gone ahead, and the thought of seeing her in the terminal filled him with pleasure.

He was taking her back to her home.

Together they would drive to Lancaster in his Morris Traveller, and to Henry's delight, Joy had invited him to stay with her. If all went well, as he felt sure it would, he planned to return the invitation in Skipton. Henry was especially looking forward to introducing Joy to Audrey and was confident that the two women would get on well. He was also looking forward to meeting Susan, Joy's daughter and her husband, Hugh. Joy had mentioned that she intended to visit soon, partly to catch up but also to talk with Susan and formally introduce Henry.

'Passengers with the colour purple luggage tags may now disembark.' Simon's cheery voice rang out, and Henry gathered his hand luggage.

As he left the ship and walked across the quay to the terminal, he heard a voice calling his name. Puzzled, he turned.

'Mr Henry! Mr Henry!'

Henry looked up and to his delight, he saw Jennifer on a lower deck, wildly waving her duster. She was beaming, her whole face alight with elation. He remembered leaving his cabin earlier, when the housekeeper had flung her body against his to hug him so tightly, he'd had difficulty in prising her off and saying goodbye.

'Thank you, Mr Henry! Thank you for everything!' Jennifer's voice, full of feeling, caught the wind.

Henry laughed and lifted a hand in return. 'Look after yourself, dear Jennifer, write to me soon and don't forget, I want to see lots of photos!'

Jennifer nodded eagerly, dabbing at her eyes with the corner of her apron. 'God bless you, Mr Henry,' she bellowed. 'My children have a future now. You have given them that.'

Their eyes met for a moment longer. Hers shining with gratitude. His aglow with pleasure.

As Henry turned towards the terminal, he thought of the Gift Deed arrangement he'd soon set up for Jennifer, after consulting with his lawyer. At Henry's request for advice, Jim had suggested this and carefully explained how it worked. Years ago, Henry's father had left him a property, which he had sold for a considerable sum. He didn't need the money, and now, at last, he'd found a purpose for it that felt right. Giving Jennifer the means to educate her children in the Philippines brought him happiness. It wasn't charity, it was gratitude for the woman's kindness and . . .

Because he could. It felt like a natural course to use something he didn't need to change someone else's life.

The terminal doors opened, and Henry hurried in. Joy was waiting for him and as he moved towards her, for the first time in what seemed like forever, Henry felt that his life had meaning and most of all, love.

* * *

In the terminal building, Joy sat with her suitcases by her side. As she watched passengers search for their luggage, she remembered a little earlier, standing on the Lido Deck of the *Emerald Dream* as the ship glided gracefully through the calm waters to enter the mouth of the River Tyne.

Beneath the early morning sky, seagulls wheeled and cried overhead, their calls echoing over the waves and welcoming home the passengers of the Arctic cruise.

As the gleam of the hull cut through the misty morning, they'd passed a sandy bay at Little Haven, and Joy saw the Inn on the Beach hotel. She remembered the cosy room that she hadn't wanted to leave, the quiet refuge where she stayed the night before she boarded the cruise. It felt like a lifetime ago, and the woman who'd set sail for the Arctic was a shadow of the one now returning.

Like a soothing balm, her days at sea had ultimately taken away her pain. The ache that she'd carried onto the ship, the weight of unhappiness, had softened and dispersed like sea spray in the wind that blew over the waves. Leticia, dear Leticia, had taken away her guilt, releasing her back into the world. And what a world awaited.

Standing at the rail, with salt air caressing her skin and South Shields coming into view, Joy had known that whatever lay ahead, she was no longer afraid to meet it. She'd felt a lightness, confidence, and most of all, love.

Henry Halliday. A man with a heart as big as the sea they'd sailed had come into her life, and she knew he was here to stay. He'd seen her for who she was and asked for nothing but the chance to walk beside her. Joy had almost laughed as the wind tugged at her hair, and reaching for the ring on her wedding finger, she tossed it into the sea. No longer haunted by her past, she thought of the days to come, knowing that she would step into her future with joy, both in name and in spirit.

And she had the Arctic cruise to thank for that.

Now, as she looked up, she saw Henry walking through the terminal towards her, a broad smile lighting up his face. For somewhere in the stillness of the northern nights, a spell had been cast, and in the magical glow of the aurora borealis, Joy had found what she hadn't even known she was looking for. A hand to hold, and a man whom she would love, her heart finally, at peace.

'Henry,' she said softly, as pulled her into his arms. 'Take me home.'

Epilogue

Twelve Months Later . . .

Beneath the Northern Lights, two hearts found their course, to sail life's sea together.

Invitation
Ms Audrey Aston requests your company:
Mulled Wine, Misfits & A Marriage Celebration

Henry and Joy were married a year to the day that they first met. In a quiet ceremony at Skipton registry office, guests included Audrey, who stood as Henry's Best Person, and Leticia, Joy's Matron of Honour. Dressed in a new shirt, tie and trousers, Audrey refused to abandon her erratically stitched, voluminous cosy cardigan. She added a corsage of hellebores and heather from her garden, pinned through one of the many holes. Leticia was resplendent in scarlet satin with diamanté beads threaded into her braids. She carried a posy of early flowering hyacinths which mirrored the white, sweet-smelling blooms in Joy's bouquet.

As guests waited for the bride to arrive, Leticia stood alone. Her fingers rubbed the stone of her ice diamond ring, and she remembered the Arctic cruise and the words Jim had whispered when he'd given her the Christmas gift. *'Let the ring be your* always . . . *for the days when I no longer will be.'*

True to the words she'd uttered that day, Leticia had never taken the ring off.

Now, wearing a wistful smile, she stared at Henry, who looked every bit the man who knew he was the luckiest pensioner alive. His face had a youthful glow, belying his seventy-one years, and he wore a perpetual grin. As Audrey leaned on his arm and whispered something to him, Leticia caught the words 'Good woman . . .' and wondered what else Henry's best friend had said.

A short distance away, Leticia recognised Joy's daughter Susan and her husband, Hugh. Timelessly elegant in her Carolina Herrera tailored suit, Susan held a clutch in one hand and fiddled with her pearls. She caught Leticia's eye and smiled, lifting her hand to wave.

Susan, the daughter, now appreciated her mum. Not out of duty but with an understanding of the truth, too late for comfort but soon enough to start again. 'I think deep down, I always knew,' Susan admitted when Joy had finally told her. 'But I didn't want to believe it of Dad.'

And that was enough for mother and daughter to begin to build a new bond.

Margaret stood out from the guests. Dressed in a well-cut hacking jacket, crisp white shirt and cravat, her pleated skirt skimmed her sensible brown boots, and she looked every inch the equestrian. But there was no Lady Eleanor by Margaret's side.

Within weeks of welcoming her new friends to her New Year's Eve Party, Lady Eleanor slipped quietly away to join her beloved Richard in their final chapter. Doctors said it was a heart attack, sudden but not unexpected. When they assembled for the funeral, Margaret told the cruise friends that Eleanor had been growing more distant, her mind often wandering to memories of Richard, and it was clear she longed to join him.

Lady Eleanor Dunmore was buried in the family grave in the churchyard in County Kildare, where friends old and new, and a large local crowd gathered to pay their respects to the legacy of a woman who through her kindness and charitable trust, had left an indelible mark.

The wedding march played, and guests turned to see Joy slowly enter the room. Wearing her gold cruise dress and a soft fur bolero, as she saw Henry, Joy's smile made it clear to everyone that she had found her forever.

Escorting the bride, with her arm tucked through his, came Jim.

Months of remission from The Beast had given him strength for this day, and Leticia glowed as she gazed at her husband, drinking in his quiet determination.

Was this down to her prayers under the aureola borealis? Every step Jim took was careful and measured, and his face showed his pride in the honour of being Joy's escort as she went to make her vows with Henry.

Doctors had told them that Jim was in remission, and Leticia and Jim had been granted more time. Not endless, but enough. Enough to witness their friend's love blossom and sufficient to know that their own happiness was complete.

The reception for the newlyweds followed at Audrey's home. It was her wedding gift, and she organised a lavish feast of festive food and drink, laid on by Yorkshire's finest caterers. Happy to combine their nuptials with Audrey's annual mulled wine party for her rainbow wrinklies, it was a colourful crowd that gathered. Audrey's parlour had been transformed with garlands and bright lanterns wound through the jungle of potted palms and ferns in their vast Victorian urns. In the fireplace, logs blazed, sending a golden glow over the guests, and on a 1950s music console, vinyl records were stacked, playing a mix of bebop and 1960s rock and roll.

Audrey had arranged congratulatory cards for the newlyweds on the mantle above the fire. At the centre stood a card bearing a photograph of Jennifer, flanked by her children in neat school uniforms, smiling brightly for the camera. Inside, the message read:

Mr and Mrs Henry, we wish you a happy marriage! From your Filipino family, we love you very much.

To Henry and Joy's surprise, there was a message from Barbara. Depicting a cruise ship cameoed in a circle of bougainvillaea and palm fronds, the inscription read: May your love be as deep as the sea that brought you together, and if it ever springs a leak, find a new partner and keep sailing!

'Good heavens,' Henry said as he read the words. 'How did Barbara find us, and where is she?'

Margaret spoke up. 'I ran across her on a cruise last month, and after we got up to speed, she gave the card to me. She was enjoying ten days in the Caribbean, shacked up with a wealthy American and occupying the Royal Emerald Suite.' Margaret was thoughtful. 'Barbara was in her element, more diamonds than a jeweller's window and cocktails flowing like a river.'

'But what has happened to Kenneth?' Joy looked puzzled.

Margaret gave a wry smile. 'Ah, Kenneth,' she said. 'He seems to have an arrangement with Barbara. Barbara told me he was at home in Cheshire, parading around the golf course in a captain's hat over his new toupee, escorted by a younger female caddy. He told anyone who'd listen that Barbara was on a luxurious spa retreat.'

'Whatever floats their boat.' Joy grinned.

'Indeed,' Henry agreed.

'Where are you two lovebirds galloping off to on honeymoon?' Margaret asked, a playful glint in her eye.

Henry and Joy held hands and exchanged a smile that spoke volumes. 'We've booked a riverboat cruise on the Nile,' they said as one, their excitement barely contained.

Margaret arched her eyebrow. 'Ah, the Nile! Marvellous! More cruise escapades. Let's hope that Hercule Poirot doesn't turn up with a murder to solve,' she snorted. 'And make sure you look out for aristocrats and heiresses who aren't what they seem.'

Margaret tapped a spoon against a glass and called the room to order.

'I propose a toast,' she announced. 'To the newlyweds, and as they embark on married life, may their love sail as

smoothly as the Arctic cruise that brought them together.'
She paused. 'And while on the Nile, don't let any pharaohs,
pyramids, or mysterious detectives get in your way.'

Glasses were raised, and as laughter rippled and Henry
and Joy turned to their friends, everyone chorused: 'Good
luck and carry on cruising!'

Can't wait to sail away on another cruise ship
adventure from Caroline James? Then turn the page
for your next escape and enjoy a sneak peek of
Caroline's new book, *The Nile Cruise*.

Coming in August 2026.

Hollywood

In the heart of the county of Cumbria, at the edge of the Lake District, where the fells melt into softer pastures, lies the hamlet of Hollywood. Named not for glittering movie stars or cinema success, but for the little village's ancient holly trees that nestle just beyond its winding lanes. Here, tucked between a large manor house and a long drystone wall, in the winding Lover's Lane, you'll find a cottage with whitewashed walls and a slate roof weathered to silver. Smoke curls from its chimney in the cooler months, and a tangle of roses clamber around the old oak doorway in summer. From beyond the garden, one can see the holly wood itself, where the dark-green, glossy leaves catch the light, highlighting the mysterious thicket that shelters the village.

At the back of the cottage, an outbuilding lies adjacent to a pond, where a solitary duck glides on the surface. A pretty blind covers an open window, and a comfortable wooden bench, overlooking the water, nestles at the top of the garden. A middle-aged man wearing a checkered woollen shirt and overalls rests his body on the bench, puffing on a roll-up, his eyes closed as he basks in the watery autumn sunshine. Beside him sits an old collie dog, her head nestling against his muddied boots. Her tail thumps as she eyes the duck.

On a breezy washing line, strung between two poles, sheets blow like sails on a choppy sea and a variety of undergarments flap like colourful flags. Lace-edged knickers tangle with dancing stockinged legs, while a generous, strap-stretching bra catches the wind, hinting at an owner who never shrinks from a hearty helping of pudding.

Welcome to Hollywood. The home of the county of Cumbria's celebrated private investigator, Hattie Mulberry.

Chapter One

Hattie Mulberry typed out a notification on the administration page of her website and hit save, then checked the live site to ensure that her instructions were clear.

H&H Investigations
We are temporarily closed
& unable to take new enquiries.
Please leave your message
on our contact form.

Perfect! Hattie thought. The message was loud and clear. For temporarily closed, read: 'The owner is completely knackered and needs to lie down for some time, in a darkened room, with copious amounts of gin and chocolate.'

Hattie yawned. She nudged the laptop aside, propped her feet on the desk and, placing a cushion behind her head, sank back into her oversized captain's chair. Folding her hands across her stomach, she closed her eyes and released a long and tired sigh that almost rattled the blinds on the window overlooking her garden. For Hattie, being a private investigator, or whatever one called the matter of meddling and mystery solving, had become an exhausting business.

When she'd launched H&H Investigations three years ago, Hattie had imagined the occasional eccentric client, perhaps a suspect suicide, or even a missing heirloom. But instead she'd dropped headfirst into a maze of puzzles that made the fictional world of *Midsummer Murders* look like a primary-school play. Mystery solving had turned out to be far more exhausting than it looked on TV.

But now, Hattie's desk was clear. She'd wrapped up the case of the husband who went out for a loaf of bread and never came back, tracked down the missing pug who'd mastered gate-latches, and solved the unpleasant Garden Gnome Dispute between neighbours in Appletree Avenue. A recent, more sinister case had involved an elderly couple who requisitioned Hattie to the rescue when their life savings went missing, and she'd discovered financial foul play in their family. That dilemma had been draining, and now, Hattie decided that she'd earned the right to let the world of investigations go on without her while she paused and took a break.

With a satisfied smile, Hattie drifted off and let her dreams carry her onto soft fluffy pillows of clouds, where she floated happily without a care in the world. Never one to let anything disturb her dozing, no matter how demanding the job, Hattie's power naps could rival a teenager's ability to sleep through a minor earthquake, and soon, she was snoring.

A loud knock rattled the open window and, startled, Hattie jolted awake, her swivel seat almost pitching her headlong out of the chair. 'What the . . .' she muttered, blinking hard as an acrid whiff of tobacco drifted in, and the heavy thump of boots could be heard on the path beyond the office door. Hattie froze.

'Anyone home?' A voice called out, muffled through the wood.

Hattie's eyes fixed on the handle as it turned. From the crack of the doorway, a hand emerged, gnarled fingers curling around the frame, the nails thick with grime.

'Bloody hell, Alf!' Hattie burst out as the rest of him shuffled into view. 'Do you have to slope about like a thief, scaring the life out of me?' Hattie regained her balance, rubbed her tired eyes, and pulled her cardigan across her chest.

'Mornin' Hattie,' Alf said as he stomped into her office, pulled out a chair and sat down. 'I'd have thought as a private dick, you would detect an intruder.' He stared at her sleepy face. 'Takin' a nap? I suppose it's to be expected at your age,' he added as the chair creaked, and Alf tugged on his moleskin trousers then settled his weight.

'My age?' Hattie exclaimed, 'I'm a good deal younger than you.' Crinkling her nose, she waved her hand to disperse smoke from Alf's cigarette.

'Nowt wrong with a nap,' Alf said, having enjoyed similar on the garden bench. He pinched the butt before placing the remains behind one ear.

'I wasn't napping, I was thinking,' Hattie lied.

'Not what your snores suggest. I could hear you from the top of the garden.' Alf placed two fingers on his lips and, letting out a sharp whistle that made Hattie wince, smiled when a collie dog nuzzled the door and ambled in to halt by her master's feet. 'Ah Ness, there's my beauty,' Alf said and scratched the old dog's head.

Hattie had little time for pets, with the exception of a tame duck who'd claimed a home in her garden. Least of all was Alf's scruffy old black and white sheepdog who looked like she could do with a hot soapy bath. She frowned as Ness nestled against Alf's knee, while Alf rummaged about in the top pocket of his shirt and, finding a treat for Ness, held it out.

Hattie leaned her chin on her hands and watched as Ness gobbled the fluff-covered snack. Shaking her head, she stared at Alf. Her gardener and handyman had been a part of her life for as long as she could remember. He lived on a nearby smallholding where he kept several sheep, and despite his grumbling ways, and his love of bedraggled animals, she was genuinely fond of the man. Their friendship, worn as smooth as the stepping stones by the pond, had stood the test of time.

'Better to nap than idly chatter,' Alf mumbled.

'Better to chatter than idly mumble,' Hattie shot back. 'Shouldn't you be out there cutting the grass or pruning a rose?'

'Nah, the wind's getting up and we're in for a storm.'

They both turned to the window where the blind had begun to clatter against the frame. Hattie reached across and drew it aside, slipping the latch into place. She lingered for a moment, wistfully gazing out. Even with the storm approaching and dark clouds gathering, she thought it looked lovely. Alf's hard work had paid off and showed in every corner. Neat flower beds, trimmed hedges, and a pretty path wound around the pond where Drake, the duck, dabbled in the water. Hattie hadn't a clue about gardening, and it was a mystery she left for Alf to tackle. But it didn't stop her from enjoying the beauty he'd created, or from perching on the bench to gaze out at the open fields beyond the stone wall, that stretched away to the holly wood.

Hattie's little cottage was transformed too and was no longer the derelict wreck she'd inherited almost four years ago, but a place that she'd made a comfortable home. As Hattie returned to her seat and plonked her ample bottom down, she thought of the sparkling new kitchen and bright and airy garden room. The cosy snug at the front of the cottage had a cheery wood burning stove that replaced a crumbling, soot blackened fireplace, where Hattie's cantankerous old aunt had warmed her hands for countless years.

As though reading her mind, Alf said, 'She'd not recognise the place; your aunt must be turning in her grave with the fancy new set-up here.'

'Well, you talked me into it. I was perfectly happy with things the way they were.'

'Hah! A likely tale.' Alf raised a bushy eyebrow. 'It was like living in a squat.'

'I don't need a fancy lifestyle,' Hattie huffed, but the glint in her eye betrayed her. She adored her comforts and as an ex-hotelier managing guests in the lap of luxury, Hattie thrilled at the sight of her own little cottage transformed from a ruin into a wonderful refuge.

'Tha needs a new bathroom,' Alf commented. He shifted in his seat and Hattie grimaced as mud, caked on his boots, scattered across the floor.

She knew that Alf was right. When the cottage had been converted, she'd insisted on keeping three bedrooms upstairs with a new shower room tacked on behind the kitchen. But Hattie was a woman who missed a long soak in a hot bubbly bath, at the end of a busy day. Standing under a jet of water that pelted her skin like bullets was no substitute, and traipsing to the loo in the dead of the night was often a tricky manoeuvre, especially if Hattie had enjoyed a tipple or two. More than once, she'd wobbled her way down, careering and cursing and praying not to be taken short as she negotiated the steep curving staircase and darkened rooms.

'Tha doesn't need three bedrooms, and with your office out the back, you can easily convert one to a bathroom upstairs.' Alf reached for another treat for Ness and the dog wolfed it down.

'You're after an expensive job,' Hattie said.

'Plenty of jobs for me in the village, and beyond,' Alf said and placed his hands on the arms of his chair as though to rise. 'Book me now or wait till spring.'

Hattie raised her fingers to her shoulder-length curls and tucked the strawberry blonde locks to one side. She eyed Alf and wondered if it was time to commission a new job. Converting the outbuildings to her office had been expensive, in addition to all the work on the cottage, but that was ages ago, and Hattie was hardly short of money. The thought of a deep roll-top bath, nestling beneath the bay window of a south facing bedroom was almost impossible to ignore. Winter was approaching and she could think of nothing nicer than submerging herself on a cold frosty day, in heavily scented bubbles, with a gin in one hand and a good book in the other.

Alf was right, she didn't need three bedrooms. Only one was occasionally used by her best friend, Jo Docherty, and Hattie's two sons had kids of their own and lived abroad, visiting Cumbria rarely. If truth be told, Hattie enjoyed travelling to see them far more than hosting lively young families in her own cosy home.

'I can make a start next week,' Alf paused, yawning with disinterest. 'After that, as I said, you'll have to wait till spring as I've a house renovation in Marland that will keep me busy all winter.'

'Intimidation that's what this is,' Hattie pouted, 'there's plenty of folk out there who can tackle a new bathroom, I can easily find your replacement.'

'Aye, but you won't.'

Alf stood up and Ness thumped her tail against his leg. He removed the butt from behind his ear and lit it. 'You'll need to be out of t'way, for a week or two.'

'What?' Hattie's mouth dropped open.

Alf raised his hand and ran his fingers along the spines of books that sat on the shelves lining one wall. 'Get yourself away on a holiday,' he said. 'It's not as though you've any current mysteries to meddle in.' He paused as he studied several volumes of Hattie's favourite author and pulling one off the shelf, held it up. Then, placing Agatha Christie's *Death on the Nile* before Hattie, he pushed it under her nose.

'A Nile cruise, something different, that's what you should do,' Alf said. 'Think on!'

* * *

Hattie thought on for several days. When her mind wasn't occupied with ordering bathroom fittings, tiles and a posh toilet seat, she contemplated Alf's advice. She'd agreed that he should start work on the new bathroom by the third week in November, which gave her two weeks to decide where she would go while the work was carried out. Hattie could stay with Jo, at one of her friend's lovely country house hotels. But she knew it would be impossible to relax in those surroundings, and she'd soon rope herself into work. November could be a cold wet month in Cumbria and Hattie felt that it would be good to go somewhere warm, to feel a bit of heat on her tired bones and refresh both her mind and body, ideally somewhere new. She would return home, relaxed and ready to review any new cases that were waiting in her inbox.

Sitting in the garden room while rain lashed down outside and thunder crashed, Hattie flicked through holiday sites on her laptop, looking for last minute inspiration. A couple of weeks in sunny Madeira looked promising, with colourful flower markets and interesting walks. Her eyes studied a snow-dusted winter chalet in the Dolomites where skiing the magnificent slopes was a highlight.

'Not a chance,' Hattie sighed, puffing out her cheeks. The thought of bundling up her body in a vice-like snowsuit and balancing on two tiny planks, to throw herself off the side of a mountain, did little to encourage a booking, although the après-ski looked tempting.

On the coffee table beside her, the book that Alf had chosen lay as though waiting for Hattie to pick it up. *Death on the Nile* was her favourite, and Hattie knew that if she began to read it again, she wouldn't stop. Outside, a storm had gathered, and lightening lit up the sky in a jagged white flash, while thunder rolled in close.

Hattie snapped her laptop shut and stared at the book. Gilt letters on the cover flickered in the light of the storm, seeming to dance. Fascinated, Hattie felt a shiver as she turned a page. The story took place on a Nile river cruise. *Was the tale inviting her in?*

'A cruise!' Hattie exclaimed. 'Of course, Alf was right!'

Hattie loved cruising, and with her second husband, Hugo, in the brief two years of their marriage, they'd travelled to many far-flung destinations. Yet somehow, a Nile cruise had never made it onto their itinerary. She visualised the slow, sunlit river winding its way from Luxor to Aswan, gliding past golden temples, whispering palms and age-old buildings. Just like a scene from her favourite novel. She felt a ripple of pleasure at the thought of exotic sights and a canopied sundeck where she could relax and unwind as the ancient world passed by.

Hattie opened her laptop again and began typing into a search engine for tour companies that offered such holidays. At least she'd be out from under Alf's feet and away from the clatter of hammers and drills and constant clouds of dust.

Yes! Hattie thought with a satisfied smile, a river cruise on the Nile. A proper, well-earned holiday!

Loved *The Arctic Cruise*? Don't miss *The Cruise Club*!

Because the best adventures are still to come . . .

Escape to the sun in a feelgood rom com full of
romance, fun and mischief, which will sweep you
away to the azure waters of the Mediterranean
with every turn of the page.

Three women.
One widowed.
One unmarried.
One almost divorced.
All aged 63, but not ready to give up on life!

It's time to seas the day

The Cruise

CAROLINE JAMES

Will the three friends find the comfort and joy they
seek aboard the *Diamond Star*?

Fern Britton *Picks*

Exclusively for **TESCO**

EXCLUSIVE ADDITIONAL CONTENT

Includes an author Q&A and details
of how to get involved *Fern's Picks*

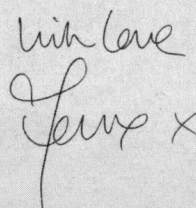

Dear lovely readers,

I'm delighted to share this month's pick with you all. This winter you can pick up this gorgeous, escapist romance and set sail with me in Norway's winter wonderland to see the spectacular Northern Lights.

The Arctic Cruise follows our heroine, Joy Bradley as she embarks upon a journey of self-discovery after the loss of her husband. Whilst navigating her grief, Joy finds unexpected companionship with the charming Henry Halliday, a retired history teacher seeking a fresh start of his own. Their love story is warm, witty and beautifully written as it explores themes of love, healing, and the courage it takes to truly embrace new beginnings.

Join Joy on the adventure of a lifetime, as she learns to let go of her past and open her heart to the possibilities of the future in this gorgeously uplifting and wonderfully atmospheric novel.

I cannot wait to hear what you think!

With love
Fem x

Look out for more books, coming soon!

For more information on the book club,
exclusive Q&As with the authors and
reading group questions, visit Fern's website
www.fern-britton.com/ferns-picks

We'd love you to join in the conversation,
so don't forget to share your thoughts using
#FernsPicks

A Q&A with
Caroline James

Warning: contains spoilers

You write about cruises so beautifully in this book, as well as in your other books *The Cruise* and *The Cruise Club*. What first drew you to cruises and inspired you to start writing about them?

My sister had always been passionate about cruises; she even got married on one. I'll admit, I was never particularly drawn to the idea myself. I used to think of cruises as little more than package holidays at sea. But when my sister suggested I try one as a guest speaker which essentially gave me the chance to experience a cruise for free, I decided to give it a go.

My first voyage was with the wonderful Fred Olsen Cruise Line, in the Mediterranean, and from the moment I stepped on board, I was captivated. The ship itself is an enclosed setting, a floating world with so many fascinating people and stories. I soon realised that a cruise is the perfect backdrop for a novel. Offering mystery, intimacy, and a constantly changing landscape. That first experience sparked an enduring love for both cruising and writing about it.

All your books are set in gorgeous places; how do you tend to approach researching a new location?

I start with thinking about places I'd like to visit, or somewhere I've really connected with. For example, I've been lucky enough to spend quite a bit of time in the Caribbean, so when I began writing *The Cruise*, it felt like the perfect setting. I could picture the islands, the people, the rhythm of life. If I don't know a place, I make a point of going there. For me, no amount of online research can replace physically being in situ. I walk the streets, taste the food, smell the air, and hear the sounds. It's those details that bring my stories to life. Often, I might notice someone by way of a gesture, a smile, or how they speak, and this will spark an idea for a character.

Norway in the winter is such an idyllic location! Where do you think might be up next on your book bucket list?

I'm taking a new group of characters on a Nile river cruise next. I'd never been to Egypt before, but I've always been fascinated by its rich history and culture. Agatha Christie's time there with her husband, Sir Max Mallowan, intrigued me as she often accompanied him on archaeological digs, and that sense of discovery really inspired me. To research the book, I went on a river cruise along the Nile from Luxor to Aswan. It was a wonderful experience, and the ever-changing scenery, ancient temples and the deep sense of history created the perfect backdrop for my next story, entitled *The Nile Cruise*.

What did your writing process look like when you were working on this book?

To capture the setting, I went on an Arctic cruise myself, and it was one of the best experiences I've had. The landscape is vast, and so humbling. I spent time on deck, wrapped up my thermals and cosy coat, watching the mountains drift past and taking in the light, which changes constantly up there. Those moments really shaped the book's atmosphere. On shore I wandered around the locations taking note of everything that happened on excursions so that I could recreate them realistically. I had already come up with the characters and once back, I began. I'm an early-morning writer and usually aim for around 2,000 words a day. Some days it flows, while other days it's more of a struggle, but that's part of the process. The key for me is to keep showing up at the page and the story will eventually complete.

What advice would you give to aspiring writers looking to pen their own novel?

My biggest piece of advice is to not wait for the perfect idea or moment. Put your rear on a chair and fingers on a keyboard and write. It may be nonsense at first, but eventually the story will reveal itself. Writing is my job, and, like any job, it has a routine. I start early, after doing my exercises and supping a coffee, then I begin. Find your 'writing time' and make it work for you without excuses. When I was running a business 24/7, I made time, late nights and early mornings. If you are determined, you will succeed. Experience as much as you can by observing and listening. Inspiration often comes from the people you meet and the places you visit. Finally, please don't be too hard on yourself. All writers doubt their work at times, but the most important thing is to keep going, even when it feels impossible. Often those days lead to the best story!

You've crafted such a lovable, eclectic cast of characters in this book. Where do you tend to find the inspiration behind all their different personalities?

Inspiration comes from people I meet, places I've been, and little moments I notice when I'm out and about. In *The Arctic Cruise,* Joy's character developed after I sat in a café and chatted to a lady who told me her husband had passed away. She said she found it so hard to travel alone, and I was deeply moved by her honesty. I thought it took great courage to keep going at a time of life when loss or misfortune can so easily diminish one's confidence. I connected emotionally with her feelings, which made it easier to bring Joy to life on the page. Sometimes a single glance can spark the idea of a character. A look or gesture, and I'll think, "That's it, there's so and so!" From there, I start to imagine their story, and before I know it, they've found their way into the book. Everyone has their own personality and quirks, and it is such a pleasure to weave and blend different behaviours and traits together into a lively, believable mix.

Do you have a favourite character from this book, and who was the most fun to write?

My favourite character in *The Arctic Cruise* is Henry because he's such a genuinely decent man. He has a great deal going for him, even though he doesn't realise it. Henry is intelligent and kind, with a hidden hint of mischief. Writing him was a pleasure, and I'd love to have a coffee with him, listening as he brings his fascinating historical knowledge to life and gives us glimpses of his hilarious and eccentric neighbour, Audrey.

Kenneth was fun to write. He's a real handful. A pompous know-it-all with an awful toupee that more or less wrote its own comedic scenes. I enjoyed placing Kenneth in amusing situations where my imagination ran wild with his antics. I hope he's the kind of character that keeps the reader amused, and he certainly kept me laughing throughout his creation.

As an insider, what tips would you give to someone who might be considering booking their own cruise holiday?

If you're considering a cruise, a good tip is to pick a ship and itinerary that really excites you. There is something for everyone, from relaxing sunny hotspots to adventurous voyages, not forgetting a wide choice of river cruises. I'd recommend researching the excursions and experiences on offer, but don't forget to be spontaneous and not miss out on hidden gems.

Even with a perfect weather forecast, the weather can change quickly at sea or in exotic destinations, so pack for all eventualities. Enjoy the simple pleasure of wandering around the ship and getting to know fellow passengers while soaking up the atmosphere. Lastly, relax and embrace the slower pace. Cruises are wonderful because they give you the chance to travel, explore, and unwind all at once.

Questions for your Book Club

Warning: contains spoilers

- Which character did you enjoy most in *The Arctic Cruise* and why? Did your initial opinion of them change during the story?

- Does the author's experience of cruising influence the writing, and do you think that first-hand knowledge of settings and locations is essential for authentic storytelling?

- Knowing that Jim is terminally ill, we see Jim and Leticia approach the cruise with positivity and happiness. How did their outlook affect you as a reader? Did Leticia and Jim's courage and love change the way you think about living life fully?

- How did you feel about housekeeper Jennifer's life as a single mother working far from her children, and about Henry's unexpected generosity? Did this moment change how you viewed either character, and what does their interaction say about empathy and the ways people can change each other's lives?

- Kenneth and Barbara add plenty of drama. Their condescending attitudes and Barbara's obsession with social climbing set them apart. How did you react to them as a couple, and what do you think their behaviour reveals about class, insecurity and the desire to impress others?

- Fitness participants on the Emerald Dream adore Kyle's wacky exercise classes. Why do you think the sessions appeal to the mature passengers, and would you enjoy taking part?

- Joy's story is one of vulnerability. As a nervous widow carrying a secret, how did you interpret her journey? What do you think her secret reveals about grief and finding strength to move forward? Did her secret, when revealed, change the way you felt about her?

- If you could be any character in the book, who would you choose to be and why?

An exclusive extract from Fern's new novel

A Cornish Legacy

CHAPTER ONE

North Cornwall, April, present day

Delia squinted through the windscreen, the sun ahead dazzling her. 'You'll see the turning on the right in a minute,' she said. 'Keep an eye out. I might miss it.'

Sammi tipped the last of the crisps into his mouth and sat up a little straighter. 'My eyes are peeled.' He pulled the sunglasses down from his head. 'Will there be some kind of landmark?'

'There's a big metal sign swinging on a post above the gates. Remember? You said it looked like a gibbet.'

Sammi chuckled. 'The gibbet! Yes, of course! Such a welcome.' He sat up straighter, alert. 'There!'

Delia saw the emerging gap amongst the tangled hedge of rhododendrons, with the rusted sign hanging from the post.

'Is that it?' asked Sammi. 'Can't read the name.'

Delia slowed, changing down through the gears. She wasn't smiling. 'Yep. This is it. Wilder Hoo.' The sight of the tatty sign that she had never wanted or expected to see again forced her stomach into a tight knot. Turning, she slowed the car and braked to a halt. 'I really don't want to be here.'

Sammi reached over for her knee and tapped it briskly. 'You're not on your own. I'm here, and those horrible people are gone. Come on.'

Delia put a hand to her chest and took a deep breath to control the old anxiety welling within. 'It's quite late. Let's go and find somewhere to stay tonight and come back tomorrow.'

'It's only half past four!'

'But it'll be getting dark soon.'

'Darling, it's April, not December.' Sammi's voice became soft and sympathetic. 'I know this is hard. But you can do it, and you will do it.'

'I don't want to do it.'

'The past is past. Dead and buried.'

Sighing heavily, Delia put the car in gear and slowly drove the winding tarmacked drive. 'Dead people can still haunt us.'

Stiff clumps of grass and dandelions had forced themselves between the cracked pitch, and in other places, huge potholes housed red, muddied puddles.

'It'll cost thousands just to repair the drive,' she said. 'Look at it.'

She knew that Sammi saw through different eyes. For him, this was an adventure. When Delia had first told him that the house had been gifted to her, he had been ready to celebrate, despite her horror of the whole thing. He seemed to feel only the thrill of an escapade.

Looking out of his side window at the ancient, rolling parkland with great oaks dotted across the scene he said, 'Delia, this is utterly captivating. Please tell me there's a lake. I'm expecting Colin Firth to stride forth in his wet breeches and shirt.'

Delia was scornful. 'If only. No lake, I'm afraid. Just a beach and all these acres of parkland. Do you know, it takes four men with a tractor each an entire week to cut all that grass? When they get to the end, they have to start again. It's a bloody money pit.' Her eyes flicked to the avenue of ivy-clad beech trees ahead, the bare branches forming a tunnel over sodden leaves. 'That ivy needs cutting back too. Argh. Who can afford all this, I ask you!'

Sammi was not listening. 'How long is this drive again?'

'It's 1.2 miles.'

'Very specific.'

Delia sighed. 'My father-in-law preferred to tell everyone it was two kilometres because that sounded longer.'

'And all this land belongs to the house?'

'Yup.'

Sammi was grinning. 'I'd love to jump on a tractor and spend a whole summer mowing all this.'

'You really wouldn't. Back in the day, there were sheep and deer to crop it.'

'Sheep and deer! Delia.' Sammi laughed. 'And all this is actually yours!'

She shrugged. She was weary and wretched. 'Not for long, I hope.'

They rattled over a cattle grid and onto a sparsely gravelled drive.

'OK. Here we go.' Delia swallowed hard. 'Round this bend, you'll see the house.' She took a nervous breath and added, 'I couldn't do this without you.'

Sammi tutted, 'I wouldn't let you come on your own, would I?'

Delia steered the last curve – and there, suddenly, was Wilder Hoo.

Available now!

Our next book club title

Sometimes the last page is just the beginning...

The Last Page *Café*

KATE STOREY

How would you write the next chapter of your life?

At fifty-four, Erin McRae feels like she's living in the margins of her own story. Her son is preparing to fly the nest, and the rent increase on the café she loves to run means she's going to have to close up shop. Her greatest escape is the mismatched book club she founded, bound together by one unusual rule: they choose their next book based solely on the last page.

But when the book club discusses what their own last pages might say, Erin and her fellow members begin to see their own lives in unexpected ways

As the club's discussions grow deeper, long-buried secrets surface, old wounds start to heal – and romance leaps off the page. With The Bookmark under threat of closure, Erin must ask herself: can she write herself a happier story?

A heartwarming novel about friendship, second chances, and the surprising ways stories shape our lives, perfect for lovers of Evie Woods, Sally Page, and Pip Williams.

SPEAK·TRUTH·TO·POWER

COMMANDER
STEVEN HAINES
ROYAL NAVY

OXFORD MONOGRAPHS IN INTERNATIONAL
HUMANITARIAN AND CRIMINAL LAW

General Editors

PAOLA GAETA

SALVATORE ZAPPALÀ

The Law of Maritime Blockade

OXFORD MONOGRAPHS IN INTERNATIONAL HUMANITARIAN AND CRIMINAL LAW

The aim of this series is to publish original and innovative books on fundamental, topical, or cutting-edge issues in international humanitarian law and international criminal justice. The primary purpose of the series is to publish books which, in addition to critically surveying existing law, also suggest new avenues for improving the law.

Special attention will be given to works by young scholars.

The Law of Maritime Blockade
Blockade

Past, Present, and Future

PHILLIP DREW

OXFORD

UNIVERSITY PRESS

Great Clarendon Street, Oxford, OX2 6DP,
United Kingdom

Oxford University Press is a department of the University of Oxford.
It furthers the University's objective of excellence in research, scholarship,
and education by publishing worldwide. Oxford is a registered trade mark of
Oxford University Press in the UK and in certain other countries

© P Drew 2017

The moral rights of the author have been asserted

First Edition published in 2017

Impression: 1

Crown copyright material is reproduced under Class Licence
Number C01P0000148 with the permission of OPSI
and the Queen's Printer for Scotland

Published in the United States of America by Oxford University Press
198 Madison Avenue, New York, NY 10016, United States of America

British Library Cataloguing in Publication Data
Data available

Library of Congress Control Number: 2017958436

ISBN 978–0–19–880843–5

Printed and bound by
CPI Group (UK) Ltd, Croydon, CR0 4YY